Fearless in Florida is dedicated to the small Florida
trailer parks in their heyday

-and to independence

Fearless in Florida

a novel
of
Florida Suspense

by Emma "Freeway" Lincoln

Fearless in Florida
Copyright 2012 by Emma "Freeway" Lincoln

Published 2012 by Awesome Book Publishing
All Rights Reserved.

ISBN: 978-0-9840538-8-9

Chapter 1

April 1999, Flamingo Park, Florida

A man crouched outside Shaye's trailer window. Shaye could smell him. They'd left the window open because of the extreme heat. Now, on the breeze that came through the screen, she smelled musky sweat and some kind of chemical- perhaps pesticide. The man leaned back against the wall. From her own angle, trying to remain unseen, she could only see the top of his head and a portion of chest exposed inside an open shirt.

Shaye listened to his breathing. She tried to keep her own breath silent, holding her mouth open as she stepped up closer to ascertain what this was about.

A lawnmower droned in the background, and she heard the sound of traffic on Flamingo Beach Parkway several blocks away. An orange plopped down off a tree, making a noticeable thump.

Shaye's heart pulsed powerfully, but no longer gyrated like when she was first roused out of bed by the intruder's presence. Her large breasts lifted, her chest moving just enough for her to breathe, and enough for her to make a move if she had to.

The prowler lit a cigarette, and he drew on it with a smacking sound as smoke curled up into her window.

Shaye focused on keeping relaxed, even as jets of adrenaline washed through her and burned her stomach. She had waited for something like this to happen. Now she was responding to a drill already much practiced in her mind.

Who was this man crouching in the Hibiscus bushes, breathing roughly and spitting out pieces of tobacco? Shaye watched the stranger furtively count a handful of money again and again. Maybe he had just robbed someone. Why else would he sit in the sewage-damp dirt, waiting out the afternoon?

Pressed up against a grainy interior wall, with one eye exposed to look through the screen, Shaye thought about the different reasons why he might be here, trespassing on her yard in this compromised neighborhood.

She had observed a crew doing yard work several lots away and maybe he was one of them, hiding here to count the day's off-the-books wages. But then why would he vault several fences to trespass in her yard?

Possibly the man was evil. Perhaps he was crouching here because he had hurt someone already, or he was planning to hurt someone now.

Shaye wondered if she could possibly defend herself if he tried to attack her. Or possibly, at his first movement to get inside the screen, she could run to the front of the rental trailer and escape onto the street.

Her heart ached with the hope that he would just go away.

A telephone with a long cord lay in the middle of Shaye's immaculate bedspread- cold, ironic comfort, because there was no way she could call the police.

1 month earlier, New Jersey Turnpike, NJ, the afternoon of Shaye Taylor's and Adam Underwood's escape from the Westchester State Hospital for Psychiatric Disorders

It was all about freedom. When Shaye's world had been crushed, and she inhabited strange days in the hospital in a netherworld between pain and fear, suddenly freedom became the most important thing.

Shaye had never thought much about freedom in her life, but now it became clear to her that freedom could be the only path to safety.

Her best friend, Adam, the only human being in the world who currently cared about her, was willing to provide that chance.

Late nights, he'd hidden in Shaye's room, and they'd concocted an elaborate escape scheme as dramatic as in the movies. Shaye and

2

Adam had been careful and secretive and the plan had actually worked.

Now, in a snowstorm, with skeins of fat snowflakes brushing against the windows of the rental car and the tires whispering along the padded ground, they and the two other inmates they had chosen to help were on the road- Shaye; Adam- the mastermind of the scheme, forty-year old Della Roman- known for her antisocial tendencies and sixteen-year Eric Watson- whose troubles were the impetous for their escape.

Today was the quintessential snow day, a day when other people stayed home from schools and jobs. Most of the people Shaye and her companions saw were required to be out, like the men driving plows and sanders, bright orange behemoths on chains, trying vainly to push away the loads of snow falling on the Turnpike.

Inside the muffled shell of their rented car, the speakers throbbed out the song by Jane's Addiction, "Been Caught Stealing", again and again.

Shaye felt the cold creeping through metal and plastic and glass, she felt the unsteadiness of bad tires on deep new snow and her mind registered annoyance each time Adam, who called himself Adam Ant, after the eighties' punk rocker, pushed in the "play" button.

Shaye was lying down in the back seat and she felt the abnormal tension in Della's thighs, which she leaned against. She smelled the reek of cigarettes off Eric's clothes and she listened to the nervous tapping of his laceless sneaker on the mat on the passenger side of the car, where it squelched each time against brown slush. Their companions' discomfort simply fueled her own nervousness more.

A gas station attendant with snow covered eyelashes gave them dirty looks when the handsome, but effete, Adam requested gas in his cherished Scarlett O'Hara imitation. Then the attendant glanced into the back seat and spied sickly thin Shaye lying across Della's legs and his face knitted up in even more disapproval. There had also been a lot of cops out this afternoon; she'd noticed many of their snow-dappled cars gliding past them as the snowstorm got worse.

It didn't help that Adam wasn't confident enough to drive over thirty miles an hour in snow, or that he talked with his hands. He pattered his hands on the steering wheel like a drumroll every time their favorite phrase came up to buoy their spirits. And he sang it out loudly each time it played- the part about walking through the door.

They all joined in singing the phrase: croaky voiced Della, jittery Eric, even Shaye in a half-hearted way and, of course, Adam leading in that unmistakable songbird voice of his.

Adam smiled politely at a police officer who passed them as he waved his hands, and he laughed melodically. He loved that line so much. After all, they *had* done it, hadn't they? They had walked right through that door. And now they were free, in this unprecedented blizzard.

"Stay with us, Babe," Adam called to Shaye from the front seat.

She still tasted the lingering sweetness of vomit tinged with blood when she'd had one of her attacks earlier, right after they escaped the State Hospital. What else could she do now but trust him? She felt too tired and sick to care.

They went into a gentle slide off the left side of the road. "Rest area," Adam announced. His voice sounded a little worn as they pulled into the crowded rest area where cars trailing tails of steam slid past each other in the sloppy snow.

"Why don't you call your Dad from here, Eric?" he suggested.

"I'm going to, definitely," Eric said. "And thanks, Adam. You know, for everything. You saved our lives." He reached over and squeezed Adam's shoulder through his wool coat and his eyes looked a little teary. They planned to drive Eric to meet his biological father in Washington DC, a man who didn't have legal custody, but who was willing to help.

Shaye saw Adam squint in the rear view mirror, as if he felt uncomfortable with this show of emotion. Or maybe it was just the weight of responsibility. This was a rescue mission, after all, and it was his idea. So suppose none of them really *were* safe to be out on their own, he must probably have wondered.

It was now Adam's judgment pitted against that of the legal and psychological establishment. But Shaye felt Adam *had* to be right. Shaye had been slowly, physically, dying in the State Hospital. Even all the doctors with their pride and their cruel treatment of her could not make that fact go away. Thinking about it, her stomach clenched with familiar fear. She willed it away, hoping that she could stay strong right now for Adam's sake.

Della leaned forward, gathering the mishmash of belongings she had run away with, and interrupted in a loud voice. "I want to buy one of those big Turnpike coffee mugs, the souvenir ones. They keep showing it on all the signs."

Della could be so crazy sometimes. But her inane comment at least broke the tension.

Adam brought the car to a halt on the cushion of snow and everyone else piled out first. Then Shaye was left to face crawling from the overheated womb of the car into an outdoors that she hadn't been free in for a year and a half. She felt dazzled at first by the bright light. Then her lungs filled with damp air that was scented with auto exhaust, but fresh anyway.

Shaye reeled back against the car with her coat open and snowflakes fell into her eyes and mouth and onto her delicate belly, where her shirt rode up. Adam straightened her up on her feet and she pressed her face into his neck, feeling his little mahogany colored whiskers and smelling yesterday's application of Cool Water cologne. Adam was always so clean and perfect; it was one of the wonderful things about him, something that made Shaye feel safe.

And she did feel safe, safer here with him than she ever had in the State Hospital, safer than in all the medical hospitals and ICU's before it.

"I'm fine," she said to him, straightening up.

After just a few minutes standing there snow already filled Shaye's shoes, burning her ankles and letting her know that she was still alive, no matter that this might possibly be the last day. It was amazing that, even with all the plowing, four inches of white slush had accumulated in the parking lot and they had to fight their way through it, man against nature, the four of them walking along with all the other families.

Adam looked once into Shaye's eyes. His eyes were big, deep and brown, with a warm reddish undertone, of the same shade as his stylishly close-cropped hair. He then handed her off onto Della's waiting arm, so that she leaned on the older woman's plushy bosom.

"I don't need help," Shaye protested.

"Take her to the ladies room, Della, please. And make sure everything she touches in there is clean," Adam said, "so that she doesn't panic."

Eric jogged into the rest area first and now Shaye and Della pushed through the heavy doors. A sharp flash of sunlight off metal momentarily blinded Shaye. Meanwhile other people in coats pushed on her to get inside and a vent released a gush of hot, suffocating air onto everyone's heads.

Germs, Shaye thought, and panic began. She whimpered, quietly, knowing the danger a full-fledged scene could put them all in right now. Her two friends got her inside, but then her body twisted in her coat trying to resist going down the broad yellow-tiled corridor that led to the ladies' room.

Luckily other people paid no notice, they were moving so fast. Shaye wondered at these other women, who seemed so alive and so oblivious to germs that could take away years of their lives, or kill them.

They talked loudly, these travelers, pulling their children and sisters and grandmothers by the sleeves into that communal ladies restroom. They brushed their trendy new coats along walls that appeared covered with slime, never washed. Possibly it did not look odd to them to see one woman holding up another; others were doing it because of the slippery footing outside.

"Don't make me take her," Della pleaded.

"She can do it," Adam said simply, and walked away.

Della weighed two hundred brawny pounds, she'd once fought off four male nurses with a butterknife, and she was afraid of nothing. But she now seemed terrified of what fragile, ninety-seven pound Shaye would do when she got into the ladies room.

"It's okay, honey," Della said to try to comfort her, and Shaye made an effort to concentrate on her friend's pink-lined lips as they entered the row of stainless steel toilet stalls that seemed to stretch forever. A helpless thread of urine trickled out of Shaye's panties as she responded to the cold, the noise and the smells of human waste that so terrified her.

Other women veered impatiently around them. Children cried. Someone had left a window open to the parking lot and very cold air washed in. The scent of this cold air served to clear Shaye's head.

Gradually some of the panic subsided and Shaye was able to stand on her own and prowl before the stalls, pushing open each of the doors with her foot and peering inside. Then she saw horrors in each stall, while Della stood patiently behind her, waiting.

This was the human condition, she thought with sickness in her soul. It was a world where women who wore five hundred dollar designer leather coats could unashamedly leave behind unspeakable bodily filth, toilets full of feces and blood that could mean death to the next person using them. And then they would pass briskly out of the bathroom, the majority of them not even washing their hands!

6

Shaye found a group of stalls that had just been cleaned; the seats were up and the floors were wet and stinking of ammonia and she judged these were safe. Everything had to be done exactly right for her to function; she closed herself inside a stall using toilet paper to touch the knob- it took a long time despite the throbbing in her bladder. What a wretch I am, she thought, as she held herself precariously six inches above the toilet. But she also felt a sense of pride- she was able to do this, after all, able to do it free of the hospital and not infect herself with germs.

Packs of women moved through in the time it took for Shaye to complete her ritual. Feeling brave, she had called to Della to go ahead without her. She emerged, shaking, with a wad of toilet paper clutched in her hand so she could safely turn on the sink.

Shaye washed her hands for several minutes and gave a tight smile to a woman next to her, who reached over her for a towel. The woman was about her age, twenty-four, and she looked happy and vibrant bundled in her winter clothes.

Shaye was surprised by her own face, which glanced back at her in the steel-framed mirror. When she used to work as a swimsuit model, people liked to say that she resembled the willowy blond actress Uma Thurman. But this was flattery, because besides being tall and dusky blond, Shaye had none of the movie star's quirkiness. Shaye had more of a Barbie doll look, with big green eyes, petite but plump lips and generous hollows under her high cheekbones.

Now, the hollows were carved out fully and her eyes seemed to jump out at you, alert and excited and brilliant-colored in the pallor of her face. Her trademark long hair was hidden by a thick men's woolen hat.

Once, Shaye was in demand as a model because of her cutesy generic look. But now her look seemed frightening, and feral.

When Shaye ventured back out into the bustling main area, she found her friends sitting at a plastic table, with food spread before them. It seemed like appalling fast food that she could not eat because of her fears, and her sudden gut feeling was envy.

Adam smiled at her, seeming proud that she had come through the crowd okay.

"I got something for you," he said, as she sat down.

He'd bought her milk in a small carton and a muffin in plastic wrap. Shaye glanced over at Eric, who gnawed on a fried sandwich with shreds of lettuce falling out; Della, sipping her souvenir coffee and Adam, picking at remnants of a chef's salad.

"It's sealed," Adam encouraged, and pushed Shaye's food toward her.

Shaye took up the muffin, controlling her breathing. If she wanted freedom, then she could do this. Adam smiled and winked when she took the first bite.

Della and Eric went off together to call their people, while Shaye and Adam stopped at a computer screen to plan the itinerary. Adam punched up information on hotel discounts between the Carolinas and Florida and then he impulsively grabbed a handful of slick pamphlets for tourist attractions.

"You know, I hate to say this," he said in Shaye's ear. "But it'll be easier for us when we get rid of those two... They're so whacked!"

He said it lightheartedly and his lips slid into a grin. Adam had always acted cheerful for the year and a half Shaye had known him. But she could sometimes sense the turbulence of his internal moods, just like now she noticed the tired purple dents under his eyes. Adam chewed on his lip, looking over detailed maps they had bought with some of their last ready cash, while Della had wasted hers in the gift shop.

"Do you know anything about Washington D.C.?" he asked. "Eric's dad supposedly lives not far from the Capitol."

Trying to help, Shaye bent over the map with him and, together, they planned a route. It would mean Adam driving until nine-o-clock at night, when they were supposed to meet up with Eric's father.

They got on a sundry shop line to buy supplies for later and Shaye noticed how, of all the people standing around them, her Adam's face seemed the most compelling. He had perfect creamy skin and high cheekbones and pouty lips like a male version of herself. Adam looked kind of like a model, in a downtown Greenwich-Villagey way. But he also had that startled deer look at times, much too boyish. Shaye had to remind herself that he was only twenty years old.

"Adam," she whispered, in case the others were in earshot. "You're trying to do too much; you can't do all this driving by yourself. I'll have to take over for a while."

Shaye knew her offer seemed ridiculous, there was so much medication poisoning her body right now that she needed help walking. She hadn't driven a car in two years, and she hadn't been very good at it even then.

Adam smiled. "Maybe you can drive tomorrow, Sweetie, or whenever. But I'm still going on adrenaline, and I'm good to go!"

His voice came out dramatically and three teenage girls standing next to them giggled, trying to flirt with him and ignoring Shaye. Of course, Adam smiled back at the girls, adoring the attention.

Shaye and Adam were basically alone in the world, even though they stood amongst other bodies. Most people probably lived a whole life without realizing how alone they really were and Shaye once had felt safe that way. Her husband had also been her talent agent, and the owner of the primary publication she modeled for. And the nature of their relationship was that he was also the person who told her what to do to survive in this world.

When Adam Underwood met her in the State Hospital he was just a schizophrenic kid thrown out by his rich parents because of one very bizarre and insistent quirk.

But, for Shaye, Adam became her rescuer. When she first came wheeled into his institutional home on a stretcher, with tubes in both arms and one big one hanging out of her nose, her long blond hair twined around her hips and half a breast exposed by a twisted hospital gown, Adam had actually gasped. "Shaye?"

And she had heard him; she opened an eye.

"Shaye Taylor," he whispered, so that none of their captors could hear. "*There's nothing so hot as a Tropical Sun!*" Adam had recognized her. He had quoted the slogan of the B-grade swimsuit publication she had modeled for.

Adam became a light in her life after that, just like the Florida sun he always wanted to carry her away to. Meanwhile her husband Riley had become worse than a stranger, turning on her and quickly divorcing her at the beginning of her illness when she was diagnosed with a strange, numbered, form of E-coli that the doctors knew little about. Shaye's husband Riley had been pragmatic enough to realize that her promising young career was lost along with her health and everything else.

The only thing left from the marriage was Shaye's diamond ring, which glittered oddly now in the rest area light. They planned to pawn it for their start in Florida.

Hopefully, Eric's biological father, and Della's boyfriend who lived in Orlando, would turn out trustworthy so that Shaye and Adam wouldn't have to keep up financial responsibility for the other two. But they would take care of the others if they had to; it was concern Eric's safety that gave them the nerve to escape the hospital in the first place.

Adam wore a loose gym shirt under his charcoal wool coat today. It gaped as he bent to suck on a milkshake, and Shaye caught a glimpse of his small rounded pecs pierced by two golden nipple rings.

Adam noticed her looking and she blushed. But he wasn't laughing. He took her by the arm.

"Shaye, Sweetie, come outside, please. I need to tell you something serious and I don't want the others to hear."

They walked out and leaned up against an outside brick wall. Shaye noticed the clouds rip apart, revealing pieces of blue sky. Adam still sipped on his milkshake but he wouldn't let her go.

"I'm only going to say this once," he said. Shaye nodded. It seemed difficult for him to say what he had to, but he forged ahead.

"I'm not well, Shaye. And I don't mean physically. In your case you're supposed to be this innocent victim of the system, locked up in the nuthouse only because you had a real physical illness and a whole string of doctors did you wrong. And I absolutely believe what you say; that's why I got you out of there. I mean, possibly you *are* a bit neurotic..."

They smiled at each other because, of course, Shaye Taylor currently *defined* the word neurotic.

"... But you're *sane*..."

Adam wouldn't let her away from the wall where she was pinned.

"Shaye, I've been on anti-psychotic medication since I was thirteen years old. And now I've gone off of it cold turkey. Right at the moment, I feel absolutely wonderful. But let's say something happens. I mean, it could."

Shaye felt all right meeting Adam's eyes. She had made the choice between life and death and the choice of breaking the law. Now, she would have to do whatever was called for, even if it meant taking care of someone else.

She wondered if she looked very reliable with her shaking body and twitchy eyes. "I'll be there for you, Adam," she said, "no matter what."

"You might have to be awfully strong all of a sudden," he said to her. "You might have to take care of those two..."

He gestured at the others who were just now coming through the doors, looking lost.

"I can do strange things when I'm off meds, Shaye, dangerous things..."

She heard what he said and yet she laughed ironically. So did Adam. His turning into some kind of monster seemed so improbable because, at the moment, he was her God, responsible for everything, even helping her shuffle across the parking lot to the car.

Adam got the car doors open; the others climbed in. People moved around busily in the parking lot while mountains loomed silently in the background. The air was very damp, like it was still filled with more snow it wanted to let out. Shaye had always hated the cold but today, finally being out, she felt like it was wonderfully invigorating.

In the hospital, in the patient lounge, they had watched a show called "Prophecies of the Millennium" and Shaye took it seriously, like she did all gloomy things these days. There was one year until the Millennium arrived, and maybe the end could come with a worldwide plague as easily as it could with a nuclear holocaust or a comet striking the earth. But, right now, she felt, really *felt* in her body, that there was nothing but time.

April 1999, Orange Blossom Trail, Orlando, FL
two days later

Adam Ant's deep dark secret was that he liked to cross dress, to dress up like a woman. Their first morning in Florida, Shaye got up and stretched, pulling herself up in the hotel bed with her hair falling around her and actually feeling luxuriant and healthy, forgetting for a moment about everything bad.

And then Adam came bounding out of the bathroom.

He wore a deep-plunging swimsuit made up of glittery silver fabric, and he started dancing for her, singing and mimicking runway moves.

"What do you think; is it me?"

Della still slept in the other bed. In an hour they were going to take her to a Denny's Restaurant here in Orlando to meet up with her boyfriend. She'd leave to live with him and then it would just be the two of them. They then planned to head back toward the East Coast of Florida, the part of the state they were both familiar with. They next planned to find work for a while in some anonymous little town and lay low there for as long as they needed to. Then, when they got all their legal trouble worked out, they'd head down to Miami, to the hip heart of South Beach, one place where, unfortunately, Adam's parents would probably be searching for him right now.

"I have to find out information. I have to find news," Shaye mumbled. "Where are we, anyway?"

"Well they call it Orange Blossom Trail," Adam chuckled. "But it ain't too pretty." He referred to the six-lane highway in front of their hotel that was lined with fast food, pawnshops and giant factory-outlet stores. This part of Florida was crowded with Office Depots, Tire Kingdoms, Sam's Clubs- a thousand un-tropical monstrosities like those and none of the quaint touristy places Shaye had expected.

A spur of Interstate 4 angled in from of their hotel. And a giant Disney billboard featuring ET the alien with enormous continuously rolling eyes looked as though it stared directly into their window. The sign had seemed ominous in the night but now it was bleached out in the soft blue sunshine. Shaye listened to the soothing noise of palm boughs brushing up against the long metal balcony where their room blended anonymously with the doors of thirty others, with two other identical floors below theirs.

All the snow had been magically stripped away the night before last as they passed through the Carolinas. Dropping Eric in DC had just been a sleepy blur for Shaye; it had been very dark, she had stayed lying in the back seat while Eric's father leaned in Adam's window to talk and to shake hands and Eric leaned back in to give Adam a hug goodbye. Big glowing white flakes had pattered down against the windows and Shaye's breath had come out steamy while she had fought not to whimper from another bout of pain in her stomach.

But today was another transformation, just like the books had promised. Alternative medicine books Shaye had taken to reading had given her the only real hope for her illness, a hope that she could be completely cured without any medication. She'd researched enough lately about everything ranging from faith healings, to herbal cures, to the miracles accomplished by witch doctors, to know that alternative cures could work. And all she wanted lately was to learn more.

"Adam," she persisted, "there must be a public library or an Internet café where we can get online to find out about the police search for us. And we could also pull up classifieds from some of the local papers to search for jobs for you."

"You know, you worry too much, girl," Adam said. "Way too much. I guarantee I'll take care of us. But, for the day, you need to just live. Can you do that? Feel some serenity and relaxation and start to heal. There's a wonderful heated pool here and who knows when we'll get the chance again. Anyway, I bought this suit for you at the thrift shop. A beautiful swimsuit for America's most glorious former swimsuit model. What do you think?"

There was something so sad in how Adam said this, something trembly in how he stood there wearing her ladies' swimsuit, like he was waiting to possibly be punished. It had been that way before, according to what he had confessed late nights they had stayed up in the lounge together. His father had started to physically punish him each time he dressed up in women's clothes. But it had been his mother who had started dressing Adam up as a joke and with the father's knowledge.

His mother had wanted a daughter to spoil and so, up until he was five years old, they had thought it cute to show their son off in public dressed up as a little girl. Then later, no matter how harsh the punishment, it became a compulsion for Adam to to dress as a female whenever he could. Each time his parents caught him he ended up back in the Children's Psychiatric Hospital.

Now that Adam was finally free, he could indulge in his compulsion as much as he liked with no one to punish him and he could finally see where it led.

And Shaye was here to support him, just as he was here to support her.

Shaye got up, a little wobbly on her feet, and touched the slippery bathing suit, which felt odd, like touching a woman. "I could try. But I don't really know if I can swim," she said, gently. "I mean, I still feel a little unsteady."

Adam seemed to feel accepted and he grinned again. "Well, first let me get you a healthy breakfast when we stop with Della at the restaurant. And then I *know* you can swim. This is Florida, Baby. I'll make sure you do it!"

Shaye had to admit that it was amazingly nice at the pool. The oversized free-form pool was a beautiful gem blue, illuminated by the sparkly Central Florida sunshine. When Shaye dipped a toe in, the water seemed to tremble before her for her entrance and analysis. Palm trees around the pool whooshed in the breeze and the sun glowed on the white concrete and white plastic chaises lounges.

This was such a simple place, yet it felt to Shaye like it represented everything and everywhere. And it felt so bittersweet to be alive. "My God!" she whispered.

"I told you you'd love it," Adam said. He'd changed into fluorescent pink swim trunks, which may not have been flashy as the glittering silver suit Shaye wore now, but he still seemed happy to be here.

At first Shaye huddled on one of the chaise lounges, wrapped up completely in a beach towel, not even realizing that she was shivering. Adam paid no attention. He had oiled his body and grinned with his eyes slanted in the sun.

Meanwhile, out of watery eyes, Shaye watched the other women, young mothers vacationing with their kids. Shaye had always been taught to prize slenderness, which had come naturally to her. But now it was plumpness she envied; tan, healthy flesh bursting unashamedly out of vivid colored bikinis, as the young women crashed around in the water with their children. Their lips and nail beds were pink; their butts, in inappropriate thong bikinis, looked brown and swollen, with water droplets beaded on them. They showed off for the old retirees and other women's thirty-something husbands around the pool. How healthy they seemed!

"Shaye," Adam hissed, "stop staring at other women's butts, or they'll think you're making a pass!"

Shaye gulped. "Am I that obvious?" she asked. "I was just thinking that I may never get my body back the way it was. You know, my skin will never be the same even if I could gain back the weight."

Adam dropped his sunglasses and looked at her seriously. "Does it really matter?" he asked. "At least you're alive. You know, there are other poor slobs in that State Hospital that are going to be there for the rest of their lives. And that is what the doctors said about you. They were telling you that your mind was gone. Now you're out. Nothing else really matters, does it, next to freedom? You can't be afraid of the honesty of life. Know what I mean?"

"Yeah, I do," Shaye answered. "What you're saying is, if this does work out, I'll have to accept life as it is, life after all the losses and the changes. I'll *have* to. Right?"

"I'm no wiser than you are, Sweetie, and this adventure is all uncharted territory," Adam said. "But all I know is there's nothing to be sad about on a day like this."

Of course, Shaye pondered- we make our own danger and our

own safety and this moment around the pool *could* be safe. So she told herself that it was.

Other women eyed Shaye's man, probably wanting to sleep with him. It amused Shaye to think what they would think if they knew Adam did want in their clothes, but for a very different reason.

Shaye got up, on her own, to go to the pool. Holding the railing tightly, she mouthed, "Microbes?"

Adam shook his head and mouthed back, "Chlorine. It makes it safe."

Tentatively Shaye lowered herself into the cool water, absorbed by the sight of sky. Another step and she felt the water wet down her hair, cleansing her in its tranquility. She took another step and then gave in and slid through the water. Closing her eyes, she glided, finding herself blissfully alone in a shadowed corner of the pool.

Shaye floated on her back, gently pulling her arms, breathing, forgetting everything. She stroked and pulled herself backward through the cool water, once, then again and again. She listened to the silvery ripples she created with her movement. She splashed her feet.

Where would they go the next day? She didn't know. But, with the sun and Adam smiling down on Shaye, she smiled, trusting to fate.

Chapter 2

Crime wasn't Shaye's and Adam's biggest worry when they looked for a place to stay. Their first priority was getting out of the public eye and going to ground for a few months until they could afford a decent legal defense. Neither of them had ever willfully hurt another living thing in their lives- but now by running away from the State Hospital, and rescuing two other patients, they had turned themselves into criminals.

Shaye and Adam laughed about it, just like they laughed about a lot of things these days, as money ran out and nights staying at Holiday Inns changed to nights at smaller chains they'd never heard of. Finally they felt lucky to afford nights in dank structures in wastelands of neighborhoods where half the storefronts sat abandoned, and the other half were barred. But they still tried to treat their trip as an adventure.

Looking for a safe place to roost, they hit the road again each day, discovering endless four or six-lane urban highways that all looked alike. Traveling, they explored a seemingly continuous grid of roads: repetitions of car lots with their flapping banners, hulking superstores, strip malls with improbable combinations of businesses and vast parking lots bristling with thousands of cars baking under the sun. Clogged intersections featured variations of the same combinations of fast food restaurants, chain drugstores and convenience store/gas stations- hundreds of nameless places like this all mirror images of each other, so that it was hard to know if you were in one city or the next.

This sprawl had no boundaries. Localities went by different names but, in physical reality, they simply merged into each other. Each town was just one more traffic light along the same garish parkway.

It was now obvious to Shaye that Florida had lost its heart. And it seemed such a shame. All development in this state was so relatively brand new- all in the nineteen hundreds, and most within the past twenty years- that it could easily have been planned right. And the state of Florida could have become the Crowning Glory of America; land developers could have learned from previous generations' mistakes. Instead, they capitalized on them and overbuilt due to greed.

At another time it may have been hard for Shaye and Adam to absorb this truth, only knowing Florida from only a few fashion shoots for her and a few club-hopping spring breaks for him. It used to be a fantasy place, dear to their hearts.

But they were different people now as they cruised these roads in the New York rent-a-car with no air conditioner and Shaye's ankle resting out the open window as she read ads out of the newspaper classifieds.

"It's different here then we thought," she said in a muted voice. "I guess we had lots of illusions."

They talked about how the developers seemed to be ruining that beachy Florida they had so cherished. It was ironic that all this sprawling retail held nothing for them as Adam discovered at interview after interview. Even the lowliest minimum wage jobs demanded a W-2 form and identification before they'd let you start work.

"I can work as a waiter, totally off the books," Adam asserted with his chin up. "We'll have to find some really small place, maybe some little bar. And everything around here seems like chains."

"Well, maybe we'll find something right on the beach," Shaye said. "That could be our best bet, amongst more laid back people. You know, I hate to get back to this... But we're going to have to get rid of this rental car soon. The police have probably traced it already..."

Shaye hated to refer to what she had discovered when she finally did get on the Internet at a Central Florida public library and she pulled up their local Westchester, New York newspaper. She'd held back on mentioning what she'd read while they dealt with more immediate concerns- like trying to score a hotel they could stay in long term or a viable job. But none of their prospects had worked out, and now was the time to share with Adam that fact that they were definitely wanted by the police. The article she found on the Internet mentioned several criminal charges including endangering the welfare of a minor. And some of the charges were felonies no matter how ridiculous or untrue they actually were.

Adam sighed after she filled him in. "I'm not completely surprised," he said. "It's just what we get for trying to be heroes." He sighed once again, making a smooth left turn on a green arrow with their wanted rental car.

"How about if we drive East to Cocoa Beach?" he suggested. "I've heard that town is somewhat quirky and touristy, kind of surfer style. So there would probably be bars we could try for work for me. If that doesn't work, Sweetie, then we can just work our way down the coast 'til we reach the Keys. We'll just discover some tiny beach town where we can walk to everything, and then we'll dump the car at one of the airports- just like they do in all your crime novels, Shaye."

Adam was so optimistic sometimes. Of course he had not been abused by the world in quite the way that Shaye had been the past two years. Even though society had ostracized and despised Adam, it had not gotten up and taken a physical piece out of his body the way it had with her. Shaye had learned not to trust anyone.

Yet she needed to trust Adam and allow him to quiet the screaming voices of her internal fears. She knew she couldn't act so panicked that it would get Adam crazy and unable to function. Because Shaye needed to stay with Adam to keep from being swallowed by this muggy, traffic-filled chaos where everybody moved too fast.

Another evening and Shaye stretched and yawned, hungry and sleepy, with a weight inside her stomach that was the fear of eating germ-infested fast food, a nagging thought of nowhere to sleep tonight and a moment of existential confusion and a questioning of "who is this man beside me and what really are his motives?"

This was paranoia; of course; it was Shaye's diagnosis. But at the same moment she was trussed up with anxiety that felt like barbed wire, she also felt limp and too tired to care. Being transient like this in this strange state of Florida had an odd effect on a person's soul. It felt like wandering this state somehow leveled you out, taking away your age and your sex and your strengths and your weaknesses and leaving you completely in the moment.

Shaye navigated for Adam, replacing the newspaper with the map and then she lifted the newspaper up again to look at ads for rentals in the Cocoa Beach area.

"I guess we'll have to find something that rents weekly," she said. "These monthly rentals are all asking for first and last months' rent, plus security deposit, and we just don't have that much money."

Adam glanced at her, absorbing the information. They had fallen into roles where he drove and looked for jobs, while Shaye was responsible for navigating, budgeting what was left of their money and securing places to stay.

"Whatever," Adam said. "I'm confident you'll find us something good. It just needs to be near somewhere I can find work."

Many of the small and timeworn mom and pop hotels used to rent to vacationing snowbirds back in Florida's heyday. But now the small hotels opened their doors to anyone, without credit or background checks. The problem was that they charged as much as five hundred dollars a week now during high season. And Shaye and Adam didn't have that.

They tried some weekly rentals that seemed affordable priced under two hundred dollars a week. But these efficiencies were located in the centers of gang-filled neighborhoods where crack cocaine was sold openly. Shaye and Adam felt desperate enough to try such hotels two separate times. Both times, after lying awake listening to the sounds of fighting and breaking glass outside, and then having no good job prospects the next morning, they looked at each other and said, "Let's just try another town."

They went to look at several nicer weekly rentals in private homes. But the middle-class landlords showed their renovated little spaces attached to their own sprawling suburban homes with a suspicious flicker of their eyes. Perhaps they were turned off by Adam's piercings, or the purple dents under Shaye's eyes. Shaye and Adam were starting to smell of desperation by now and the landlords acted as though they were afraid they would catch something. When they handed over rental applications including employment, credit and criminal background checks, Shaye and Adam had to give up.

Shaye would gaze wistfully at another screened porch, or pretty palm tree or vibrant hibiscus bush that wouldn't be theirs. Even where they didn't encounter rental applications, they were crippled by cost. One landlord added insult to injury by telling them that, including security, he wanted fifteen hundred dollars for them to move in.

"Fifteen hundred dollars to rent a weekly room! Remember that one?" Shaye reminisced.

Adam yawned, not sleepy, but just fatigued "Let's just get to the beach," he said. "And we'll just take any apartment we can get before our money runs out. It might have to be in a not-so-good neighborhood. But it'll only have to be for a little while, Shaye. What do you think?"

He knew that Shaye was very aware of crime and bad neighborhoods; he knew that her mental state at the moment made her hyper-aware of all dangers, so whether they could stay in a place would, ultimately, be her call.

"I think," she said, "I'm more afraid of the police catching up with us if we keep the car. We could stay anywhere for a little while, I guess and just lie low."

And she looked back down at the newspaper in her lap, even though it was getting toward sunset, too late to visit any more rentals tonight.

"What are all these places," she mused, looking over a section of rental ads she hadn't noticed before. "Oceanside and Flamingo Park. I've never heard of either of those places, but it looks like both towns have a bunch of weekly rentals. They must be wonderful places," she added, cynically. "'*Flamingo Park. Lo move-in. Privacy*'," she read to him. "It sounds sinister- like someplace out of one of my true crime books…"

Adam made a face as she read the rest of the ads to him. Then Shaye went back to that first ad and, as she read it again to herself, gooseflesh went up on her arms. It was turning night and getting colder.

Adam noticed her shiver. "We can avoid those places if you want to," Adam said.

But Shaye suspected he was just being nice; she had a very strong feeling that Oceanside or Flamingo Park was their next destination.

Shaye was right. She made the first call to one of the Flamingo

Park rentals from the ad a half hour later. The outdoor payphone at the Publix supermarket they chose felt suspiciously slimy to Shaye and she first had to clean it up with alcohol before she could make the call. Stilling her trembling, she punched out the number.

"A&H Investments" a wheezy man's voice said into the answering machine. And then followed a curt message on what you had to do to get one of the company's many weekly rentals. The man's voice sounded currupt to Shaye and too close to the phone. Behind her she heard the mundane clattering of shoppers' carts on concrete- the sounds of strangers' wellbeing. Shaye took some comfort in it as she scrawled down the impersonal directions given over the phone. The rental office wouldn't open again until Monday, and it didn't bother Shaye one bit that they had to wait that long to go there.

Shaye reported the progress of the phone call and then she and Adam sat down on a bench and ate a nice meal. Adam had asked an employee at the deli to microwave a factory wrapped sandwich for Shaye, and this was the first warm food that she'd eaten in weeks. The Publix parking lot was lit up with yellow lights, while the strip of woods around it was velvety dark. Insects thrummed from out of these woods while meanwhile shoppers did a quiet dance putting their groceries into cars. There was an unreality to the scene, an odd peace, Shaye thought.

She and Adam drove to the beach at Cocoa Beach late the next morning. The first thing they did after emptying their bladders was to try a sandpitted payphone in sight of the beach to call more of the Flamingo Park rentals. As the newspaper fluttered around her in the strong beach breeze, Shaye only reached more answering machines. Shaye and Adam shrugged to each other and decided that they might as well stay here for the moment, close to the phone and Tiki-style bar and grill.

And they both filled their lungs with refresing air and turned comfortably in the direction of the beach.

"Adam," Shaye said in wonderment. "This is what I was talking about!"

The beach, and this moment here, in the mostly deserted parking lot, felt glorious. Shaye's senses registered the call of sea gulls, the rustle of greenery and delicate sea oats, but most of all the incredible wash of air around them. She inflated her lungs and then the sparkling Florida winter breeze caught up her long hair and violently tugged it free.

Shaye watched her companion's face register the sight of her with wonderment. All the photo shoots she had been flown to various beaches for- all the times she had been set up in front of the water with a whole crew of people poking at her to make her hair fly in the breeze had been contrived to achieve this result!

But Shaye had been too much a product of civilization then, she realized now instinctively; she'd been just a girl, laughing at it all. Maybe nature could only embrace you when you truly had nowhere else to go. And now the message was not anything that could be manipulated- to look sexy, for example, like the beach was supposed to make her look in the swimsuit catalogs. The real message was more raw; you'd have to take it where it chose to lead you.

Shaye looked at Adam. "I've got it, right? Is that what you're thinking?"

"You're magnificent, Shaye."

"No, Adam. The *beach* is magnificent!"

She smiled and then spun and jogged towards a little wooden crossover where the blue horizon beckoned. They hiked over it quickly, Shaye leading. Then she ripped off her sneakers and jumped down into the sand. She stumbled and almost fell, because her balance was still altered from residual medication in her bloodstream. But she righted hersef and hurried forward.

Walking in the sand tired Shaye and made her pant, but the sounds of the birds and the frilly sound the water made coming to shore urged her on irresistibly. She and Adam came to stand at the water's edge breathless while small breakers slammed up, threatening, and then the water curled away just missing their feet.

"I mean," Shaye said, "I've finally figured things out. That was all bullshit, Adam, that *Tropical Sun* catalog. My whole former career. I mean, real life is frightening every minute- that's what I'm finding out. But meanwhile, it's like I'm finding out other things, too, like the best things are somehow granted to those most in trouble. I mean, Adam, I think I never really *saw* the beach before…"

Adam smiled at her indulgently. Either he had this all figured out already or else he was in a different place altogether, with different issues. He rubbed at his hair, which was already stiffening with salt, and he teased her.

"I remember that *Tropical Sun* catalog." He grinned as they plopped down together near the surf. "You were my idol," he said. "You were like the flesh and blood essence of femininity, Shaye, wearing those tiny swimsuits with your boobs hanging half the way out, showing off your long trashy nails and just looking innocent and confused. I so much got off on looking at you, I hoarded those catalogs and, when I saw you in person I almost died."

"So you liked me because I was dumb!" Shaye made a show of pouting, yet she was able to laugh.

They rolled over on their stomachs to watch some teenagers walk onto the beach, the guys carrying surfboards.

"You know," Shaye said, telling herself as well as Adam, "I don't think I would ever want to be famous and naïve again. All I want now is to be free of all the fears I have. I always took safety for granted before. You know, before I knew how treacherous the world could really be. But now I think I'd have to earn that feeling of safety- I mean, make my way through in this horrible world that I've discovered. There are heartbreakingly wonderful places like this beach right now. And I never would have appreciated it. Even though sometimes I don't know from moment to moment now if I'll make it. Sometimes I don't know what fears are in my head and which are really out there."

She would have liked to cry but the warm sun on her back wouldn't quite let her.

"Don't worry so much," Adam said. "Try to take things one step at a time. We've just got to wait a few months and then my trust fund will come through. And as soon as it does, we'll hire a good lawyer who can get us off the criminal charges. You just need to be strong enough that you can get up on a witness stand and let a judge see that you no longer have to be locked up in a loony bin. We'll work on that, Shaye. But first we have to get you physically healthy, get your ulcer cured and get you eating again.

"Your fears may not all go away," he said, "but I believe we can get you functioning. I believe you can live a wonderful life. And you know, Shaye, that's been more important to me than my own future. The thing that would make me the happiest would be to see Shaye Taylor healthy once again- and living a glorious life."

Shaye looked out to sea, and the breeze turned suddenly strong. So strong that it snatched the words of reply out of her mouth. So strong that it stung her eyes, making them painfully water as she gazed out into the distance.

Fearless in Florida

Later that day, Flamingo Park Florida

The first thing that Shaye noticed about Flamingo Park, the sprawling trailer park so large that it represented its own municipality, was that today was obviously trash day. Couches with exposed springs and assorted items of furniture beyond salvage were piled high at every driveway. As she'd dreaded, Shaye observed old cars on blocks and long strips of bent aluminum hanging off the sides of some trailers. Seemingly impenetrable brush broke up the crowded homes, vegetation that looked like it had never been trimmed or tamed.

It was quiet at the moment. In fact, so far Shaye hadn't seen one human being since they'd turned into the park off Flamingo Beach Parkway. A few of the trailers in the shabby area seemed surprisingly neat- with Florida-style lawn ornaments and carefully tended plants. And the mood of quiet, although oppressive, didn't seem necessarily foreboding, she tried to convince herself.

The next thing that Shaye noticed as they explored the maze of short streets were the dogs of Flamingo Park- mutts with orange coats and square jowls, others that appeared to mix Rottweiler and some other protective breed, all wandering aimlessly in the streets. These streets were dirt, and the mixture of the flying dust and the listless panting dogs gave an Old Southern appearance to the area. Shaye and Adam drove past a little canal that was partly obscured by brush.

"I wonder what's in that canal," Shaye said, biting her lip. "Alligators, maybe. So that's a danger we have to consider." She looked over the garbage in front of all the trailers and shuddered. "And maybe rats, too. You know, rats in a place like this could carry bubonic plague."

"I know,"Adam said with a sigh. And Shaye realized he was humoring her even as she eyed the vacant lots, the areas that were crowded in some spots and consisted of empty desolate space in others.

"I wonder if it might be safe here, though," he said, with some aspect of hopefulness betrayed in his voice. "Safe enough for a little while."

The first weekly rental that Adam and Shaye went to look at was a travel trailer situated about an arm's length away from its neighbor. The landlord emerged from this second trailer where he lived. He was a young man, shirtless, with one eye shut and blackened.

He finished a beer and the first thing he did was to extend another unopened can to Adam.

"You fish?" he asked. "I do a lot of fishing."

Adam declined the offer of the beer and sidestepped when the guy tried to lean on him. There seemed something too familiar in the landlord's approach.

His good eye roved between Adam and Shaye. "You guys party?" he asked. "Selling any weed? 'Cause I can't get shit around here lately!"

While he spoke to them, he left the door of his trailer open, allowing the bugs to fly in and one cat after another to slowly wander out. Shaye and Adam backed away. The landlord didn't seem to notice; he just closed his good eye tightly, leaned his head back and sucked on the extra beer that had been meant for Adam.

"Oh *no*!" Shaye said as they turned down another street, leaving the rental behind.

"The sad part is," Adam added, "that guy seems to think in well around here."

Shaye knitted her brow.

"Maybe we do at this point," she commented after a moment had gone by, and Adam let the comment hang in the air offering her no reply.

They crisscrossed the expansive trailer park, quickly driving past some of the rentals they were supposed to be viewing today because the mobile homes simply looked too rundown to stop at. One home in the approximate center of the park stood out. It seemed a showplace among the others, relatively small but of a doublewide construction with a unique lattice-style cinderblock wall in front, a close-cropped lawn and several mature banana trees and a big palm in the well-tended yard.

"Now that one looks pretty sweet," Shaye commented. "Relatively."

Adam uncrinkled the classifieds. "That one's on our list, Shaye," he said. "It's the one from the holding company we called. I thought you didn't want to see it because you said the absentee landlord sounded like a mobster."

He had slowed the car down in front of the mobile home and a young woman with long blond hair and bare dusty feet smiled at them as she passed on the street. Silence enveloped them as they pulled up onto the lawn in front of the trailer.

"I guess we could look."

Shaye's voice was quiet as though respecting the greater mood as they padded around the vacant trailer, peering into windows. Inside it looked dingy, but livable, and outside it was lush. Shaye especially liked the screen of trees.

Some of the neighbors they saw looked young and gave the impression of being alcoholics and potheads, with bleached hair and leathery tans that came from spending hours outside, working and playing. The few older residents looked like long term alcoholics that had reached the end of their useful lives here, living in the only rentals that allowed them to support their habits.

This park seemed like a place where Adam and Shaye might safely vanish for a while. And the holding company was only asking two hundred dollars a week for rent. Adam and Shaye headed inland that afternoon to drop off their rent and three weeks' security deposit, and they moved into the trailer that night.

They got back with the key and then the half rusted lock put up a fight. You had to jiggle it a certain way just to get it open, and Shaye felt exposed and vulnerable waiting for Adam to figure it out. She decided to make herself useful by unloading the car. Leaning in to load up with the possessions they had accumulated during their travels, she felt even more spotlighted and exposed.

It was early evening and little Manatee St. was filling up with people now. Four pickup trucks on extra high wheels parked in the driveway across from theirs, and shirtless men milled around while the long-haired blond woman held a beer can and chased kids around the street.

Every now and then one of the kids would get too close to Shaye, trying to lean into the car with her, and the woman with the blond hair would yell at the child and then call out an apology. At times a mottled mongrel dog also came to snuffle around Shaye's heels. She rushed forward to the house with an armload of stuff.

"Adam," she hissed between clenched teeth. "Get the damn door open! Those people are all over me. It frightens me!"

"I'm trying," he said. "The lock is broken. Just another thing that's unsafe around here. There," he said as the door burst open, allowing out a smell of old human perspiration.

"Uuugh!" Shaye exclaimed in horror. She had to hold back tears as she leaned on the doorframe and tiny raindrops started splashing through the vegetation onto her. The smell of the place was truly sickening, like someone had curled up in here to die, she thought. "I don't know if I can do this!"

Panic bubbled up inside her again and then came fear of the panic. Before the doctors had called Shaye paranoid/schizophrenic, they had first labeled her as agorophobic, which meant that she had a fear of everything or, more specifically, a fear of fear itself. Her frequent panic attacks would set off physical symptoms and, if the panic attacks went too long unchecked they could aggravate her bleeding ulcers.

Whenever Shaye saw the coffee-colored blood this, in turn, set off more fear, forcibly controlled in the hospital by powerful medications the doctors forced on her. But there was nobody here to sedate her now, to restrain her, to keep her from physically damaging herself. Right now there were only cold hard, little droplets of rain.

Shaye squeezed her eyes tight shut, until the panic inside her shrunk down to a hard concentrated ball in her gut.

When she opened her eyes, she saw Adam looking at her with compassion. Shaye listened to an adult spanking a child in the street, and she tried to remember how she had learned to do Zen meditation in the past few months from her books. Just listen to each sound for what it is, she told herself; it can't touch you any more than those germs in the trailer can. She could clean the trailer, she reasoned and those people in the street would not hurt her; in fact, they hardly noticed her. In all things she had time.

"Shaye," Adam said. "I'm sorry about this. You have to understand that I'm as scared as you are." Adam shuddered as he looked into the interior, which was chilly despite the ninety-degree heat outside. The trailer wafted its dank smell onto his clean body and was darkened inside by cloaking dusty draperies.

"I'll do what I can to get a waiter job," he said. "And you can check the newspapers on the Internet and find out how hot South Beach is for us. After a month, maybe even less than that, we can get out of here. I'm not going to let anything hurt you, Shaye. You're my only friend in this world."

At the moment Shaye felt, literally, like a cornered animal. She stood here wrestling with the smell of enemies, some gone, some still here, the old human odors now mixed with the fumes of carbuerator cleaner, someone repairing a truck across the street.

"Then why are you laughing?" she snapped as she noticed a smile starting to form on Adam's handsome lips. Her voice raised above the revving of the neighbors' engine.

"Oh," Adam said. Then he laughed again and couldn't stop laughing for a moment. He contained himself enough to speak. "I'm sorry," he said, finally. "It's just that my father used to say to me that if I kept cross-dressing I'd end up in some trailer like this, in some neighborhood like this, with no job. And then some steroid psycho biker would come in the night and slit my throat because I didn't want to be his bitch. And my father said he'd laugh when it happened…"

Shaye just walked away from Adam, shaking her head fretfully. Maybe he didn't realize how disgusted with him she felt at the moment. Sometimes it seemed that Adam had to make everything about his gender identity- someone could be killing them and he'd still be screaming about whether people were willing to accept him with mascara and women's underwear! But, as quickly as it came, Shaye allowed her impatience to be replaced with amusement. After all, what could she and Adam expect of eachother when they each had their own mental illness and their own obsessions?

At a few minutes past five, when Shaye made her final trip to unload the car, a low rider car with four men filthy from working brushed by her on the street, their arms hanging negligently out the windows so that they almost touched her. She gazed after the car as it drove off trailing black exhaust and she pondered that working men and day laborers probably used their little street, Manatee Street, as a favorite shortcut because of its proximity to Flamingo Beach Parkway.

"Wonderful," Shaye mumbled.

From deep in the maze of streets, Shaye heard another of their new neighbors.

"You touch my fucking dog," his drunken voice yelled, "and I'll burn down your muthafuckin' trailer!"

A group of men laughed uproariously and another man teased the first speaker. "No one's touching your piece of shit dog. It's your *woman* you gotta worry about…"

Then came the noise of a scuffle behind a trailer, the sounds of beer bottles breaking and men laughing.

The long-haired woman that looked like Shaye raised her voice, calling to the men. "Why don't you shut the fuck up, guys? You're gonna make our new neighbors think we're trash around here."

Now some of the grimy male faces looked up, eyes peering at Shaye, where she leaned in the vehicle, her face only partially obscured by the lightly tinted windows.

"That chick looks just like Darlene!" one of the men said. Shaye knew for a fact they were talking about her. It was nothing bad, she realized, not yet. But it promised to be a very long month.

As she straightened up out of the car, which was now emptied of junk and could be dropped off at the International Airport tomorrow, the dog the group had been talking about came padding across the street. It was a big friendly, red hound dog and it happily sprayed yellow piss all over the side of the white rental car.

Shaye was scowling at the spectacle when the next vehicle cruised up the street. A local blue and white police car, it moved through the street like it did this many times each day, expertly avoiding the dog and a metal trash can on its side that rolled lazily in the dust.

The officer inside hunched down, drinking a big takeout soda and enjoying the car's air conditioning with the windows run up. Darlene and some of the men waved to him, but he ignored them. And then he stopped the car.

He looked straight at Shaye. The officer was a dark young Italian and he looked deeply tired and somewhat impatient. Shaye noticed all of this because, ironically, he was exactly the type she used to be attracted to in high school, when she and her girlfriends from Westchester County used to dress up and use fake ID's to get into dance clubs in the city when she was young. The young cop resembled her first serious high school boyfriend and many of the other boys she'd had crushes on and she wondered what someone like him was doing working in this desolate trailer park in Florida.

He looked like he had been here forever, so tired that he was living off the caffeine in the soda. His brown eyes locked on hers, soulful yet also suspicious. Finally he drove away, but not before his look made it clear he had noticed her.

Adam came to stand next to her. "The overhead lights don't work in the trailer," he said. "We need to pick up some kind of lamps. And you better look inside. I think you may want to throw out what's inside and buy some new clean bedding..."

"A cop just went by," was Shaye's comment, made in a wooden inflection, as she watched the dust settle in the street following the squad car's progress.

Shaye and Adam stayed out late shopping and it was very tense knowing that if Adam didn't get the job tomorrow, they could only make one more week's rent. But Shaye felt she absolutely needed cleaning supplies, for their rental was obviously a nexus of previous tenants' germs.

In an older Publix supermarket at the corner of US 1 and Flamingo Beach Parkway, people looked at Shaye strangely as she frantically piled bleach and yellow rubber gloves in their cart, instructing Adam rather shrilly, "We've got to make at least a ten percent solution of bleach to clean with. That'll kill even Hepatitis B germs. I've researched it. We've got to sterilize everything!"

Adam had stopped to put on makeup before they went out, just mascara, lipgloss and eye shadow, but he had insisted. "If I'm going to risk my freedom for this, I might as well do it," he said. "Anyway, I walked around in public like this when I went to performing arts high school, and I never had a problem with it."

Contrary to what it might seem, with all the weirdos who lived in the state, Florida was not at all progressive. In the supermarket, Adam, with his makeup and flamboyant ways, got many hateful looks that made Shaye cringe. But it wasn't like she could say anything; they constantly indulged her phobias and now they were indulging Adam's needs.

And at least Adam could be happy with what he did.

When they drove back to their trailer it was late and quite dark. A phosphorescent glow seemed to come from the canal on Caiman Street and Shaye peered deeply into the mysterious water as they passed.

"I saw something move, Adam," she said. "I think it was an alligator. Just another danger. Another danger lurking for us..."

Chapter 3

Adam got a job interview lined up for the next day and, that afternoon, he insisted that they stop at a thrift shop so he could purchase an outfit. Shaye felt restless and overtired after their first night. All through the night she had listened to constant noise in the neighborhood; a truck with a bad muffler circling the block again and again and far off men's voices yelling. And then there was a suspicious noise that sounded like something scraping the metal screening of her bedroom window.

Every time Shaye heard the sound, more tired each time as the night wore on, she dutifully got up and checked every latch and window. The 1970's vintage mobile home featured many of these, including weird vent-like windows made of metal. The assorted windows served as their only ventilation at night, since the central air conditioning in the trailer didn't work.

Adam didn't seem surprised when Shaye padded through his room at two, and then at three in the morning to check his open window for prowlers outside. Adam wasn't sleeping either. Instead, Shaye found him sitting up, biting his nails and staring out towards the streetlight like he was thinking deeply.

At 4:00 am Shaye's fears about contagious disease outstripped her fears of intruders and she got down on hands and knees, equipped with bleach and rubber gloves to scrub out the tiny bathroom off her bedroom. At five in the morning she tried to settle down again, but her bed still felt grainy to her, as though the previous tenants had left unspeakable filth in it. Sleeping on spread newspaper the way the landlord had left it wasn't going to be enough. Shaye stripped the mattress and made a crude patchwork covering of black garbage bags to seal it off. All the while she felt a creepy feeling, as though someone was spying on her activity though the inadequately covered window. She peered out at the blackness of the back yard, suddenly aware of how vulnerable she must look.

Only when dawn lightened the sky and a fresh thread of breeze cleared out some of the menace in the air, did she feel free to lay her beach towel over the garbage bag sealed mattress and curl into fetal position and sleep. She felt any of the night's crimes had already been committed; daylight had made it safe.

And then came bad dreams, even worse than she had experienced in the hospital.

"I can't cook in this kitchen," Shaye told Adam in the morning.

"I wanted coffee," he said, going for an old kettle left on the stove, just like many of the tourist efficiencies by the beach left you dishes.

"Please!" Shaye said intently. "Don't touch that! Don't touch anything until I've had a chance to clean this place properly. Please let me take care of it." She pushed at her hair ineffectually. "I tried to clean my bathroom during the night."

She hung her head and extended to her roommate a pathetic offering, a Pop Tart that was stone cold after being kept overnight in the refrigerator. "I'm sorry," she said. "I thought I saw roaches during the night, so I put all of our groceries in there."

"Oh," Adam said simply and then he chamged the subject. "Please come to the thrift store with me, Baby. It will give me confidence if I can go to the interview looking good."

Adam had located a local Salvation Army Superstore, something Shaye had never seen before. As they approached the doors, they had to dodge several overweight shoppers in shorts dragging heavy pieces of furniture out to their vehicles. Two scruffy men in their thirties sat on the stoop sharing a cigarette and they leaned into eachother and laughed, pointing after Shaye's long legs and long blond hair as she passed.

There wasn't much cool air conditioning inside the store and Shaye felt dizzy following Adam through row after row of musty clothes. Oblivious, Adam excitedly filled bags with cheap clothes for himself and his female *doppleganger*, a persona he liked to call Eden.

"Grab something for yourself, Baby," he encouraged. "It's a

dollar an item!"

Adam selected a gray silk shirt and dress trousers for his job interview, designer castoffs, while telling Shaye what he knew about the cross-gender nightclub called Foxy Lady where he was going to apply.

"And this job is just for a waiter?" Shaye asked. "It sounds a little off, you know?"

"You never know," Adam said, trying to make light of it. "Maybe Foxy Lady does sound a bit unsavory, and it's weird that they have a bar like that all the way out in the countryside. But, you know, dressing up nice, even if it's in *guy's* clothes like this, gives me heart in any situation!"

For herself, Shaye picked out a few oversized souvenier-style T-shirts with iron-ons of different Florida animals. The animals reminded her of the street names in their trailer park, where the planners had seemed to use up the cute names like Manatee and Ibis and Conch and then had to extend to naming streets after native menaces. Gator and Barracuda Streets, for example were main thoroughfares in the park.

Because of her dizziness, Shaye had trouble seeing her T-shirts very well. She kept licking her lips and blinking because her vision was getting funny.

"Are you okay?"Adam asked as they stepped back into the oven-like parking lot and plopped into the rental car without air. He twisted around to shove four full bags into the back seat. "You need something to eat or drink?"

"I'll be okay," Shaye said. "I think it's just the heat."

She felt a little better as he got the car moving. They drove further west, then south. The scenery changed to woods, swampy fields and abandoned looking industrial lots.

"Where *are* we?" she asked twenty minutes later.

"Supposedly the club is all the way out here. The kind of business it does, it has to be outside city limits. Are you sure you don't need to stop to eat something?"

"No, you'll be late for your interview," she said. "I'll get something later."

Stupidly, Shaye hadn't brought bottled water with her; now she could not accept any food or drink until they could find a convenience store where the product would be sealed.

"Is this it?" Adam asked disturbing her from her reverie. They had pulled up in from of a decrepit peach-colored strip mall that contained an adult book and novelty store, an incongruous medical supply shop and a tinted door flanked on either side by windows covered by closed hurricane shutters. Curvaceous white lettering on the door read, "Foxy Lady."

It was odd how the club was miles from anywhere. On one side there was a farmstead, on the other a Stor-All facility with a group of large U-Haul trucks, some missing tires, parked in front. The row of individual storage units seemed to stretch a mile back, exuding a greasy industrial smell. Aside from double-rig tractor-trailers flying by on the county road, it seemed like no living thing had passed this way in a long time.

Adam glanced at Shaye, who slumped in her seat.

"Are you sure you're going to be okay?" he asked.

Just then two strikingly trampy looking women came striding out of the club, giggling and leaning into each other, counting money. Shaye grimaced.

"I'll be fine," she reassured Adam. "Go ahead in, you look great."

One of the women was maybe five foot seven, a few inches shorter than her red-haired friend and she had a slim exciting figure that caught the eye. She strutted along, with each move intentionally attention-grabbing, sporting black leather ankle boots with metal spike heels and delicate chains around the ankles. She had a big head of glossy black waves, dusky skin and she favored intense wine-colored lipstick. She turned around fully to stare at Adam as he walked into the club.

"Where you been all my life, brother?" she called after him in a husky Cuban accented voice, just loud enough to impress her friend. Then she caught sight of Shaye sitting in the car and watching her. She flashed a look in Shaye's direction. "You got some problem with that, girlfriend?" she challenged. Her voice was so melodic that it made even her anger seem somewhat charming.

Shaye wasn't after a fight. It seemed ironic- the world had already won its contest with her and she would have thought that it showed in her face.

She just sighed, hoping the woman would go away. And then her attention was distracted by a dark male form she noticed lurking at the end of a row of storage units. And the sun felt so awfully hot.

"Madeline, come on," the Hispanic girl's friend pleaded. She pulled Madeline over to stand in front of the medical supply store and then she leaned over and whispered to her, obviously trying to dissuade her from bothering Shaye.

The redhead, despite the retro Farah Fawcett bigness of her hair, seemed more mature and extremely tired. Her makeup looked cakey and failed to cover the deep lines around her eyes. As the women stood conferring, a new midnight blue Infiniti sedan driven by a whitehaired man in a silk dress shirt pulled up beside them and she nudged her friend and then leaned into the window to speak to him.

Shaye noticed how the woman's dress was skintight and lipstick red and marveled how incongruous it seemed for the hookers to be working at noontime with commodes and canes behind them.

Lost in thought, Shaye must have missed something. One moment the two women were flirting with the driver; the next moment the car burned rubber out of the parking lot and the redhead yelled after it, "I ain't doing nothing for less than fifty, you old faggot!"

The two girls laughed together in surprisingly deep voices.

Suddenly Shaye felt like she was losing consciousness; she felt herself dropping against the window frame. Next thing she knew the hookers were by her at the window staring at her with concern. She was overwhelmed by their big mascara-accented eyes, their cakey makeup and glittery dresses.

"Wake up! Are you okay?" The redhead roughly nudged her, offering her a cold soda. Shaye felt for it, her hand trembling against the condensation. She smelled perfume and body heat, *male* body heat. The two hookers were right up in her face and looked so belligerently female- and yet her nose told her they were male!

Shaye looked up blearily again into the faces, feeling like Dorothy from *The Wizard of Oz*. The Spanish one had such soft blurry features, really pretty, but it was possible if you looked at her from a certain angle that she could be a guy, probably no older than twenty, Adam's age.

The redhead with her craggier features- yes, she was definitely a guy. Shaye was surprised she hadn't noticed it before.

"I can't take the soda," Shaye's voice came out as a dry whisper. "Unless it's screw top. And the seal can't be broken. It has to be sterile, because I can't risk the germs."

"But you're dehydrated, Honey" the redhead protested.

"Leave her alone," her Spanish friend said. "Or get her the

bottled soda like she wants. How do you think she *got* this way?"

Shaye didn't care about the insults. When the redhead brought her a fresh soda from the bar she drank it in one long desperate drink.

After sucking down the soda she said, "Thank you," and extended a dollar bill to reimburse her for it, trying not to meet either woman's eyes for too long, because meeting new people lately terrified her.

The redhead was going to respect her privacy and walk away. But her Hispanic friend paused. "Wait," she said and leaned back in the window, with breasts that looked very real showing inches of cleavage.

"Is that your man?" she asked Shaye, her voice deepening just slightly as some of her act was dropped. "If he is, I'll back off. I was just messing with you and I know we're going to have to work with him. So, is he yours?"

"He's my friend. We live together." Shaye said, feeling bleary and far from reality.

"What's his name?"

"Adam. Or Adam Ant; that's his stage name."

The transsexual cracked her gum. "So, are you doing him?"

It took Shaye a while to figure out what was meant. Miserably, she shook her head. Two years ago, back when she modeled swimsuits, Shaye had been the quintessential boy toy; she used to be *good*. Now, emaciated, she no longer even got her period.

"No, I'm not doing him," she answered, hanging her head.

The "girls" glanced at each other.

"Is he gay or is he straight?" the darker one persisted.

Shaye had wondered about this herself. Because, at times, even though she no longer had sexual feelings in any normal sense and even though she knew from what he told her and showed her that Adam was as female as she was, there were sometimes incongruities that troubled her. Like when he used to sneak into her room in the hospital and lie down on the narrow bed beside her to whisper through the night, she used to sometimes feel something she shouldn't, something inside her that was disturbing.

"I don't know if he's gay," she said, honestly. "We never really talk about that. You could ask him, you know. He's really open. We just never got around to talking about that, a lot was happening…"

The transsexuals shook their heads at her in awe. Even these people thought she was nuts.

"My name's Madeline." The dark haired one laughed. "And you're fucked in the head!" Madeline then twitched off on her heels, laughing, going straight for Adam who was coming out of the club.

"Don't sweat it," the redhead said to Shaye. "He's just on PMS." And then she reached out and tousled Shaye's hair. "You've got pretty hair, you know. You're a really pretty girl." And she looked at Shaye like she didn't quite understand her.

Adam talked with the two transsexuals for a few minutes, and then he gave them a theatrical kiss goodbye before jumping into the car with Shaye and pulling out of the parking area.

"Let's go get you some food," he said. "Rochelle told me you almost passed out."

"How do you do it?" Shaye asked. "How can you get people to love you in ten seconds flat, Adam? I just create aggression in that much time." She laughed at herself.

"I got the job," Adam said, without additional comment. "And the girls are coming by tomorrow night to give me a ride. They're performers. Is it all okay with you?"

"I guess."

Then Adam turned to look directly at Shaye and the car veered all over the road.

"Did you just tell them I was gay?"

"Just that I didn't know," Shaye said in a small voice, feeling uncomfortable talking about this. For some reason she felt ashamed. She tried to say innocently, "I mean, I *don't* know…"

Adam suddenly seemed angry with her, although she really didn't know why. "Well, if you don't know, why bother asking, right?" he said. Dusky red spots bloomed on his alabaster cheeks.

Shaye hated the sudden feeling of distance between them, but she chose to just let things go and let them resolve themselves. She gazed out the window, watching for alligators and snakes in the miles of stagnant water at the side of the road. Adam finally broke her reverie.

"Do you think you'll be okay in that trailer at night, Shaye while I'm working? I'll get my first pay two weeks from now, and some tips each night. The problem is, I don't think you can hang around the Foxy Lady waiting for me. The place isn't real wholesome; you know what I mean? Things go on there…"

Shaye noticed the dark shadows that had formed under Adam's

eyes and she imagined her own face had the corresponding look. She had no real desire to see what went on inside Foxy Lady's tinted door.

It was quiet when they returned home to Flamingo Park, walking after having dropped the car off at the airport and then alighting from the County bus at the local bus stop. They both breathed shallowly in the heat. In her peripheral vision Shaye took in the details of Caiman Street, which was their shortcut into the park. Some of the trailers on this little street looked tipped over at an angle, while a dinette set laid out for dinner sprawled in the bare red dirt of one neglected front yard. Children wearing diapers played near overflowing garbage cans while, nearby, a shockingly red bird pecked at the marshy grass along the side of the canal.

"What *is* that?" Shaye asked.

"A scarlet ibis, I think. It's native to Florida" Adam seemed to relax into Shaye's relaxation now. They rounded a few corners and were then welcomed by the frond-covered fortress of their own trailer.

It was fairly late; since it had taken a while to drop the car off at the airport and make the bus connections for their return. Then they had to pick up a bag of food at the local supermarket. Now Shaye watched headlights flicker past occasionally on Manatee Street while she prepared dinner, thinking of how this would be their last dinner together for a while. The next night Adam was going to be starting work as a waiter for the dinner shift at Foxy Lady.

"I'm tired," Shaye said as she sipped on cocoa after dinner and Adam finished his coffee.

"I know, Sweetie. So am I," he said.

They went to their respective rooms, his in the front of the trailer, hers in the back where their lot connected with that of the neighbors.

Shaye started cleaning and made up the bed with her new comforter. She was interrupted suddenly by a sound like a gunshot that seemed to come from several blocks away.

Immediately, she flattened against a wall and then hurried through the darkened living room and burst into Adam's room without knocking.

She found him lying on his new striped comforter faced away from her curled into a fetal position, his lips moving along with music from his boom box turned so low you could barely hear it.

He didn't even startle when she ran in, just rolled slightly to see her.

Shaye felt embarrassed. "That noise," she asked. "You think it was a gunshot?"

It was an inauspicious start to their evening. Instead of sleeping, Shaye sat down on Adam's mattress and talked, subjects ranging from her fears in the park to both of their fears of being arrested and both of their destroyed relationships with their families. They got up late the next morning.

But the mornings always managed to seem more cheerful. It was a rural setting, after all; the air was fresh and birds sang amongst the trees.

After cleaning some more inside, Shaye and Adam went out and began pruning the greenery in their yard, then excitedly transferring plants from one side of property to another, festooning trees with air plants and dragging suitable furniture outside.

By afternoon, Shaye had exactly what she wanted, a little outdoor room behind the lattice that was covered by enough greenery to protect her from view and yet clear enough to give her a vantage point on the street.

"You see that guy?" she asked Adam while peeking through the spyhole in the concrete blocks. She indicated a middle-aged black man with baggy green trousers and worn down shoes who slowly passed their trailer, darting furtive glances.

"This is the third time he's passed here in an hour," Shaye said. "And he did the same thing yesterday. There's something wrong about him and it frightens me."

Shaye had noticed yesterday how the man's eyes looked glazed and wild, and she had memorized his features so that she could be alert if he ever came around here again. But today he turned the corner and stayed away.

When the light started fading Adam went in to shower and dress and Shaye settled down in the outdoor room. It would be intolerably frightening with Adam being away until two in the morning. But taking action like this, sitting down to her vigil before he left somehow made it easier.

Adam gave Shaye a hug goodbye.

"Make sure to eat something," he said, before he jogged off to catch his ride. Waiting in the car, a little blue Escort, Rochelle waved happily at Shaye before she and Adam drove off.

As it got later, Shaye locked up the trailer airtight despite the heat. She turned out most of the lights so that she would not be silhouetted in the windows. Then she sat down to wait, listening to the on and off grumble of the old refrigerator while pondering.

Noises mounted in the neighborhood- fighting voices, car engines and drunken laughter- and fear seemed to carry Shaye out of the trailer and above the neighborhood on its wings. She could already visualize where most of the streets lay in relation to each other and imagination filled in for her what kind of incidents the sounds represented.

Shaye felt homesickness well inside her. It wasn't her ex-husband Riley and her glamourous career she missed right now, but rather her parents and their unconditional love. She pined for the safety of their big traditional home in Westchester County, New York, where her own room sat, probably still untouched since she had left it six years ago.

But now Shaye was tainted and no longer welcome in that fancy pink and cream bedroom of her childhood. Her dear parents had come to visit her in the State Hospital towards the beginning of her illness and a choice was made clear to her- take the medicine the psychiatrists prescribed and get better like they claimed she should, or else lose their love and protection. Shaye's parents watched her refuse the doctors' poisons. They grimaced as she stubbornly shut her mouth tight and thrust against her captors' restraints, accepting only those drugs shot or dripped into her screaming veins.

Her mother and father paled as they watched Shaye scream in rage, tossing her head and flinging bloodied vomit and drool in every direction. With each Sunday afternoon visit, Shaye noticed the fear grow stronger in her beloved parents' eyes, along with sadness. And she felt so very sad herself when they finally stopped coming to see her at all, sending only the occasional greeting card embellished with flowers and butterflies- the things Shaye Celestia Banks used to love.

Now Shaye allowed herself the luxury of a few tears in the darkness. She was so ready to protect herself against any intruder in the trailer that she found herself holding a kitchen knife at her side. But what was she protecting, really?

What did she have to look forward to? Adam had all kinds of schemes. He would go to college for psychology, he was sure on some days. Other days he thought he'd pursue a career as a pop recording artist. Adam was going to get his trust fund when he turned twenty-one, so it was possible his schemes could work.

Shaye could start college too, couldn't she? She had recently discovered the Internet and she seemed to come alive in its anonymity and richness of knowledge. She worked over plans in her mind. She could go to a community college, train to work with computers and then never have to deal with people face to face if she didn't want to. That is, she could attend college as soon as she and Adam could clear themselves of felony charges for escaping the State Hospital and supposedly abducting a mentally impaired person and a minor...

Those charges were ridiculous- as though any of the hospital staff had actually cared what happened to Eric or Della! The staff had physically abused them, and she and Adam had saved them! And now *they* were the ones being blamed...

Shaye's nose and ears and muscles twitched nervously, jumping at every nighttime movement in the neighborhood as her mind raced. By the time she heard Rochelle's Escort stop in the street, Shaye's senses were already so strained that she'd acclimated to the dark. It actually felt like sensory overload when Adam came in reeking of smoke and cologne and he seemed to be speaking to her in such a loud, excited voice.

"It went really well tonight," he announced.

Now that Adam had safely returned home, Shaye went into her room and lowered herself onto the cool surface of the comforter she'd bought yesterday. No parents were coming tonight to collect their little girl; the past was over now and the present could never be as good.

Somewhere out there, just across US 1, crack cocaine was being smoked and whores were working their corners. In the park nearer her people were drinking and threatening each other, their hate spilling from condemned trailers into the street.

But inside the room was total stillness, fear but no reality to back it up, a heart thumping inside Shaye's chest which seemed like the loudest sound in the world now, asserting that she was alive and alright. And, like a child that is abandoned but has cried itself out, Shaye curled up and slept.

Later, as she kept track of her days in her particular way, this one would be remembered as the last peaceful night. The next afternoon she would observe the furtive gardener lurking in her backyard under her window.

From that moment on, although the prowler would leave without doing anything, she would continuously tell Adam, "There's going to be a murder, Adam! I sense it. Maybe not that guy in our yard, but someone's going to do it. Somebody's going to kill someone in this park…"

A few mornings later, after Adam's first night working at Foxy Lady, Shaye woke in a more positive frame of mind because Adam had agreed to take her to the nearest public library where she could get on the Internet.

Shaye's plan was to find out more about the neighborhood they were renting in, believing that more information could make it safer for them. Meanwhile she wanted to learn more about obtaining fake ID.

While they were out, Adam planned to use a pay phone and a calling card to call friends in Miami. Their best hope was an open-minded young man named Jeff Freeman, who had once employed Adam at a gay nightclub he owned in New York City. Freeman also owned another club in South Beach and Adam believed he might be willing to take them in and help them with a new start.

Although Adam said he was eager to speak to his friend, and even more eager to get out of this horrible little community, in ways he also seemed to be dragging his feet. He was actually doing Shaye a favor by getting up this early because he had started a habit of sleeping during the days to make up for his late nights working.

Shaye was in a good mood, despite the fact that she leaned into one of the tiny windows and narrowed her eyes at a slow-moving rusty white truck that navigated the street. Its large rear bed was filled with cut palmetto fronds and resigned looking Hispanic lawn workers wearing green trousers and open shirts.

Two men in their thirties sat up in the cab, the bosses apparently. To Shaye's intently peering eyes they looked bigger and more muscular than their employees. They also seemed much more confident, with their sleeves rolled up and their mouths open to grin and talk while the short men in back hunched over, silent, perhaps conserving energy.

One of the bosses was blond; the other had raven-black hair like the workers. Unlike the workers though, he had flawless lightly tanned skin and a handsome craggy face, probably a cross between American and Hispanic heritage.

"That's the truck," Shaye said to Adam, gesturing for him to look out the window. "The guy sitting farthest back in the truck bed is the same one I saw the other day hiding out in our back yard! I recognize the outfit, Adam. They do lots of lawns in this neighborhood, especially some of the large commericial properties. I've been observing every day. And I'm still not entirely sure, but I think they might have something to do with that new construction project, that big new supermarket plaza that's going up across US 1. The turf is dug up and I noticed this truck pulled up there on the side of the road, although the men weren't working at the moment. So maybe they're bidding for the job. Do you think?"

The words rolled out of Shaye all in a bunch and then she indicated the window again for Adam to bend down and look.

Adam glanced out at the beefy landscape truck as it slowly rumbled past their trailer. "It's amazing you know all this," he said, with his serious tone managing to convey respect combined with concern. "But you can drive yourself nuts watching everything like this, Shaye."

"No I won't," she said. "I'm fine."

After the drama of the truck's passing was over and the crew had turned the corner, Shaye straightened up and refocused on her preparations for their trip to the Oceanside public library.

First she ducked into her small bedroom to change into one of the T-shirts from the thrift shop. It had a big silly cartoon shark emblazoned on the front. The shark was surfing on a bright yellow surfboard and wore red trunks; it was kind of kitschy.

"You like it?" Shaye asked, smoothing down the shirt in front of the only full-length mirror in their trailer, the one on the back of her bedroom door.

For a moment Shaye thought that she looked good, brighter anyway. She moved around, looking at her body from different angles and brushing out her hair.

Adam joined her in the mirror, clipping a black fall that he got God-knows-where into the back of his hair and adjusting a wide orange hair elastic around it. It was the beginning of his transformation to female for the day. Shaye just watched him, dumbstruck, while she worked the tangles out of her long hair.

Adam kind of laughed and adjusted the volume up on the alternative music station he listened to. But he was watching her closely as he always did.

"You look great, Shaye," he said, cautiously and turned her a bit so he could look at her better. "You look *different*. It's, like, all coming together today. You're looking so cute in that shirt. I've been suspecting but I didn't want to say anything, but at this point you can't deny it. I think you're gaining weight here in Florida. At least ten pounds, and you're definitely putting on some muscle." He smiled warmly. "This is the healthiest you've looked since I've known you."

Shaye looked into the mirror and smiled at her reflection proudly. She *was* filling out a little inside the shirt. Her body seemed to have some kind of substance. Sure, one hundred and ten pounds was not quite normal for a woman of five-nine but it was different from the freakish ninety pounds she had been when she had left the hospital. It was as if she had crossed some critical line back into healthy. She raised a sleeve to expose her upper arm and saw a shade of definition there, a slight shape of muscle. She grinned more.

"You're right, Adam, maybe."

"Definitely, Shaye! Look at you!"

She noticed how her hair seemed springier and less dull than it had in years and how her eyes looked green and alert- not as glassy and jumpy as they had been. She leaned in further and the green eyes in the mirror blinked at her complacently, as if saying, "Yes, why are you looking at me?"

This new her was frightening in a way. Her skin was smoothed over and slightly sandy colored. It was nothing like her dark caramel tan that used to set off neon bright bikinis in the *Tropical Sun* catalog, but it was definitely a change in color, a result of healthy time outdoors.

"This is real, isn't it?" Shaye murmured, understanding that she'd have to get used to her new skin. She plopped down in a chair. "I look like Darlene across the street!" she said with a laugh.

Then she watched Adam perform his transformation to looking like a girl, and she had to acknowledge that he was truly extraordinary. Watching Adam dress in drag was enough to totally play with a person's head. Adam had warned her about this and she now watched him stoically and analytically. Adam watched her watching him in the mirror and she knew he'd spot any sign of discomfort or condemnation.

Shaye sometimes feared he'd find out she *did* condemn him. But Shaye's negativity was not for the reason he might think. She cared about Adam and accepted him deeply to the bottom of her soul. Gender didn't matter in a place where his caring had saved her life. And yet she resented her best friend sometimes for his happy preoccupation with himself. Couldn't he see that they were in danger here in Flamingo Park? Why did she have to feel at times like she was in this alone?

Maybe Adam sensed her impatience. He was pretty shrewd. Or maybe he just knew better than she did that things somehow would work out right.

"What?" he said to her, turning to her with the head of a woman and still shirtless in baggy sweats because he had done makeup and hair first. "Our situation scares me, too, you know."

"I, um…" Shaye laughed. It felt quite awkward talking to Adam when he looked this way. And yet it felt good to be alive. She had eaten some toast and was now licking yogurt off of a spoon. And it was staying down.

"Okay, how do you do it?" she asked, grinning. "What are your trade secrets?" She knew that he liked that she asked. And, if they were both murdered in this trailer tomorrow, she would have at least been nice to him today.

"It's simple, actually," Adam boasted, straightening up from a shame filled posture to a stance that was visibly proud. He efficiently pulled on an orange halter-type women's top. It had bra cups built in, which gave his pectoral area some definition. And it left a little bit of white belly peeking out, just like all the trendy teenaged girls.

Adam ducked inside the bathroom, modestly changing into women's panties, Shaye knew. And then he walked out sporting a pair of low-rise women's bellbottoms.

"Just regular clothes," he said as he added the finishing touches, chunky black platform shoes and an orange and black choker made of beads shaped into daisies. Now he could have been her teenaged girlfriend, getting ready to spend a day with her at the mall.

"The secret is that I don't try too hard," he explained triumphantly. "People are looking at me expecting to see a woman and so they make everything fit their expectations. I go for a natural look. Or where's the fun of it? Fuck 'em if they can't take a joke!"

Her girlfriend Eden, as he called himself when he was in drag. He was perfect. He hesitantly laid an arm over her shoulder to walk her to the door.

"Let's not be silly, Adam," she protested as they left the trailer.

Shaye thought Adam was going to demand they to skip all the way to the bus stop or something and she was not *that* comfortable.

Meanwhile the neighbors were up and clanging dishes across the street- she knew they could see them through their open window.

But, oddly, Shaye didn't worry.

According to Adam, after years of dressing in drag no one had ever made out his secret.

And now as he walked beside her, complete down to orange nail polish on fingers and toes and the delicate scents of peach body spray and vanilla lipgloss, his secret was impenetrable. For, right now, Adam Ant Underwood *was* a woman.

If anyone in the Flamingo Park figured out that he was a cross-dresser he and Shaye might have been in real physical danger. But it wouldn't go like that. Their neighbors would all think one guy and two girls lived in their trailer. This had to be true. Shaye dreaded any other possibility.

On Hibiscus Street, right on the corner of Caiman, which was the cross street to Flamingo Beach Parkway, two young men dressed in the style of gang members leaned up against a van in a yard that reeked of marsh and improperly drained sewage. They traded off something in downturned hands.

The one with a goatee turned and saw Shaye and Adam on their way to the bus stop and Adam sort of waggled his hips while coyly turning his head away and snapping gum. The youth took a few steps forward.

"You wanna play someone, Baby?" he called out. "Why don't you come over and play this!" He grabbed at the crotch of his baggy jeans and he and his friend broke down laughing.

Adam giggled in the temptingly melodic voice he used when he was cross-dressing as he and Shaye hurried away. "Those guys totally think I'm a girl!" he boasted. Can you believe they're hitting on me?"

"I can't believe you're *proud*!" Shaye snapped at him.

They ran across Flamingo Beach Parkway, and then continued across US1, dodging traffic. They had to sidestep a curly-haired homeless man, who sat beside a bicycle at the side of the ditch, eating pizza crust. He glanced up and literally growled at Shaye as she passed him. Shaye shuddered. Sometimes she felt like she was talking to herself, for all Adam understood her.

"Are you actually *proud* that you're attracting that kind of scum back in the park?" she persisted.

"You don't get the *point*, Shaye," Adam said. "I'm male and they don't *know* it. The right clothes have that kind of power. Isn't that metaphysically awesome?"

No, their whole life was metaphysically disturbing. And Adam was the one who didn't get the point, Shaye realized. They kicked at raw dirt with wooden stakes in it, behind a newly formed curb of still wet cement. The vast shopping center behind them was just a half-formed concrete shell at this point. A hundred workers climbed around on the site, hammering and carrying things, their well-formed muscles glistening in the distance.

Shaye wondered who these men were and how many of them took shortcuts through the trailer park. Already, some stopped work to peer at them, with body postures of primal lust that were evident even at a distance.

Again, she shuddered.

In the public library she felt much more confident and secure. She typed her way rapidly into the world of the Internet and discovered that Jeff Freeman, Adam's former employer, published an underground newsletter, as well as owning the chain of gay clubs. It was easy for her to find the website. Adam waited impatiently for her to find him a telephone number and, when she did, he hurried outside to try to call Jeff.

Meanwhile, Shaye began her own investigations.

Her gold mine was a site she found called realtorsecrets.com- a way she could find out more about Flamingo Park. The site gave descriptions of communities all over the country for people looking to buy real estate. The only drawback she found was that the authors of the site tended to be unrealistically upbeat because they were trying to sell properties. The egregious example read as follows:

"Flamingo Park, Florida is a one-of-a-kind community on the Atlantic Coast... Once dirt-farm homesteads and small citrus orchards, the area now is home to an array of colorful Florida locals..."

After cringing, Shaye continued scanning the write-up. One interesting fact that she was able to dig up was that a quarter of the park belonged to one owner, although many machinations had been tried to hide it. The owner was her own landlord, the elusive A&H Investments, listed as being licensed out of Houston, Texas.

Shaye had been extremely quick and efficient doing her research but all she could glean was that the park was being considered for several different futures. One possibility was purchase by private developers and total demolition, followed, she assumed by gentrification. Another scenario involved Flamingo

Park being annexed by the neighboring town of Oceanside. Either way, any changes that would make the area safer were likely to come years down the road.

Unfortunately she now became distracted by an old favorite site she couldn't resist checking into, DoctorIzIn.com This extremely graphic site was devoted to "unusual medical problems that your family doctor may fail to diagnose" and Shaye's total immersion in it took up the rest of her time in the library.

In fact, Adam had to pull her away from the computer so that they could get back to the bus and he could make it to work.

"I called Jeff Freeman," he said. "And there's good news and bad."

"What's the bad?" Shaye asked.

Adam chewed on a painted fingernail and gave Shaye a dirty look; then he proceeded with his story the way he wanted to tell it.

"The *good* news," he said, "is that Jeff is going to make some connections in Miami for ID for us, and he thinks that in a few weeks he'll also have a house that we can stay in with some other people. They're like eight drag queens, but, so what, it'll be an experience…"

"And the bad news?" Shaye prodded.

"Oh yeah, that." Adam giggled, trying to make light of it. He made so much of a show with his dramatically feminine gestures that the mature bus driver glanced appreciatively back in the mirror. Adam waited for him to look away before he whispered, "Jeff's club has been crawling with cops looking for us!"

"*Why?*" Shaye demanded. "I mean, why us out of everybody?"

"It's my father," Adam said. "Jeff told me that my father is in Miami right now looking for me personally. It's the money thing, Shaye. I'm going to own a big part of the family business this summer when I turn twenty-one, and that intimidates him. My father would prefer to have me locked away in mental institutions all my life where I can't make any of the business decisions. That's all his concern's about; it's not like he's worried about me or anything."

Shaye thought she saw a little glaze of moisture over Adam's eyes.

"So," she asked, "does this mean we can't go down to Miami at all?"

"No, Shaye. Don't worry. I told Jeff how badly we want out of this trailer and he said he thinks that within a week, or two weeks at the most, the worst of it will be over. He'll buy some fake ID's and send them to us. By the end of the month, he's going to close on that house in North Miami and we can stay there for free. All we need to do is to change our appearance a little and nobody will make the connection. Jeff wants us to keep in touch until we come down. He gave me one of his friends' numbers where we can get a message to him anytime."

Adam wrote out the telephone number and they slipped it from his purse to Shaye's shorts pockets.

"Adam, I found out some facts about Flamingo Park," she said.

She told him about A&H Investments owning much of the park and then she couldn't help reporting to Adam what she had found on the other site, the medical site that so obsessed her.

"I learned all about something called brain-eating diseases," she recited. "There's a whole class of them. They're worse than viral; the infective particles are called prions and nothing kills them, not heat, not freezing…"

Adam had told Shaye that her continued obsession with illness was probably a way of coping with her fears because it gave her a sense of control. In the past Shaye Taylor had never been a knowledgeable person. She had usually taken others' word for things. That's why she had felt so betrayed when she contracted the infectious disease and all of medical science had failed her.

Adam had given her an idea when she sat in the hospital rec lounge in a kind of stupor repeating, "I just don't know how I caught the E-coli. I can't figure out anything."

"Research it," he had said.

"But how?"

First Adam had friends of his bring in gifts of medical books. Shaye, whose previous reading had been fashion magazines and the occasional bestselling romance, took on a new sense of power from deciphering the facts in these intricate texts.

She struggled grimly with the medical terms, cross-referencing indices and dictionaries like she had been a student all her life. Adam liked to laugh because he was so expert in psychology; he had studied it diligently for years, both inside and outside of school, trying to get a handle on his own illness as well as his strange obsession.

"You and I could be partners," he would laugh. "You can be a doctor and work on their bodies and I can be a therapist and work on their heads."

But Shaye hadn't been laughing. "This isn't enough, Adam. The information in these books isn't up to date. Would the Internet be better?" she had asked.

Adam had looked surprised because Shaye had told him she was scared of computers.

"My husband used to use the Internet all the time for his business," she explained. "I just avoided it because it seemed so complex. If only I had learned to use the computer then!"

Adam had grinned because he thought up a plan. One of the hospital volunteers, a bored housewife, found him cute. All he had to do was flirt with her to convince her to bring in her laptop computer several evenings a week so some of the higher functioning patients could play games on it. And he asked her to teach Shaye to use the Internet. As Adam chatted up the volunteer, distracting her, Shaye learned to become more and more proficient at finding information she needed on the computer, seeing in this a potential for a new kind of freedom.

Shaye got very quick at finding information. She'd hunch over the laptop while other patients leaned over her, gaping at how fast the different graphics overlaid each other as she diligently searched.

Shaye learned to pull up the exotic medical sites in a nanosecond and then, if one of the nurses checked on them, to cover it just as quickly with some other site they approved of- fashion or careers. The staff had only approved the computer on the condition that the patients didn't access anything "sensitive or non-therapeutic" and they particularly didn't want Shaye, with her obsession, probing in medical matters. But of course Shaye did; she found out about real-life medical horrors that most people had never dreamed about. And, strangely, her ability to do this gave her some feeling of control.

One night, when everyone had left the lounge and Shaye leaned on an empty table gazing out the window, Adam had come up behind her and hugged her.

"You did it, Babe," he said. "You've become a virtuoso. You could get to anything on that little computer."

Now, sitting shoulder to shoulder with her friend in the bus, Shaye contemplated that maybe her talent using the Internet could prove of some use to them because it was the only talent she had these days, and they needed something.

She knew things were bad at the moment; she knew big things would be demanded of her. For her fears had been right, her worst suspicion. After living in the trailer only one day over a week, Shaye would discover that, as she and Adam had slept their fitful sleep, a woman was murdered only blocks away in Flamingo Park.

Chapter 4

Shaye found out the news at the coolest and mistiest hour of the next day, seven am, when the temperature had dropped to its low for the night.

She had come outside warily like she always did, while yawning, to look for her newspaper. She struggled with several locks on the metal door and then padded out to the "patio" wearing socks, short shorts and a long jersey shirt. Fresh milk and cereal were set out on the dinette top and she wanted to hurry back. But she liked to get the paper very early because it was a secret bonus, sort of. Not really theirs, it was still getting delivered for the family that lived there before. Shaye would get up early and devour it, every story front to back, before Adam was up.

The sun slipped into the patio making a bronzy coating over the foliage and all the leaves, especially those on the big fat banana plant, were still silvery wet with dew. The moisture put its chill into the air.

Possibly it had rained. The newspaper was rolled up tightly in its plastic sleeve, lying on the crabgrass, with a coating of wet sand along one side.

Shaye bent and reached for it and snaked it slowly to her behind the cinderblocks. Her leg muscles quivered but she didn't want the neighborhood seeing half her butt cheeks hanging out of Adam's gym shorts, which she only used to sleep in.

Usually Shaye would eat first and then read the paper after she was dressed. But today she wanted to get a quick peek at the headlines.

She pulled the paper from its sleeve just as activity began in her neighbor's yard. One of the men from across the street hawked phlegm while a white puppy with black blotches tugged determinedly at the corner of a black garbage bag at the curb.

"*Trailer Park Murder*," the headline read.

Suddenly it seemed to become very cold outside. It felt like it was twenty degrees.

Shaye was still momentarily perplexed. Those were her last few seconds of sanity.

She remembered with clarity a loud bang coming from across the street and the man's voice raised. "Fucking motherfucker!" he cursed at whatever he was doing. Then she heard a metallic scraping noise again and again.

Shaye feared the murderer would come for her. Her heartbeat increased, clogging her throat and her consciousness ebbed for a second as the next line of bold print swelled and receded before her eyes.

"*Young woman found dead by Flamingo Park Canal.*"

The neighbor was dragging something huge and scraping across the street towards her. Shaye flinched back, hearing the air come out of her like a hissing cat.

She had dropped the paper and held onto the doorframe while backing inside. Her breath heaved heavily out of her. Her eyes told her that what was being dragged onto their side of the street and leaned onto the garbage pile was only an incongruous object, the white and fuschia door off a 4x4 truck, being disposed of for some reason. And the puppy was still tugging at a swollen garbage bag.

The neighbor who had a toothpick sticking out of his mouth nodded his wolfish head at Shaye.

"Mornin'!" he said.

He could see her clearly even in her hiding place.

Shaye's brain cleared enough so that she could think and she blinked her eyes, realizing that she wanted to go back and read the article. But her stomach was now swaying and cramping with nausea.

Shaye was in the grip of vertigo, and could hardly walk a straight line back to get the paper. When she made it she bent and retrieved the portion with the headline.

"*Murder*," it said. "*Murder*."

She read it again and again so that she could get the words into her head past the fear and make them just ordinary facts.

"Murder in Trailer Park..."

Her eyes finally made it down to the article itself.

"A grisly find yesterday afternoon as Department of Transportation workers unearthed the nude bloated body of a young woman from a shallow grave beside a Flamingo Park drainage canal.

"DOT workers were shoring up the banks of the drainage canal on Caiman Street following complaints of refuse in the canal and water overflowing into neighboring yards. Complaints of drug activity have also been common in this unincorporated community known for its lax law enforcement and deteriorating properties.

"Some residents said that they had also noticed a strange odor in the area but they told police and reporters yesterday that this is not uncommon.

"'There's always animals killing each other down by that canal, alligators and stray dogs and cats. But nobody does nothing," long-term resident Hank Wood told reporters.

"Impressions like this seemed to be a common theme among residents of Caiman Street when they heard about the murder.

"'This used to be a nice safe neighborhood. But now I don't feel safe to let my children go out and play,' said Amber McClurry, who lives in a singlewide trailer on nearby Hibiscus Street.

"While police are stating that the cause of death was apparently homicide, they are not are not releasing further details.

"Oceanside mayor Adrian Walker, who has been at the center of much recent political controversy, would not comment on whether the victim had been identified and would not give any more details on the victim. Mayor Walker stated that more information would be available today.

"The mayor told reporters, 'Right now, I've got men out combing the neighborhood and they'll be out all night. We hope to make an arrest on this right away.'

"Yesterday afternoon, the municipality of Flamingo Park's only two police officers, Glenn Chow and Frank Danielo, interviewed locals at the scene.

"'This is sad, very sad,' said Officer Danielo. 'A lot goes on around here. But we'll catch the scum that did this!'

"Despite Mayor Walker's assurances that the municipality is doing it's best to police the area, he did say that only two officers

assigned to Flamingo Park simply cannot keep pace with the influx of drugs into the neighborhood. Mayor Walker also said he often fields complaints about the negligence of absentee owners in leaving abandoned structures as nests for criminal activity. 'But the City of Oceanside has no jurisdiction over Flamingo Park,' he explained. 'The town council of Flamingo Park will have to make some tough decisions about the management of their town.'

"Residents seemed to have trouble understanding why no one wanted to take responsibility for their community.

"'You see these two cops?' one outspoken resident yelled as coroner's personnel removed the victim's body. 'They're the only cops we got out here for a park with two thousand people. You do the math. That ain't right!'"

"Insuffient policing in this Old Florida neighborhood has been a problem for many years, and the issue may not be resolved any time soon. Only one thing is sure- the diverse residents of this working class neighborhood will certainly be sleeping with fear tonight."

Shaye looked over the front page photo which showed bright yellow crime scene tape enclosing a grisly tableau- crime scene technicians climbing the incline up from the canal, their human burden covered in black plastic and strapped onto a stretcher.

Two police officers with their backs to the camera held back a small group of residents.

Looking over this group, Shaye's heart gave a lurch because two of the faces stood out. She recognized the young man with shorn hair and a goatee wearing baggy shorts and a white tank top, his teeth seeming to curl in a snarl as he gazed directly into the camera. Next to him stood his young friend with the coffee colored skin. He looked guiltily down to the side, just as he had a few days ago when they exchanged drugs and the more aggressive friend proposited Adam only one lot down from the site of the murder.

The caption on the photo read, *"Local police question Flamingo Park residents at the crime scene".*

Shaye wondered why, in a group of only ten or so residents, those two boys would stand around the scene like that, why they would risk being seen by police unless this scene had some particular fascination. Immediately, they became suspects to her.

And now Shaye was possessed by the feeling that this was no way going to stop here, that this killer, or killer, was a serial killer, a killer of women, come to prey on the park in a reign of blood and terror.

"I am not imagining this," she said to herself as her fingers brushed lightly over the gritty picture. Her mind was a complete blank as to what she could do now.

For a while she kept her legs curled under herself while she just gazed at the picture. Then she leaned forward to snap on the small television that had come with the trailer, hoping for local news.

She watched patiently while her breakfast soured on the table. Finally a news show came on, but it was national news and there was no mention of the murder. She raised her eyes wearily when Adam came to stand over her, holding out her empty bowl accusingly.

Her voice came out a whisper, grainy and low-pitched.

"There was a murder, Adam, just like I said there would be. It was a young woman. Down by that canal on Caiman Street..."

Pages of the newspaper were strewn all over Shaye's lap and the television droned on. If ever there was a time for tears, this would be it, but Shaye couldn't cry.

Adam glanced down at the frontpage headline balanced on Shaye's legs.

"What do you want? What do you need? I'll call Jeff again... We'll make plans to leave here," Adam said. Yet he seemed relatively helpless in the face of what she had told him. "I'll stay home with you tonight, whatever..."

"You know," Shaye said, still without looking directly at Adam. "I have an idea who might have killed that woman. Those two boys, the sleazy teenagers that hit on us the other day on our way to the bus stop. I know it sounds crazy, but it's possible. Not that I know how we could do anything or let anyone know..."

She sighed, her eyes glittering with unshed tears. "It all seems so hopeless, you know. All everybody ever did in the State Hospital was call me paranoid and now it's all coming true! My worst nightmares... we wanted to believe they were just products of my fevered mind... but now they're coming true, in real life, in my neighborhood!"

Rather than trying to argue with her, Adam changed the subject. "Shaye, you didn't eat."

Shaye shook her head, frustrated and wiped at the corner of her eye. "I *couldn't* eat. I just can't."

She got up and backed away from Adam. The fear blinded her and numbed her. All she felt was an irrational need to run with no plan beyond that. When Shaye spoke and heard her voice it sounded tense but rather rational, at least to her. Possibly it truly sounded overexcited and crazed. But Shaye couldn't judge.

"I've got to go out, Adam," she said. "I need to be alone. It feels like I'll die otherwise... It feels like the end..."

Where does the soul go when it is no longer inside you, she wondered. How can time stop when you're still alive? It's supposed to happen once you are dead. When it happens and there is no light to go to, where can you go?

Shaye walked, her empty stomach sprouting little rivulets and veins of blood, like exclamations of feeling. But her eyes looked empty. She left the trailer, walking mechanically, and if the killer had brushed shoulders with her, she would not have flinched. Something had turned all of her pain sensors off.

It was a beautiful day, cloudy but not too humid or hot. Shaye walked all the way down Manatee and then used Egret as a cross street, avoiding Hibiscus Street and the canal. But as she walked she could smell the presence of the crime scene even though it was hidden from her eyes by trailers and vegetation. Shaye's route took her far out of her way, but she didn't feel it.

She couldn't avoid stepping in red mud; it was smeared all over the construction site by the bus stop, fanned out into the road. Shaye hardly noticed.

She escaped to the beach at the end of Flamingo Beach Parkway. Locals usually avoided this beach because it charged ten dollars admission as part of the state park, and county residents held tight to their modest incomes.

Shaye got to the water but didn't remember paying, or even walking past a guard shack. She sat alone on the small white beach located past the nature center, where the only human activity in the park took place. Up on the deck several park rangers polished glass cases featuring taxidermied Florida animals, swept off the cedar deck that really didn't need sweeping and flirted with each other happily while paying no attention to her.

Shaye wore wide-legged blue jeans borrowed from Adam, their edges caked with red clay mud from the construction site, paired with a skimpy camisole top, which she must also have borrowed from him. She wore no bra at the moment; in her shock about the killing she had forgotten this, too.

Shaye's loose long hair spread over her whole body as she crouched in the damp sand hugging her legs. She made a forlorn little package on the sand, alone, rocking in time to the insistent hissing and pushing of the waves.

A light drizzle passed over, darkening the sand more and dampening Shaye, but only her eyes moved. This ocean provided no specific answers. But, in itself, it could be an answer she sensed, if she could only figure it out. As the hours passed she didn't think persay about being resigned to die; but she was.

The last thing Shaye clearly remembered was stretching all the way out this morning and feeling every muscle working to reel in the newspaper.

"Baby," a soft male voice said behind her.

"Don't make this end," Shaye said, refusing to turn her head from the ocean. "If you weren't here to get me, no one would..."

"It's not easy to die," Adam said. "They don't let you. I'll take you home now, Shaye; it's not really safe out here. You're probably safer behind locked doors at our trailer. And I'll be with you."

Now, as it turned twilight, she let herself be helped to her feet.

Adam took her up to the nature center where he leaned against the wall indolently, making his telephone calls from a pay phone with one hand stretched over her shoulder like a boyfriend. He looked nervous and worried and chewed roughly on his lip, while waiting for a call to Jeff's friend, which never went through.

"It's no good," he said. "There's no answer right now. And we can't risk leaving a message."

All his day had been spent looking for her when she ran away and he was showing five-o-clock shadow; the first time Shaye had seen him like this since the day they ran away from the State Hospital.

She stared at her friend, fascinated by what a chameleon he could be. He didn't have the time to dress up in drag today so he was all guy, wearing baggy jeans shorts and a tight tank top that lay flat on his muscular stomach. He pawed frustratedly with one big unlaced sneaker against the other as he waited for someone to answer at the Foxy Lady.

"I'm not coming in," Adam said, when the phone was answered. "My roommate's sick." He raised his voice to be heard.

The park rangers angled dirty looks in their direction. A shame, Shaye thought because the pay phone here was really clean, it was one of the few public phones that seemed immaculate. If she ever again needed a pay phone, she would want to return here.

Maybe the rangers didn't like her bedraggled appearance with the oddly long strands of hair coated with salt that she sucked nervously between parched lips. Or maybe it was Adam, so intense and edgy today that he looked like a gang banger.

"What?" he asked, uncurling off the wall and tightening his arm around her neck. He seemed slightly accusing and angry. "My manager's pissed," he said. "Maybe I'll lose the job..." Then abruptly his focus changed and he sounded ultra gentle again. "You haven't eaten anything all day, you haven't even had water."

They had to hike a ways down the road because the bus didn't stop exactly at the park; it stopped and turned off half a mile short of it.

"You walked this, Shaye?" Adam asked incredulously when they finally reached the corner where the bus picked up.

"I don't remember," she said.

Adam pulled her to him and laughed, then kissed her on the top of the head. Shaye suddenly pushed him off.

"Don't do that!" she snapped.

She felt brittle and didn't feel like being touched today. But it was more than that. Fear had dulled all her senses today, except for the oddest effect- she felt disturbingly sensitive to desire. Adam's too-familiar touch had made her wriggle violently, like a heated up little snake- like one of the living denizens in the glass cases behind them.

Sometimes it seemed like Adam Ant was teasing her, playing with her in some awful incomprehensible way. Like he was gay, but leading her to do some inappropriate thing, and then she'd finally step over the line into madness.

She clung to her own thoughts during the meandering bus ride back, her gaze sliding over mobile homes inadequately lighted in the growing dusk. She noticed three Hispanic men in tan uniforms pedaling their child-sized bicycles toward the heart of the park. They balanced metal lunchboxes on the handlebars; probably returning home from work- that was all.

An unfamiliar man of about thirty dressed in dark clothing stood idly on the sidewalk before a stretch of shady woods and, as their bus passed, he threw a smoldering cigarette butt onto a pile of them in the street. Shaye knew that no more than a block behind him, as the crow flew, was the murder site. But this man was not the same one she had seen shuffling past their trailer on several occasions.

She hadn't seen that wild-eyed individual in a couple of days and now she wondered where he had vanished. But she didn't voice that concern to Adam.

She did tell him, "I'm not walking on Caiman and Hibiscus to get home. That would take us past the crime scene, and I just can't do that..."

"No problem," he said. "We could even get a cab."

"No. I know we don't have the money. And it's not quite dark yet."

At the bus stop two young women loitered around, watching traffic and making no move toward the bus after Adam and Shaye got out. One of the women blatantly adjusted her denim miniskirt and cracked a smile, breathing out cigarette-scented breath. The other one, in faded jeans, was barefoot. They both eyed the couple hungrily and Adam pushed Shaye forward.

"Walk," he whispered.

The area was so heavily treed and undeveloped that the wide-open construction site at her side produced an odd feeling, like a sucking pressure, disturbing- it pulled at your attention even though you couldn't see into it. And it tugged at your nostrils with the smell of the disturbed and tainted earth.

"Those two women are prostitutes, aren't they?"

"Yeah, I guess," Adam said, "but usually those white girls stay in the park. Some black girls usually work up here near the bus stop. Madeline and Rochelle told me."

"What are they, experts?" Shaye smirked. She and Adam grinned and then they began laughing, holding onto each other's arms like gossipy girlfriends.

"I guess they do know a little bit about it." Adam snickered.

"That's gross, Adam. That's so bad!"

They were laughing loudly and just stepping casually across the grass to cross US1 on the light when the sound came.

"Get up!" it sounded like, a deep make voice, sibilant, coming from the dark brush.

Then a ragged old man leaped at them, standing up from a murky depression where he must have been curled all along. "Get up, get out of here!" He raised his voice angrily. Now they could see his light colored clothing, his pale white skin and scruffy beard.

It happened in a split second. The man barreled forward at them, Shaye grabbed tighter onto Adam's arm and he ran, pulling her with him through the unprotected intersection. All around them headlights glared, their hot smell warming the darkness of coming night.

Shaye and Adam ran and, halfway across, the light changed in their favor. The homeless man sank back into his ditch and they skipped onto the sidewalk, safe on the other side of the road. Bizarrely, they laughed even harder, the synapses in their brains mixed up somehow between the absurd images of Adam's transsexual colleagues turning tricks and then the sudden danger flinging itself out of the darkness in the form of the homeless man who seemed more animal than human.

"Maybe it was that guy," Shaye said. "He's aggressive. Maybe he's the killer."

She was shaking hard. All of her body shook, and they hadn't even turned off of Flamingo Beach Parkway onto Egret St. and the park itself.

Adam patted down Shaye's arms. "Don't worry about it so much," he said. "You're gonna be okay."

Just then an old green truck rattled by them, slowing with a blinker on for the park and yard implements clanging in its open back.

"Hey!" the man in the passenger seat yelled over the noise.

He was a white guy with a bandana tied on his head and tattoos fully covering the arm that hung out the window brandishing a can of beer.

"Hey, Blondie. You got some gorgeous tits! Where do you live?" he demanded. And then he spat out the word, "Bitch," when she didn't answer.

The truck then spun out in its turn down Egret Street and he was gone. Shaye watched the taillights vanish in the distance. She gulped and it tasted like she had swallowed a small mouthful of blood. "I can't do this," she said once again.

She and Adam made it safely to the trailer with no further incident. They carefully entered, turned on lights and cracked some of the small windows for air. The newspaper was still littered all over but Adam directed Shaye to the couch and he snapped on the television.

"I know you're going to want to watch local news. And it's six-o-clock now. I'll just take over cooking tonight."

Shaye knew he was going to try to trick her into eating. He began scrambling eggs for a fancy frittata. But it smelled faintly nauseating to her as she focused on the news.

The phone shrilled. Shaye's panic had invaded Adam; he dropped the spatula. Then he steadied himself and picked up the phone.

"Yo," he said with a defensive edge. Then he smiled and nodded, indicating to Shaye that all was okay. "Yeah, Madeline, Honey" he said, in a voice that sounded like he was humoring her. "No, Shaye's not dead or anything. No, your voodoo didn't work!"

Adam laughed and Shaye heard the shrill voice protesting through the phone. Twenty minutes of local news passed and she listened to Adam talking to his cross-dresser friend about evening dresses.

Then Shaye's body stiffened to the newscaster's words.

"A shallow grave. That's how some people are referring to the tragic discovery that was made last night in an Oceanside trailer park. An unidentified woman was murdered Thursday or Friday night in Flamingo Park and her body buried in a shallow grave beside a drainage canal.

"Police are now able to tell us that the victim was approximately twenty-five years old, either white or light-skinned Hispanic, and she had extremely long black hair. Police still don't have a positive identity on the victim. They are calling her Jane Doe and believe she may have been a prostitute known in the trailer park.

"While they are stating now that the victim was stabbed to death, they aren't releasing specifics about the weapon. They also cannot tell us whether robbery or sexual assault were involved in the late-night attack or whether the victim knew her assailant.

"Police have been actively canvassing the park, which used to be a family neighborhood, but has recently been plagued by prostitution and crack cocaine. This is an area close to the beach where many residents walk or use bicycles for transportation and children often play in the unpaved streets. But tonight many residents expressed fear, as well as outrage that the area is not adequately policed..."

The news station showed an interview. A fat lady with large breasts squeezed into a sport bra gestured to a canal and a dirt yard where her tow-headed children played. "Things ain't right no more," she said. "Things just ain't right."

"You know," Shaye said when Adam sat down next to her eating the frittata she had refused and a spatter of rain hit against the windows. "I don't feel like he's out there tonight. I feel as though I have some sort of radar for this killer and somehow I don't feel he's around tonight."

"You can't obsess about this, Baby," Adam said. "We'll just have to get out of this place. Obviously we made a mistake coming here; like all we make lately is fucking mistakes!"

They stared at each other. Adam rubbed at his face and then grimaced at his silver painted toenails, which had somehow got lost in the mix. "This is all bullshit," he said. "Who the fuck am I kidding? None of this is your fault, Shaye."

Shaye sunk back against the couch, just blinking while the loud-mufflered truck roamed the street. Adam made her feel like such a little girl. Did he want to return her to the State Hospital? She felt too healthy to go back and yet not healthy enough for anything else. But what *was* she going to do- go out and get a job? She was wanted by the police and a killer was circling her neighborhood- maybe her yard.

The windowpanes looked so dark. From the inside you could see nothing, but from the outside she knew their enemies could see everything. Shaye stood up and shut off the light.

It was felt frightening to be alone here with Adam, especially when she had no answers for him and he was so obviously struggling.

Then Adam eyed her strangely and suddenly demanded, "You think I'm just like them, don't you? You don't have to tell me how you despise me. I can smell it sometimes!"

"Like *who*?" she asked, truly not getting it.

All she smelled was her own reek filling the darkened room, sea salt on her hair and clothing, sickly sweat and a hint of the oily mud that she had let stain her friend's precious girl's jeans.

Inside her body her pulse thudded, with each beat timing out the seconds of the wait. The killer was coming. Coming around here. Maybe not tonight. But, one way or another, he was coming.

The little television quietly babbled on. Adam glanced at her, just wet flickering eyes in the darkness.

Shaye had thwarted death once; that particular strain of E-coli that infected her had simultaneously infected four other victims who lived scattered around the country. The only thing they shared in common was a weekend festival in Gulfport Mississippi; a laid back occasion that was supposed to be fun.

Two of the others had been professionals. One was a woman- a forty-four year old family court judge known for her dedication to charitable causes. The second was a fifty year-old professor known for founding the nation's most innovative Arts College. Before his illness, he had often made headlines because of the generous scholarships and community outreach programs his school sponsored.

The last two victims may not have been as influential in society, but they were surrounded by love in their personal lives. The third victim was a twenty nine-year-old cherub-faced housewife from Iowa who left behind unconsolable grief. Her extended family and the congregation of her rural church choir mourned her. So did her husband, who was stationed overseas in the army. Her three children under five years old were too young to really know what happened, yet they were plagued with crying and nightmares after their mother's death.

But most memorable was the E-coli's fourth victim- a seven year-old boy with a shining Norman Rockwell smile. His family and his small Northern California community held candlelight vigils, while all of America prayed for him as national television documented his losing struggle against the disease.

Shaye Taylor was the only victim who was famous before the rare disease. But Shaye had never changed the world; she had never even changed anybody's life.

Unlike the other four, who had surrended to the disease in agony, Shaye, who had survived, had been nobody except for a pretty face and a tight ass. So, of all of them, she was probably the one who should have died. Instead, against all odds, she had been the only one who lived. But the violent illness, along with the cruel treatment by the medical community, had torn down her sanity. And now perhaps fate had played with her, letting her out here on a leash.

During her drawn-out illness, after she was institutionalized, Shaye had attempted suicide ten separate times. She and her friends from the ward used to laugh about it because she held the record for a dorm full of very sick people.

Between her paranoia, her suicidal tendency and her anorexia, as well as barely managed bleeding ulcers and possible damage to her liver and kidneys, the doctors had given Shaye an extremely poor prognosis. Like Adam had said, they'd discussed keeping her in institutions for life. A quote from one doctor to another when she had been spying: "If that girl leaves these walls, she'll be dead within the day."

Well, here she was, so terrified that death would have been a relief, and yet she had lost all of her guts. She idly contemplated using the rusty kitchen knife tucked under her thigh on her own wrists. But she couldn't. Shaye clung to life now, defending it.

Maybe the killer in the park was meant to be her executioner. She pictured him as rough and animalistic, a larger man. She didn't picture any sexual violation because killing would be violation enough. She pictured herself in the musky smelling darkness looking up into the man's face, as he prepared to slash. The image was so appalling she trembled with it.

"Adam, you're fine," she said. Whatever comfort she could have given him, anything, she would have done it. "You know, I'm the sicker one here."

It was quiet for a long time. In silence he made and offered her hot chocolate, which she turned away, even though the past few days it had been a favorite. Her eyes were fixed on a palmetto across the street where a shadow moved rhythmically in a splash of yellow.

"It's like I'm hallucinating all the time, seeing dark shapes moving in the street."

Adam bent forward closer to the window, checking it out. "No, you're not. You don't hallucinate."

Then his voice got softer. "But you're right. Sometimes I think it's so horrible to be inside this ugly body that's neither man nor woman and I think about you and your sexy gorgeous body and I just want to be you. But meanwhile you're hurting so much, Shaye. I don't even know what it's like. I'm sorry."

Now she gulped back tears. There was still no solution. And it was only nine o'clock. Her vigil would just be starting.

Not sleeping three hours later, she lay on her back in bed, the knife between her breasts, and she counted unfairnesses. She remembered each landlord on their way down here that had turned them away and each rental application designed to exclude them. If these things hadn't happened, they wouldn't be living here now.

But neither would many others in this park if it wasn't for

unfairness. Society was supposedly concerned with the betterment of people, but really it wasn't. Flesh and blood people lived out their lives in Flamingo Park in tin pens, struggling in terror each day against against the sea of poverty that threatened to drown them. Their terror was considered okay. So was allowing your neighbors- children, the elderly, veterans- to sleep out in ditches every night fearing for their lives. Suffering each and every day of life was legal- only attempting to kill yourself to end that suffering was not.

Later that night Shaye tensed when she heard a rustle in the grass out behind her bedroom and she rolled closer to the window to check it out but couldn't see anything. She heard Adam turning in his sleep on the couch where he had slept to be closer to her, guilty for acting insensitive earlier.

Shaye clearly remembered the small Hispanic man that had hidden outside her window last Thursday, coincidentally on the day of the murder. She could remember the smell of chemicals on his clothes and the sound of his breath. She wondered if maybe he was the killer, if he had been that close to them, and she tried to impress the memory of his features on her mind, in case the description might be needed for evidence.

"What can I do?" she whispered to herself.

Shaye stayed inside, napping during the day, lying awake at night. The only new news item in the paper was a recap of last night's television newscast, only this one had a police artist's sketch of Jane Doe. The victim had jutting cheekbones, nondescript eyes and loads of slick black hair, with only the hair looking distinctive.

Shaye scuttled time and time again window to window, checking the comings and goings on the street. She didn't bathe, afraid that the shower would make a noise that would cover the noise of an intruder's entrance.

Adam stayed with her as she requested for several days. But on Friday with no further news of the killer, he stood over her, looking at her seriously, although she seemed so nervy she could meet no one's eyes.

"I have to work this weekend or else we're on the street, Shaye. We've got no rent... There is one thing going on, a possibility at the bar where I could make some money. We could be out of here sooner..."

"Just let me get into the shower," Shaye said tersely, not

explaining what was going through her mind, that if she was going to die, she wanted to face it being clean.

She got out of the shower with a towel wrapped around her hair and Adam helped her lock up before leaving. And then Shaye was left alone with the sounds of the night.

Chapter 5

She was awakened at four thirty in the morning by the sounds of throaty laughter, the refrigerator slamming, ice clinking and soda pouring, then more laughter closer to her doorway- someone sitting down on the couch which backed up against her bedroom wall.

Shaye's bladder was tight- to the point where she had almost voided when the voices woke her. On a night like this, she had never thought she'd sleep. But apparently sleep had taken her away- sometime before the abysmal, and most dangerous, four o'clock hour. And why hadn't Adam come home before that, anyway?

Shaye stumbled to the bathroom off of her bedroom, pulling on a pair of shorts over her bare legs and making it to the toilet just in time. Her head still seemed a little foggy and confused, from staying up so many hours worrying and then finally falling asleep so deeply.

If Adam was finally home, why had he brought guests? And why was he making it a habit to get back later each night he worked?

It was just too paranoid to think that the person who had let himself in with a key, and was now serving soda to guests in the rental trailer's dingy living room was anyone but her roommate Adam. But Shaye had to make sure anyway. She kept her light off and cracked the bedroom door. The incandescent lights outside seemed to glare. Angled off the couch, she caught sight of a calf in pink fishnet stockings kicking up and down, and a glass resting on the fishnet-stockinged knee.

"So, I told him…" the voice purred with familiar laughter. "… I told him, Poppi- it don't matter if I'm a man or a woman- because you so poor- you can't afford neither!"

Across the room two other women, or men dressed as woman, leaned together, perched on the two fifties' style barstools that had come with the trailer, and exploded into raucous laughter.

"Madeline, one of these days you're gonna be arrested- telling all these old geezers where to jump off..." This was Rochelle speaking; although she faced backwards, Shaye recognized her by her distinctive head of red hair.

The other woman, or man dressed as a woman, wore a big-haired wig in neon pink. She also wore fishnet stockings, along with a leather miniskirt, both black. The mini stretched tight on muscular thighs and, as she spread them undemurely over the cushiony square seat of the barstool, Shaye looked away.

This third transsexual dancer that Shaye had never met leaned forward, splaying herself over the kitchen counter, and stretched out long hands with long pink fingernails to reach for Adam.

"Come'ere, Honey," she said to Adam in a gravelly voice meant to be sexy, but sounding a bit more male than female. Shaye hadn't even seen Adam, because he had been leaning into the refrigerator, blocked from view by the dancer's piles of faux pink hair.

Now he straightened up, with a single bottle of beer in his hand and an embarrassed hectic flush on both cheeks.

"Now this man, this Adam Ant," the dancer said sleepily, almost intimately, "is every girl's dream man. He's so young and sweet."

Rochelle stepped forward in friendly fashion to ruffle Adam's hair, distilling some of the other dancer's sexual overtones. "Adam is sweet, and he certainly makes a woman feel safe."

Hiding behind the door, standing with her bare toes on questionably clean carpet, Shaye seethed.

Nothing was safe in this neighborhood, and Shaye couldn't believe these dancers couldn't feel it. They just wanted to sit here, laughing like silly women that had been born women, trying to squeeze a little fun out of this last miserable hour of their miserable evening.

Madeline sprang to her feet, theatrically pushing the pink-haired dancer who reached for Adam around the other side of his neck. "And you stay away from Adam Ant!" she said. "Whenever he decides to give it up, this boy is mine!"

She went for Adam, standing quite a few inches taller than he was in her heels and grasping him around the neck, trying to press his head against her cleavage. Adam struggled out of her embrace-but laughingly. Then he looked toward the doorway with a suddenly alert expression as though he could see Shaye hiding there.

"Listen girls, seriously. It's late. Let's keep it down so my roommate can sleep."

Now Shaye felt even more mortified, as well as disturbed and troubled, even though she knew no one could see her. She had lain through the hours terrified. And Adam cared; he had just shown that by mentioning her, and the expression in his eyes made clear that she was his first concern.

So, why couldn't she just go out and join the party? Madeline always acted snippy with her- but that was more for show-off than anything. Right now, other than Adam, Rochelle and Madeline were actually the only friends Shaye had.

She stuck her foot through the open doorway, like a cat inserting its paw to test the air. The cool and dampness of her darkened room pressed into the middle of her back like the hand of fate. Easy enough to escape the fear- just step forward.

Madeline gave another cackle. "Adam's worried that 'Trailer Park Barbie' is sleeping okay. Ain't that sweet? He's just like a big brother..."

"Oh, be nice," Rochelle said, and Adam said, "Cool it."

Everybody argued and giggled and shouted to be heard over one another. And Shaye delicately pulled her foot back in and closed the door on the darkness that enclosed her.

The next morning Shaye grimaced as she watched Adam skipping around lightly on bare feet in the kitchen preparing breakfast, she was sure, for both of them. He was singing "It's Raining Men!" in that sweet engaging voice that couldn't be repressed. Adam wanted to be an entertainer. And who couldn't love him? His singing used to always make Shaye smile, back in the dark days in the State Hospital. Sometimes it was just a secret thing between them- a few lines of some pop tune whispered to her as she was being wheeled off to surgery or ICU, or buckled down in restraints.

Now his choice of song made her dizzy. After all, it was of his world- a world she could not share. If it weren't for her, Shaye had no doubt Adam could simply move in with his transsexual friends, collect his trust fund in a few months and live his girlish life.

Instead, he was frying eggs for a paranoid outcast and skipping around in time to a gay club tune while his bare feet dodged cockroaches that they just could not eradicate from the trailer.

Shaye brushed past him wordlessly, and collected her newspaper outside. She scanned the headlines for news of new murders, but found none. So she climbed the stairs and silently shouldered into the kitchen, collecting a big cup of black coffee- one of the food items she was never supposed to touch with her ulcers.

Adam stood holding a plateful of steaming food, tailored to her bland diet needs, and his soulful eyes opened wide, looking like they were going to contain tears.

"Okay, Shaye, so fine. You were up last night- and you overheard us out here and you're pissed. It's understandable. Madeline can certainly act bitchy. But Rochelle and Candy Cane are good people. They're fun to hang around. Look, is that what's bothering you? Me having the girls over?"

Shaye raised an eyebrow, crumbling her paper to her chest and sipping at coffee that went down like lava.

"Girls? Or freaks?" she said.

"What??" Adam set down the china plate because he was trembling so hard. He stepped around to the other side of the jutting counter. "What are you saying?"

"Or am I the freak?" Shaye persisted, swallowing hard around a second sip of the strong coffee that could prove suicide for her. "Maybe you don't like to be around someone crazy like me."

Adam seemed to pant to get out his words. "That's ridiculous, Shaye. But since when do you mind transsexuals? Since when were you ever not open-minded?"

Shaye suddenly stood up straight and roared, as loud as her reedy voice would let her. "Who cares whether I'm open minded, Adam? I don't care either way about your she-male friends. I don't care even if you're turning tricks at the Foxy Lady, just like they are!" She gasped to get her breath, and then she defiantly gulped another sip of coffee. "All I care about right now is that our home is being terrorized by a killer!"

Suddenly, Adam's eyes seemed to glow with a fury Shaye had never seen. With no warning he lunged forward and violently slapped the full mug of coffee out of her hand. It splashed hot liquid over both of them, dented the refrigerator and painted its surface brown before finally shattering on the floor.

Shaye glanced at it, but Adam pursued her.

"I am *not* fucking turning tricks!" he yelled. He stood right up in her face, puffing up his small but muscular chest, and Shaye had never seen anger like what burned in his eyes. "I'm not turning tricks and I don't care about your fucking killer!"

Adam violently ripped at the local newspaper that Shaye clutched to her bosom. His hands assailed like claws, ripping it in to tatters. Shaye fought, clinging to it, even though her rational mind told her that there was nothing about the murder on the front page, so there was probably nothing inside either.

They struggled with pants and grunts, but no words, until the newspaper was a shredded mess at their bare feet.

Shaye finally let go of the last couple of strips and she backed up toward her bedroom, bending to retrieve her sneakers. Hopping towards the front door, she pulled them onto her heels, then turned back towards Adam who had slid his slim body down to rest against the edge of the counter, underneath the ledge.

He looked pale and small and unsure as he gazed at her.

Shaye would never leave him for good; Adam was the only real family she had ever had. Yet she was stubborn. She felt like she was the wronged party in all of this.

"I'm going to the library to research 'my killer', Adam, like you like to call him. I'll be proven right when the next murder happens," she said in a shaky voice. And then she raised a finger to point at Adam. "And you're crazy. You really are crazy."

Adam raised his eyes to her and spoke out of a tremulous, pouting lip.

"I told you that, Shaye. I warned you of that."

Shaye could have doubled or angled all around the park, but anger was an effective antidote to fear. For the moment, it blocked everything out and she chose the shortest route to the bus stop, the one she had been avoiding. Shaye wasn't even aware of much of the scenery she saw. And the three-dollar canvas tennis shoes she had purchased at the local supermarket carried her like they had a Greek god's mythical wings attached.

Shaye Taylor seemed to fly on magical wings through the dejected and damaged trailer park. She wasn't even surprised at the scenery when she found she had taken the most direct route-Hibiscus to Caiman street. She saw the crime scene tape around the corner lot and the newly dredged canal. She seemed to hover over it like she had magical powers to stay above the ground. She observed the crisp slick yellow tape dispassionately, remembering when the most frightening thing she had imagined in this canal was an alligator.

Now she could practically smell death, the odor seeming to permeate the slick of ruddy earth. Shaye tamped at the earth with her foot, watching it squealch underneath. In fact, the ground was so sodden that some of the impression of her tennis shoe was lost when she lifted her foot. She pondered. If there was a struggle down there in the greenery by the canal, she had to assume that not much evidence of it would be left.

But she felt curious anyhow. Shaye glanced around her and, other than the up and down fanning of wide overhanging palmetto fronds in the strong breeze, she noted no movement- and no one to see her here.

She delicately stepped to one side, off of the muddy area and onto some tamped down vegetation beside the canal. She glanced at it but assumed it only showed where the heavy county machinery had pulled off to the side of the road.

She took another glance back at the street and then she ducked under the crime scene tape. She carefully moved along the bank of the canal, keeping her back to the water. Small trees and leafy vines shaded her, scraping at her back, yet concealing her from casual view.

From the short video clip on TV, and the photos in the newspaper, Shaye knew that the mudered girl's body had been discovered toward the back end of the lot, where tall grasses concealed the steep lip of the canal.

Holding in her breath and biting her lip, she made her way towards this area. Then she crouched and ducked down, sweeping her hand around to try to part the long grasses.

Anything could be here. Her mind raged. She knew all the diseases she could expose herself to by coming into contact with the victim's blood- or the killer's. And there was even a chance he could be here, now, behind the dilapidated trailer on the lot that this one backed up to, or even in the canal itself, submerged like a big lizard up to his eyes. Shaye glanced around again warily, and again saw nothing.

It would have been so easy to perpetrate a murder here, she thought. Nobody had passed on the street in the past ten minutes. Even if they did, she doubted that they would spot her here in the grassy shadows. What if she had to call for help? No one would respond. There were r om shouts and screams all over this park at every hour of the day and night.

The residents just perceived the screams of pain and fury as background noise.

And the two cops - Danielo and Chow? Shaye got the impressions from the sarcastic comments of the locals, and what she had seen of Danielo slouching in his car on desultory patrol, that they were only biding their time here. If they passed on the street right now, she doubted that they would glance back to see her hovering by the crime scene.

What would she say if they did? She didn't know. She looked down at her light colored T-shirt and saw the coffee stains left by Adam. Breaking the cup, he was only trying to protect her from herself, she knew. Trying to keep her from recklessly injuring her stomach. But yet their conflict still tore at her heart. And she really didn't care about the risk from the cops. For she wanted to catch the killer. If she could do that, she thought, then she could bring some control to absolute danger and madness. She could recover and take her life back. Shaye Taylor could be somebody again.

Shaye's heart seemed to stop. For she saw the cop car nosing its way onto Caiman Street. She flattened further in the grasses, and watched the car veer drunkenly on the dirt surface of the street at five miles an hour. The dark haired officer in the passenger seat- she assumed it was Frank Danielo- stared fixedly straight ahead.

Minutes after the car had passed, Shaye straightened up from her flattened position and then padded slowly along the brink of the canal bank. The police certainly hadn't cleaned up the crime scene. On the banks of the canal, Shaye found beer cans, a thousand old cigarette filters, remnants of old campfires and even used condoms that she cringed away from, fearing the HIV virus.

Up here, on the bank, was an area where homeless and people up to no good obviously hung out. With some amusement, Shaye even turned up old soda bottles in a style used in the nineteen seventies. But there was no sign of any struggle on the slightly packed ground.

On the level just below this, where the ground slanted towards the water, she had no trouble finding where the victim had been buried. A shallow grave, they had said. And a sandy excavation was dug out, with an inner circle of police tape ringing it. This is where the victim had lain in her final rest.

Shaye inched her way down near the grave, legs bent and sliding. She had a hard time stopping and almost fell in, and her heart stopped for a minute, feeling her terror and aloneness. Her toes pointed to the very brink, resting on an area that looked like it had been scraped at, or raked. Shaye examined this more closely. The whole area, the whole grave, looked as though it had been raked up- small strokes, about six inches wide.

Heart hammering, Shaye pondered this. Some of the strokes nearest her looked like they could even be tinged slightly with the victim's blood. She looked as closely as she could tolerate, while terror spun her mind momentarily out of control. Thinking more rationally, she wished she had the tools of a crime lab to really analyze the scene.

Why had the killer bothered to bury his victim? Not to keep her hidden surely, since his primary defense from being apprehended was anonymity, both his and that of his victim. If he did want to hide the body, though, why had he buried it so shallowly?

Shaye's heart choked up in her throat. In the grave lay a crude blood-tipped cross, about four inches long, fashioned of dried grass that the killer must have pulled out and braided right here. The eerie feeling shot up like freezing water through every nerve pathway in Shaye's body. This grave must have been ceremonial, then. The killer must have wanted his victim to be found- and wanted it to be observed that he had buried her.

Buried her like some sacrifice it would seem.

Shaye inched a little further from the hole, for a moment imagining what it would be like to just lie down there, and let it be over. For Jane Doe, her misery must have ended. Shaye wondered if she had died in terror, struggling for life, or simply accepted her fate and an end to the pain.

Shaye's heart ached for the woman, to the point that sudden tears fell out of her eyes, here with no one here to see.

Something caught her eye further down by the canal bank, deeper into the park and all the way into the next lot- a small piece of paper, fluttering around halfway in the water. Several pieces of paper actually- one blue and one green.

She scrabbled lower on the bank, not really thinking, but in pursuit. She had to walk a ways, under more shadowy branches, and felt almost overpowered by the rotten oily smell of the water. Mucky ground with grasses embedded sucked loudly at her shoes with each step.

Mosquitoes started to bite and Shaye whimpered, fearing malaria and encephalitis. She swatted at them fiercely, smearing her own blood on her shoulders. But, perversely, she pushed on.

"I will not be afraid," she chanted to herself over and over, like a soldier walking into battle. "I will not be afraid."

She reached the item on the riverbank and crouched down to see it, knowing already from the moment she had spotted it what it was. It was money. Shaye brushed it with her fingers as lightly as though she was touching an elusive butterfly's wing. A fifty dollar bill. This had to be the victim's. And it brought with it tremendous implications.

People around here were poor, so the victim probably hadn't arrived here carrying the fifty. It was probably the pay the killer had used to entice her. And then he hadn't taken it back. As though it was not important to him. If this was all true, then robbery of the prostitute was not the motive. This pointed more to a serial killer who simply killed for the pleasure of it, as Shaye had feared all along.

She looked around more. Embedded in the ruddy canal side she also saw something metallic. Most of it sat an inch deep in the muck, but Shaye used a twig to raise one corner- a little tweezer- for plucking eyelashes or facial hair- and not at all rusty. This had to be the victim's as well. Perhaps her pocketbook had gotten upended up there by the grave. Possessions must have scattered all over and the police had obviously retrieved most of them, but not all.

Some items had rolled down the incline and then been carried along by a lazy current. With the well-advertised sloppy police work and lack of manpower around here, it was not that great a surprise that half the victim's possessions had been missed.

Shaye wondered how diligently the police were investigating the murder of a transient hooker anyway. The idea of their laxity made her fear more for her own safety, and made her more determined to retrieve the next piece of evidence- the blue cardboard business card that sat halfway in the reeking stream of water.

Shaye retrieved the nearest rickety dried branch, coating her hands with slime. Then a spindly daddy longlegs spider crawled over her fingers. She squealed like she was burned, but still fished with the branch until it snapped just as the card drifted toward her. Shaye went for the card and dragged it out of the stream, shaking water from it.

Much of the ink was gone from its soaking but the photo was still clear enough, and the unemotional face of the victim stared back at Shaye. Elvira Ramirez was her name. Twenty-six years old, according to the birth date on the card. She had long, inky black hair, just like in the artist's sketch and pasty white skin. *"Phoenix House, Oceanside- Women in Renewal"* the card read.

Shaye bit her lip. There was no sense trying to wipe her fingerprints from the card, for it was soaking. Instead, she dabbed it dry on her pants, adding stains from the ink to the ruin already imposed by grass stains and muck. She would throw the pants out when she got back to the trailer. And she would find out more about Phoenix House.

From what she could get from the headlines, the police believed the victim and the killer had been strangers to each other. But maybe someone at the halfway house could point Shaye in the direction of where Elvira Ramirez hung out- where she might have picked up her killer, or what kind of men she liked to date. This would be a start to figuring out the puzzle, at least.

And, at the moment, Shaye felt that she must figure out the puzzle. For, only by finding out why the killer had selected Elvira Ramierez as a victim, would she know how to keep herself safe.

Shaye found a shortcut across the park by following the canal behind the crime scene. She crept along the banks observing the strange backs of trailers, sheds and broken fences. She peered into people's homes, but no one saw her. Not even when a wire cage full of pit mix dogs exploded in barking. She emerged out on a half-block long street, Roseate Spoonbill, which she guessed connected with Egret. And her guess proved right.

She hurried down Spoonbill, turned the corner onto Egret and then tried to move as though she was in a hurry, but still nonchalant. The odor of the canal clung to her, wafting off her hair and clothes, and her entire appearance was disheveled. No one seemed to notice, and all the trailers looked closed-up and silent- unusual for Egret Street at any time of day.

Trying not to breathe hard, but starting to pant with the speed she was walking, Shaye turned back onto their street, Manatee.

She almost ran into the local squad car jackknifed across the middle of the road, and she heard staccato voices arguing by the trailer across the street. Shaye jogged forward, instinctively sliding towards the vegetation by her side of the block, where she was less likely to be noticed.

The voices raised even louder. Two cops had their backs to her, standing in the yard across the street by the open trailer door. They argued with Shaye's lookalike, Darlene, and a middle-aged man with no shirt, a booming voice and a very big beer belly.

"I told you guys to leave, us alone!" Darlene protested. "Harold ain't done nothing."

"So let him tell us that," officer Danielo said, the first time Shaye had heard his voice. She slipped back into their own yard, and rested on an upturned cinderblock under a palmetto frond near their garbage cans. No one saw her, and she took the chance to ascertain what was going on.

"I ain't tellin' you fuckers nothing," the big man boomed at Frank Danielo, sounding drunk. "Ya'll can't come into a man's yard, middle a the day, and tell me ya wanna fuckin rip apart my house..."

"We're not trying to rip up your house," Officer Chow said, in his small sensible voice. "We need to go through your mobile home to get backyard access. Now, since there's been a problem, we need to take a census of what people are living in the home."

"What?" Darlene and the man exclaimed simultaneously.

"This is fuckin America," the man raged. He literally foamed at the mouth as he came down off the steps to get right up in the cops' faces. "You can't take no fuckin census... and tell me who's all in my home. That's *my* home, man..."

Officer Danielo sneered at him like a rude bad boy from the city, and something tightened in Shaye in attraction. Against her will, Officer Danielo, with all his testosterone, suddenly reminded her she was a girl.

"You are so pathetic, mister," Danielo said to Darlene's bearish boyfriend, with a strong New York City accent. "Maybe I should just taser your lard ass and get it over with!"

"You can't hurt my boyfriend," Darlene shrilled.

Two smaller men came out the trailer, kids cried and the big man bellowed in his defense like a fighting walrus, his words unintelligible now.

Officer Chow tried to break the small crowd up, giving instructions in an intense monotone. Meanwhile Danielo poked at the trailer residents with a nightstick, laughing like this whole scene made him high.

Now doors began creaking open, and the other residents of Manatee St. started pouring into the street, crowding in the police car.

Shaye backed up to her trailer. Under the shaded canopy of plants, and behind the partial wall of cut out brick, she jiggled the stubborn key in the lock.

"Come on," she urged, under her breath.

Several long moments later, the door opened and she practically tumbled in.

"Adam," she called out, wanting to forget that they were fighting. "I have some information about the murder! I was just at the crime scene."

There was no reply. The trailer seemed stuffy, yet chill, and all the lights were off. She thought she sensed his presence at home, but maybe Adam had gone away right after she did. Maybe he went off again with his friends. Assertively, she barged into his room.

And she found Adam hanging from the light fixture, choking. He was alive. His eyes swung to Shaye as she walked in, and his cheeks looked swollen and bright red.

Shaye became silent, she couldn't scream. She assessed every aspect of the scene. Adam's neck, ringed round with stretched pantyhose. His eyes bugging and his skin turning blue.

There was a vinyl chair next to the Formica covered vanity and Shaye shoved it under him. Then she ran for the kitchen and retrieved a steak knife. She ran back, knowing Adam might be in his last seconds of life. She clambered onto the rickety vinyl chair. It swayed, but she grabbed for Adam's body, trying to take some of his weight.

Adam had peed himself, and the wetness chilled Shaye through her shirt. She clutched him to her harder, as the chair underneath her righted itself and she sawed at the pantyhose, taking clumps of Adam's auburn hair. She cut through and they both fell to the floor, jarring every bone in Shaye's body.

Adam's eyes rolled back, as his head lolled in her lap. She slapped at his cheeks. "Breathe!" she begged.

Adam gasped, and gave a little dry cough. Then he wheezed, then gave another. Then he started wheezing more strongly, taking in squeaking breaths that frightened her. He coughed and gagged again.

Shaye looked at the red and black bruises forming around his delicate neck, and listened to his breathing that struggled to normalize.

"The cops are right outside," she declared, making the decision that Adam's life was more important than their freedom. "I'll go get them."

Adam clutched her arm, and then made the effort to stroke it once or twice in appeasement. "No, Honey," he whispered. "I'm an asshole. But I'm fine... no cops! Never. Never any cops."

Chapter 6

Shaye stared at Adam, more frightened than she could recall being throughout her entire illness, or the year and a half of abuse in the loony bin while she ailed. Oddly though, Shaye's face showed not much emotion, just blankness, her big green eyes open wide in true confusion.

"Why did you do this, Adam?" she asked. "Because of me? What I said?"

She reached out her hand in hesitation, as though unsure if her touch might hurt him. "What do you need now? Do you want some water? You want me to help you into bed?"

Adam gave a token shake of his head. He couldn't speak, but tears trailed out of his eyes. He gulped and swallowed. So did Shaye.

"I'm useless," he murmured, adjusting his legs and glancing up toward the curtained window and the shouting of cops and residents from across the street. "Like you said, Shaye, like my parents said. I'm just a freak."

"How can you say that *you're* useless? That you're a freak?" Shaye exclaimed. "*I'm* the one that's useless, Adam. And you're such a good person. You're worth a thousand of me!"

Pushing his roughened vocal cords Adam said, "Shaye, I want you to know that I'm not turning tricks at Foxy Lady. Okay? I'm not."

"Adam," Shaye said, "I wouldn't care if you *were* turning tricks. Don't you understand?"

"You're the one that doesn't understand," Adam said glumly. He struggled up to his feet, straightening out his slim body. He and Shaye both reeled together in the direction of the bed, with it unclear which of them needed the help in standing. When they reached the bed Shaye lowered Adam down on his back, and his eyes opened wider, sweetly sentimental in their expression of tragedy- almost poetic in a gothic way.

"It doesn't matter," Adam said. "You know my diagnosis. Schizophrenic. I see and hear things that aren't there. I've been trying to hold it together since we've come here. But it's getting worse now."

Shaye sat on the edge of the bed and shook out her hair, which seemed to reek of curdled mud from the crime scene by the canal. Thoughts raged in her head like *she* was the one who was schizophrenic, not Adam.

"So, what do you want?" she asked in a strained voice. "Do you need psychotropic meds again? Because I can find some way to get them... I'm not going to let you kill yourself!"

Adam reached up and tucked a long strand of her mud-crusted hair behind one of Shaye's ears. "Where on earth were you?" he asked.

The tragic reflection in the dark pools of his eyes seemed like he already suspected.

"I went to the crime scene," Shaye said. "I was looking for evidence and I actually found some information on the victim. I know her name now and think I might be able to track down her killer. I could turn in the information to the cops secretly so we wouldn't have to get involved..."

Adam seemed weak and disoriented in the big bed, very pale and swimming in a sea of languor. His eyes met hers with more cynicism than she could have imagined. "You're really losing it, aren't you Shaye?"

"I'm not losing it!"

Adam answered in a painfully raspy voice. "I know you're not crazy, Shaye. But you're putting yourself in danger in this park now. Can't you promise me you won't do this? That you'll stop digging into this crime? I just need a little time to recover. These 'spells' of mine come in waves, and I can pretty much predict the duration. It's happened all my life."

Adam turned on his side in fetal position and Shaye rested a hand on the side of his body helplessly, suspecting that, if their roles were reversed, he would know better what to do now. She wished she could do more, but all she could do right now was stand guard and wait.

"So, you think you'll be all right again?" she asked him after a few minutes of silence.

"I'll be all right, Sweetie" Adam said. "Just help me through it. And don't take any chances out there, please, when I can't help you."

The tragic aspect in Adam's tone made Shaye have to struggle to sound optimistic, and not dissolve in tears.

"You like hot cocoa, right, Adam? I'll make you a cup. Maybe that will make your throat feel better."

Adam smiled, seeming to convey that her caring had momentarily broken through. He acknowledged with his eyes that he appreciated her offer, and he squeezed her hand with long cold fingers.

When Shaye returned, Adam's velvety brown eyes stared up at the ceiling almost sightlessly. His cracked lips moved as he murmured to himself, or someone else that he imagined.

Shaye padded over, holding out the unbroken mug of their matched pair, filled with warm cocoa. She thought Adam might be too far gone at the moment to recognize her. But he surprised her, speaking even as he continued to stare at the fixed point at the ceiling.

"Shaye," he rasped softly. "Don't be afraid. Come over and give me my hot cocoa. I see some freaky hallucinations at times like this. Like right now I see this woman- like mythological looking with long black hair down to her ankles. Very long, very black hair. And she's talking to me…"

A vision? Or a ghost?

Shaye shivered, thinking of the distinctive hair of the murder victim Elvira Ramierez. Despite her sudden chill she held the cocoa steady, resting the cup's warm base on her flattened palm, an offering for the old friend she cared so deeply about.

Now Adam looked at her, and pulled back his plump lips in a crinkly smile.

"You're so brave, Shaye. I hope you know I'd never hurt you or anybody else. It's funny how, at the worst, I've always acted out like a sissy, like a girl would. Yet because of my histrionics the authorities had to lock me away on and off for probably half my life…"

"If you acted out, Adam, maybe you had a reason," Shaye said. "Maybe it was more their unfair treatment than your hallucinations that made you have your nervous breakdowns."

Now Adam's eyes met hers and he seemed totally engaged with reality. "These visions hurt so much, Shaye. Sometimes I want to cry, or scream or tear my own head off to take out my second-hand brain. But I've always thought it's like when someone is high on recreational drugs- or even alcohol. The chemicals can't really make you do what you wouldn't anyway, you know? They just drop your inhibitions.

"So, it's the same way with my hallucinations. The visions seem real. But another part of me knows they're not. Maybe I'm not the strongest guy. But I've always been able to fight it, even without the medications. If anyone would have ever just given me a chance... If they would've just let me grow up like a normal boy..."

Shaye slowly and patiently fed him the cocoa "You'll be okay," she said, stroking his hair, his shoulders and his legs as he sat up, leaning on the cracked Formica headboard. "You'll have nothing but freedom now, your new testing ground. This will be the year of Adam Ant!"

Adam fought to get down a last sip of the cocoa that seemed agonizing on his bruised throat. Then he gently pushed the mug away. Shaye leaned forward to set it on a bedside table, leaving her face inches from his pale and bruised looking one.

"Isn't it weird? You're afraid of so many things, Shaye. And yet you're really not afraid of me?"

Shaye shook her head with absolute conviction. "Never, Adam. Not at all. I'll just get you better, whatever it takes. Even if you need to go back in the hospital..."

Adam shook his head.

"...I'm just saying," she said, "if you ever *want* to go the hospital, then say the word and I'll take you." And she meant it, even though the thought of venturing anywhere near a hospital terrified her. "If you don't want a hospital, then I promise I'll stay right here and do whatever you say you need until you're stronger and feel you can face things."

Adam flexed his cracked lips in an attempt at a smile. "It might be a week, Shaye, or maybe longer until this episode runs its course. And I feel safest staying away from people, just hiding here inside."

"That's fine," Shaye breathed, through her own cracked lips. "I'm here. Remember, you always stayed with me in the hospital when I was at my worst. You were the one who saved my life, Adam."

Adam took Shaye's hand. But something inside him looked a thousand miles away. It seemed almost like she could see moving pictures deep within the crystal balls of his eyes. He laughed. And then he coughed on it, hard.

"You know what? I peed on myself when I was hanging, Shaye." He shadowed his eyes with his long eyelashes in shame in this lucid moment. "I don't want to be filthy here in the bed. Please, I want to get up and clean up a little."

"I'll help you," Shaye offered valiantly, with her terror of bodily fluids seeming to evaporate through the roof. All she cared about was preventing Adam from trying to kill himself again. The oxygen loss from the hanging had left him still too dizzy and disoriented for her to allow him to minister to himself- especially in a little bathroom with a lock on the door.

She insisted on helping him, and Adam relented, laughing for a second at himself and her and their predicament.

Then they staggered to the closet-sized bathroom in a strange embrace, with Shaye supporting Adam's graceful weight, while carrying a pair of clean jogging pants and boxer briefs for him bunched in her palm.

Out in the street, park residents and police officers yelled louder.

"I'm looking for a murderer, dude, and you're telling me I shouldn't arrest you for an unlicensed handgun?" That was Frank Danielo.

"I use it to shoot fuckin' raccoons!" the tenant, Harold, countered. "This park is infested!"

Oh, goddamn you!" Danielo cursed.

Then she heard the sounds of a struggle and a large body being thrown against a car hood. "Now get your fat ass self in the squad car."

"We'll sue you for police brutality," a female voice screeched.

"I don't care," Danielo yelled back. "I'll arrest every man in your family, Darlene, just so you skank bitches in this park can sleep in peace tonight!"

More cursing and arguing erupted. Then someone threw a beer bottle, which shattered against the squad car. The voices raised even more and the curses got filthier.

Adam talked to himself as he and Shaye crowded together in the shadowy bathroom. Shaye let him rest his troubled head on her bosom as she slid off his soaking pants and replaced them with the dry jogging pants, ministering to him like she was his mother.

"Shhh, Little Baby," Shaye murmured to her friend. "There's nothing to be afraid of now. It will all be all right."

Shaye stood guard, allowing the days to blend together, but never losing her vigilance or the courage it gave her. The first night, after cleaning him up, she got Adam back to bed and he began talking to himself furiously for hours. There was more crying, and then some gasping for breath. Shaye tried to keep them secret in the room using no overhead lights. She feared that the police might barge in here while they were arresting half the family across the street but, mercifully, they never did.

That night Shaye remained remarkably clearheaded, although possibly not all of her thoughts made perfect sense. She cradled Adam's curled up body, feeling the bones of his spine and the lines of each individual rib. She stroked him and rocked him as he cried and argued with enemies that were not even there.

At each sound of struggle in the street, she gazed up in the dimness toward the small window, holding her chin and nostrils like an alert dog guarding its owner.

If she and Adam were caught and returned to the State Hospital, it wasn't going to be on her watch she determined!

Adam's words at one point became indecipherable, and he seemed to choke on them. Shaye rolled his unprotesting body over so that he lay on his back, and she gasped at the darkening necklace of self-inflicted bruises on his throat.

She ran to kitchen and returned with a flashlight, which she played over the damaged flesh, checking him over. Adam giggled.

That was his last moment of lucidity for a while.

The ruckus went on in the street until approximately two in the morning, and Adam writhed in the bed the whole time. Sometimes he talked so that Shaye could understand; mostly it was gibberish, along with pitiful sobs and sheets of tears that soaked both of them.

The night cooled in the trailer and Shaye felt the chill settle onto the bare skin of her arms. The weight of it seemed to rest in the small of her back.

This was madness, just like Adam had said. Shaye Taylor had been physically sick; she'd also been depressed. Then she'd turned suicidal and she still was afraid of every living thing that moved, including every microbe. Shaye Taylor was definitely no longer anyone's candidate for Model of the Year. But she held a tight ball of sanity within herself that seemed as fiery as the burning lava within the center of the earth.

Shaye couldn't have explained it, but seeing Adam in this state filled her with dread. For she held that core of sanity and she sensed he did not. As much as she loved him, it was hard for her to relate to this.

Adam stood close to the edge of madness, the edge of the earth or the edge of the universe- the vacuum. At the moment, Shaye held onto sanity for both of them for safekeeping. If she didn't hold it- and hold him- when he came back she sensed he might be lost.

At around four that morning, Adam fell asleep and so did Shaye, half sitting, half lying, draped over his side.

The next day, in the morning things were somewhat better. Adam was vacant-eyed, but quiet. When Shaye walked him to the bathroom, he paused to stare at the horrific ring of bruises around his neck, with his eyes resembling dark troubled water.

"Am I supposed to die?" he asked Shaye. "Am I going to?"

She smiled her best model smile that she used on all the *Tropical Sun* jobs, deliberately holding her head up high to fuel his morale. "Adam, you're golden!"

The old Adam would have laughed. This one simply sulked and lowered his head, shuffling back to the bed.

Shaye checked in on him every few minutes, meanwhile running out to straighten up and make them snacks. She compulsively checked the TV news as well, and she was rewarded by mention at noon of the conflict between police and residents in the park. The newscast made it seem quite serious, rather than the farce it had actually been.

Although she cooked, neither she nor Adam ate much. Just before four, the day after he attempted suicide she took it upon herself to call Adam's job at the Foxy Lady, to tell the manager that he was sick and couldn't make it in for work that night.

While she waited for the manager, listening to Foxy Lady's throbbing music, someone decided to call Madeline to the phone.

"Hey, Barbie," Madeline said, obviously more than a little drunk.

Adam had confided to Shaye that Madeline had to get herself drunk in order to face going with the johns. If so, Shaye didn't understand why she didn't just stop doing it. After all, there were so many sexually transmitted diseases. No matter how you protected yourself, it could still be a shortcut to dying.

"Please don't call me Barbie," Shaye said, trying to act compassionate and at the same time not alert anyone in the club that there was something irregular going on with Adam. After all, they desperately needed his job.

"You are Barbie, though," Madeline slurred. "You look just like my favorite blond Barbie doll I kept under my pillow when I was a little boy. Now whatsa matter with my sweetie, Adam Ant today, Barbie?"

"He's just ill," Shaye said. "He has a really bad migraine, and so he can't even talk. He gets these sometimes and sometimes it takes a few days…"

"Why don't I come over there?" Madeline urged. "I can nurse him and all. I've got a woman's touch."

"*I'm* a woman, Madeline," Shaye said. "Just please tell the manager Adam's not coming in. He and I are fine here, taking care of ourselves. We don't need you here right now."

Abruptly the transsexual's voice changed, to become more awake, deeper and more admonishing.

"Shaye," she said. "Adam Ant told us all about you. How you act totally petrified around illness. I'm worried about him when he's sick 'cause maybe you can't handle it."

"I can…"

"I get off work at two-thirty tonight. I could still hop a bus…" Madeline wheedled, sounding drunk again. "I think I know where your bus stop is…"

Someone else took the phone. Once again, it was Rochelle to the rescue.

"Shaye, I don't want Madeline getting' on a bus, in the condition she's in tonight."

"I'm fine," Madeline yelled in the background.

"She's just like a real girl," Rochelle said to Shaye. "She's so vulnerable. But I'm tired and we gotta drive all the way back to our apartment and then back here for the morning shift tomorrow. Does Adam really need us, Honey?"

"No, not at all," Shaye asserted, with the wheels in her mind racing. Something eluded her, just at the corner of consciousness and planning. But she lost it and went on with her explanation. "I tried to explain that to Madeline. Adam's just got a migraine headache. Please try to buy us a couple of days with the boss..."

Rochelle assured she could smooth over things with the manager, and that the "girls" would try to drive out to visit on the weekend if Adam still wasn't better.

Shaye prayed to herself that he would be. Only when she got off the phone, and was heading back to Adam's bedroom with a tray, did she realize that when she had referred to Adam's illness, she'd asked Rochelle to buy "us" time with the boss, like it was her illness, too.

Four days into his psychotic "spell" Adam, sounding a lot more like himself, requested that he take a bath.

"I'm filthy, Shaye- my body, my mind and my soul," he said. "And you scrubbed out that bathroom so beautifully, just like you did everything in the house. It shines, like I wish this whole neighborhood could shine. It's my little spa oasis!"

Shaye looked at him with crinkled brow.

"Shaye, Sweetie, I'm kidding."

Shaye's mind darkened with images of languid forms with slit wrists lying in blood-red water. She herself had tried the method three separate times in the hospital, even though she had never gotten it right. The nurses had always burst in just as she hovered at the edge of sleeping before her eternal Emerald City, and they'd pulled her back to the gritty reality of her real vida loca.

"Adam, I don't think a bath is such a great idea," Shaye said. "I want to be able to watch you. I haven't even taken a shower myself since this started."

Adam laughed. "So, you're filthy dirty, too. How's that gonna help us?"

Shaye rocked side to side, trying to deeply examine his eyes. Perhaps the "real" Adam was back and things were safe. After all, he was joking. But no, she thought. His eyes still looked off-kilter and strangely shadowed.

"Get real," Adam persisted, losing the languid stance momentarily and standing up to her. "I'm going to my bathroom. I'm gonna strip. Then I'm taking a shower. You're welcome to watch, wash me, join me, Shaye- whatever. Otherwise we're going to rot in this bedroom."

Adam flicked his shoulder in annoyance as he turned. Then he snatched up a towel and marched for the shower.

Shaye pursued, kicking her tennis shoes off, preparing for a soaking wet struggle if Adam attempted to hurt himself. She stepped into the small bathroom and was surprised to face his hard butt cheeks, as he stood naked, singing and berating his reflection in the mirror.

"What is the measure of a man?" Adam asked himself. "Is it how he looks? What he calls himself: boy or girl? Is it the things he would do? Or is it the things he would *never* do?" And he screeched out a falsetto varient of the line about the man in the mirror from the Michael Jackson song.

Shaye jumped back on her bare feet as he swung around to face her.

Adam's eyes looked dark and sleepy, like a dangerously potent vintage wine.

He stepped toward her and took Shaye's hand, making her look at him staring at himself in the mirror. She'd seen the naked front of his body and she hadn't even blushed. Now she brushed the silky bare skin of his back and arm and shoulder as she leaned forward. But his troubled eyes mesmerized her today, just like they seemed to mesmerize him.

"Why can't a man be like his father?" Adam intoned. "Or like Our Father in Heaven? Why can't a man be like all the generations of fathers in between? Men made to be men? Why can't a man see clear to see himself?"

Suddenly Adam turned back to her, and stamped the floor, like an angry child. "And why can't you ever see clear to give up on me, Shaye?"

His outburst was simply so weird that Shaye stood her ground, with undecided expression, like she had much of the week.

Adam looked down at himself and noticed his penis bouncing up and down as he threw his angry tantrum. He stopped and suddenly sputtered out a laugh. Shaye laughed, too.

Adam climbed into the shower, now flicking his tight tail. "I know; I'm pathetic," he said. "Let's see if I can still remember how to turn on the water without scalding myself."

Shaye wondered for a brief second if Adam was teasing, trying to entice her into the shower to finally get to see her naked. But he was gay, wasn't he, she thought. Worse than that; Adam was *female* at heart. So how could she think he *wasn't* gay? How could she think her nude body could have an effect on him?

As she stood undecided, Adam sighed deeply with pleasure as the water hit him, and then started belting out, "*Singing in the Rain*".

When he heard nothing from her for a few minutes, he peeked his head out of the curtain, blinking water droplets from his big doe eyes.

"Shaye, I've basically already seen you nude in the swimsuit catalog," he said. "If you want, though, get in here with your bra and panties. At least that way you'll get clean. And I won't have to feel so guilty."

Shaye breathed out a sigh, like a weight had left her. He was a friend getting back to himself, it seemed. And so why did she always have to be so paranoid? Adam had no more sexual interest in her than he would a little sister.

Shyly, Shaye dropped her shorts and oversized T-shirt. She wore her only bra, a pretty pink lace one from the old days that bunched in the front where she had lost so much weight. Her panties were new, cotton, white. Adam had actually bought them for her in a package at the dollar store next door to the local supermarket.

Shaye climbed tentatively into the shower, as Adam reached out a slick hand to help her in. Her climbing was unsteady, so he curved a hand around the small of her back, a gesture almost as though they were dancing.

Shaye gasped as the front of her body pressed momentarily against his. Water dripped down from his thick hair over his eyelashes, his soft nose and hard cheekbones. It slid over his lush plump lips, which he held parted as though out of breath.

"*Are you gay?*" Shaye wanted to ask, once and for all. She fantasized saying, "*I know you love me. But would you stop loving me if you knew that sometimes this tattered body talks, wanting you to be the man that you never wanted to be? When you touch me, Adam, what do you feel?*"

Instead, Shaye found breath in her body for only one question.

"Adam," she breathed. "Are you getting better now? Are the visions going away?"

Adam gulped. She watched anguish twist his face as their bodies brushed each other in the warm running water.

"I think I am!" he said.

Suddenly he lowered his head and began to cry, leaning into her so that his chest brushed her breasts, so that his semi-hard penis leaned against her nervous belly. "Oh God," he sobbed. "Oh, God.

I've been so afraid, Shaye. I'm sorry I tried to kill myself. I've been so afraid of going back to the State Hospital!"

Still crying, with his touch passionate yet completely equivocal, Adam slid down against her. His lips brushed her wet belly and the fronts of her thighs. He kissed her skin and clutched her knees, kissing them, while she tangled her hand in his silky wet hair.

"Oh my God, Adam. Oh my God," she said, as they held each other, rocking under the water.

That night, Shaye peeled off her wet bra and underwear and crawled into her own bed, nude. In a way right now she felt pretty. In a way she felt powerful, like she and her partner had cruised the dizzying and dangerous expanses of the universe this week, almost gone, yet they had come back safe. The important thing was that Adam was going to be okay now. Triumphant, Shaye finally felt that she could sleep.

The noises of the neighborhood did not disturb her. She slept straight through the night, angled across the bed under the covers, not even rising to use the bathroom. When she rolled over groggily in the morning, she truly did not know what time it was, but it felt warm and stuffy and she suspected it was quite late.

Shaye pulled on a T-shirt and panties and padded out to check on Adam.

He was not home. Centered on his neatly made bed, Shaye found a note. "You were sleeping so peacefully. So I went to get groceries. I want to make us a wonderful lunch before I go to work!"

Shaye smiled, feeling almost a languor of well-being as she returned to the living area, realizing that unlike on the other days, there was nothing she was responsible for do. The lack of tension felt good, and she casually contemplated whether she wanted to eat some cereal, or just wait for Adam to get back with real food.

She swung by the television, which Adam had left playing , a bit surprised that it was already noon, for the local news was on. She started to walk away. But something deep within Shaye's heart sensed the headline even before she heard it.

"Murder!" The newcaster declared. *"**Another 'woman of the night' murdered in Flamingo Park.**"*

Chapter 7

Shaye left their home and her feet led her, automatically and of their own accord, in the direction of the new crime scene. It was as if this was all she had been destined for, all along. Shaye Taylor, a pretty young woman, not intended to have success as a swimsuit model as it would have seemed, not intended to rest in the bosom of her suburban family's love on a mild early winter afternoon like today.

No, instead, there was malice in the air. There was a man in this bleak, dirt-covered square of ground stalking and killing unwanted women. And Shaye Taylor was following his trail.

The noon news hadn't said much, only mentioning that this murder had taken place "on the other side of the park" from the first crime. Using her own trailer as a compass point, Shaye knew that the first murder happened just southeast of where she and Adam lived. Reversing that, logically, would mean northwest. If she went to look for this crime scene, it would bring her into a section with the most derelict trailers, a section that appeared shaded even in the height of daytime- into the very bowels of the park.

Shaye Taylor was afraid of shadows; Shaye sometimes scared herself when she moved too fast and caught a glimpse of the movement in the cloudy bathroom mirror. And she hadn't eaten today, even though it was past noontime. Soon, her stomach without medication in it might start to secrete acids, would start to turn on itself. There could be pain and blood, with Shaye curled in the bed for days just like Adam had been.

But none of it seemed to matter. For it seemed like Shaye alone was destined for this thing. Shaye Taylor, under these strange circumstances, had been brought to this desolate place to stop this killer.

So, this noontime, she had calmly snapped off the TV and pulled her dusty Keds on and started out northwest, looking for a crime scene.

As she took the shaded shortcut up familiar Spoonbill Street, Shaye heard voices. She pulled back under an overhanging palmetto frond, quickly assessing the streets in every direction.

Instinct easily told her who was sharing the area with her on this dusty noontime- two of the particular men she was most afraid of- her two strongest suspects for the murders.

The two young men wore the same clothes that they always did- oversized white T-shirts and baggy greyed denim shorts, also oversized. They stood in a break in a thicket beside an abandoned trailer just diagonal to Shaye. And although the younger of the men, the one with light mocha colored skin and curly hair, kept watch, he had to shield his eyes. Shaye realized that he was looking directly into the sun and that his lookout was completely ineffective.

She dared to take a few steps forward to improve her own position of spying. And she was disgusted with what she saw. For the two men were not alone. The white guy with a goatee had his back to her, and his back was straining. Squashed behind him, up against the moldy siding of the old trailer, Shaye now spotted a woman.

And the young man was screwing her.

With his buddy keeping watch.

"Oh, Oh, Daddy!" Shaye heard the woman pant, like she was reciting lines.

She was plump, with medium length blond curls that poufed out against the trailer wall as the young man vigorously pumped her up and down. She curled one dirty bare foot up against the back of his baggy shorts to brace herself, grunted and took a pull on a cigarette. Her smeared bright red lipstick looked almost like a wound. Her plump flesh, half in/half out of her thin summer clothes, jiggled all over the man she was servicing.

"Fuck. Fuck you girl," he panted. "Just take it!"

"Fuckin' hurry, dude," his friend said to him. "We don't need Danielo and Chow over here."

"Then tell this fat ass bitch to do her job," the one with the goatee, the obvious leader of the pair, grunted. "Move your ass, lady!"

"First gimmee my rock like you said!" the prostitute protested.

She pushed her wiry customer off and prissily pulled the loose top of her peasant blouse back over her large naked breasts.

Goatee backed off and shook his head. "I don't know what y'all are so antsy about anyway. We'll all smoke together soon."

"No thanks," said his friend, pacing to get a better vantage point on the street, but still not noticing Shaye. Then he stepped back to the circle of well-trodden dust where the other two stood, squared off. "Why don't you just break out the rock now, Troy?"

Troy with the goatee looked up, and his eyes seemed to glitter. And Shaye took one step back, contemplating how quickly she could escape through the brush if she had to. She noticed the young man had a chain conspicuously hanging out of his shorts' pocket. This probably attached to a case for a large knife, and Shaye wondered if this could be the murder weapon. She envisioned him snagging her by the legs as she ran, bringing her down, face down into the brush and then cutting her...

The prostitute's voice rang out, shrill and complaining in the quiet setting. "Troy and Byron, you said you'd gimmee some rock. I only came out here for that. And how come you boys gotta get laid right where Josie was killed last night?"

"That's bullshit," Troy mumbled, while setting up a crack pipe with shaking hands.

"It's true," she protested, with a voice that seemed sharp enough to drive the birds out of the trees. The stout woman abruptly squatted, hiking up her flouncy miniskirt. She then peed into the dust like this was an everyday occurrence. Then she straightened up and leaned into the young men again. "Josie was raked to death," she said ominously. "The fuckin' psycho tore my girl up with a garden rake! I don't care what the police say. I saw her body this morning when they took her out of here."

Suddenly, she stepped back and took a drunken squint into the two young men's faces. "You know, it coulda been you boys that did it," she said.

Byron, the darker skinned young man simply pulled back and his expression turned stony.

"For real," the prostitute slurred. "How come you'all are hanging out this side of the park anyway?"

Troy stepped up suddenly and pushed her, hard, against the trailer. He fumbled in his pocket to threaten her with a small hunting knife that glinted in the sun. "You scared, Pollyanna?" he taunted. "If you're so scared, why don't you get your ass out of here?"

Shaye weighed her options. She could charge Troy. At least that would stop him before he cut the prostitute's throat. Or she could back up and run for her telephone to call the cops.

Neither was necessary.

"I ain't going anywheres," the hooker called Pollyanna squealed, grabbing for the crack pipe. "I want my rock!"

Troy didn't use the knife on her. Instead he slapped her, knocking her off balance. Byron got into the fray, pulling on his friend. "Come on Troy," he said. "Let's just get outta here."

The hooker snatched the crack pipe and Troy swatted her upside the head, before allowed Byron to pull him away.

"Come on man, come on!" Byron urged, seeming a hundred times more nervous than his friend.

Finally, sulky Troy gave up fighting for the crack pipe. He shrugged out of his friend's grasp and conspicuously dusted off his T-shirt like he was above all of this. "Fuckin' stupid cops," he muttered as he stamped off. "They won't find who killed those two hookers. Fuckin' bitches deserved it!"

Shay flattened herself instinctively down on the ground and a moist bed of broken fronds. Her body slid naturally, like the chilly curves of a snake. Concealment was her only chance at safety. Shaye barely breathed as the young men's sneakers trampled within feet of where she lay.

"Tore up with a garden rake!" Troy laughed raucously. "Pollyanna oughta be tore up with a rake!"

Then Shaye could not believe what she heard next- and it came from quiet Byron. "They *all* deserve it," Byron muttered. "All these whores in this park do."

Shaye lay in her place of concealment. Birds skittered around her, clawing up old leaves. A green Florida anole lizard hurried around before her face, then stopped and raised his head up and down, showing a red wattle, a lizard mating dance.

Across the dirt drive, the prostitute Pollyanna relaxed back against the siding of the trailer sucking on the glass crack pipe. She closed her eyes tight, as if all the cares of the world were retreating, and she seemed to lose complete track of time. So did Shaye, although she remained afraid to step out from her place of cover.

The sun shifted a bit, and a familiar cop car rolled onto the street. From her vantage point, all Shaye saw were the underinflated tires squatting down lower in the dust as the two officers got out. She saw their pantlegs and their shoes. She heard their radios crackle. Officer Chow spoke up, identifying their position and one of them- she assumed Danielo- spat in the dust.

Officer Chow bent down and took one of the prostitute's arms.

"Come on, Pollyanna," he said. "We need to take you into custody. Think of it as protection for you."

The hooker wearily shook her head, trying to crawl free of his grasp. "No way," she said. "I ain't going with you guys. I ain't done nothing wrong."

Shaye watched officer Danielo step into the picture. He grasped the woman's other plump arm none too gently and hauled her to her feet so that she yelped. Then he got behind her and walked her like an overbearing dance partner to the squad car- the second highly physical arrest Shaye had watched him make this week. But, despite his eagerness, he still he wasn't arresting the killer. He hadn't even found him.

After securing Pollyanna inside, Danielo and Chow leaned up against the squad car and the two smoked cigarettes almost furtively. Their body posture seemed like they might be former smokers, just slipping off the wagon in this week's stress.

"Do you think Pollyanna knows anything about this Josie Swank that was killed?" Chow asked Danielo. "If so, we should try to interview her before we bring her in."

"They *all* know each other," said Danielo, with his usual tone of slight annoyance. "They like to pick up their tricks at the bus stop across US1. Then they find a cozy spot in the park to entertain them."

"So, what I'm saying is, Pollyanna was just turning a trick right behind the trailer where the other girl was killed last night," Chow said. "So why was she spared and the other one taken? I didn't even recognize that girl, although I know most of the regulars around here. The funny thing is- I didn't recognize Elvira Ramirez either. Don't you think that's strange, Danny?"

Danielo scrunched up his youthfully attractive face. He pulled a piece of tobacco off his tongue and then threw it in the dirt. "You're right, Glenn," he said. "I'll talk to some of my informants up in here. But so far, I think you're right. Nobody so far said they know these girls. Maybe the girls weren't currently working. Or maybe they're from down the road or something…"

"And," Chow persisted, "how about that elaborate grave display back there with all the flowers, Danny? It looks like something from the Mexican Day of the Dead! Like pseudo-religious. Catholic, but with a Mexican flair. It's like in the movies where the serial killer has some special ritual that he does each time that represents something in his own demented mind. What do you think, Danny? I bet you used to see this kind of thing in New York City all the time. I bet they left all the interesting stuff for you detectives."

Officer Danielo threw his cigarette into the dirt at his feet and snapped at his partner.

"You're implying I should be back in New York City, working as a detective? That I *would* still be there if I didn't screw up?"

"Danny, at least you were there, man. At least you once were a detective," Chow said. "I've never been anywhere but here."

"Who cares?" Danielo said. "I really don't. Why can't you just be content where you are, and we just do our time here?"

Slightly built Officer Chow turned to his partner, and his Oriental face did not look inscrutable. Shaye saw it twist with pain. "I just thought maybe I could do some real detective work on this case, finally do something useful," he mumbled.

Danielo's tawny eyes glimmered in the full sun as he grinned. Then he put his reflectorized shades back on. "So, you can worry about the Mexican grave display, partner. Be my guest. Research it, do whatever you wanna do. As for me, I simply notice one thing at the moment. We've had two killings with the same M/O, two hookers, but neither one a working regular. And they both have really long black hair. So, I'm not into all that profiling crap- but I don't care for coincidence either. I think we need to be keeping chicks with long black hair inside at night in this park. And I can do that if Adrian Walker lets me speak to the press! Now let's go see that grave of yours again…"

Shaye's long hair fanned out around her like a stream of gold interweaving with the grasses. Shaye's very, very, very long hair.

She crept backward, backpedaling with the heels of her hands like an animal. Mud and earth caressed her bare legs as she crept, parallel to the cop car, heading for the crime scene just behind the tilted trailer where Troy had just pounded his body into the hooker's.

Should I tell them, Shaye contemplated, about Troy and Byron? The young men were drug dealers, and hostile. They patronized prostitutes and Troy had a hunting knife. He'd threatened Pollyanna with it. Did that mean anything? Today they had talked like they wanted prostitutes murdered. Did that mean *they* were the ones doing the killing?

It would be simple enough, Shaye thought, as she kept pace with the cop car, cutting through the underbrush. When the police officers' backs were turned she could just step out of here, brush herself off and casually tell them that she had seen the two young men acting threatening with Pollyanna. And she could also relate how she'd seen them hanging around the crime scene on Caiman Street.

Nervously, Shaye hunched along, half standing, half bent, preparing to disembark from the trees.

Meanwhile the police car slid incredibly sluggishly toward the crime scene. Danielo, at the wheel, talked on his car phone while gesturing with his hands. "Baby," he said to someone on the phone, pushing up at his stylishly cropped black hair in frustration. "You gotta let me do my job here. Shari is perfectly safe. And you're safe, too, Lorrine. The only thing in this trailer park is skanky whores. Like I told you, Baby. And this fucker preys on them, end of story."

His wife, Shaye assumed, said something on the other end. Shaye could hear her reedy panicked voice.

"Our subdivision's perfectly safe," Danielo answered. "It's a whole 'nother world from this. That's what we paid for when we bought our house... Fine, you go stay at your mom's overnight. Whatever makes you feel safer..."

He hung up the phone, and then threw up his arms helplessly as he addressed his partner. "It's ironic," he said, "that it's the middle class women around here who are so scared about this, and they're the only ones taking precautions. Meanwhile, the pathetic excuses for females in this park are just sitting around letting themselves get picked off..."

"I really think we oughtta arrest all of them," he said. "Seriously, any female in this trailer park that's young with long hair. Most of them have some kind of charges hanging over them. Just bring 'em all to jail tonight. Every skanky bitch in here. It'd be for their own good."

Shaye glimpsed Danielo's partner look at him in semi-shock. Then Chow delicately laughed, as if choosing to take the comments as a joke was the safed route for himself. Shaye settled back on her haunches in the woods. Considering Officer Danielo's current vigilante mood, she imagined that her stepping out of the brush and talking to him about her suspicions would be the absolutely worst thing she could do. Mysterious women with warrants out for their arrest were probably not his favorite thing at the moment. And there was no doubt her long hair would be just the thing to set him off.

The police car pulled around and stopped. The officers got out again, adjusting radios and gun holsters. This time they also took out a notepad and a cumbersome Polaroid camera.

Shaye stood shadowed amongst the fronds and small trees. She peered over their shoulders past the yellow tape of the crime scene. And, before the dark empty doorway of an abandoned taupe colored trailer, she saw something stranger and more horrible than even she could have imagined.

It was a fancy funeral arch- constructed Mexican-style of white paper shreds and many white, green and blood red carnations. In the last hours of nighttime, after brutally raking a long-haired woman to death, the killer had stood here and taken the time to decorate the door to the place of slaughter in this delicate, and almost hopeful, religious fashion. In the strong sunshine, amidst the weeds and trash and broken vinyl sided-home, the funeral bier looked almost beautiful.

"The Story of the Victims" the next day's newspaper read. *"Elvira 'Mami' Ramierez... A successful graduate of Phoenix House... twenty-eight years old... Found in her purse at the crime scene- an envelope with a generous money order made out to her family in her small hometown in Mexico."*

The article went on to give details about the mountain village, and the Mexican relatives who now grieved for Elvira. Relatives said she had been raised a devout Catholic, and they refused to believe that she had ever been involved in prostitution in America, even though they knew she sent money home while never revealing how she earned it.

Shaye clutched her newspaper, holding it open to the two-page feature on her tightly bunched up legs on the sofa. Around her the trailer was closed up tight, even though it was now steadily warming in the morning sun that caressed it from the east. At eight in the morning Adam still slept the sleep of the righteous in the front bedroom, and Shaye didn't want to disturb him. What would be the use of it?

Yesterday afternoon she had been late getting back from hiding from the police at the crime scene.

She'd walked in to find a beautifully made sandwich under tightly-stretched Saran wrap, and a note from Adam saying he apologized for missing her, but he had to get to work. Shaye had climbed up on a stool, contemplating the bread- an authentic Italian ciabatta roll with a taut golden crust. She couldn't imagine how Adam had found the gourmet roll around here, and suddenly the sight of it had brought uncontrolled sheets of tears slipping from her eyes.

So she had resolved not to burden him with news of the second murder right now- not until he heard about it and mentioned it himself. Or unless there was some reason- some immediate danger- that meant she absolutely had to tell him.

Shaye pulled the newspaper closer, thumbing the edges that were already starting to tatter from the many times she had read over the information today- starting before the light of dawn when she had first retrieved it.

The most striking fact was that "Mami" Ramierez had been gainfully employed, working as a secretary out of a temp agency not far from US 1... Working at respectable jobs other than prostitution, it seemed.

This news surprised Shaye, mostly since it didn't make sense. The newspaper justified the earlier labeling of the victim as a prostitute as a case about people making assumptions based on the neighborhood and someone's ethnic heritage. Whether "Mami" Ramierez had ever turned tricks in the past seemed to be left deliberately vague by the reporter. And then there was the fact that Shaye had found the fifty-dollar bill down by the canal. No other explanation seemed as plausible as the victim providing sex for money...

And something else seemed a little odd- the nickname Mami. The article mentioned that other "working" girls in the neighborhood had called Elvira this because she was "helpful to them", and "like a mother to them."

Shaye chewed on her plump, yet dried out, lower lip as she read, once again, the description of the second victim.

Name- Josie Swank. Possibly not her real name, but this is what she had called herself. Age- twenty-seven. Exactly one more year closer to Shaye's age.

Shaye closely examined the photo of the victim when she was alive. Slightly thinner than the last victim, she had sheets of dead-straight raven black hair down both sides of her winsome, high-cheekboned face and a look of strain in her dark blue eyes. The photo looked like it was paid for at a photo studio. The victim posed in a fluffy white sweater, holding a nubby white teddy bear against one side of her face, and balancing a smiling dark haired, wide cheeked baby boy on her knee.

A second photo, showing Josie Swank looking much gaunter, appeared to be a mugshot.

Biting her lip, Shaye went on to read more about the victim.

No one knew exactly Ms. Swank's true identity. She had, apparently, come from Texas, near the Mexican border. Then she'd moved around from Illinois to New York and then to Florida, working in aspects of the sex industry from massage parlors to peep shows. She'd also starred in a few low-budget porn films.

Ms. Swank was HIV positive- one fact that had jumped out at Shaye when she read it. Disease. How could the woman walk around the park offering her body for money when she carried the deadly disease? Did her customers know? Did she use protection? Universal precautions? How many years had gone by before she herself had found out?

Possibly, settling in Flamingo Park had been the end of the road for Josie Swank. Her HIV status had caught the attention of Department of Children and Families and they were actively supervising her and her kids. The article emphasized that Josie Swank had valued her two children, a two and a four-year old, immensely. And, apparently, she'd had actually proved a good parent to them. So much so that her Children and Families caseworker allowed her to keep them in her home under close supervision.

This meant that Josie Swank probably *hadn't* been turning tricks when she died despite how it appeared. Josie had been living on welfare and taking pills to build up her antibodies. The article made it sound like when she was last heard from she was fairly healthy, living in the back end of a doublewide mobile home, which she cleaned in exchange for the room. Josie's landlady was quoted as saying she didn't know anything about Josie tricks.

The special section on the victims went on to plead for information on Josie Swank's family or background. Unless relatives came forth, the children would have to leave the landlady's home and go into foster care, the article said.

The home where Swank and her children had lived was located on a double lot on Anhinga Street, right at the edge of the park, on the corner of Flamingo Beach Parkway. Shaye shivered because she knew which home the paper was referring to. Indeed, she'd walked past it, and noticed it was one of the biggest and best looking manufactured homes in the area.

So the second victim had lived right here in the park. Just as she did. Shaye fiddled with her own very long tawny blond hair, twisting it and using the rough ends like a broom on her shoulders and chest. Then she chewed on these ends just like she used to as a young girl.

She wondered if Adam woke up and found her here with the newspaper and the description of the second victim, whether he would insist she cut her hair. What an easy solution. Adam's caring about her would certainly win out over any vanity about her beauty. Many he'd take up the scissors and do the task himself, even as tears would roll down his face.

Shaye wouldn't let it happen, she resolved, lovingly arranging her spectacular long hair all around her shoulders like a delicate cloak. Like Sampson, she wanted to believe, superstitiously, that this hair could shield her from trouble. She peered out from behind the medieval veil of it to read the rest of the article.

Part Two detailed the crime scenes. And what the newspaper left out was as telling as what it revealed. At first the text simply rambled on and on with graphic descriptions of the squalor of the community that Shaye and Adam now called home.

Been there; done that, Shaye thought impatiently, eager for more. But there weren't many hard facts provided. Conspicuously, the newspaper never mentioned the murder weapon- never even hinted anything about it. Shaye had always savored crime novels, reading hundreds of them back in the State Hospital, where the pink lady volunteers gave out such books for free. And she would have bet the specific murder weapon was the clue that the cops were holding back for only the real killer to know.

But Pollyanna had said it was a garden rake. Her friend, Josie, had been raked to death, she'd said. Where could Shaye find out more about this? For she felt that, with the right forensic expertise, the weapon could possibly be the key to solving the murder. It seemed gruesome, yes. But *everything* in Shaye's life for the past two years had turned from pretty and sunny and glitzy to gruesome. And she was tired of being afraid to look at things directly.

If someone could match up the victim's wounds with the exact type of weapon, maybe such a tool would be rare. A rake, powerful enough to cause the wounds, but not full length or else the killer could not have positioned it. Who in this area owned one? If the cops could find a tool that matched exactly with the wounds in a suspect's possession, then they would have found the killer and solved the case, protecting other vulnerable individuals...

Who exactly did Shaye think was vulnerable around here? She bit back a little sound that seemed like it could possibly turn to a sob, and she struggled not to go down that particular road of imagining and worry. For, in that direction, lay certain madness. Shaye took herself a plastic cup of coffee, diluted with much cool milk to hopefully insulate her stomach. She curled back into the sour smelling couch cushions, tamping down her well-worn newspaper.

The article also mentioned tire tracks- broad tire tracks. This could be another lead. The text said that it was too soon for police to determine if the heavy truck tracks might have something to do with the killer, or if they belonged to the utility workers- possible witnesses. The reporter said this was one area the police would be devoting a lot of time to investigating.

Then followed sketchy descriptions of the grave displays, the second including brightly colored carnation heads in springtime hues scattered around the mattress on the old trailer floor where Josie Swank's body was left. And Shaye had seen the bizarre flowery bier outside- seemingly fit for a Mexican deity- or a queen. She swallowed hard, around a sore esophagus that hated to take down the coffee while reading on such subjects. For she knew the image of the peculiar funereal display she had seen at the crime scene would stick with her forever.

The paper said that the fact flowers and quilts were brought to the scene indicated that the killer had some sort of vehicle. Maybe the large truck in question? Interestingly, similar materials, including flowers and many of the reed-woven crosses, had also been removed from the first crime scene.

The last portion of the article was titled "The Lawmen". Two uninspired photos showed Officers Chow and Danielo, both looking a bit fresher and wearing dress uniforms straight out of police academy. Under each photo was placed a narrow strip of text.

Now Shaye's lips parted in a grim attempt at laughter as she read- for the journalist most likely wanted readers to laugh- or smirk. His descriptions of the two young cops' lackluster and weird career paths bordered on sarcasm- barely disguised.

Reading these descriptions, time and time again, until she had them almost memorized, started Shaye off on a plan.

When Adam padded out of the bedroom, yawning from a much-needed sleep that had lasted to almost two in the afternoon, he discovered Shaye standing unnaturally quietly behind the bathroom door.

He cracked open the door and then he stared at her. For a very long time they both stood staring tensely. For Shaye had been standing there nervously poised, holding the end of her long tail of hair in one hand and a sharpened pair of scissors in the other, about to start snipping.

Chapter 8

Shaye kept her hair. At the last minute, she hadn't been able to cut it, settling for other ways of protecting herself.

She jogged down the metal trailer steps, through the seating area and past the peek-a-boo stone wall with it bouncing on her back in a new long fat braid that Adam had crafted. Yes, she might lose everything- but not today. She was determined to accomplish something today.

Out on the street she immediately walked into officer Frank Danielo. He stood in her yard, half hidden by the adolescent banana tree, smoking a cigarette and squinting his eyes in contemplation.

"Blondie," he said, in what she thought of as a smoky barroom "last call" voice- peremptory, yet tired. "Come over here for a minute."

Shaye stood her ground. A cicada ticked in the overgrowing grass, marking time.

"I'm not kidding," Danielo said, puffing up somewhat in his full blue uniform to make a show of authority.

Shaye, about an inch taller than he was, met his eyes and didn't budge. Nothing he could show her could make her any more skittish than the eerie funereal display she'd seen yesterday. Just like nothing he could say could make her queasier than the rare bacteria that had ambushed her, eating away at her delicate insides, taking away everything good in her life starting two years ago.

Now, as for those pathetic remnants remaining of Shaye Taylor, she felt strutting young Frank Danielo could have it if he wanted. What was a prison cell any more than the prison of her own body anyway? Being branded a criminal couldn't take any more of her dignity away than when she was being branded as mad.

"Officer," she inquired calmly, "can I help you?"

Danielo chuckled dryly. "Can I help you?" he imitated. "Yeah, you can fuckin' help me! What you need to do is help yourself." His voice raised and thickened with his native Brooklyn accent. Then he took several steps toward Shaye and looked her body over up and down impolitely. "You know, you're not bad lookin' at all," he said.

Shaye snapped at him, "Is that a professional judgment?"

Danielo noticeably winced. Then he took another step forward and snagged her rope of braid in one hand, as if testing it for weight. He dropped it down in disgust.

"It's your hair, Blondie. It's down to your ass. There are only a couple of girls in Flamingo Park with hair this long. One lives right across the street from you, with her family of lazy ass drunks..." He pointed in the direction of Darlene's trailer, which seemed shut up tight, now that most of the men in the family had been arrested. "Two of the others happen to be dead. Two ex-hookers with extremely long hair were murdered by a serial killer in this park in the past two weeks, Mami Ramierez and Josie Swank."

As Danielo spoke, intensity fired up his pale brown eyes and a few drops of spittle flew from his lips. One hit Shaye's lower lip, and she wiped it off, emphatically. Their eyes suddenly connected in an odd way, like for a millisecond the Flamingo Park world was forgotten. In fact, all the world could have been forgotten this instant. For Shaye sensed Frank Danielo had little more in his life to be proud of than she had in hers. And fantasy might be a relief for both of them

She drew in a breath and Danielo watched her lips as she did it. She didn't know if he was able to read the very mixed signals in her big green eyes. In recent years, as a "prisoner" in the State Hospital, and especially after her own family had turned on her, she had learned to keep her feelings safely veiled, learned to hide away her naturally trusting self from people.

Shaye tamped the earth down with one tennis shoe. It didn't seem like Danielo was here to arrest her. He just seemed to want to make her squirm. "So, what do you want of me?" she asked.

Danielo sighed in annoyance. "Did you hear what I said? About your hair? Girls with long hair being killed? Maybe you'll be next!"

"But not if the local cops catch the killer. Not if you guys follow the forensic evidence properly," Shaye replied in an uncharacteristically smoky voice. She then took a chance and brushed past him boldly, heading for the street, wanting to fake him out.

Danielo called her attention back.

"Listen, Blondie," he said, pointing at their trailer and aiming right at the frosted louvered window that Adam was probably right now peeking out of. He held his index finger aggressively like a pointed gun. "I know something's seriously strange in this trailer here with you and your roommate in there. I'm just too concerned with young women's safety right at the moment to worry about it."

Shaye felt herself unravel into terror for herself and Adam. If this police officer acted so afraid for their physical safety, then how scared should she be? Yet she knew she couldn't show it. Even telling Officer Danielo her suspicions about Byron and Troy and what she had witnessed yesterday morning didn't seem possible at the moment. She just had to make him go away.

So Shaye made her voice haughty. Icy.

"Officer Danielo, you know what? I think you should concentrate on the residents who don't read the news if you're so concerned. There are plenty of people like that in this park. But my friend and I are fine. We never hurt anyone, and we don't take chances. Please let me go right now. I have some important research I have to do."

Shaye backed away. Then she turned, flipped her hair and walked, the braid bouncing on the center of her back, wishing she could just fly away like one of the Florida birds that streets in this park were named after. She told herself that her aggressive bluffing had to work. She could practically feel Danielo's eyes crawling over her back and butt as she sauntered down the street in retreat from him.

Danielo allowed her to go, but then he followed her, annoyingly, in his cop car, watching her from under sleepy eyelids and grinning sardonically to himself. Shaye plunged ahead in the direction of the city bus stop, walking as fast as she could. She needed to get to the public library to look up Byron and Troy, and any previous arrests on them if possible. In other words- she was determined to do this appalling local cop's work for him.

Anger infused her thinking about it, and it came out in the way she panted when she walked.

Danielo applied his brakes when Shaye reached busy Flamingo Beach Parkway. She stopped walking also, for just a second feeling unsure. And perhaps he saw something reachable in her eyes, because his eyes seemed to soften as well. He smiled and fished out a grubby business card from the glove compartment.

"I don't even know your name," he said. "But I don't get a good feeling at the moment. I seriously sense danger around you- no kidding. And I'm here to protect people. My name's Frank Danielo, if you don't already know. But everybody around here calls me Danny. When things get down to the wire, I hope you'll use this card..."

He curled Shaye's chilly hand around the card and patted it. Then he gave a wave, a wink and a beep of the horn as he drove away.

Shaye reeled the rest of the way up the road, with a feeling of vertigo.

She picked her way through disturbed earth near the city bus stop, noticing how much the wet red dirt, tossed onto blades of grass, resembled blood at the crime scenes. Not that she had actually seen the blood, she reminded herself.

Here, the whole area was in a state of transition, with the big, stone-sided shopping plaza just starting to go up at the back of a ragged, naked lot. Shaye shielded her eyes and scanned every direction of this plaza, watching the various crews of men working.

Suddenly she felt what seemed like breath on her shoulder. She stiffened and turned around, facing a small Hispanic man with twitchy eyes and a sweat soaked workshirt.

"Sorry, senorita," he mumbled. "Excuse me." He bent towards her feet to stake down a pitiful looking sapling that seemed like it could never survive under these harsh roadside conditions.

He straightened up and dared to nervously look up into her face again. She didn't know what he was seeing. Maybe he was mesmerized by her looks, which used to have this effect on most men before she went downhill.

Another look and Shaye realized she recognized him. Her heart flared up painfully, causing her to take a step back, and she thought she might faint. For this was the same man who had huddled in the dirt outside her bedroom window for several hours right at the time of the last homocide.

He'd looked guilty and furtive then, too.

Shaye looked around for possible backup or protection. She saw several of the man's coworkers, one digging, one laying turf, another sucking down lemonade out of a cooler in the back of their boss' pickup truck. They all looked smiley and well-adjusted. Shaye had to admit that even this guy didn't look that bad now that she confronted him face-to-face.

He looked too sedate and comfortable with his condition in life to be a demented killer.

Shaye had never spoken Spanish. Her husband Riley had been fluent, however. He used to show it off, ordering around waiters and hotel employees whenever they shot a new catalog down in South Beach. Riley had told Shaye she didn't need to bother to learn, for he would take care of everything.

Well, he hadn't. Now she stood beside an illegal lawn worker who was half a foot shorter than she was, and grinning shyly like an idiot. A man who might have already torn apart two women's bodies with a small garden rake, similar to the one he was holding in one dark-skinned hand which now hung indecisively at his side.

"Trabaja aqui in esta plaza?" Shaye heard herself piece together, trying to ask whether he worked on this plaza. "Por cuanto tiempo?" she persisted. For how long?

The man looked blank for a moment. Possibly her words hadn't made sense. Then he took a step closer to her, almost confidentially and began to rattle off a breathless stream of Spanish, the words fuzzy and heavily accented.

Yes, he worked here, he made clear. But it might not be long.

Shaye cocked an eyebrow. "Porque?" she asked- why- feeling she was on a roll, and actually getting some information. "Qual es el problema? What is the problem?"

The worker pointed to varying corners of the plaza, his agitation seeming to increase. He pointed out certain construction crews, ones that seemed very well equipped, with employees who were either white or black- no Spanish.

"They only like Americans to work here," he explained in Spanish.

Now the discourse became more complex, with Shaye only picking out words here and there. The gist seemed to be that this was one of the biggest construction projects going on in the area. For men like him, who were desperate to help their families back home, it could make all the difference in life.

Suddenly he spun around, pointing out a truck- the big white landscaping truck with the redwood sides that Shaye had watched jounce down her street several times a day. A man sat in the driver's seat with bronzed arms like hardwood and light brown eyes that seemed to bore into Shaye and the worker.

"Quien es?" she asked, attempting to find out more about the man who owned the landscaping company. He had caught her attention several times before, so she didn't feel she should let it go.

"Es mi jefe," my boss, the lawn worker said. He gestured with a wobbly sapling clutched in his hand, with the leaves bobbing for emphasis. "Jorge Colon- George," the man explained. He went on to explain that Colon was in America legally and he always employed Mexican workers- helping them to get established. At first the county had promised Colon this contract- it would have meant many, many thousands of dollars for his company and years of steady work.

Then something happened. Colon was thrown off the job and the Americans on the crew took over.

The worker raised a trembling hand, pointing at the Mack truck as it drove away. Something in his eyes said he feared retribution.

"Jorge Colon is a good man," Shaye understood him to say. "He helped many of us to become citizens and bring our families. He put much of his money into buying equipment for this job. Then the county threw him out. They weren't fair. Everyone was upset, everyone was angry. Many men have no jobs now. But I, and a few others who are citizens, were permitted to stay just long enough to plant these trees. Then they might fire us, too. Who knows? Jorge called us traders because we stayed, and now he's angry. He drives by the site many times like that, looking at the progress the gringos make."

Shaye shook her head to clear it, for she had gotten too much information at once.

"I understand," she said to the man in a mixture of English and Spanish, truly trying to understand it. "It seems it's all about politics; and that makes people angry."

Her eyes followed the beefy-looking white truck as it growled down the street, like an angry wrestler leaving the ring. Now she understood the overintense stares of its driver. Like everyone else in this transitional area around Flamingo Park, Jorge Colon had his own beef. Was his anger with how building contracts were awarded enough to make him kill prostitutes in the park? Shaye certainly couldn't make a plausible connection- but there was something about his eyes-and the tightly strung way he held his sinewy body that made her file away the image of Jorge Colon in her mind.

The little man standing before her innocently rambling certainly didn't seem like a killer. Yet his highly personal glance did not suggest the greatest respect for women, either.

Now Shaye noticed a pair of hookers picking their way in the direction of the bus stop after being dropped off by a gray sedan with tinted windows.

The overheated lawn worker seemed to notice them too.

"Them," he said, in Spanish slang. "They're just cheap whores. Not clean. But you are beautiful! You're very nice talking to me, also... You know, I make lots of money here, planting these trees all around..."

He actually dug in his pocket to display an earth-stained wad of cash. Shaye stood in ghastly awe as he then asked her shyly, "Do you ever go on a date? I'll pay real good..."

Shaye recoiled a step back. Maybe this guy *was* the murderer! Whatever he was, with his lewd suggestions, she'd never let him anywhere near her again. She'd make him terrified like she had to be terrified every day.

In righteous fury, Shaye crouched and grabbed one of his two-foot saplings. She tossed it violently at him, showering him with earth. Then she bent and threw another and another, as the man grunted and raised his hands to protect himself.

"You leave los mujeres alone!" Leave the ladies alone!" She yelled at him, mustering the most Spanish she could. "You lewd little pervert. I'll call the policia on you- Officer Frank Danielo! Stay away from women! Don't ever hurt or scare any women again! And stay away from Flamingo Park. Now vamos! Go!"

The man, looking appalled, bent to retrieve some of his trees. Then he scuttled back in the direction of the work truck. She heard him calling on God and using the word, "Loca", which meant crazy. Shaye had to laugh. Yes, she was crazy. There was no doubt about that.

Her breath heaved her chest up and down, while adrenalin sang through her aching veins. But she felt suddenly proud. She had just chased a man away- a possible suspect for the killer. Now she watched the two prostitutes who had safely made it to stand beside her as the county bus pulled into view, blocking the sun and opening its door wide to allow them into its momentary womb of protection. Perhaps Shaye had saved them all. For once, just now, just for this moment, she had acted completely brave.

"Hi Adam," Shaye said in a rough whisper, calling him later from the payphone outside the public library.

"Oh, so you're not in jail yet?" he teased, his voice sounding very effeminate and snide. "Homeboy didn't take you in before?"

Shaye had little patience. "Look," she said. "I did research and found one arrest report on the Internet for the guy named Byron. It's for an attempted carjacking. And that's a violent crime."

"Of course it's violent, Shaye. But why on earth are you looking into this? There's no point in it."

"I can't find anything on Byron's friend Troy," she said, brushing off his question. "But I think that might be because he was a juvenile. The accomplice in the carjacking was the one who actually grabbed the women- and the one who threatened her with a knife. You see where I'm going with this?"

"That the accomplice that threatened the woman was Troy? So what? Shaye, you have to be out of your mind investigating this. I'd tell you to tell that cop from today about these guys, but you can't. If we make a report, he'll focus on us."

"Well, that's not entirely true," Shaye said cryptically, smiling with what she had learned in the library. "I think there's a way we can make this one certain cop do anything we need him to do. With some of the information I found on him today, I think I can get Officer Frank Danielo to open up all of his resources to me. I can figure out the killer's identity and all Officer Danielo has to do is put handcuffs on him. And then we'll feel safe again."

Adam sighed. "Honey, whatever you have on a policeman won't be enough to gain us any power."

"Not necessarily." Shaye giggled with a slightly jagged sound. "You might not think so if you just read what I did on the Internet. I'm printing the newspaper article up for you right now, Adam, and then I'm on my way home."

"**NYPD Vice Cop's Brothel's Best Customer- On Department Cash!**" read the front page *New York Daily News* article dated two years back.

Adam set down the photocopied microfilm Shaye had brought him, and he chuckled.

Shaye did as well, watching his reaction. Adam wordlessly stabbed his finger against the accompanying large photograph, trying to contain what seemed like it might become explosive laughter. They both leaned back on the couch. The more they looked at the outrageous photo, the more they laughed, until Shaye finally had to hold her legs together to contain her bladder and Adam imitated her gesture, even though he was a guy. He wiped tears from his eyes and sucked back his laughter.

"I'm sorry, but Officer Danny is really such a joke," he said. "Who on earth lets a *Daily News* photographer get a picture of him with five hookers in a heart-shaped hot tub? Is that seriously possible? Or did he actually *want* the publicity?"

Shaye gently removed the sheets from his hands, sucking in her own laughter, which had left her rib cage feeling much more relaxed. She sighed.

"I doubt he wanted that publicity, Adam. Because I really don't think Danielo's too thrilled to be assigned to Flamingo Park. And he's got a wife and daughter... Maybe he took this job because of them, just trying to keep their life together somewhat. The article says he cost the New York City Police Department fifty thousand dollars with his 'high priced sexcapades'. I wonder if he's in financial trouble, and whether he's being made to pay any of that money back."

"Shaye, you are not gonna say we're gonna give him money?"

"No, no." Shaye shook her head emphatically. "But did you read the part about him being a sex addict?"

Adam held up a page. "You mean this part that says, 'rather than facing prosecution and a possible prison term, Officer Danielo was court-ordered to attend mandatory counseling for his disease of sex-addiction'? Do you want me to read the rest of it, Shaye? How about the little inset that gives information about 'sex addiction-symptoms and treatments'?"

Shaye gave a quick impatient grin in reply. "Adam, there's no need. Because, the point is, Officer Danny, as he told me to call him, is probably up to his old tricks again here in Flamingo Park! He's gotta be. In an out of the way beat like this, where he deals with hookers every single day? What do you think? He has to be doing *something* he wouldn't want to get out."

"You're not really talking about blackmail, Shaye? Are you, for real, saying you intend to blackmail this crooked cop?"

Shaye grinned, a little oddly, a little devilishly. "I think it might work."

Adam slept the next morning as Shaye slipped out of the house, with her long hair twisted, rubber-banded and tucked up under a cap. She deliberately carried no identification. But she did have a water bottle, a pocket full of dollar bills and a small digital camera. Her first task was to hurry up Hibiscus and then down Caiman, past the first crime scene. Without turning her head, she hiked athletically. Then, after taking a quick glance around, she ducked into the trees at the opposite side of the road with the grace of a spirit.

Shaye leaped over a smelly drainage ditch, and hunched down as she hurried diagonally through the underbrush. She knew that woods like this could be infested with deadly spiders, like the brown recluse and poisonous snakes she'd been studying, like southern copperheads, or possibly rabid raccoons. And, of course, the killer of women could be hiding here as well. He might hunt at night and then sleep hidden in the brush during the day.

Shaye dodged all the possible dangers alertly, like a commando. She was getting used to it, with all her slipping around of late. And, oddly, being out here and doing something made her feel so much less afraid than just sitting waiting in the trailer, or in locked in some state hospital, for doom to approach.

She could hear her own breathing, and she sought to contain it, for she wanted to remain absolutely silent. If her planning last night was correct, she would end up sitting within the cloak of unchecked Florida vegetation only feet away from Officer Danielo's favorite speed trap. And she was correct. As she neared Flamingo Beach Parkway, she caught a metallic glint of sunlight off the patrol car seen through the almost impenetrable brush. She lowered herself smoothly to one knee, moving the camera around to see if she could find a window for a shot if there was need to take one.

Shaye bit her lip.

Unfortunately she'd have to get even closer if she wanted to photograph anything. And that, perhaps, would mean losing her cover. For she was already so close that she could hear Officer Danielo mumbling to himself in his car. She knew he couldn't detect her, however. One of the side effects of Shaye's illness had been hightened sensitivity in all her senses and she heard and smelled things that a normal person wouldn't.

Danielo seemed preoccupied right now. Shaye stood on tiptoes to watch him fiddling with his new department-issued laptop, huffing and puffing and cursing under his breath.

"Goddamn thing," he muttered to himself. "They want us to be so good with computers, why don't they just put a robot in the cop car?" Stabbing at the computer, looking like he'd rather break it than coax out its precious wealth of information, he said, "That way, if their damn robot gets shot, they won't have to pay a widow's pension."

Danielo slapped the laptop shut so hard Shaye trembled for it, like it was a poor animate creature. She also drooled at the thought of getting her hands on something so state of the art.

Danielo then flung himself back against the seat and shut his eyes, all in a gesture of fruitlessness. "Who am I kidding?" he asked out loud. "This computer is probably worth more to the department than I am. Who the fuck am I kidding?"

A voice answered him- a young playful blond girl of about twenty years old who jogged across the street and leaned in his driver's window. "What, you kidding somebody Danny Baby? You not really a cop?"

Danielo's right hand moved instinctively for his holster, but his visitor didn't see it. Shaye's body also tensed for fight or flight.

Apparently, Danielo knew the girl and he relaxed.

"Hey, Sunny," he said to her, his voice strangely throaty. "What you doin' out here, still? You were supposed to hop on a bus," he gestured in the direction of US 1, "and go back home to Oklahoma, back to your parents. Remember that?"

The girl pouted. Her thin pink cut-off sweatshirt top gaped so that her exposed breasts hung down almost in his face. Tucked into her bra, sitting on her bony chest between her breasts, was an opened soft pack of cigarettes, along with a small rolled wad of cash. Shaye noticed an incongruous old scar along one of the girl's smooth white cheeks, in contrast with the soft seductiveness of her pouty grin.

"Remember I said I'd arrest you if I caught you out here working again?" Danielo asked.

The girl chuckled and stuck a cigarette between her lips. "And remember how I got off that time? Remember how *you* got off, Officer Danny?"

Danielo looked even more annoyed and put upon than he had before, if that was possible. He grasped the laptop and flung it impatiently into the back seat of the squad car.

"You know what, Sunny?" he said. "Just get in! If you wanna do this, in this park with a serial killer murdering hookers, then that's just fine with me."

Shaye could not believe what she was seeing. The young prostitute left the driver's window and pranced toward the passenger side- in the process hiking up her miniskirt and climbing out of her panties! In broad daylight! Shaye, staring in awe and horror, snapped about ten pictures.

"You want to fuck me this time?" the prostitute named Sunny called out indiscreetly.

Maybe Danielo just wanted to get caught and finally get booted out of this job for good, for he didn't even seem to care. He pushed the pink panties back at Suuny as he popped the door and swung it open for her entrance.

"I don't care to die young, Sunny," he said. "You know I won't fuck with you Flamingo Park girls. Just a hand-job. Five minutes. And no smoking in my squad car this time!"

Sunny laughed and pouted again, reaching up to set her smokes on the dashboard, and then she efficiently reached for Danielo's uniform pants. "Maybe you should handcuff me, then, so I don't smoke."

Danielo scowled, glanced around and then rolled up the power windows to give them privacy.

"Damn" Shaye said to herself, under her breath. With her heart hammering, both in fear and disgust, she crept even closer to the car.

Adam had begged her not to try to blackmail the cop last night. He had told her, realistically, that a man who once defrauded his department out of tens of thousands to pay for hookers might also use his gun against someone expendable like Shaye- and easily get away with calling it self defense. But adrenaline drove her past his warning.

Shaye broke free of the vegetation and snapped one quick picture through the windshield. She thought she caught a shot of the cop with his eyes tight shut- she could only hope- and the young hooker bending her head to... Shaye didn't want to think about it.

After snapping five photos she hopped back into the brush, lying down and pulling some palmetto fronds over herself like blankets.

From her nest, she cringed at the sound of Danielo's words, as the squad car door cracked open a few minutes later.

"Now this time for real, Sunny, try to stay off the streets. And don't be running up to this car all the time. Next time it might be my prissy-ass partner in here!"

Shaye peered through the frond and watched Sunny climb out of the squad car, grabbing her cigarettes.

She lit one and saluted Danielo. "Well, you better keep him on a leash, then. 'Til we meet again, Officer D.!" Then she turned and headed back towards US 1, hopping merrily into her panties.

"'Til we meet again, or the killer rakes you to death, you stupid whore!" Danielo muttered under his breath.

Then he got out, walked around to the passenger side of his car for no apparent reason and stretched. His shadowed dark eyes gazed into the woods.

Shaye felt sure he couldn't see her.

But then he unsheathed his gun and drew it slowly across his belly. Slowly, also, he lifted it and aimed.

"Okay," he said, just loud enough to reach her. "You in the woods with the camera. You figure I'm a bad enough cop to get a hand job from a hooker, you better believe I'm a bad enough cop to shoot you right now. Whatever your game is, it's up. You come out, hands up, or I'll come in and execute you!"

Shaye stayed where she was. It was strange but, with all her myriad fears, the thought of a sudden bloody end to her life did not scare her. In a whisper, she said a quick prayer, even though she had stopped praying somewhere during the terrible year and a half of her illness.

Danielo strode closer to the very edge of the foliage, with the stance of an old-time gunfighter.

"Goddamn it," he said, almost gently. "C'mon out of there. I can see you under that palmetto... I really don't want to shoot."

Shaye gritted her teeth and didn't move.

Danielo stepped right up to the very edge of her leafy armor, somehow able to accurately guess that she wasn't armed. He kicked the frond off of her, revealing her blinking face.

"Fuck!" he said.

They remained in this strange position, with her splayed on her belly, yet sullen-eyed, and him standing over her indecisively for several painful minutes.

Finally Shaye curled around, so she was sitting cross-legged in the leaves with her camera held protectively against her belly.

"You won't find my extra flashcard," she said. "Unless you and your partner dig up these woods like archaeologists. And I doubt you guys will do that. You're the ones who forgot one of the reed crosses and some of the victim's ID at the first crime scene. Plus a fifty dollar bill," she added with her chin stuck up stubbornly.

Danielo smirked, holstered his gun and put his hands impatiently on both hips, like he was dealing with a misbehaving little girl. "Well, it's too bad I forgot the fifty. I coulda bought myself something. Maybe a good time with a woman. And what the hell's a flash card anyway?"

So Shaye's threats had been lost on his ignorance. She got to her feet and tilted the camera to show him. "My camera's digital, Officer Danielo. It's new technology that you obviously don't like any more than you like that poor laptop in your squad car. The card is the camera's memory, so there's no need for film. In short, I have photos- I can show you right now on that laptop of yours what you were doing five minutes ago on police department time."

"And who wants to know?" Danielo asked, stepping closer. He examined her eyes curiously and then reached forward and tilted her cap so it fell off. His eyes wearily followed the twisting spiral of her braid. "Oh, Blondie," he sighed. "You are so fucked. You know, I thought you were another reporter at first. But you, you're in so much trouble now!"

He seemed both amused and horrified at her.

Shaye huffed. For some reason, she addressed him intimately, like they had known each other forever and she had the right.

"So you would've shot a reporter, if that's what I had been?"

Danielo took a step back and pointed his finger instead of the gun. "You know I wouldn't shoot anybody, except maybe the serial killer. And then only if he didn't surrender."

He ran his hand through his short, cropped hair. "What you don't understand Blondie, and why should I expect you to- is that I'm actually a dedicated cop. I really care about this job. I just need to be left in peace. And I need that flash card or whatever from you. Seriously. I have no clue what your game is, Blondie, but you know you can't go to my department with your photos."

"I would," Shaye mumbled. "If I had to."

Danielo raised his voice over hers. "No. You would not. I think cops scare you shitless. You, and your roommate, too, are probably wanted for something. And I'm almost curious enough now to start digging. So, what do you say? It's been a long day already, and it's not even noontime. Why don't you sit down with me and grab some lunch and stop acting crazy? Maybe we can work something out."

Danielo gestured for Shaye to follow and she did, gingerly. They stepped out of the woods together, with Shaye blinking in the light. "C'mon," he said, opening the passenger door for her with just a bit more chivalry than he had done for the hooker a few minutes ago. He helped Shaye inside with one hand on her protecting her head, like she was a suspect, and with the other guiding her shoulder as gently as though she was his decked-out prom date.

He plopped down in his seat so that it jarred the car. Then he made a completely false call back to his station about what he was up to and he smiled, watching Shaye as she examined all the gadgets.

"So, have you ever been in a cop car before? In the *front* seat?" he teased. "It seems to get you off, huh? Do you like the radio best? Or are you more into the handcuffs?" He jingled a pair in front of her and then started up the car and pulled out. "So, how'd you like it if I treat you to lunch at Donut Gator? Right there across the street." He pointed. "They have great hamburgers. And why not take down your hair now?"

Shaye examined Danielo seriously, wondering what she could say to make him understand things. In the closed cab, the smell of his cologne seemed overpowering- yet enticing. Being this close to Danny felt dangerous, and Shaye, feeling queasy, had to admit it to herself as they smoothly slid through traffic. She knew ninety percent of why she had come to him was about catching the killer. And the other ten percent had to be this mad attraction she was feeling.

Danielo stared at her the same way, driving using his peripheral vision while his brown eyes gazed at her and his parted lips looked slick with desire. He gasped out a breath, more desire than exasperation.

"So, what, Blondie? Is someone paying you to get me in trouble? A newspaper or something?"

"No," she said softly, still keeping firm hold on her camera. "I want to help you find the serial killer. I don't believe you can do it on your own."

They pulled into the parking lot of a strange Florida attraction. It looked like an ice cream stand dominated by a twenty-foot plastic alligator on the roof, wearing pants and chewing a red plastic donut the size of a pool float. Perspiring patrons gnawed their lunches at bright red rubbish-littered plastic tables arrayed around the stand

and back into the damp shade behind it. Shaye glanced around in panic.

"I can't eat here," she blurted suddenly. "Their hamburgers could kill someone... What if they're not properly cooked. They could have E-coli bacteria, and it could be deadly! You're a cop. Why don't you investigate this place?"

Shaye's voice came out reedy, a squeal, as she lost all control over it.

She couldn't help herself. She jumped from the squad car, backing into an overflowing garbage receptacle. The trashcan teetered, spewing paper plates and napkins and a swell of flies rose up around her. And Shaye keened in animal panic.

She ran for a table by the woods and then she crouched down hugging the seat, with her head half under the table, gasping. This was her worst panic attack in months. And in front of Frank Danielo. So there went her scheme of acting tough and blackmailing him, she thought. He'd probably cuff her now and take her to the psych ward.

In the shade of the pine trees, Shaye felt his hands touch her shoulders and she straightened up. He examined her face with his sunglasses off and concern showed clearly in his light brown eyes. Delicately, and professionally, he wiped cold beads of sweat from her brow.

"What is this, Blondie?" he asked. "You tripping on me? Are you on drugs?"

Shaye shook her head and coughed out her words, taking a second to find her natural voice. "No," she said. "I don't use drugs. It's not that. I'm obsessive-compulsive, Officer Danielo..."

"Why not call me Danny like everyone else does?"

"Danny," she said, more assertively. "I'm obsessive-compulsive. I almost died of E-coli two years ago, from contaminated food. Anything questionable brings things back. Fears I have. Usually I stay in my house, away from people. And I'm more comfortable with the computer than anything face to face. But now I feel like I've got to do something. I've been looking into your case, and I already found out some information about Mami Ramierez. I also found two guys who may be suspects. If we don't catch the killer, I feel he'll get me. You understand?"

She stared directly into Danny's eyes, and he stared back.

He reached back behind her gently and undid her hair and arranged it around her shoulders. Then he dabbed her forehead with a napkin, balled it up and threw it unerringly into the nearest trash receptical.

"So what's your name?" he asked. "You never told me."

"My name's Shaye."

"No last name?"

"Not now."

He shook his head.

"You know, I can't just have you work on the case with me, Shaye. It isn't done that way. You could be helping this killer, for all I know."

"But you sense that's not true, Danny. Don't you?"

He sighed in exasperation. "All I sense right now is that you're the prettiest woman I've ever come across in real life. And that's gotten you a lot farther than anyone else could. Has anyone ever told you that you're beautiful like that before?'

Shaye cracked a small, ironical smile. "Well, I think men *have* noticed my looks in the past. You know, just a little."

Danielo leaned back and against the table and blew air out his lips. "You got me, you know. Totally."

Shaye shook her head. "Listen, Danny, I guess that's flattering. But I'm not here flirting with you, whatever you think. I don't even know how to say this, because it's so embarrassing. But people like me don't have sex. I don't have those feelings anymore after my illness. Just, day-to-day, fear. I live in fear. I'm *crazy*."

He cracked a smile, showing nice white teeth.

"I can see you're crazy."

"It's not a joke."

Danielo fiddled with his keys. "I know it's not a joke. I don't think you'd be living in a trailer in Flamingo Park if things were okay with you."

He took her hand inpulsively.

"Can't we just be friends?"

"Then will you let me help you, Danny? Keep it secret from your partner and from Mayor Walker? If you could just let me use that police computer so I can get into the FBI database for the serial killer profile. You could let me help you with research- all the things you're not good at. Please?"

Without answering, Danielo got up and walked away. He returned with a tray with a steaming burger, a giant iced-coffee and a serving-sized bag of chips. Then he ate while he mulled Shaye's proposition over in silence. Ten minutes into his meal he offered her a bite of the hamburger. She backed away like it was a hissing cobra. Silently, he threw the bag of chips into her lap.

Shaye sat and contemplated it, with her eyes lowered as though meditating.

Danielo finished and wiped his greasy mouth.

"You're not gonna eat those?"

"Maybe later," she said.

Danielo went to dump his tray. He came back and stood over her in disturbingly masculine posture for a few seconds. Then he sat down.

"Do you know my whole history?" he asked. "I used to be a detective back in Manhattan. The newspapers only talk about the money I lost the department. But they never mentioned that I brought in millions in seizures. And I did so many good things... I really helped people and and everybody knew I was a good vice cop.

"My future was going to be so amazing that it makes me sick to think about it, Shaye. I've hardly had a friend since then. I betrayed my wife and I brought shame upon her so she hates me. Now I live in this kind of sick probation. I mean, sometimes I let the local hookers get me off like you saw. But nobody cares what I do anymore, I think. I know my wife feels sick when she looks at me. And I'm sick myself a lot, just being me. So, you know what, Shaye? I'm not here lusting after you. I don't *want* to fuck you. I actually don't want to..."

He touched her cheekbone with a playful little punch. "I can see you're in pain. I can see how thin and unhealthy you are. I can see how scared. And I can also see your passion about this case. So I don't want you to sleep with me. Okay? But I do want you to let me in. Eat my potato chips now, Shaye. Look in my eyes. And say that we're friends..."

They sat staring at each other for a while. Danielo looked a little pale. Outside their patch of shade the sun was baking and, as the days progressed, it would only get hotter. Shaye felt her overwhelming fear rise within her. How did she know she could work with this cop and actually be effective? And, what was more scary, the thought of bumbling into the killer's arms as she investigated or the thought of this stranger reaching out to her emotionally now?

Seriously, and deliberately, Shaye ripped open the bag of chips. The sound was loud, like the world ripping. She crunched one between her front teeth.

She lifted her eyes, finally, to meet Danielo's. "Okay," she breathed. "I want us to be friends."

Danny allowed himself to grin. "In that case, I think you've come to the right police officer."

Chapter 9

Shaye eagerly dug in her pockets while Danielo sipped at his oversized red cup of iced coffee. She had been up most of the night working on this project, until the point that she was confident that she had it right.

"Look," she said, handing over two ragged, and many times erased-over, sheets of paper. She had drawn two familiar faces.

"These are the two young men that I think are suspects," she said. "Troy Reid and Byron Hanes."

Danielo took the sketches from her without a word, and Shaye quickly described what she had seen in the last weeks- the two young men selling drugs, hanging around both crime scenes, threatening a prostitute with a knife and even propositioning herself and her roommate. Shaye did not mention that Adam was a man, dressed up as a woman, at the moment that the two called their lewd suggestions to them. Right now that fact was immaterial, and she was just getting the police officer to like her- she didn't want to ruin that.

It turned out that none of it mattered.

A small grin tugged the corner of Danielo's lips as he tucked the sketches away in a pocket. "I'm sorry that you went to all this trouble, Shaye. No, actually," he contemplated, "I'm glad. But I didn't really need a sketch, because Officer Chow and I already know these jokers real well."

"I read some of their history on the Internet," Shaye said.

"Well, the thing is that they're both walking around on probation right now. And one of the terms of that probation, for both of them, is that they don't associate with each other anymore. You see, we know that they're dealing drugs and it's no surprise they're threatening hookers. Troy is a real sadistic motherfucker and my impression is he leads Byron to do anything he says. The only problem is catching them red-handed. That's the whole problem with our criminal justice system these days. Glenn Chow and I can't be in ten places in the park all at the same time... We'd need more manpower. Anyway," he said, "getting back to the point. The good part is- you've seen them openly hanging out together. I don't have to prove the drug dealing right away. If I can catch them together, that's enough to put them back behind bars."

"What do you think of them doing the killings?" Shaye asked hesitantly.

Danielo gazed at her with enigmatic eyes.

"What do *you* think?" he asked. "Really?"

She drew in a breath.

"I want it to be them," she said. "I want to feel somewhat safe again."

Danielo winked. "But as a hot, sexy supersleuth you have doubts, don't you?"

It was hard for her to smile. "It's just that profile of serial killers, you know," she said. "I've read so many detective novels..." She wanted to say, "in the mental hospital," but, wisely she stopped herself.

"...In my free time," she continued. "And the profilers always differentiate between "organized" and "unorganized" killings. I think, with the funeral flowers and crosses that these two Flamingo Park murders were quite organized. Possibly organized could apply to Byron's personality. Maybe. But it's hard to imagine it with Troy. He seems so out of control and impulsive. And then there's the Mexican aspect."

"Mexican?"

Could these cops have really not noticed the aspect of Mexican religion in the grave displays, and the fact that at least one of the victims was Mexican?

Shaye gave Danny a pitying look and he ignored it.

"I'll study the Mexican funeral ceremonies," she said. "And I know a tiny bit of Spanish. Do you know any?"

He shook his head.

"Okay, I can brush up on it," Shaye said, "just in case I have to talk to anybody. I can also learn more about profiling."

Danielo stood and patted her on the shoulder. "Do what you want," he said. "I'll go pick up Glenn Chow right now. And we'll head out to the northwest section of the park where you saw Hanes and Reid to see if we can arrest them. In the meantime..." He dug into a side pocket, and pulled out a cellular phone in a black case. Then he handed it over, recitng a phone number.

"Don't lose this phone, Shaye. The number I gave you is a personal line to me. I used to use it for the girlies, but those days are over now, so we might as well use it for police work between us."

Danny winked as he dropped Shaye off on Egret Street a few blocks from her trailer.

"Try to stay close to home until I get those bozos off the street. But call me if you see anything else interesting. I'll check back with you soon."

"Okay," Shaye said, feeling odd as she stepped down onto the dirt street, not knowing what to do now.

"And please don't let anybody know I gave you that telephone..."

Shaye had avoided confronting Adam until the next day at noontime, when he emerged from his room and found her on the couch, poring over a library book called *Everyday Spanish*.

Adam surprised her a little, belted into a deep green satin half robe. She hadn't seen him dress feminine for a while and now they stood at a stalemate, eyeing eachother.

"Espanol?" he inquired. "Are you planning on talking to some murder suspects in the neighborhood, senorita?"

Shaye sighed, and reached forward. "Come here, Adam. Sit down."

Adam sat beside her and she noticed that his face was made up and his eyes lined. She scrunched her brow, but didn't say anything. Instead she told him about her meeting with Danielo the day before.

Adam closed his eyes, not realizing that he was displaying glitter shadow on the lids, and he rubbed his forehead like he had an awful headache. When he looked up at her, his eyes seemed darker than she had ever seen them.

"Let me ask you something, Shaye. Suppose I told you I have a way that we can make enough money to leave this park, and live in a nice condo in Miami until I get my trust fund? Would you even leave at this point? Or have you become too obsessed with this case and this park? Honestly?"

Adam's eyes beseeched her. Shaye wanted to lean forward and curl into his lap for cuddles to make everything all right. But his sexy female look disquieted her, and made her recoil a bit. She supposed her obsession with tracking a killer was probably making him feel distant from her as well. And his question had stopped her thoughts dead in her mind, had just frozen everything. For, what on earth *did* she feel? Did some twisted part of her actually *want* to confront the killer?

She stared at Adam with her mouth open.

"Shaye." He grinned, finally, making it seem like things could possibly be all right again. "I, of anyone, know you're not a naïve girl. In your bio in the *Tropical Sun* magazines, it tells how you started modeling, and traveling the world, at age sixteen. And then the gossip mags used to show you dating all those celebrities."

Shaye blushed. It was so long ago. It had to, literally, be another girl. A girl who used to be wanton.

"You followed my life since you were a child. Isn't that peculiar?"

Adam grinned, and batted eyelashes thick with mascara. But, at the moment, he didn't look like anything but an older brother who was concerned for her.

"Officer Danielo is a sleaze," Adam said, "and he wants your body. Which is an especial insult, since you were once voted the sexiest women in America and he's just a bottom-feeding sex addict. He'd chase everything. And he didn't even do *that* right in New York City!"

Shaye tried to act soft, and make light of everything. "So, Adam, *who* voted me sexiest in America? And how come I never heard of that one?"

Adam had to crinkle the corner of his eyes in a grin. "It was Swimsuit Models' of American Convention, or something like that. And I used to follow all of that stuff. I used keep hundreds of your photos up in this really neat collage around my bedroom when I was a kid."

Shaye gave him a playful punch in his arm. "That is truly sick!"

"Is it sick?" Adam asked. "In the end I cared more about your career than your husband did."

Shaye nodded. Although it had been meant as a joke, they both stared ahead somberly for a bit.

Adam resumed. "Shaye, it's not normal if Officer Danny is going to allow you access to police records," he said. "He could get fired, or go to jail, for letting you help with the case. So, you really think he doesn't expect to sleep with you?"

Shaye looked at Adam strangely. She glanced down at her skinny legs lying on the couch, looked down at her scraped knees and blistered heels in Keds that were now scuffed and blackened from all the crawling through the woods. Adam's question hurt and offended her. What kind of girl did he think that she was? That she would sell herself for anything? For the chance to help on a murder case?

Did he think she sold herself in the past for her successful modeling career?

Yes, Shaye knew she used to act a little free with her body. And she'd acted so stupid and naïve in the past that now she sometimes felt that those days were all a dream. But she wouldn't sell herself for anything! She knew that. At the moment, doing right seemed more important to her than anything else in the world, more important than life itself.

It took many moments that Shaye stared at Adam.

"Okay," he said finally. "You win. I know you're not naïve anymore. I suppose maybe Officer Danny genuinely likes you. Or maybe this murder case is so fucked that he actually feels he needs your help." He shook his head. "Now that would be bad."

Shaye's outrage abated a bit and the pain that had been gnawing in her stomach dialed down a few notches.

"Let's check the noon news," Adam said. "In a perfect world, based on your tip, Officer Danny would have caught the killers already."

Both their mouths dropped at the scene on TV as the picture came into focus. For, sure enough, the noon news cameras caught a shot of Officers Chow and Danielo struggling with two suspects-Byron Hanes and Troy Reid!

"Yikes!" Adam said, and gave a giggle as they watched Troy Reid try to head butt Danny on TV. The two ended up on the ground, wrestling. Officer Chow handcuffed Byron Hanes, leaned him up against the squad car and came to his partner's rescue. Then the two cops dragged Troy by the handcuffs like a hooked fish. Apparently the officers discouraged the cameraman then, for suddenly a background scene came into focus- the gaping door of a seedy apartment, along a strip of similar dejected ones.

The newswoman on the scene then reported, "In this apartment, 6A, only blocks from the last Flamingo Park murder, Byron Hanes and Troy Reid have apparently been running a center of drugs and underage prostitution."

Shaye noticed the contrast of the newswoman in her pastel blue suit with tapered jacket and miniskirt, and the grim facts she was relating. And even her perky smile couldn't hide the fact that she felt disturbed.

"In addition to selling crack cocaine out of this apartment," the newswoman said, "the boys were apparently offering underage girls for prostitution, including one who is reportedly a sister of one of the suspects. Police would confirm nothing further, but there are speculations that Reid and Hanes might also be suspects in the Flamingo Park prostitute murders. With their arrest today, park residents might be sleeping a whole lot safer!"

Adam and Shaye just stared at each other. Then they uttered, "Yes!" in unison and jumped to their feet to hug, each taking a turn to be spun with their feet off the floor.

They parted for breath and then Shaye thought to ask Adam a question.

"Adam?" she said. "You didn't say before. But what's the new job? The one that'll get us so much money? Is there one?"

Adam's eyes looked dark and liquid as he patted down his satin robe, almost mincingly.

"Shaye," he said. "I'm getting dressed up because I'm going to be performing at Foxy Lady. From now on I'm going to make a lot more money than my waiter job- and we can get out of Flamingo Park so much sooner. It's mostly dancing, and dressing up- as a female impersonator. But I get to sing a little, too. And I'll actually get paid for it, Shaye. It could be the start of something good."

Early that evening, Shaye lay on the stiff yet squishy surface of her bed that she had doctored to be sterile by wrapping it in garbage bags. The room was dimming around her and she listened to the clear sounds ringing out through the grid of streets in Flamingo Park. This time of evening people had already been home from work for a few hours, had already been drinking and perhaps contemplating their exhausting and futile lives for too long, dwelling on the injustices and turning on the family members who stood near…

Just because Byron Hanes and Troy Reid were off the streets didn't stop the comings and goings and all the sad and sinister trades and barters that took place at this time of evening.

Perhaps there would be peace now.

And, even though Adam didn't realize that he had broken her heart by accepting the job dancing, maybe there was indeed an upside to it. The male dancers, impersonating as campy females, always got great tips. And Adam did look beautiful- flawless- pretending to be a woman. Maybe the clientele would really appreciate the art of it- and maybe he would never have to let anyone touch him the way Madeline and Rochelle and the others did.

Shaye shuddered at the thought of it. But she had to trust that Adam had a good head on his shoulders. Enough not to jeopardize his safety- and his life- by doing anything risky. And she must trust him. Adam had said that they might only have to wait a few more days. And then they were out of here.

Shaye rolled over, staring at the low ceiling tiles and loose hanging fixture, and she sighed. She didn't really have to call Frank Danielo right now. It looked like the suspects she had turned him onto really might be the murderers. If so, the case, and their affiliation, could be over before it started. So much the better, she thought. She had just wanted to keep things safe. Here in the park. And for herself and Adam.

She played with Danny's cell phone now, testing its weight in her hands. She didn't really have to call. And yet it seemed the nice thing to do. Also there was the fact that the walls of this room, and the sounds of the park, seemed to be closing in on her. She hated to feel more evenings like she had experienced in the past weeks- hated to feel this helpless and crazy huddling here in the dark, amidst the sounds of vehicles and voices and crime and the pain of a thousand unseen neighbors.

Shaye hated the evenings.

Heart hammering nervously, she dialed the only number in the cell phone's memory.

"Danny here," a voice answered, seeming blurry and right up against the mouthpiece. "That you, Blondie?"

Shaye pulled her mouth away from the phone to let out a breath, and some tension. "Yeah, it's me," she said, feeling glad now to be connected to him through the phone.

"Yo. I'm at Oceanside station," he said. "Give me a second and let me get some privacy. I'll take you into the john with me. Nobody's gonna listen there."

Shaye listened patiently to the busy background sounds of the police station. In a way she felt like she was there with him. And, in a way, she wished she was.

"Okay," Danny said, still using a relatively quiet voice. But he sounded happy and bright, able to talk more freely. "So, did you hear? We arrested Hanes and Reid. Shaye, you wouldn't believe what all we found in their apartment. They might really be the guys for the murders. We're hoping. Reid tried to resist arrest and we had to beat the crap out of him… It was crazy…"

Shaye could envision Danny smiling on the other end of the phone, for the first time in perhaps years feeling lighthearted. He could barely pause in between his words to get a breath.

"This was a really important arrest," he said. "Hanes and Reid were dealing crack cocaine out of that apartment and now we have tips on their suppliers- really big guys that we're gonna bust next. That kind of thing is right up my alley, Shaye, my expertise. We also saved some young girls and that was awful. The guys were keeping them imprisoned, feeding them drugs and then turning them out as hookers- basically using them like slaves. One of the chicks was even Reid's fourteen-year old sister!"

"I know," Shaye said softly, keeping her voice down though she did not know why. "I saw the arrest on the news today."

Suddenly a howl went up a distance away in the night. Shaye could not tell if the source was canine or human. It might as well have been a werewolf, with what her uncontrolled fear told her. She clutched the phone closer to her face, like she wanted to blot out everything else.

"Hey," Danielo said. "So how you doing today? I didn't forget about you or anything. It was just non-stop, you know, so I didn't get to call. First, Chow and I fought with Troy Reid. So everybody had to go to the hospital to be checked out. I guess the department doesn't want his lawyers claiming police brutality later on. But, everything checks out fine. Except, of course, I've got a black eye now…"

He chuckled expansively. "You know what? I'm loving it now. It's like, for the moment here, I'm finally vindicated. This is the single most important arrest *ever* by Flamingo Park police- in all time. People are talking like, if I follow this through, they'll probably move me to Oceanside- a real police department. And, you know, I might make detective again. And it's thanks to you, Shaye. I'm not forgetting..."

"You did the police work," she said. "You apprehended them."

Her chest tightened, hoping so badly that Hanes and Reid, indeed, had been the killers and this reign of terror would be over. It seemed hard for her to remember now a time she had lived free of these sounds in the night, and the omniscient expectation of violence.

She let out a sound that was like an interruption, but also like a vague little cough. "Are there any loose ends, Danny?" she managed to ask. "Is there still stuff you have to do- to prove stuff?"

There was a second of silence, and expectation.

"Well, Shaye," Danny sighed. "There's lots of detective work. Chow and I will be tied up with it for days. Weeks or even months, possibly, because this is big. And I know what I'm doing with all the detective work, so that's no problem. Glenn is excited to finally be exposed to a case like this. It can change his career, too."

"But, Danny, is there something not perfect?" Shaye asked, breathing out her suspicions quietly in the crypt of a room that smelled of mildew and human fatigue.

"Just the usual," Danielo said, but now his voice sounded resigned, like the beaten young man he had been when she met him the day before. "I don't want to say everything's all tied up until it is. We took a ton of evidence out of that apartment, including DNA evidence from the suspects and the young women on the scene.

"Here's the thing," he whispered, much quieter even than before, with much more confidential information. "On one of the beds, we found some blood and some long female hair..."

"What?" Shaye gasped. So this really could be it. Troy and Byron really could be the killers.

"We can't jump to any conclusions until we match the DNA with the victims'. There were a lot of girls staying in that place, and nobody looked like they'd be real good with their monthly hygiene. It could just be that. I've walked into that kind of scenario before."

Shaye found it interesting how much in his element Frank Danielo seemed. He really did sound professional and she could imagine that detective work really had been his passion in New York City. She wondered if she had made some noise out loud, for he asked, "What?"

"Oh, I was just liking how you sounded," Shaye said. "How knowlegeable as a police officer. It's good to know that. It makes me feel safe."

Danielo chuckled. "Okay," he said. "It's funny, because suddenly my wife is impressed, too. I think this is the first time since my shame in New York that she called me up during work just to say hi."

"Oh," Shaye said, "that's good."

Danielo laughed at her. "You sound really sincere."

Shaye felt genuinely shocked. "I don't?"

He evaded. "You know, you make me smile," Danielo said. "Here's the thing, a favor I want to ask. Would you still be careful, there in the park, Shaye? Until we match up the DNA evidence?"

"Sure."

"And one more thing."

"Yeah."

"Do you happen to know anything about the murder weapon, Shaye? We never released any information on that publically."

"I overheard what it was. A handheld garden rake, right?"

"Damn," Danielo said. "It's nice how you found out all this shit so easily. Anyway, we do believe a hand-held cultivator was the weapon- and it may be a signature for this freaky killer. Both girls suffered from rake type wounds, several inches deep and extremely violent. Now we went through Byron and Troy's hideout apartment, and the yard there, all the surrounding areas. Shaye, we got some knives off the boys. And we literally took a whole pickup bed full of rusty tools from behind the rental property. But nothing that looks, offhand, like that murder weapon. Now we first have to test every single item for blood and trace evidence..."

"Yes," Shaye said, sensing that there was more.

"Have you ever learned anything about forensics, along with all your other personal researches?"

"Well," Shaye stammered, not really wanting to reveal how completely obsessive she was. "I have studied a lot of medical things. Wounds and any kind of insult to the human body. Actually," she confessed. "I probably know more about ways a person can die than some doctors. I don't want to get into why and how. But I'm a quick learner also. I can learn about police forensic science if I can just get to a library and get on the Internet."

Danny lowered his voice once again. She heard noises in the background. He said hello to somebody, and then finally he resumed their conversation.

"I believe you can learn it, Shaye," he said. "And I want to go with a hunch I have, and let you do some research for me. Here's what I'd like you to do. I have over fifty pages of reports specifically about the victims' wounds and the trace chemicals found in them, and I want to copy those reports for you. I also have coroner's opinions on how the victim's bodies shut down and also quite a few detailed photos. This is all extremely classified information, Shaye. Do you understand that if anyone finds out I'm giving it to you, it would mean my job? Plus probably criminal prosecution for me?"

"Danny, you know I'm discreet," Shaye said. "And I'd never want to cost you your job. You're actually one of my only friends," she ventured.

Danielo paused for a beat. "That's cool. So which do you think is safest? Should I email you the information, or drive by and slip copies into your mailbox tonight?"

Shaye scrunched her brow. "Nothing on the Internet is perfectly safe, Danny. Don't let it scare you or anything but I, just for example, could easily hack into your personal email account. Possibly your department one as well. And now, not to sound insulting, but you never know when Internal Affairs might be looking over what you do, so you should probably be extra careful."

Danielo chuckled. "Unfortunately, no police department in fifty miles of here is even big enough to have their own Internal Affairs department. But I get your drift, and I'm grateful you're concerned."

"I guess I am," Shaye said.

"So, I'll come by at around dawn in my personal car, and I'll throw the pages by your porch wrapped in a newspaper so no one sees. I'm sorry I can't just stop in, but we're expecting to be working all night, and Chow always hangs all over me, trying to learn something. I just don't have the time, and I can't risk being seen around you."

"I'll watch for the photocopies," Shaye said, "whenever you get them here. Then I'll start work on the research tomorrow, as soon as I can get on a computer. But Danny, can you tell me exactly what you're looking for?"

"Okay," he said. "I've seen things like this on television all the time, but it all seems like science fiction to me. And I never investigated a murder before. So this is my question: could you possibly use the computer to construct a detailed picture of the murder weapon, Shaye, based on the injuries?"

"I guess," she breathed. "I've read about it being done, and seen it done in movies. I guess I could find a way."

"Good. Also, based on the chemical traces in the wounds, could you find the weapon's manufacturer, Shaye? And then is there any way to go on the Internet and find someone around here that sells the item?"

"That's a lot," Shaye said. "I think finding that information would take your department weeks, if it can be done at all."

"I think you're right about that," Danielo said.

"So, you're scaring me," Shaye said suddenly. "Why would you want *me* doing it, then? Why would you possibly trust me to do something like that?"

"Shaye," Frank Danielo said, in a voice much more somber than any he had used yet. "It's key that we connect that weapon to the killer or killers. Honey, I'm praying that Troy Reid and Byron Hanes are the killers and it's as simple as that. If those two did the crimes, we still need that weapon, or proof of how they got it, for evidence…"

"I understand," Shaye said, swallowing hard, for she now felt afraid. She knew that there was more. She knew that Danielo didn't really feel in his heart that he had the killers in custody. Instead, he was now entrusting finding the real killer to her.

"Oh, and, I'm going out tomorrow," he said. "The mayor is taking Chow and I out for happy hour to celebrate this bust. I might be unreachable for a little while…"

Neither he nor Shaye could seem to articulate the unsaid- that she still couldn't sleep safe at night.

Danny came as close as he could. "I'll check on you late tomorrow night. Just to get an update on your evidence… And, you know, to check that you're okay. All right, Baby? Just stay safe for me."

Late that night, Shaye sat out in the outdoor room, breaking the growing silence in the park with the scuff of her sandals only to return inside several times to pee. Things were still noisy; suspicious sounds came from many different corners of the park up until around one. By one-thirty or so, things had quieted down and she could almost think that it was bedtime in some sleepy upscale subdivision, similar to where she had grown up, and all was right in the world.

At around three, Rochelle's coughing little Escort sputtered up to the curb, and Adam climbed out from the front seat. For a moment, Shaye heard the girls' silly dance station playing, and she even got a whiff of Madeline and Rochelle's perfume on the heavy humid air that hung over the park in its stillness.

The car sputtered off and Adam's heels scraped on the concrete as he approached the outdoor room. Shaye noticed that he wore a champagne-colored evening dress that clung to his slim body in a twisted fluted column tonight. It must be just another thrift shop find, something that cost less than ten dollars- but it lit up the night almost painfully, like a sudden stab of Hollywood glamour from one of the forties' screen goddesses.

Shaye stared up at Adam, almost in awe.

"You look beautiful," she said.

Adam gave a tight little smile in response that only moved the corners of his mouth. Then he reached forward some wadded up money to her, all twenties and fifties, unlike the dollar tips he had been bringing home as a waiter.

"You have a good night?" she asked, with eyes big and innocent, hoping that she and Adam could stay innocent and that none of the dark stuff had happened.

"Sure," he said, matching her whisper so that they wouldn't catch anyone's attention or, God forbid, wake someone. "It's good getting up and singing and all, but I wish it was a nicer club."

"I know," Shaye said, trying to convey that she felt understanding.

"What are you doing out here?" he asked. "Are you worrying again?"

"No," Shaye said. "I'm actually waiting for Officer Danny to drop off some paperwork. He's gonna throw it wrapped in the newspaper whenever it's late enough for him to get away."

Adam raised an eyebrow. He stood there over her for a moment, looking relatively tall in his high heels. Then he yawned, and rubbed at mascara that was just starting to smudge. "Well, I'm tired. You stay safe, and I'll see you in the morning."

Adam leaned down to give Shaye a goodnight kiss on the cheek. With the satin gown, and the scent of subtle cologne it reminded Shaye of her mother, checking in on her those late nights when her parents got home and relieved her nanny. Sleepy, Shaye used to accept the airy goodnight peck without opening her eyes and then wonder about those mysterious gala parties her parents had attended and the unbridgeable distance between herself and her regal, socially pedigreed mother.

She now watched Adam delicately click into the house, swaying the bell like bottom of his dress under his trim ass and sashaying the flower-petal hem over his sculpted calves. There were no mysteries after all she pondered now, other than those impressions and illusions set up by our own minds. If Adam's female impersonating had taught her one thing, it had taught her that.

Shaye gathered her legs up to her, hugging them, on the wire seat of her little outdoor chair. She sighed and the big banana leaves around her rustled and sighed as though in sympathy.

She heard a scuffing sound down on the street and looked forward into the lighted area from her comfortably cloaking pool of darkness within her greenery screen. She made out a man's figure and thought she recognized the cavernous set of the chest, and the slumping set of the shoulders. The man had dark skin, and what looked like brown clothing- a Dickies uniform with the nametag torn off- the same older black man that had reconnoitered the neighborhood trip after trip before the first slaying.

Now he bent to examine some garbage in front of Darlene's trailer. He came up with a plastic crate half full with various items. And then he looked in Shaye's direction as though he sensed someone watching.

Stubbornly, she stayed still and silent, knowing that she could definitely outlast him. The fear she had felt the first days she had seen him felt like it had completely evaporated. What did it matter if he was wandering the streets at three in the morning, after all? She had already faced up to the worst, that any man she saw in this park might be a murderer. She supposed what she felt at the moment was, "well, bring it on!" for she was tired of being afraid.

Byron Hanes and Troy Reid were behind bars now. And the killing was supposed to be over. The ragged man in the street, the hobo scavenger with the paranoid tilt of chin, finally lowered his head and walked on.

Trembling just a little, Shaye Taylor remained.

Danielo came at a quarter to five, swaying down the street in a wine colored Dodge Intrepid with a ragged rear bumper. Running down a tinted window, he reached out an arm and flung a big thick newspaper sheathed in plastic. With a thump, the paper hit the lattice wall, and the car swerved out of sight. Shaye smiled and uncurled her legs to go get her gift of evidence.

Shaye read over the reports diligently in her bedroom and, at seven thirty in the morning, she suited up in T-shirt and shorts and Keds to head out to accomplish the second part of her task. In her arms she carried a manila folder containing photocopies of some of the most horrible images she had ever experienced, photos of women torn apart with a garden rake. She had stayed up the remainder of the night examining the grisly photos.

The body is a temple, she knew. But she knew all too well how that temple could be torn apart, piece by piece, centimeter by centimeter, sinew by blood cell, by fearful curling tissue, recoiling from an invader, whether that invader be a mutated strain of bacteria, or an invading piece of metal- a garden rake guided by a vicious man's hand.

A yellow-orange school bus clattered over the potholes in the dirt drive, and Shaye had to step onto the damp grass at the shoulder of Caiman St. to avoid it. When she stepped back onto the street, and glanced through the fog toward the site of the first crime scene, she was not surprised at all to find the black man in coveralls from last night there. He crouched over his crate and a small fire by the side of the stream. His eyes bored through layers of morning mist, as though challenging Shaye to possibly understand.

It didn't matter, she thought. She looked forward and walked straight ahead.

At nine that evening, on a computer screen made blurry by twelve hours of staring, an image revolved before Shaye- a computer composite she had created. It was four and a half inches wide, with five three-inch teeth. Shaye watched the image of the cultivator slip end over end, doing a lazy dance, as though choosing its course in outer space. Should I come to earth, it seemed to ask? Should I land there in Flamingo Park, Florida and make so much trouble?

Shaye felt a touch on her shoulder and jumped in her seat.

The solidly built middle-aged librarian smelled like powder and sported gray hair, jaggedly cut, and glasses on a fake pearl chain.

But her eyes showed unexpected intensity and deep curiosity at what Shaye had been doing.

Shaye's fingers went defensively to the keyboard to save the conclusion of her work to floppy disc. The librarian squinted at the image on the screen in bottomless curiosity that could find no healthy and normal words to express itself.

"You've been working at this computer for twelve hours straight, Honey," she said, in a voice that crackled. "Are you okay?"

Shaye slipped out the floppy, and blinked her eyes a few times.

"I'm fine," she said.

The librarian straightened up, a little less alarmed looking now that a "Reading is the Coolest!" screen saver replaced the disturbing image of the rake that had been revolving before Shaye for hours as she tweaked it.

"The library is closed," the librarian said, pointing to the fact that the building was empty. "Are you sure you're okay?"

Shaye pocketed her bright red floppy disc that she had hand labeled "Murder Weapon." She stood and stretched out her long torso and her long legs that had fallen asleep. She glanced at the darkness outside the library windows and turned around, getting her bearings.

She'd have to catch the last bus of the night. And then she'd have to cut right in front of the crime scene on Caiman street on her way home. But that was okay. Her heart beat faster, for in her pocket, she held a new piece of evidence. Shaye Taylor now knew something about the murder weapon, something that distinguished it from millions of other garden tools on the market. In fact, Shaye knew some facts about the weapon that only one other person could know- and that person was the man who had used it to kill.

Chapter 10

After her walk that evening Shaye stood outside her own home, surrounded by a chorus of strumming cicadas, and gazing at the three small, lighted windows of the living room. They seemed like an oasis of warmth, in the damp, chilly night and the starless darkness.

One of the windows was cranked open for air and Shaye got glimpses of several people inside. She thought she heard laughter and the clink of glasses, as though a party was going on. She had to squeeze between two cars parked right up next to each other- Rochelle's Escort and Officer Frank Danielo's Intrepid.

For a few minutes, Shaye stood at attention amongst the fronds of the outdoor room, listening in at their window like a prowler. Inside they were laughing and singing out "For He's a Jolly Good Fellow." Shaye heard Frank Danielo's low-pitched laugh along with female voices- rather harsh female voices- which made sense if you knew that Adam's buddies really were men.

When the song ended and the laughter resumed, Shaye finally stepped inside.

She found Danielo sitting on the couch with a flushed face, his dress uniform shirt unbuttoned and his policeman's hat set at a rakish angle. The "girls" seemed to hang over him, one on either side. They bounced on the cushions, laughed uproariously and gave a blurred impression of gowns, sparkly platform heels, feather boas, big hair and fishnet stockings. Tonight's tableau didn't look that different, she reflected, than the lurid photo in the *Daily News*. The

147

only difference was that, in this scenario, in her pitiful excuse for a home, there was no hot tub involved.

Adam met Shaye at the door, trying to serve her some sparking water in a wineglass. His female impersonator look was much more classy than the others'. He wore a short black cocktail dress with his short hair brushed into a neat Audrey Hepburn style. His unreadable eyes were ringed round and round in circles of smudged kohl makeup, and Shaye had to ask herself who the heck this person was.

Meanwhile Frank Danielo drunkenly waved a champagne bottle by its neck.

"C'mon, Blondie," he urged. "Come join the party. We've all been waiting for you for hours!"

Madeline, sitting on his right side, looked up from the champagne glass that she sipped from with a pink flamingo cocktail straw. She batted false eyelashes and swung off the veil of her thick sleek hair to make sure that Shaye saw the defiance in her eyes.

"Why not join us, Shaye?" she asked, in a voice that could be interpreted either as bedroom, or flat out masculine, depending on what one knew. "Why not come over and sit by your cop friend and join the fun?"

Shaye took another step inside, but not before turning to carefully lock up the door, to lock out whatever dangers might be lurking outside. Then she carefully set down the wineglass full of water that Adam had given her, and perched on a stool to face those unexpected dangers that sat in her living room right now.

Adam leaned across the counter to stare at her with little owl's eyes, ringed in makeup. He did look beautiful, indistinguishable from some young female gamine, only one hundred and thirty pounds, but carrying an unmistakable load of heartbreak at age twenty.

It surprised her in a sense that Danielo would spend his time with three such individuals. He didn't seem that open minded. Unless he actually felt they were all females. Was that possible?

"So, Shaye," Adam said sarcastically, leaving his tail in the short dress perched in the direction of the living room. "We now know all there is to know about Officer Frank Danielo, budding Oceanside detective! And what's most interesting, Sweetie, is that now Danny's big case is cracked, he's still here. He spent the evening celebrating with the mayor, but that wasn't enough, Shaye.

The department's party was still going strong, but he chose to come up here and spend time with you instead."

Shaye grimaced. So that was what this was all about. Jealousy. Albeit a strange kind, considering this was Adam, dressed as a girl.

She could have told him that she hated Danny nosing around here, but that wouldn't have gone over so well with Danny. And he was "the man", after all.

Danny was sloppy drunk, lying on his back and fighting off Rochelle and Madeline as they tickled him to try to snag the champagne bottle.

"Of course, Officer Danny's got a crush on Shaye," Madeline pouted. "But we're trying to get him interested in the three of us. We've got moves that Shaye couldn't imagine."

"I'll bet," Shaye muttered, feeling about to choke in the close atmosphere. Staring at Madeline playing over officer Danny, with her long hair falling all over his body, some thought nibbled at Shaye, something to do with the case and the killer. But it seemed ephemeral and she couldn't grasp it, not right now. The more she tried, the further it floated away, like smoke.

Danny parted Madeline's hair to grin at Shaye. He seemed to get the vibe that she didn't like their rowdy company, and he tried to sound a little serious.

"Shaye," he said. "I can't believe you didn't tell me anything about your roommate, Eden. She and I had a whole long talk." He struggled to sit up, maneuvering Madeline's loose body to one side. "Now I feel like I really know you girls."

Adam smirked at Shaye, before turning with a catlike languor.

So, Danny really *didn't* know.

"My roommate *Eden*," Shaye said, her voice icy cold. "So, you've met 'Eden', and you approve?"

"Sure I approve!"

Rochelle pulled Madeline over to her own side of the couch, sticking a palm between Madeline's lipstick-smeared lips to shush her laughter.

"I'm a cop," he continued. "If you don't want to be forthcoming about yourself, I get the information somewhere else. In this case your roommate Eden, who seems like a very wise and perceptive girl, told me all about you. She says she knows you better than anyone else in the world, and I think I believe that."

"Yeah, well, 'Eden'", Shaye growled. "*Eden* is sometimes so busy worrying about me that I think she forgets to wonder who she is."

The insult aimed at Adam made Madeline prostrate herself in Rochelle's lap, literally rolling with laughter, as Rochelle tried to gag her. Rochelle waved at her eyes, as though to dry tears of sudden emotion from her eye makeup.

"Well, girls will be girls," she croaked, fighting back her own laughter. "We're just too intuitive. Shaye and Eden make us all emotional, too."

Madeline rolled to the floor, stuffing hormone-enhanced little breasts back into her tight bustier. "I'm gonna piss," she squealed, "if I don't stop laughing. I've gotta use your little girls' room, Eden."

She ran for Adam's room, ruffled miniskirt swinging, thumping the unsteady floor of the trailer with her undelicate weight.

Shaye advanced around the counter, teeth clenched together. It was hard to talk to three drunk people. Adam, who never let himself go farther than a social buzz, was even harder to look at with his soft enigmatic eyes.

Shaye looked between Adam and Danny. "Well, 'Eden' *is* my best friend" she said. "But she doesn't know everything. That's why I turned to you, Danny. Because you're a cop and I wanted you to keep everybody safe. But now the threat's over, and I think the party's over, too."

Adam simply glared at Shaye, with what looked like embers shimmering deep within his eyes.

And Madeline came tripping into the room, clutching a glossy magazine to her stomach. "The party's *not* over! Not yet"

She threw the magazine to Danielo, who neatly caught it. Then Danny patted his knee and Adam made his way toward him. Shaye couldn't believe what she was seeing. Adam sat down delicately on Danielo's lap, while Rochelle and Madeline leaned eagerly on both sides of him.

And Danielo spread the pages of the magazine, opening to a centerfold. "I can't believe you didn't tell me, Shaye. Look at this. Shaye Taylor! 'As hot as the Tropical Sun' it calls you."

It was the *Tropical Sun* catalog! They were looking at her, posed in a golden bikini, with tanned skin and tendrils of spun gold hair trailing all the way around her curvy breasts and buttocks down around tight calves, and almost down to her golden ankle bracelet and painted toenails.

Shaye gasped, and she felt her world darkening and spinning around her. She felt she might fall through the trailer floor and into the ground, down to a vortex where, hopefully, her heartache would end.

Where had they found it? Where had they found an old *Tropical Sun* catalog? But she knew. There was only one place they *could* have found it.

She couldn't even walk, she shook so hard.

"Why would you let him see that?" she gasped at Adam, knees feeling weak at this treachery.

Adam tried to make his face stay sullen, even though Shaye's pain obviously stung him. "I didn't do it deliberately," he said. "Madeline was in my stuff before, looking for makeup to borrow, and she found it. What's the big deal?"

"I didn't even know you had it," Shaye said. She stepped closer now, gingerly, peering at hundreds of photos of herself as Danielo flipped pages. "I haven't seen one of the catalogs in over a year."

"Oh, of course not," Madeline sniped. "Like you're just so modest, Shaye, just the poor martyr!"

She stabbed at a particular photo with a long nail. It showed Shaye slung over a wet gray boulder, her long opalescent nails demurely covering about a third of her nude breasts and her lower body decked out in a shimmering mermaid's tail. The title "Tropical Ecstasy/ Tropical Fantasy" was emblazoned above the photo.

The next page showed Shaye in a bikini top made of nothing but two giant shells. She was shown pouting and licking a multicolored ice cream cone, while her spectacular breasts swelled to fill the page on both sides. "Tropical Treat," the caption read said. All in the room stared, mesmerized. Shaye remembered the advertised bikini cost over one thousand dollars, yet people used to buy it eagerly because of that photo.

Danny flicked over to the next page. Now his eyes accused Shaye as she stood over him. He found his place in the text beneath a full-page close up of her face in shimmery beach glow makeup.

"*Shaye Taylor*," he read. "*America's new voluptuous ingénue. Shaye is a cross between sly supermodel and cuddly cutey, with all the sexy vulnerability of a young Marilyn Monroe! Ms. Taylor is the exclusive cover model for* Tropical Sun Magazine *five years running. Named in national fashion and celebrity magazines to have* the 'hottest body in a bikini', Shaye's been photographed in creative spreads on sumptuous beaches all over the world. She's a photographer's darling, and also a magnet for naughtiness, caught frolicking with celebrities such as..."

It went on to name two of the most lusted-after male stars of the moment, but then wrapped up by saying, "But above all, Shaye's slavishly devoted to husband and hotshot international talent agent Riley Taylor..."

"So, you're married, Shaye?" Danielo accused.

"No, I'm not married," she said, "my husband left me when I got sick. When I became no longer marketable."

"Oh, poor baby," Madeline interjected, flipping to the next page of the story.

Then she read out loud. "'This may be the last year for the men of America to indulge in so many sizzling hot photos of Shaye in the Tropical Sun catalog. Because rumor has it that Shaye's been approached about certain national, six-figure deals for next summer...'"

"So, you're a supermodel, aren't you, Trailer Park Barbie?" Madeline accused. "A real life friggin supermodel!"

Danielo nudged Madeline. "Hey, don't be cruel," he said.

"No, of course not," Madeline snapped. "Shaye can always wrap men around her little finger and make them feel sorry for her craziness. Now we see why," she said, viciously flipping pages to give them all the overwhelming show.

Shaye stepped up and snatched the catalog away, her whole body trembling.

"Why would you let them get this?" she shrilled at Adam. "You think I'm so paranoid? Well, maybe I'm right to be paranoid!" Her fear and fury spun out of control so she could not stop yelling. She turned on the two she-males, Madeline in particular. "You really, honestly, think I'm a rich supermodel, Madeline? Well, the fact is my husband took every penny from me. Whatever didn't go on two years worth of medical bills!"

Shaye paced the carpet for a moment, scuffing her Keds and growling like a hurt animal. Then she came back near them. "Just look at me," she said, spreading her scrawny arms wide, like a crucifixion. "Does anybody really think I look like a happy healthy supermodel?

"And you." Shaye's eyes rolled down towards Danny. "I hope you got you're fill of looking at sexy pictures and playing with my roommate's ass. Because you can be so incredibly stupid. He's not a girl, Danny! His name's not Eden. It's Adam! And he's sitting there laughing at you! And despising you. They all are, because you wanna act just like the typical man. They think you're a real hoot!"

Danielo's skin paled a few shades. He cringed out from underneath Adam. As he got to his feet he swayed ridiculously, with the liquor hitting him. "So, what is real here?" he slurred. He poked at Adam. "This guy's a man?"

Adam grinned maliciously and stuck out his chin.

"He is a man, and what he did here is shameful," Shaye said. "All of them. And you, too, Danny, for what you had in your mind!"

"In my mind?" he said. "All I was thinking about was you. And it seems like half the men in America did that anyway."

"Watch it," Adam said to him.

Madeline reeled to her feet on her high heels, flinging back her long messy locks. Rochelle got to her feet regally, fluffed her curls and joined her friend, an arm over her shoulder.

"It don't matter about Shaye, Officer Danny," Madeline pouted and purred. "What we got to offer can't be matched. Check it out!"

Suddenly, she began to bump and grind, squawking out the words to "We Are Family" until Rochelle, and then Adam joined her, adding their voices, tossing hair and flouncy skirts, kicking up their legs like cancan girls and shaking the house. The two she-males sang out defiantly, with Adam in the middle, all circling drunken, disoriented Officer Danny.

Shaye slumped back against the counter. "Stop it," she repeated weakly, again and again, until finally her voice rose in fury. She clutched her hands against both ears, trying to block the noise and the swirling confusing motion. Then she stumbled into the middle of the Bacchanal.

"It's not a joke," she said. "None of this is a joke. Women have been getting killed around here!"

Suddenly her eyes rolled, taking in Madeline, who seemed to epitomize the worst of them. Biologically a man, yet with her hair mussed and her overdone lipstick smeared, a cocktease and a loudmouth, literally- a bitch.

Shaye faced the other "woman", approximately the same height, and she suddenly went for Madeline's precious hair, pulling at it roughly in the belief that it was a wig.

"Oww!" Madeline yipped, struggling against Shaye.

Danny fell back, laughing uproariously.

"That's my real hair, you little puta!" Madeline yelled, trying to claw at Shaye.

"Girlfight, girlfight!" Danny laughed.

"Let her go, Barbie!" Rochelle yelled.

Shaye and Madeline swung out from the others. "Okay, fine," Shaye said, calling to Danny. "You want to see. You want to see what you've been playing with, here, instead of doing police work, you sick pervert?"

"No!" Madeline squealed, as Shaye reached for her miniskirt and panties. Shaye didn't know where she got the strength, for Madeline fought like a hellcat. But Shaye grabbed her by the belly and lifted her, even as Madeline violently kicked out churning legs. "Let me go, puta!"

"See what she's working with, Danny!" Shaye said. "You love sex so damn much, why don't you look at what these 'girls' are working with!"

Shaye pulled down Madeline's red lace panties and pulled up her miniskirt. Everyone stopped singing. Danny, and even Adam and Rochelle, stared aghast.

Suddenly, Madeline decided to take it philosophically. She stopped fighting and simply pouted. "She don't like my candy," she said. "Why can't I get anybody to try my candy?"

Then she gave a little laugh at herself. Danny fell to the floor, laughing so hard that he started wheezing. "This is a trip. This is such a trip!"

Madeline grabbed onto the champagne bottle and gulped some down to drown her sorrows. Meanwhile Rochelle came over to fix her friend's skirt.

Adam was the only one who still looked classy and untouched. He squeezed Rochelle on the shoulder. "You know what, you girls better go," he said. "This is getting to the point where it's no longer cool."

Shaye stalked over beside Danny. She dropped a large manilla envelope on the floor beside him. "There's your research," she said. "A little murder weapon picture to occupy you when you're not slumming."

Danny reached out to pull on Shaye's leg as she tried to step away. "Get back here," he said. "You better not go."

Adam stepped between them, making Danny release her. "Leave her alone," he warned.

154

Shaye stalked into her bedroom, walking into the darkness and slamming shut the rickety door so the trailer shook. She felt like she was a million miles up. She wished she could be in the moment, absorbed in the petty conflict out in the living room. But she could not be. She felt like she was up in space somewhere now. Up in the empty galaxies, which were dark like her room. She couldn't even feel she could connect with the photos of that beautiful woman that she had seen in the wrinkled old *Tropical Sun* catalog. For, wasn't that women dead? Hadn't the rare strain of e-coli that had seared through her insides left her dead?

Vaguely, Shaye heard something through the thin trailer walls. It was just another fantasy. Shouting. Men's voices.

"You need to leave Shaye alone!" Adam yelled at Danny. "You don't understand her. Not at all."

"Well, you all don't understand me, *Eden*," Danny said. "I'm a detective, and I'm not gonna be made a laughingstock."

"Oh," Adam smirked. "Then why don't you go lock up a hooker killer and do something useful? After you sober up, that is."

"I'll leave," Danny said, "but not without that magazine. I'm keeping that forever."

Suddenly, there came a long silence.

"No," Adam said, in icy seriousness. "Over my dead body."

There was another silence.

Then came Adam's voice again. "Let me show you the door."

Shaye then heard the door slam, and Danny's car engine roared as he tromped on the gas.

Next came the quiet again, and a high melodious voice. Adam was straightening up from the party, and singing sweetly to himself- an old Billie Holiday blues song about lost love.

Chapter 11

Adam came to sit on Shaye's bed early the next morning. She blinked up at him with big green eyes, and he was the first thing she saw. She took a breath and they just continued to stare at each other for a moment.

Then Adam shook his head. "He's just such a typical man, Shaye. Haven't you seen it all before? Haven't you hated it?"

Shaye yawned, and sat up, just feeling tired and not knowing if it was Adam that she was peeved at, or Danny, or both. Whether it was the "girls" out in the living room last night, or really all men. For years, she hadn't realized it, but weren't they all always taking advantage of her every time boys from six to sixty devoured one of her photos with their eyes- and sniggered?

"Adam, what do you want me to say? I thought I had Danny understanding me. And then you had to go and provide him with those photographs. What do you expect?"

Adam dropped his head. "I'm sorry," he said.

"It doesn't matter," Shaye said. "I understand your motives, and I know your boyhood obsession with me was pure- in its own sick way…"

They both giggled, a little shadow of what their friendship used to be at its best.

Shaye continued. "But don't you see, Adam, the irony of it? My own husband was one of those guys you talk about. Lots worse than Danny, in fact. It's pretty easy to love a sixteen-year-old girl with a 34 DD-24-34 figure who's willing to do anything for you. Who's stupid like I was … "

Adam leaned forward and stroked Shaye's hair gently away from her face. "You don't need to go into it, Honey. When I saw those catalogs, I saw the best in you."

"That's because you were looking at the *swimsuits*, Adam!"

Adam sighed.

"My husband really did have ulterior motives. So many of them did." Shaye felt sullen. She thumped her body back against the headboard, loving her new physically unattractive self that could pursue men instead of being pursued. "In their hearts, Adam, philosophically I mean, how many men are really woman killers?"

Adam opened eyes and mouth wide and sat back speechless, with no answer.

Before he could talk, to offer her some hot cocoa, some milk, a nice soft-boiled egg or some other inane physical comfort, Shaye gestured to the lopsided dresser in the corner of the room, where her copy of the case file sat.

"Adam, get that, please," she said.

Adam reached for it, not even having to get up, and delivered it to Shaye. She paged through it until she pulled out her computer replication of the serial killer's murder weapon. Adam took the sheet and gave a gasp. He held the sheet up, with the morning sun bathing it, so they both could look.

They had to stare in silence for a moment.

"This is what you wanted to show Danny last night?" he asked. "And he was messing around?"

Shaye nodded. "That's right."

"So this is the murder weapon?" he asked. "A cultivator shaped like a rooster claw?"

"A hand rake shaped like a rooster's claw- carved of pure silver, Adam!" Shaye showed him her crime scene photos, her laboratory reports and pages and pages of research and calculations. "This was fairly easy forensic work," she explained. "Based on the chemicals found in the wound, there was no doubt that the weapon was made of pure silver- very rare. Any other traces in the wounds, I believe were left by garbage at the crime scenes. But to have large amounts of silver show up in a wound- and on both victims- that couldn't just be chance…"

Adam stood up, ran his fingers through his short hair, and started to pace in small circles, looking like he doubted just about everything in life. He would turn to Shaye to speak, then sigh and turn away again instead. Puffiness showed out under his pretty eyes, and he seemed to age as he stood there. Shaye wondered idly how silly it would be if her beloved Adam were actually the killer here. After all, he was completely crazy. He'd said it himself and she'd seen his paranoia, seen him dissociate from himself.

But Adam couldn't be a killer. She knew that. Although he did seem to, now, carry the guilt for the whole male race. More and more every moment. And he seemed confused at what to do.

"Okay," he said finally. "So you're sure about it being silver? Even though the police lab hasn't yet figured this out?"

"They will," Shaye put in. "But it may take a while. That's why Danny handed the project to me."

"Oh," Adam said. His tone easily could have been suspected to be humoring her.

Shaye perked up a little anyway, getting to the exciting part, the first contribution to society her skill had made in the past years- perhaps, honestly, in her entire life.

"I figured out the rooster claw design you see reconstructing up from the patterns of the victim's wounds."

Adam gaped again. "How did you do that, Shaye? How would you know how?"

"Danny left me passwords for some police forensic sites, which include tables and calculators. Plus I have a few somewhat unusual medical sites I like to visit for my own pleasure and they came in handy here."

Adam's eyes seemed to glaze over. "You are so crazy, Shaye. Like other people look at porn, you look at medical sites. Autopsies now!"

There was nothing she could say anymore to comfort him. She knew her compulsions scared him, and they scared her, too. And, even though she had a couple of days feeling productive because Frank Danielo had entrusted her with this, now she realized Danielo had probably been humoring her as well. He just probably wanted to be around her long hair, and plump lips and plump boobs while she played neurotic Nancy Drew. He was probably just as revolted by her taste for tragedy and illness as everyone else was.

But she couldn't help it. She hadn't made this killer. But now maybe only she could stop him. The chances that Byron Hanes and Troy Reid had somehow found a silver hand cultivator cast as a rooster claw were pretty slim. In fact, Shaye surmised that the weapon had been lovingly custom made for a single individual. Yes, silver could be cast in any shape. But, in this case, the fighting cock probably symbolized something particular to the killer. And probably so did gardening itself. And not every silversmith could forge such a quality item- like precious jewelry, almost icon-like, and yet strong enough to actually work with.

And strong enough to kill with.

For a moment, Shaye's heart ached. She really wished that she could call Frank Danielo right now to talk about this. But, after his performance last night, she had to admit that Adam was probably right about him. Weak, and driven by his hormones, he was scum.

Anyway, he had that manila file now- her complete report. He could come to any conclusions, and do anything he had to do. Meanwhile, she was going to the library. She stretched and stood on shaky legs, to Adam's curious stare.

"Adam," she said. "I have to go to the town library again. I have to find where a claw like that could have been manufactured."

She leaned into her closet to dress demurely. Then she turned to brush out her hair. Adam stepped forward, wordlessly, to braid it and help her tuck it under her cap.

"Be careful," he said. "Nothing says Danny is going to protect you."

Shaye grimaced. "I know. But I have to do this."

Walking past the first murder site on Caiman St. that fresh morning, Shaye again saw the derelict in coveralls, sitting under the fronds of trees and preparing what might have been his breakfast coffee. He had expanded his campsite to include another night's hoard of collected trash. And he sat, less than five feet from where Mami Ramierez's body had begun to decompose not three weeks ago, boiling water in a tin can over the smoky embers of a tiny campfire.

If he was the killer, he certainly showed quite a lot of gall.

And if he was the killer, where was Officer Danny not to notice him here, and at least question him? "Oh, yeah," Shaye said out loud to herself. "I forgot. Danny likes to sleep late. He had a rough night with the 'ladies' at our little party." So, how about Officer Chow, she wondered. And was all of this even real, or just a product of her own paranoid imagination?

She stared boldly at the derelict, and he raised his eyes, dark eyes blending into dark skin, blending into dark shadows. She had trouble making out his expression in the shadows but she saw him raise up his arm, pointing accusingly in her direction.

"I didn't kill nobody," he said to her in a deep, yet tremulous, voice, the voice of a long term alcoholic, or an old-school biblical prophet- or some old New Orleans hoodoo man. "I see you lookin' at me, girlie. And I know what you thinkin', Chickadee. But them cops don't bother me. Cause they know I didn't do nuthin'"

Keeping an eye on him, Shaye delicately began to pad backwards, up the street, towards the relative safety of Flamingo Beach Parkway. From a distance, she heard his crackling laughter. And she fancied she heard something else, but she couldn't be sure. Shaye thought she heard him say, "But I know who did do it!"

She trembled all the way to the bus stop, and all the way to the library. She thought about going back. She thought about bringing Adam with her, or even trying once more with Danielo. At least he would have a gun. She doubted the derelict was the killer. He wouldn't possess a silver hand rake and he wouldn't have constructed elaborate, Mexican-style grave displays.

But maybe he had seen something. After all, he wandered the park at all hours. She knew that. Why hadn't she simply approached him and tried to interrogate him? Shaye had to admit that she was afraid. Even the smell of the man's old coveralls and the reek of something greasy cooking over his smoky campfire knotted her stomach with fear.

Shaye debated. Waiting outside the library, waiting for it to open up in the suddenly oppressive and marshy-smelling air, she made a decision. On their "special" phone, Shaye jabbed out Danny's number. When his sleepy voice answered, she took no time to identify herself, no time even to breathe.

"Danny," she said curtly, "you need to go to the murder scene on Caiman St. right now."

"Shaye, listen…" Danny said.

She cut him off, turning the cell phone off and, without letting herself think about it further, headed into the library that was just opening.

The librarian recognized Shaye, greeted her and immediately asked her if she could be of help, her gray complexion seeming invigorated by extreme curiosity now. Shaye shook her head absently and hurried to the same computer as yesterday. Only after she sat down, and logged in, did she remember to look up. "No thank you," she said. "Maybe later."

It turned out some of the material she needed was not to be found on the Internet after all, but in huge photograph-filled books on Mexican culture. About noontime, when Shaye's Internet search led her in the direction of these books, the solitary librarian flushed with pleasure.

"We actually have one of the most comprehensive sections on Mexican culture of any library on Florida's east coast," she boasted. "In fact, it may be the best such section in all of Florida."

Now Shaye gaped. The whole library was smaller than Shaye and her husband's bedroom used to be- and there were never many patrons. Just herself and the middle-aged librarian on a weekday afternoon like this.

"A collection like that? That's fascinating," she said with a little awe, as the librarian started stacking volumes the size of slabs of concrete one on top of the other on a wide wooden table.

The older woman nodded her head vigorously. "That's right. Some of these were a donation from a private individual. They're beautiful books," she said. "This one..." She lifted one to demonstrate. "...has beautiful photographs from the Mayan culture. The others detail day-to-day life, especially in the rural communities..."

"Rural," Shaye said. "So, would one of these include information about roosters? Specifically- symbols of roosters? Art involving roosters? Designs of roosters?"

She looked towards the librarian hopefully, and the librarian didn't look at her as though she was crazy at all. She looked a little curious, but she smiled and extracted another large book from the stack. "This one includes folklore, and folkloric art," she said. "I'm sure you'd find a rooster design in it somewhere."

Shaye lowered herself before the stack of books, cracking open the glossy pages of the enormous book on folklore.

Only about fifteen minutes later did she remember to look up and thank the librarian. The motherly woman only accepted her thanks and then asked, "Honey, are you hungry? We had a Friends of the Library Meeting last night and we have plenty of leftovers in the refrigerator- vegetable lasagna, egg rolls, homemade quiche..."

Hearing the list of food, Shaye blanched. She imagined matrons, each in their own kitchen rolling dough with bare hands, carrying the covered dishes in the backs of hot cars, allowing bacteria to begin breeding. Then she envisioned the assortment of warm foods left out last night on an oversized table to fester for hours while all the biddies gossiped about library politics. Well intentioned, of course. They would have carelessly allowed the hot food to cool to room temperature and then, rather than disposing of it in sterile fashion, they had preserved it. Waiting to be fed to somebody like her. Shaye didn't have to be pursued by the killer this morning, for she would be killed at noontime by a casserole prepared by a librarian.

Shaye fainted. She woke with her head on the table and the librarian standing over her, rubbing her back. "Honey, honey are you all right?" she asked. "I can call the paramedics- I can call the police."

Shaye straightened up, protectively pulling her giant Mexico book back towards her. "No," she said, her words a little fuzzy. "Do not call any cops! Don't do that!" She looked up into the librarian's concerned brown eyes. They resembled her mother's when her mother had first come to visit her in the mental ward- and found a weeping skeleton tied down in restraints that she had trouble recognizing, except for the very long, very greasy hair.

Carefully, Shaye controlled her tone. "It's just that I don't want any food," she said. "You see, I'm on a diet. A very strict diet." She batted her eyes and made a little joke, for her own appreciation only, as the librarian backed tactfully away. "I work as a model," Shaye said. "I'm actually a swimsuit model."

As soon as the threat of the bacteria laden food was removed, Shaye found it easy to breathe again. She breathed in the astringent smell of pages that had never been cracked, and she flipped through colorful and extraordinary photographs. Many showed religious icons- saints and crucifixes. It took her only about five minutes to find something that resembled the reed cross at the first crime scene. It took her five more minutes to find photographs of floral decorated grave displays- actually carnival displays from the Mexican Day of the Dead, intended to honor the spirits of the departed.

And then Shaye gasped when she was twenty minutes into the book. For she was looking at an image etched on a red background, an elongate, almost Scandinavian-style, caricature of a rooster, with a twinkle in its eye that resembled a gargoyle or angry Chinese dragon. At the back tips of its feet, curved like Moroccan slippers or the little cleft feet of a demon, were long stylized spurs. Underneath the illustration was a caption, which said in an indigenous Indian dialect of Spanish- "The Silver Heel of the Rooster."

Shaye felt a sharp spike of pain in her stomach. She chided herself mentally, for she knew Adam would want her to put down the book when she experienced stress like this- to do her biofeedback exercises and allow her adrenalin to return to normal. If a book made her stomach ache like this, Adam would say to run away and avoid it forever.

She was on no medication whatsoever, not even over-the-counter ulcer medication like Pepcid. Her only hope in controlling her chronic ulcerative gastritis was in controlling her emotions.

Not listening to Adam's admonitions inside her skull, Shaye dived back into the book, even though she knew she might be seeking more trouble.

A section from an American anthropologist's volume from the nineteen thirties read as followed:

"There is the legend in Mexico, in the north central mountain regions, of this spur of the rooster, called The Silver Heel. The men of the region hand down from generation to generation the notion of equating the rooster with courage, strength and tenacity, as well as male virility. In the legend, Silver Heel, a courageous fighting rooster well past his prime clawed the drought-packed earth outside of the ring, dirt which would later form his own shallow grave. Silver Heel fought in the ring with great bravery, defending his mujeres- his ladies- and the ground that was all their sustenance. And he was defeated through cowardice and treachery.

As the old cock fought his last battle that day, his spurs moved so fast and so hard, they were forged into silver. His opponent, brought to the ring by foreigners- gringos- was helped to defeat Silver Heel unfairly, his spurs tipped with poison. But the valiant rooster of the legend fought to the end and went into the ground with his silver heels as his testament.

To this day, in the region the silver heel represents integrity and courage. It also, for this indigenous people, represents an intrinsic link with the earth. It is not uncommon for peasants of the region, when the father of a family is sent on a journey, to send him off with a talisman of silver, fashioned into the shape of a rooster spur, around his neck.

A man who wears this spur announces that he is filled with courage and loves the earth so much that he would die for it. If a head of the family dies making a dangerous journey and he's discovered wearing a silver heel talisman and buried with it it confers great honor to the people of his small village and the surviving family. For this is a man who would die for his beliefs and would not be cuckholded."

Shaye shook her head a few times to try to clear it. What had she just read? She searched desperately for additional clarification in the remainder of the book, but she found nothing immediately pertinent, just additional chapters, each focusing on other little-known Mexican folklore icons.

But Shaye was hooked, looking back again at the sketch of the rooster with the Silver Heel. She could feel hairs stand up on her neck, and on her forearms, with the certainty that she had found something that only the serial killer knew. It gave her a bizarre feeling of intimacy, and the weight of the knowledge felt like the weight of the world.

Or, it could all be imaginings, after all.

Once again, Shaye stayed in the library until closing. She read every bit of information on rural Mexico until her vision blurred and her eyes ached. Most of the books were new and glossy and filled with photographs, obviously donated by the library's generous benefactor. Others looked like old children's textbooks, with cracked leather covers and cracked and browning pages. She saw sketches of pirates and bandits and Mexican cowboys, and she struggled with hand-sketched maps of Mexico's geography.

She was looking for one thing- the name of the particular town where the legend of the Silver Heel originated.

By the time darkness began to settle outside the library she had found it. There was a unique mountain region in North Central Mexico called Santasemana where ten individual villages ranged in circular pattern around a mountain peak called *El Viejo*- The Old Man. Each village was people by approximately three hundred individuals of primarily Indian heritage, and they'd held on to their myths and customs virtually unchanged from hundreds of years ago. The men of these villages, throughout history, had been renowned as undefeatable warriors, in one of the few areas that resisted overthrow by Cortes.

The people in the region still lived as farmers. In the relatively inhospitable terrain of the mountain plateau they displayed an almost mythical talent for making things grow. They were talented botanists, creating a verdant mountain paradise, and raising some crops that existed only in the region. As for livestock- the mainstay of the diet, and the economy, of the Santasemana region was- poultry! Chickens. One of the books even went so far to say that many of their legends centered around roosters, which were considered to take on an almost mystical importance in the region.

And what was the other export from this intriguing region? Nothing else but silver!

The reason that these remote villages had grown up with such a unique and powerful culture, and the reason for the odd symmetry of their geographical location had to do with one thing. An ancient silver mine.

This mine, in the very bowels of the central peak of El Viejo, was said to have existed thousands of years ago. Legend had it that tribes mined it long before their Spanish conquerers' fascination with silver mining and forging. It was said that a whole moon-oriented culture once existed there, included stories of slaves working the mines, and tales of religious human sacrifice.

It didn't matter to Shaye if any of this was true. What did matter is that the abandoned mine still held silver, and that the elders of the region were said to be able to forge it into remarkable artifacts-"even utilitarian items". Shaye yelped out loud when she read this quote.

Utilitarian items. This silver garden rake, in the shape of the rooster's claw, had probably come from a small village in Mexico, in a region with no more than three thousand residents! The smith who crafted it probably still resided there. And there was a strong likelihood that he knew the exact identity of the person that had purchased it. Not Byron Hanes or Troy Reid, but someone of Mexican heritage, someone born to be a warrior. Someone with some connection to farming or landscaping. And someone who probably lived, or worked, in Flamingo Park right now.

Shaye pushed the books away from her, her breath coming heavy and her eyes flashing. She staggered a bit as she tried to carry a stack of them over to the copier. The librarian was cleaning up, preparatory to closing and she came to watch Shaye, standing at a respectable distance.

"Those books can be borrowed," she volunteered helpfully. "None of them are reference books."

Shaye looked up with her shiny wild eyes.

"I don't have a library card," she said, and added, "and I don't have any ID on me."

The librarian gazed at her with a strange look of wisdom. She padded over behind the front desk, and took out some paperwork.

"Just give me your name and address," she said.

Shaye bit her lip, taking the forms while juggling the books that she wanted. She carefully wrote out the name of Frank Danielo's wife- Lorrine Danielo. She didn't really know if Danny would appreciate the humor. She'd find out soon enough, for she *had* to contact him now. She had to hope that he would trust her information, for she had no way to contact silversmiths in a remote Mexican village. But the police department could. Records that were not available to her, for example the names of men who had legally immigrated to America from that region, would be easy for Danielo to find. Maybe even the names of every man born there.

Shaye had to hope.

The librarian offered to drive Shaye home. Shaye wriggled around with confusion. It was hard for her to trust anyone. On the other hand she was carrying about thirty pounds of books, the night was starless and dark and then there was that derelict crouching by the canal at the crime scene. She didn't know whether Danielo and Chow had gone to Caiman St. and removed him, or maybe Danny had simply ignored her call.

The librarian ran her silver Toyota Camray at the curb, with the door held open and the smell of vanilla wafting out.

"Lorrine," she said. "I'd feel better driving you. I don't know if you've heard about it, but there's been a serial killer right in the area where you live. It certainly scares me!" Shaye still hesitated. "Really," the librarian said. "I won't sleep tonight if I don't know you got home safely."

Shaye's heart tumbled, another go round of the roller coaster-fear, then the easing of fear. A danger, then a savior. One long endless night that never seemed to end.

She swung her books into the backseat and climbed into the comfortable car.

The librarian waved a friendly goodbye as Shaye disembarked at a random trailer she had selected further down her street, nearer Spoonbill, just as a precaution to hide her true identity. As Susan Hall drove off, Shaye could see the cheerful lights of her own trailer home peeking out from the patio greenery further down the street.

She hoisted her books up, and stepped off the grass curb onto the dust to walk the half block necessary, examining the shadowed greenery on both sides of the road just to be safe. The trailer she had selected to pretend was hers was abandoned, and now Shaye heard an aluminum door creak. She upped her pace, not running, but briskly race-walking until she had gained her own yard. Shaye stood by the banana tree, squinting back out at the street.

And then eyes peered around the tree and stared at her.

Shaye gasped.

It was the derelict again. The black man with the mechanic's coveralls that she had tried to get thrown in jail this morning. He leered at her, with very white teeth- probably false- showing in his dark complexion and he wheezed with an old rural man's laughter, his arms filled with trash.

"So, you don't like me much. Huh, Chickadee?" He sniggered and laughed again as Shaye shrank back half inside the tree. It was hard to tell if he was laughing or choking. "You sent dem cops on me, today. I know it was you, Chickadee. Just havin' my morning coffee, I was, peaceful as anything in my new spot. And then dem cops come rollin' up, right after I seen you." He raised his voice in ire. "Now you tell me dat ain't no coincidence!"

Shaye cleared her throat and found her voice. She could have run for the trailer, yet she found she was becoming tired of always running.

"Yes, I sent the police," she said. "You said something, as I was leaving, about knowing something about the crime. I thought they should ask you some questions."

The derelict grinned like a demon, using his bright white teeth to rip into some food he had collected in his armful. After taking a satisfying bite, he allowed self-satisfied laughter to intersperse with his exaggerated chewing.

Then he pointed, with long nail and swollen knuckle, right at Shaye's trailer. "They lookin' for some funny bizness in Flamingo Park, they need go no futha than this here mobile home."

"That's the last place they should go!" Shaye asserted, feeling her skin crawl at the scent of the man on the breeze, a scent similar to that of the garbage he always collected. She feared germs, bacteria or pests that his unfortunate living habits might make him carry. But she also feared turning her back.

The derelict ignored her assertion. "Mens dressed as wimin. That type o' thing. Funny biznis, I say."

Madness seemed to swirl around Shaye's head like some celestial corona in the Florida darkness. It seemed to buzz just like the electrical transformer above Darlene's trailer did right now, just perceivable.

Shaye sighed. "Lifestyle is not a crime - any more than yours is," she said, genuinely wanting to placate the man. "But what was it that you saw down at the crime scene, please? It's really important. Did you tell the police today?"

"No ma'am. I didn't tell them police nuthin. The fuzz. The pigs. The man. They don't care bout nuthin but puttin' some homeless veteran in prison!" He spat down at the sidewalk, revoltingly.

Shaye's stomach lurched, and she had to take a step back. The derelict didn't seem to notice her discomfort. Instead, he set his trash almost lovingly on the ground, like a little shaped nest, and he pulled up an upended cinderblock to take a seat.

He looked up at Shaye with moist eyes that shone in the flickering streetlight. "Officer Glenn Chow," he said, "comes out swingin' his handcuffs, wanna read me my rights. Then Officer Danny says, 'No, lets offer this boy some money, tell us what he saw.' Well, I don' need they filthy money!"

He spat into the grass again, and Shaye had to shake off gooseflesh that sprung up all over her body. "But you want to tell me?"

"Thas right, Chickadee."

"*Why?*" Shaye couldn't help asking.

The man rubbed his hands on his uniform pants and gave an obscure answer.

"You remind me of some of my buddies back in the war- back in 'Nam. You got crazy eyes like those guys- eyes lookin' all every which way. But you know evil when you see it. And you hate evil! You want ta stop it..."

Shaye felt like the air was pushed out of herself. She trembled, yet she felt quite brave. Without moving too much to spook him, she gently lowered her stack of books onto another cinderblock.

"Did you see the killer?" she asked baldly.

The derelict bobbed his head, first one direction, then the other. "Yes an no," he said. "I seen Mami Ramierez every day, Chickadee. I seen her back six years ago when she was all raggedy, turnin' tricks in this park..."

Shaye nodded as they both stopped for an interruption, a woman screaming in the trailer across the street. "Well, if you don't want your goddamn dinner, take it on your head then!" They heard a thump, a crash and a scuffle and then heard a man's voice roar. But nothing disturbed them in their little jungle oasis of evil tales where they sat.

"She went away for a long time- in rehab or somethin'," the derelict continued. Then I seen Mami come back aroun', actin' all high and mighty."

"What do you mean?" Shaye asked.

"She workin' at some job in town, dressin' pretty, tryin' to look just like some white woman. All the time, right before she died, I seen her walkin' aroun' this park *with her boyfriend*!"

"Her *what*?" Shaye stuttered.

The man suddenly looked up at her like an afterthought. "You got some food?" he asked. "I like hot dogs and taters, little bit o' ketchup. Coffee. Maybe some beans. Good food a man can make over a campfire."

Shaye saw his sincerity and she felt sorry for him. Giving him food wouldn't really help, because it would promote his terrible lifestyle. Yet, what could it hurt?

"I'll give you all our food," Shaye said. "When we get done talking. I'll give you a few more dollars for the store also."

"How about whiskey?" he asked. "You got that?"

Shaye felt her world seem to tilt again. She so hated to be a party to things that weren't right. But she needed this man's information. She sensed she was closing in on the truth and that she still had the chance to save innocent lives. Anyway, maybe giving their booze away would stop Adam's aggravating entertaining.

"You know what," Shaye said. "I don't drink. But we might have some liquor in the house. You can wait outside and I'll bring whatever I can find out to you. Now you need to tell me why you think you saw Mami Ramierez with a boyfriend. How can you tell that it wasn't just a…" She hesitated, not knowing how to put the concept delicately. "A business customer?"

The derelict smiled to himself. "He weren't no customer, Chickadee. Not that one. Walked around with that handsome face, and them lizard boots, carryin' them gardin tools. Chased me off my canal more than once, that one did. Thinks he some Spanish prince, and Mami his lady now. Like they own the place. Playin' aroun' down by my little canal. They go on that way coupla months. And then she dead."

Shaye was compelled to pull up a block at his level, although she sat back far enough not to be touched by his eagerly flying spittle.

"Okay," she said, breathlessly. "You're sure he was her boyfriend?"

"Sure walked aroun' like he was."

"How old was he?" Shaye asked.

"Older than her."

"Thirties?"

"Older than that. Forty, more likely. Good condition, though. Got dem eagle eyes."

This man had a lot to say about eyes. Shaye's were crazy, in his opinion. So were the killer's. Nice, she thought.

"Eagle eyes? Dark, you mean? Intent?"

The derelict nodded.

"Was he Hispanic then? Dark complexion? What exactly did he look like?"

"Lotsa Mexicans, Guatemalans 'roun this park," the man answered obliquely. "They all dark skin, slump shoulders. Little men. Walk around wi' they heads down mosta the time. Not this guy. He stand tall. Pressed pants, shined up boots. He come over an' cover up my campfire. Throws dirt all over it wi' a spade. Then stands there like the devil. Mami standin' behin' him, tellin' me he's gonna own the land, and I better take a hike."

"He owned the land?" Shaye almost squealed.

The derelict gave a giggle. "Don' own nuthin' now. Cops roped the motha off. Now it's only here for me and dead people!"

He was lost for a while in paroxysms of his personal amusement.

Shaye had to interrupt him. "Do you think he owned it?"

"Don' think so," he said. "Not really. For like a week or so, I didn't see him an' Mami together no more. Saw him only once. Showed up like a ghost, gave me a bad look, me campin' at the lot again. He looked bad that time wearin' a T-shirt, and all beardy. Looked different."

"Did you know his name?" Shaye thought to ask.

He shook his head. "No, ma'am."

Her mind swirled, as she glanced toward her books and back. Her suspect was Mexican. There had to be a way all of this tied in.

"This man," she said. "This boyfriend. He didn't act like the other Hispanics, you said. But could he have been Hispanic? Any chance he could have been Mexican?"

The derelict sighed. "Didn' talk wi' no accent. Talked all high an' mighty- kinda like you."

Shaye took a breath, perhaps ready to protest, but he continued. "He was real careful wi his words, though- talkin' slow an careful- and loud. Yeah, he looked white, but he coulda been an immigrant."

He started wheezing with laughter again and rubbed at his face to stop himself.

"What's funny?" Shaye asked, almost in a whisper.

"If he really a Mexican, pretending to be American. Served Mami right, maybe. Mami came back off drugs an she thought she was too good for dark men anymore!"

Shaye stepped indoors, where Adam had kindly left an incandescent light on. She had left her new friend, Willie Jeremiah he had told her his name was- Willie from the name on his coveralls- and Jeremiah for the prophet- out at the curb, while she scrounged for food for him.

She walked out juggling a flashlight, and a bag brimful with groceries. She had also included a blanket. He took the gifts and, as an afterthought, Shaye handed him the flashlight, as well.

"You can probably use this," she said. "On a dark night like this."

They looked at each other strangely and then finally Willie hung his head, like he had said the beaten immigrant men did.

"You need to find Mami's boyfriend, Chickadee," he said.

"Why?" Shaye asked again, softly. "Why me?"

When the strange derelict Willie looked up, his eyes were wet. "'Cause the man knows where I live. He knows I seen him wi Mami. And I think he's coming back…"

Without another word, Willie turned, straightened his shoulders and shuffled back onto Manatee St. He was headed right back in the direction of Caiman.

Chapter 12

Frank Danielo picked up when Shaye rang their private cell phone- and said nothing.

"Hi," Shaye said.

She could hear him breathing, and she knew he knew it was her. But he continued to play possum.

Shaye sighed. "Okay, so let's pretend last night in our trailer never happened. It was a bad dream, whatever. But you need to come over again tonight- now! There are some things in some books I have to show you, Danny. I know much more about the case now, about the murder weapon and the man that it was made for. And I need you now. You have to do the police work. And you'll find him this time; I swear you will."

Now, Danny snickered. It made Shaye jump, because the sound was so intimate it seemed like he was right in the room with her.

"So you've found the killer," he said. "Who, Shaye? Stinkin' ole Willie Jeremiah? You managed to find him?"

Anger rose up through Shaye's face. She felt herself flush. Perversely, she felt like she could sob. She used her hands to try to articulate, tucking the cell phone between shoulder and chin. There were a million things she could have said, but she chose to put the good of the many ahead of the good of the few- or the one.

"Please, Danny," she said, in an intense whisper. "Please- did you see my computer simulations of the murder weapon? I know where the weapon came from now- the exact town in Mexio. Please, come over..."

She waited through another long silence, broken by a sound that seemed like ex-smoker Danny lighting a cigarette. He gave a little cough, and a little chuckle.

"Fine," he said. "Fine. I'll be over. Princess Shaye's wish is my command."

Shaye didn't know why, but for some reason she began to shiver after she hung up the phone. Real shivers, with her teeth chattering and all. She padded around the trailer quickly, looking hopefully for Adam, even though she knew he would have come to the door earlier when she came in to collect the food if he was around. She hoped he'd left her a note. Maybe one saying that he was planning to get home early tonight. But there was no such thing.

Shaye hurried into her own bedroom, where she'd left the light off, to vigilantly check the back window and the back yard. Then she retrieved a charcoal gray fleece hoodie that she had purchased at the thrift shop.

She snuggled into it, wrapping it tight over her breasts and her T-shirt and folding her arms. Her bare legs remained gooseflesh covered as she padded, in her Keds, once again across the trailer. She'd wait in Adam's room, she decided, where she had a better idea what was going on in the street.

Again, preferring to see out, rather than letting others peek in, Shaye left the lamps off. The glow from the living room end table lamps was enough for Shaye to find the bed, and a jersey shirt from Adam's male wardrobe that he had left on the bed. She imagined him in the process of getting dressed and Rochelle outside in her Escort, responding to Madeline's urging and leaning on the horm. Adam, who usually took the time to meticulously put everything away would have scampered to finish getting dressed in his diva's costume, leaving this little relic of his maleness abandoned as he hurried off.

Shaye cherished it. Like a puppy left behind with a blanket, she tucked it up under her chin, inhaling Adam's cool fresh scent that smelled like faraway oceans. Lovely young Adam, who had named himself after the first man on the earth, her friend and her savior. She wished so he was here with her right now.

For some reason, the prospect of being alone with Frank Danielo made her nervous. She'd never felt that way about him before. In fact, she'd been pretty fearless when it came to manipulating Danny. But now something seemed to press on her, something about being alone in the night.

Shaye lay back on the bed, kneading the fabric of Adam's jersey between tense fingers and thinking. She had no idea how long had passed before she heard the weight of a vehicle bump over the border of dirt and grass into her yard. She sprang up and tiptoed in front of the miniature window to see Danny's patrol car turning into their driveway with all the lights out.

She took a hesitant breath.

That was strange. Why the patrol car, she wondered, rather than his personal car. And why the secrecy of all the lights out? He jounced along, and she heard the squad car going all the way back, stopping in back of the trailer, where the bad septic left the yard spongy. Why there, Danny, she wondered. She knew he was hiding the fact he was here from any curious neighbors. But then why bring the squad car at all?

In the moments that she waited for him to arrive Shaye, plastered up against the front wall in hiding, let a million thoughts rush through her mind for consideration. Maybe this mysterious officer wasn't Frank Danielo at all. Maybe it was someone else-someone she should fear.

Or maybe Danny's wife had needed their car tonight and he had just let her take it so as not to seem suspicious. After all, he wasn't going to take Lorrine on this errand. Shaye felt a strange feeling of shame swell in her throat. She and Danny were truly more than just partners in an investigation, she knew. They had never touched, but anyone seeing the way Danny looked at her, especially his wife, would think they had already done much more than that.

They had shared extraordinary intimacies together. But a different kind of intimacy. Shaye hated herself for her own fevered imaginings. For a crazy second she imagined Danny taking her into his arms, rubbing his warm commanding hands up and down her cool flanks. She imagined him burying his face in the warm nest underneath her hair and murmuring, "I love you." She imagined him possessing her, not saying a word, simply laying her down on the floor and entering her, making every single one of her fears go away, including her fear of him.

Shaye panted with her own lurid fantasy that felt like it was choking her and then she seized with fear when Danny pounded on the door. The entire wall shook. A whole other part of her, one she didn't even know she possessed, made her run for the kitchen to retrieve the butcher knife.

"Shaye Celestia Taylor," Danny bellowed in a deep voice, "Police! Open the door or I'll break it down."

Shaye regained her hiding place behind the door while Danny yelled and pounded. She could tell by the darkness and aggression in his voice that he wasn't joking. He wanted to hurt her. Was he actually trying to arrest her? She didn't know. She doubted that. Did he think *she* was the serial killer because of her obsession? Or even poor Adam?

She heard Danny insert a pry bar and the metal door squealed as he attempted to work it. There was no way out of here except past him. But she liked to think she had just a few IQ points on Danny. He'd run for the bedrooms and every hiding place, like a dark Spanish bull looking for his red cape.

Meanwhile Shaye would simply slip out. Where to then? First, she could run through Darlene's back yard and she could cut through the woods. She could even wade through the canal on Caiman- the same canal that, not long ago, drained away Elvira Ramierez's blood. Then, if she could get to a telephone in cover of night, she'd call Foxy Lady. Rochelle would be willing to pick her up, and maybe even drive her and Adam to North Miami if she had to. Then Adam's friend Jeff would hide them, as they'd planned all along. All Shaye knew was that she had to get out of here and get to Adam before Danny got to him.

Dread knotted Shaye's stomach as she wondered if Danny already had Adam...

And the door burst in. It fell down into living room and Danielo, wearing black combat boots, tromped on it. Shaye instinctively flattened in her hiding spot as Danny stormed around in circles, with his voice gravelly and slurred with alcohol, yelling for her. He swung a large black automatic rifle.

"Shaye! Shaye Celestial Banks Taylor," he intoned. "Twenty-four years old. Born in Westchester, New York. Mother- Lucille Banks- homemaker and socialite. Father- Brian Banks- venture capitalist..."

He swung the gun again, swaying on his feet, and it looked as though he was looking directly at her. But he didn't seem to see.

"Shaye Taylor. Depressed. Paranoid schizophrenic," his voice hammered on. "Wanted by the New York State Police for escape from a State Mental Hospital. Also for kidnapping, and endangering the welfare of two other patients, one underage... Yes, that's right, Shaye, Baby," he hollered. "I've got five individual felony counts against you, and a warrant out of New York for your arrest..."

Danny laughed and Shaye felt like holding her ears as the trailer echoed with his noise. She didn't want to cut him with the butcher knife, but she'd have to if he tried to grab her. She looked directly into the shadowed eyes of the man she cared about- and felt betrayed. In fact, this betrayal hurt so much more deeply than when her husband had done it that it almost felt bittersweet.

Danny still didn't see her. Crouching, he slunk toward the back corridor, heading for her room.

Shaye took the chance to run and she almost made it, but then he swung toward her. "Dammit," he mumbled. Shaye got as far as the wide-open doorway, when Danny swung the butt of the gun and thumped her in the side of her head.

The impact knocked Shaye down the metal stairs, where her hands scraped along the concrete to keep her face from hitting. Danny immediately grabbed her by her long hair and bodily lifted her back up the stairs and into the trailer. No one from outside had seen anything.

Shaye tried to squirm free, but Danny climbed on top of her back, crushing her with what felt like enormous weight. He painfully locked her hands behind her back and snapped them into handcuffs. Then he dragged her back further, scraping her upturned chin against the gritty carpet. He dragged her until he was able to prop the broken front door back over the doorway.

Then he used a toe of his combat boot to roll her onto her back.

Shaye gasped as she squinted at him in his demented combination of dress and SWAT uniforms, with parts of the clothes unfastened. He set down the assault rifle to rest against the couch.

"You're under arrest, Shaye Taylor for escape, kidnapping, endangering the welfare of a minor..."

He droned on, and Shaye could smell the alcohol wafting off of him.

She knew a lot about cops from all she had read during her confinement and she didn't believe a single thing about this arrest. Danny wasn't even on duty tonight. Yes, he had clearly found out about the charges against her. But she was sure no one else in his department knew anything about it. She was also pretty sure they had no idea where their squad car was, or the location of seriously intoxicated Flamingo Park cop Frank Danielo, for that matter.

"You're under arrest," he repeated again, with a self-important hiccup.

They faced each other down. Shaye's eyes didn't flinch, except when she followed his, to glance down at the shiny butcher knife she had dropped.

His handsome face glowed; his eyes twinkled. "Add some more charges for tonight. Assault on a law enforcement officer," he said, pointing to the knife. "Resisting arrest. Attempted *murder* of a law enforcement officer."

Shaye's voice came out a little trembly. Maybe the blow to her head had done something. But she still sounded more rational and assertive than he did.

"That's not playing fair, Danny," she said, in a cross between humoring him and despising him.

Danielo lowered himself on the couch, leaned his head all the way back, sighed and then leaned forward to stare at her. "Life's not fair, Shaye. Haven't you learned that yet?"

"I thought you were fair," Shaye said, before she could stop herself.

Danny shook his head sadly.

"And I thought you were beautiful," he said. He looked pointedly at her golden hair spread under and around her on the floor. "And I still do." He said it regretfully, like she was already dead.

Shaye struggled to a sitting position, uncomfortable under his stare as Danny switched a light back on.

"How did you find out about me?" she asked.

"It was as easy as running your name, Baby," Danielo said. "After seeing the *Tropical Sun* catalog, I checked for outstanding warrants on you. I always suspected something, Shaye, since I first got a glimpse of gorgeous you outside this pitiful trailer. I guess I just never actually wanted to know the truth."

Shaye tried to read his expression in the pale incandescent light.

"It's not what it looks like, Danny," she said. "I know you're fundamentally an honest cop. And none of those charges against me are what they seem. Adam and I were just trying to do a good deed, helping the others. Eric Watson was sixteen years old, and one of the staff members at the State Hospital had been sexually assaulting him. Adam and I always liked to plot to escape on our own. But it was just talk, though, just pie-in-the-sky. And then Eric begged us to help him. Della, too. And we felt we couldn't turn them away."

Danny just stared, bemusedly, and Shaye couldn't read his expression at all.

"We actually plan to turn ourselves in, Danny. In a few months, when Adam can afford a lawyer. Those charges won't come out as felonies. Maybe misdemeanors. Maybe nothing. In my case, the doctors were making all kinds of medical errors. They did repeated unnecessary surgeries, and almost cost me my life. And when I protested, they medicated me so I was helpless. And no one would stand up for me back then, not even my own parents..."

Shaye couldn't believe it, but she started crying. Silent sheets of tears ran down her cheeks, chin and neck, drenching the front of her T-shirt. But Danny still gazed at her, looking impassive and stoic.

Slowly, he got to his feet. He reached out for her moist cheeks and her heart leapt. Maybe he was taking pity. Instead, he crouched beside her and shook his head.

"Maybe it's like those she-males said, Shaye. You're always looking for some man to save you. Your buddy Adam Underwood wants to save you. With all his money... That's right, Shaye," he answered her curious eyes. "I know that your little roommate's an even bigger wacko than you are. Little queer son of a bitch, but I bet he'll spend all of his five million dollars trying to get you a lawyer..."

Shaye's jaw dropped. "*Five million?*"

Danny tightened the corners of his mouth and smirked. "Like you didn't know."

She shook her head slowly. "I didn't, Danny. Honest. I knew Adam was supposed to take over the family business and that he had trust funds but... no... I didn't."

Danny nodded slowly. Then he took back Shaye's hair and fisted it behind her head with the liberty of a caveman. "Well, now you do know," he said. "Now you'll really run to choose him over me."

"Danny," Shaye whispered hectically, trying to roll her eyes in her stretched forehead so she could properly see him. "Please. I don't even know what you want from me. But please let me show you my library books. I found out that the murder weapon probably came from the Santasemana Mountain Region of Central Mexico. You need to find an elder silversmith, who forged that hand rake in the shape of a rooster's claw. And then find the man he sold it to. And then you'll probably find that man in Flamingo Park right now, Danny. And he's the killer. Not Byron Hanes and Troy Reid."

Danielo let her hair go. He sat down beside her on the floor and shucked his bulletproof vest. He crawled closer and washed her with the reek of liquor. Then he started up a cigarette, throwing the spent match on the carpet. "I already know those guys didn't do it, Baby. I know everything," he slurred. "I chased down your little derelict by the Caiman St. canal today. Wise-ass stinkpot phony veteran. And then I found out Hanes and Reid have an alibi for the first murder. Pretty airtight. And pretty fuckin' disgusting also."

Shaye looked up with interest, hanging on his every word. Danny sighed, pulling at the cigarette philosophically.

"Shaye, on the day Mami Ramierez was killed, Troy Reid had to take his little fourteen-year old sister into Orlando for an abortion."

Shaye's jaw dropped further. Danny offered her a drag of the cigarette and Shaye recoiled.

"That's your call if you don't want to have a smoke now," he said. "I just figured it'll be a long night for you after I take you to jail."

Shaye stuck out her jaw in a try at mirthful defiance. "You're not going to arrest me. You're bluffing."

"We'll see," Danny said ominously. Then he continued. "Anyway, you see, Troy Reid was the baby's father."

"What?" Shaye gasped, although no sound came out.

"That's why he didn't tell nobody at first. But anyway, those two little pricks sat in an Orlando abortion clinic all day. Then Heather Reid had complications, so they waited in the Orlando Regional Emergency Room most of the night. I checked on all of this, Shaye. Even come morning, the two punks had alibis all along I-4- car trouble, harassing people, pissing on convenience store gas pumps and getting chased away. They couldn't have designed it better to make a cop look like an asshole…"

Danny gazed at Shaye and she saw how his eyes looked glazed, ready to cry for himself.

"Does Mayor Walker know this yet? Does Glenn Chow know? Danny- does your own partner know that those two were a dead end and the real killer's still out there? Is anybody even looking right now?"

Danny crushed out his cigarette on the carpet inches from Shaye's thigh. He threw back his head into Shaye's lap and he sputtered with laughter.

"*You're* looking. You, Baby. My little paranoid schizophrenic bikini model." Danny rolled to his stomach, propping himself on his elbows. He pushed Shaye down so he could crawl up and gaze into her face.

Drunkenly, he tried to make his eyes meet hers. "Do you know I hate you right now, Shaye? Do you know I hate you 'cause I can't have you? I guess you're used to that, though..."

"That's not fair..." Shaye tried to say.

Danny caught her by the back of the neck in an iron grip and he gave her a small shake to get her attention. "I'm taking you to jail tonight, Shaye, unless you convince me not to."

Sudden terror made Shaye silent. Was there once a time when she used to be a reckless siren? At age sixteen Shaye could prance around and entertain an entire reserved dance club with a pole dance done on a dare. At sixteen and a half she was able to seduce a jaded thirty-six year old husband, who'd joked he'd turn her away if he ever spotted another model or starlet who could make him hornier.

Now, at twenty four, inches away from the guy who excited her more than any man ever had, all Shaye could do was leak stinging urine into her plain white Dollar Store panties bought by her roommate in a pack of six. She couldn't even remember how to smile. Her lips were dry and cracked. Shaye, who had grown up on makeup, was now a virgin of it for almost two years and her skin was pale and cool.

Danny peeled back her gray hoodie from the thrift shop. Then he used the butcher knife to slit down the center of her favorite T-shirt with the cartoon shark, and through the middle of her old pink bra.

Shaye's voluptuous breasts dropped out and he gazed at them, letting the knife drop.

Her eyes leaked tears.

"Would it matter if I told you that I liked you?" Shaye said. "That I really considered you my friend?" She gulped as Danny climbed out of his uniform shirt and pants, huffing out big liquor-scented breaths. He approached on his knees, wearing pale blue boxer briefs that showed off his tight hairy body and his big hard-on.

Shaye lay there on the golden puddle of her hair, sobbing out loud now. Danny crawled up to her. He crawled up to her face.

"I can't trust you, Shaye," he said. "And you can't trust me." He pushed forward more, bumping against her shoulder with that part of his body she didn't want to think about. "I won't make you fuck me tonight, Shaye. Just blow me. Just blow me and then we're even. I'll let you and Adam go on your way."

He bumped her again, for her attention. Shaye turned his way, the tears dried up. Danny's eyes looked moist as well.

"Why, Danny?" she breathed, hardly able to gasp out the words.

His reply came out not much stronger. "So I can say I made somebody famous do it."

"But I'm not famous anymore. You know my life is destroyed."

"I guess that's why," he said, tremulously. "So I can make *you* do it."

They continued to stare at each other. Danny took his hard penis out, holding it in his hand and readying it.

Shaye didn't bother to look at it, just continued to stare at the eyes that she'd never be able to forget.

"I can't, Danny," she said, finally. "I can't. Shoot me, arrest me. Do whatever you have to do. But I can't do it."

"Adam will go back to jail, also. Both of you will rot in the mental hospital. You especially, Shaye."

Shaye turned her head away.

"Do what you've gotta do," she whispered.

Danny stayed above her, staring, for a very long time. But Shaye didn't move. Her body froze on itself, and she went very very far away- back to the home of her girlhood, of twittering birds and collector Barbie dolls and Mommy and Daddy giving her bouquets of white and pink roses, almost too big for her to hold up, after she won every Little Miss Beauty Pageant.

Shaye remembered the songs and the ballet shoes, and the powdered stage floors, and the glare of stage lights and camera flashes making her little eyes tear, just like they did now. Just like now.

Frank Danielo abruptly turned and vomited on the carpet beside her, and then he crawled to his feet. He abandoned his jacket and bulletproof vest, his favorite black leather belt and the pack of cigarettes he had bought tonight. And he threw the handcuff keys down in front of Shaye's unblinking long lashes.

Then he shut out the light and lurched out the corner of the propped-up door. As an afterthought, he staggered back in to retrieve both his guns and Shaye's butcher knife and then she heard him drive away. Shaye's eyes stayed open and her lips stayed parted, seeming to smile perfectly- and she held the pose in total stillness. Just like a little beauty contest winner she used to be.

Chapter 13

After he left the trailer Frank Danielo's squad car slipped slowly through Flamingo Park with no headlights, shadowed by the cavern of overhanging foliage that waved in a turbulent wind. The wheels seemed to splay and slip on the muddy dirt track near Caiman St., while the officer behind the wheel hunched over drunkenly, mumbling into his car phone and paying no attention to driving.

Suddenly, a long-haired woman rushed out of the bushes straight at him. Danny hit the brakes and the car stopped, yet slid, guaging even deeper tracks in the red mud. The young woman, dressed in a tight white pleather mini and matching midriff top, flung herself onto the hood of the car reaching for Danny, as though for his help. She was slender and long snaky strands of her glossy black hair pasted themselves all over the windshield. Danny saw her frightened doe eyes, and her plump lips greasy with smudged bright red lipstick.

The woman was a hooker, and she was crying.

"Help me!" she cried. "Officer, please help me."

Shaye lay on the floor for hours, with the torn open doorway admitting a restless breeze. The breeze carried away the sounds of her gentle singing to herself, just like all the songs of yesterday- Shaye's days of glory.

Somewhere in all of it, she broke free from her spell, and raised herself slowly and gracefully to her feet. First, she lifted up the broken door, pushing the bent hinges back into place with an urgent strength that did not seem her own. She tightened the pins efficiently with a screwdriver left from a previous tenant.

Then Shaye helped herself to a small swig of Adam's Scotch out of a coffee mug. She had decided not to set Willie Jeremiah up with liquor earlier, so they still had the bottle. Now it scorched going down into her compromised stomach. Shaye's liver was compromised after her illness and she had been told that, in this lifetime, she could never safely drink again.

Not that she cared. Back in her club-hopping days she was just a pawn for others, after all. And Shaye had never really even liked drinking. It was just something all the popular fashion and showbiz people had done. But now Adam kept her safe, kept her away from all the dangerous things.

Anyway, she just took a little fortifying sip.

Coffee, the vice that she preferred, would have driven her into screaming madness right now. The Scotch, however, managed to settle her. She took one more stinging sip, placed the mug gently down in the stainless steel sink, and went into the cabinet underneath to prepare for her next task- big yellow plastic cleaning gloves. Shaye knelt down in the living room and cleaned up Frank Danielo's vomit.

She gathered together her torn shark T-shirt and her bra and she deposited them in her bedroom. She also hid away the set of handcuffs and key that Danielo had left, feeling that they might be of use to her somehow.

Shaye spun on her heels in the center of the room a few times, feeling disoriented. But then her bearings came to her again. Right now there were things she felt she had to do, and she didn't want Adam to find out what had happened here tonight until she was ready to tell him.

Shaye dropped her shorts and panties and the sweater she had gathered around her. Leaving the bedroom dark, she stepped into the bathroom shower stall to wash the indignities of the evening from her body. Washing off like a rape victim, washing for an hour even though Danny hadn't actually physically violated her.

But he *had* hurt her. In the end, it was not the microbes, not her illness, not even the serial killer, but the man that she cared for that had done this.

She listened to the mournful and turbulent sounds of Flamingo Park that carried over the rush of water over her body. She knew the killer was near, and she knew even more surely that she would be the one confronting him alone. Sure, Danny might come around again in the end. But it didn't matter. For Shaye understood now that this had become her personal battle.

Byron Hanes and Troy Reid hadn't done the killing. The man with the silver rooster's claw had. And the crimes were just too sinister for police like Danielo and Chow to take care of. Shaye understood, deep in her gut, that the curse was on her, the compromised one.

Shaye experienced a strange hour in the coffin-like shower that she had kept darkened, breathing in the scent of hot sulfurous well water as it sluiced over her. Her hands slid over her body in mesmerized respect- finding her skin fantastically silky, her breasts, though no longer perfect, still surprisingly firm, her nipples standing up pertly like something had woken them up tonight. Did they sense danger? Or challenge? Or just something humorous?

Shaye grunted out a solitary laugh and ran her palm over their hardness with a stranger's curiosity. One in a million she was, with her looks; that was what the statistics said. In fact, Shaye had been blessed with everything in life. A beautiful only child, slim strong and athletic. Cheerleader, tennis team, junior prom queen. She'd slept in a room decorated with wall murals of springtime, and a fat red-bellied robin perching on a nest. It was Shaye's fantasy room and her parents had commissioned a local artist to paint it.

Little Shaye Celestia Banks had slept peacefully under Robin Redbreast while the whole world strained and quarreled. She received kisses from her parents when they returned late at night from their charity galas. First her mother with her smell of Chanel No. 5 whispering, "I love you more than anything, Shaye." Then her father, loosening his bowtie, repeating the same exact words, completely unrehearsed.

Bouquets of her mom's prize roses were placed on Shaye's bedside table every single day of spring, every day a different color. The only thing her socialite mother consistently worked to do.

Was that life real? Really hers?

Shaye recalled losing her virginity at age fourteen and a half. She was traveling on her own for the first time as one of the finalists in a teen beauty pageant in Aruba. The boy was French, literally descended from French Colonial Royalty who still owned an exotic palace in Morocco. Shaye had loved his accent, and the way he brought her out on his father's private yacht, just the two of them. She'd always remember the feel of that private midnight cruise, standing together on the deck, while wind snapped in her billowy couture gauze skirt.

Afterwards, she and the teenaged Moroccan prince had returned to her private room, opened the terrace doors and lit scented candles all over the room. She remembered the handsome boy piercing her virgin insides and, surprisingly, it had hurt. And now that memory of that mysterious and surprising hurt that she felt deep inside that night, squeezing her eyes shut, was like the key to everything. For now everything felt like that pain- mysterious and so deep inside.

Shaye felt like howling with the pain now- pain she still couldn't understand.

She remembered her dark-haired teenaged prince scattering flower petals all through her golden hair afterward, sighing and swearing his undying love, wanting her to run away and marry him in his country.

But she had demurred and had returned home after the pageant, tanned and tired. For Shaye had always preferred safety to wild things. When she disembarked from her limo, her father had swung her around in the driveway. Then her reticent mother had joined the embrace with happy tears in her eyes, with a sprig of purple irises clutched in one hand.

Both smiled and gushed, with no clue that their precious daughter had sexually compromised herself on her adventure. For, of course, they only knew the headlines. Shaye had triumphed once again; winning the beauty contest for America.

As they greeted her, Shaye had smiled at the sight of the sprawling three-story house that she had missed so much, even while recalling the exotic locale she had traveled to and her first taste of illicit romance. And her parents had hurried to the limo to retrieve her bags, bags heavy with all the upscale island treasures and trinkets she had purchased on their credit card. And they were genuinely happy for her.

Later, Shaye's girlfriends, all the most popular and pretty in her private high school, had gasped with envy when she told them the true story of her adventure with an actual prince. Then she confided that she hadn't thought to use birth control- and they had shivered. That could be disaster. But nothing bad ended up happening. Not to Shaye Celestia Banks. For nothing bad ever happened to her when she was young. She was one in a million.

So was the deadly e-coli. A strain that even the scientists knew nothing about until it made its first appearance in Shaye and several other victims. Literally, the chances of contracting this particular strain were one in hundreds of millions, they said almost gloatingly as they poked and prodded her and invaded her body with needles and scalpels and tubes. Only five people in the Americas had been infected during the Gulfport outbreak. In the space of two weeks, four were dead. From that point on Shaye Banks Taylor was no longer stared at for her beauty. Jaws no longer dropped for that. Now she was famous for quite a different reason. Lost in the bedclothes of a remote University Hospital ICU, secreted away from the public behind layers of sterile plastic, Shaye received a different kind of stare.

She was glassed in, like in the bottom of a fishbowl. Monitors and live video feeds ran on her all day. The pitiful fluids she excreted were displayed high up, in clear plastic bags for all the world to see. But no one touched Shaye anymore. They simply stared. When she cracked her eyes, unsticking the long false lashes from layers of crusty mucus, she saw a gallery of curious eyes staring in.

The isolation ICU was like science fiction. The most sinister place in the world. Or, was it another world, she wondered. The life support machines breathed like hissing monsters and she was surrounded by a deep cold that she would never forget. A cold that approximated the cold of death. And then, where night and day were no different, and days blended together, visitors arrived, a team from the Centers for Disease Control, in white crinkly plastic suits with spaceman heads. Shaye attempted to smile at them. Within their plastic bubble heads, she watched human faces gape at her body that had become skeletal in the space of days.

She saw a strange terror in their eyes, perhaps even worse than the terror she felt for herself. She heard them communicate to each other through metallic sounding walkie-talkies inside their suits.

"She's one in a hundred million!" one of the doctors said.

Another shook their bulbous, suited head. "She shouldn't be alive. The others all died so quickly." Shaye heard a sigh. "Every minute she lives from this point on makes her more extraordinary- she'll go down in the record books."

The five doctors shook their swollen plastic-covered heads and the one closest drew some thick blackish blood from Shaye's ankle. "I doubt she'll last the night," he said dispassionately.

Shaye swung her eyes up to the gallery of unlookers- young residents in blue scrubs and poufy blue beret hats. She swore they seemed to step back when they saw her looking. In a last attempt at seeking human comfort, Shaye extended a blue and veiny hand toward one of the doctors- one that seemed young and female- perhaps her own age. She tried to touch the doctor's heavy white rubber glove. But the hand recoiled. The doctors retreated. And she was left with the sounds of the steadily beeping machines.

She thought she could still hear them in her head now.

Shaye finished washing off her body. She finished drying it carefully, inhaling the detergent scented cleanliness of her towel.

She kept it dark, and she didn't know if she could face her own room, or the living room, ever again.

Instead, she headed straight for Adam's bedroom. She slipped into the jersey that she had been cuddling earlier. It felt like the rest of tonight could've all been a bad dream. She made just one more stop in the kitchen to retrieve a fresh butcher knife. Then she cuddled down with it in Adam's bed and went to sleep.

Adam came home only twenty minutes later- early by Foxy Lady standards. He smiled when he saw Shaye in his bed, and he turned on one of the warm incandescent lights on his dresser to remove his makeup and his work costume.

In the mirror he then caught the slivers of Shaye's eyes opening up, as she turned to watch him fondly.

"I remind you of Mommy, huh?" he asked.

Shaye spoke in a voice warm with sleep. "You're prettier," she said.

Adam turned to her, wearing panties and with his eye makeup only half off; one eye looking male and the other female.

"You know, sometimes I feel silly doing this."

Shaye looked at him quite strangely. "Well," she said finally. "I really don't know what to say to *that* particular comment, Adam."

Adam changed his tone and spoke brightly while finishing cleaning off his face. "Get this, Shaye. A real, honest-to-God record producer from LA heard me singing tonight and he thinks I'm talented."

Shaye sighed, making that her comment.

"I know," Adam said. "You're thinking I ought to be cynical. But I know this guy. I know *of* him, anyway. He was on the last Forbes 500 list and my parents always talk about his amazing success. He was just like, passing through tonight and he thought Foxy Lady was a straight club. He said he would've left immediately, but he heard me sing."

"And?" Shaye asked.

Adam turned back toward her and sighed. For modesty, he stepped into the bathroom to change to boy's underwear. When he stepped out in the soft glow of light, he seemed to light up the room.

"Well, meeting him makes me feel that life's not all bad," Adam said. "He'd like me to try to record music as a boy. He thinks I'm a real talent and he could market me to make money. Who knows, Shaye, maybe I'd do it. But yet I'd like to be a psychologist too, and save poor people like us from the establishment someday. And then there's my grandfather's business when I inherit this summer. You and I have to take that really seriously, Shaye, and do things right. Because I'd like to be mature and make a success of everything from this point on... If nothing else, just to piss off my father."

Adam, in his upbeat mood- more like the 'old' Adam than he had seemed in weeks- suddenly cocked his head. "Are you okay, Shaye, or is something wrong here?"

Shaye liked his sensitivity, and she had no idea how well she could bluff. But, with Adam here right now, she suddenly felt all warm and fuzzy.

"Just serial killer stuff," she said. "Just problems with that."

Adam giggled. "Oh well, same old same old."

He shut the light off, and crawled in next to Shaye, his bare legs bumping against hers under the covers. He angled his face near hers so that she saw his soft eyes and soft lips illuminated in the streetlight. Being next to him felt very natural. But he looked at her with a little suspicion.

"So I get this phone call at Foxy Lady tonight. From Officer Glenn Chow," he said.

"What?"

Adam gave an off-kilter smile. "Officer Chow says to me, 'Please give this exact message to your roommate. "She doesn't have to run. Her secret's safe."' She'll know what I mean.' Apparently, this cryptic message came from Officer Danny."

Adam faced her almost with accusation. And she felt like backing away and/or shouldering the blame. It seemed to always feel like there was something dirty between her and Frank Danielo, something deeply secretive. And Adam seemed to know it.

However, knowing they didn't have to run from the park was a great relief. For, unfortunately, Shaye had been so determined to do what she planned on doing tomorrow that she had no intention of telling Adam the danger they were in with Danny, the danger of arrest.

Now, only two inches from her face and sharing every breath in comfortable unison with her, Adam gazed at Shaye like he understood it all.

Shaye woke naturally at eight in the morning and watched Adam for a few minutes as he slept like an angel in the glow that lit up the bed. She watched him with curiosity and then backed off, stripping off his jersey and tossing it at the hamper, so that she stood nude.

Shaye faced herself in Adam's baroque vanity mirror, which was so much larger and grander than the small wall mirror in her room. Everything glowed today, almost like a morning out of mythology, and Shaye stared with curiosity at her own long smooth body, which also resembled something out of mythology.

Squinting at herself, she raised her arms gracefully and half spun, lifting her hair to see her haunches and buttocks. Everything looked smooth, glowing golden pink. The ends of her hair tickled the sensitive upper butt cheeks, and one of her cheeks flinched.

Shaye spared a little smile for herself- this slender languid creature that resembled a mermaid, or a Lorelei or one of the Three Graces. She examined the delicate curve of her neck and her flanks, the slightly upturned breasts, the skin a mix of pink and gold that resembled the inside of a seashell. The sun lit the ends of her hair, which she slid over her breasts playfully to hide them. The slight frizz that stood off her very straight hair was lit from behind in sunshine, lighting her whole delicately curved shape in a golden yellow glow.

Shaye bent forward, examining her pouty lips and endlessly curious green eyes. She stared at her unblemished golden tan skin over her notoriously high cheekbones. She assessed each of her features with an eye for something that she had not considered in years.

And then she began to make up. Adam's dresser was strewn with cosmetics- chosen for his coloring, yes, but all subtle, trendy and of excellent quality. Shaye squinted, and bit her lip with concentration starting on her plan of attack. How had they done her for the catalog, she tried to remember. And what would be the very best way of making up now? What would be really the right way to do it, now that she had the choice- and the whole world- all to herself?

Shaye bent forward, with her exceptionally long legs and exceptionally high and rounded ass cheeks pointed out to her best friend Adam- the first thing he should see if he woke up.

This was done deliberately. Shaye felt that she needed something. She felt she'd like to see Adam's wise, yet innocent, smile locked on the sight of her absolutely nude. It felt like last night Danny had soiled her, doing perhaps irrevocable damage. Instinctively Shaye felt that Adam's patient glance could soothe that. And whatever part of her body it touched would receive a benediction.

Plus, a part of Shaye was actually a flirt. She and Adam had flirted last night and it made her feel great, just like he always made her feel great. Adam would never hurt her. And she sensed he'd get a kick out of seeing her like this. He had always thought she was so beautiful. He deserved to see her like this, to enjoy the almost mythical, almost spiritual pleasure. They could be together here, smiling in their naughty pleasure and totally shielded, totally safe from the world.

But Adam did not awaken as Shaye was making up. She bent down to his girl's underwear drawer, after just peeking into the guy's side. Either drawer held more than she had- the six pairs of plain white panties. Adam owned them in every color of the rainbow. Only her dear roommate could have managed to acquire this much lingerie in three weeks time- while they were supposedly saving every penny to run from the police.

But, instead of being mad, Shaye grinned like the spoiled teen princess she once was, seeing all the vibrant pink and red and purple panties. She sighed and giggled, pawing through silks and satins, panties decorated with lace and sequins and sparkles. She found a pair of neon-pink lace-trimmed boy cuts, and pulled them up her sleek long legs.

Shaye actually gasped when she glanced back in the mirror and saw the way they curved on her rump, with the lace sticking out like some invitation. She hiked up her tail and shook it, trying to shake the lace and make it dance and and she giggled wickedly to herself.

Adam woke up.

"Fuck me!" he exclaimed, as a turn of phrase- dark eyes wide as if what he was seeing was not real. But, at the same time Shaye never actually surprised him. His exclamation was only teasing and his tone sounded like he was witnessing the most down to earth spectacle in the world.

Shaye faced him, shielding her breasts with her hair, even as her pink nipples struggled behind the shifting gold curtain to try to poke out and say hello.

She flicked her thickly mascara'd eyelashes over big luminous green eyes. "Do you *want* to fuck me, Adam?"

Adam's lips instinctively dropped and pouted just like hers did, and his eyes shone. He was definitely no innocent.

He crawled up to a sitting position under the covers. His eyes slanted down with a slight look of cynicism, and his voice came out part tenderness, part challenge, part sneer. "So how would you like to do it, Shaye, my love? Do you want to climb on top of me and look beautiful and remember your *Tropical Sun* days? Or maybe I should take you from behind and play like you're a guy. Even better, why not dress in something of mine that looks just like a bikini, and then I could finally say I had you…"

Shaye held the hair over herself and put her feet together demurely. In a way she felt glad that he was backing down. Unlike Danny, Adam truly loved her. He understood.

"So, you don't want me?" she breathed.

Adam threw the covers off himself and she saw that he was hard, poking part way out of his boxer briefs. He patted the bed encouragingly and she padded over, perching on the edge so some of her hair spilled over him.

"Actually, Shaye, I really do want you." He stretched up and planted a kiss on her forehead. He pulled her leg over and planted a loud kiss on her knee, then one on her belly, so that she giggled. Her pleasure made him smile. "If you had come in here this morning, Shaye, wearing your shark T-shirt and Keds, as usual, I would've been allover you."

Shaye gulped and blinked her eyes, suddenly tearing up.

Adam caressed her shoulder under her silky hair. "That's as I thought," he said in response to her sudden display of emotion. "I know you too well, Shaye. And I have some secret ammunition. Last night, before I came in here, I walked into your room. On your bed, shoved halfway under your pillow, I found your favorite shirt-

and your only bra, slashed down the middle and destroyed. I also found a pair of handcuffs..."

Shaye sighed and tried to curl up on herself. Adam just pulled her down close to him, stroking her, but allowing her to look up towards the ceiling and not have to face him. She trembled, but he was giving her exactly what she needed. Perhaps he really could save her.

"And earlier Glenn Chow had called with that cryptic phone call," Adam continued. "So I did what you usually do and played detective..."

Shaye rolled to face Adam and, in the process, her breast slid against his chest. They both glanced down there, embarrassed, yet knowingly. Then Adam's glance returned to her eyes.

"Shaye, I know that you've been crushing on Officer Danny the sex maniac ever since you met him..."

"How did you know that?" Shaye asked.

"Duh!" Adam giggled. He gave her just one beat to contradict him, and she didn't. He resumed absently stroking her hair and he let one hand trail to gently probe one of her wrists, which was bruised. "It kills me to think that he handcuffed you, and that he destroyed your favorite clothes, which I know you never would have wanted willingly."

Adam slid his hand up again to gently cup Shaye's chin. "I could've gone after Danny last night, or I could've even got him arrested, even though that would mean us arrested, too. But I decided to trust your judgment, and the fact you didn't want to tell me about this.

"My guess is that the dude chickened out midway through trying to rape you. My guess also is that you still want to protect him, even though I don't know why. And, my guess is that you want me to make love to you this morning just to remind you of what it *should* be like."

Adam pulled Shaye closer to him and he planted a kiss on her lips that inflamed her whole body- Adam was just sexy and skilled in ways that Danny could never be. His voice became softer and even more intimate.

"And I will make love to you, Shaye. I'll do it tonight, but only if you still want it after you've had the day to clear your head." Then Adam reached down and snapped the pink underwear on her hip. "And don't think the fact that Shaye Taylor the ubermodel is back is gonna sway me!"

Adam returned under the covers and she thought he might have started subtly stroking himself as he watched her dress for today just like an adoring father might. But, if what he did was a bit kinky, Shaye didn't mind, for she had certainly stepped over that line herself just now.

She wanted him to watch her dress. Because today was a milestone, a transformation. Shaye of the trailer in Flamingo Park was facing down her demons.

She selected a tight denim miniskirt of Adam's with a frayed edge. She slipped it on and then sleeked body glitter all the way up and down her legs, squatting just a bit to get at her inner thighs.

Adam sighed and squirmed in the bed, squeezing his eyes shut for a minute until she stopped and then complaining, "Shit, girl, you can be wicked!"

Shaye winked at him playfully. She selected a pair of his hot pink strappy heels. Luckily, she was tall and her feet were almost as large as his. Almost, but not quite, and she knew she'd be wobbling down the dirt road on her way to the bus stop today. But she didn't care. The outfit would fit perfectly the part she intended to play, and she had it all figured out.

Lastly, she pulled on a little sleeveless top of dusty pink rope-like crochet, which was interwoven with shots of sparkling gold thread. She had to do without a bra.

But she did slick on plenty of juicy lipgloss.

Adam groaned. Coming out of his male reverie, he asked her, "You're not going to pretend to be a hooker, are you Shaye, to attract that killer? Because no matter how bad you want to screw over Officer Danny, I'll draw the line at that!"

Shaye shook her head. She collected a purse from Adam, made of hot pink leather in the shape of a shell. She clipped her hair up only for the walk through the park. And she smiled.

"No Adam," she said. "Actually, I'm going to Phoenix House, where Mami Ramierez got her drug treatment. And I think it's kinda poetic justice for the day, because I'm going introduce myself as a battered woman."

Adam gazed at Shaye with a half-dreamy, half-resigned expression of caring. "Just be safe, Sweetie," he said. "I'll only work the lunch shift, so I'll be home at four in the afternoon. Just come back to me!"

Shaye understood exactly what was at stake so, as she walked into the communal women's dining hall at Phoenix House, she was able to stay calm and focused. The room was long and narrow, with women crowded onto long benches- white, black, Hispanic, young and old all sitting together. And every pair of eyes watched her warily. Shaye attempted to meet the eyes and half smile, the kind of look that the women here seemed to give eachother. Not really friendly. But rather an indication of empathy and benigness.

In a hundred different ways, these women's eyes seemed to say, "Yes, we come from the street. But today we are laying down our weapons. No longer a danger to each other, we are all seeking sanctuary here from the dangers of the world- the dangers of men."

At the first table Shaye passed, she noticed women who visibly slumped over. One had bruises around her eye. Another's knobby vertebrae stood out through her threadbare T-shirt. The women at this table did not make conversation with each other. One bit her nails. Another bent over and sobbed quietly.

Shaye drew in a breath, assessing that these women were fresh off the street. They had probably come in today and were told that they could go ahead and enjoy the free lunch. Then they would go through an exhaustive intake interview with the resident social worker later.

This is exactly what happened when Shaye had walked in. It was still early, and she imagined that they could have processed her immediately. Instead the social worker had eyed her with immediate suspicion, as well as some kind of disdain.

The social worker, Marabelle Sanchez, looked exactly Shaye's age. But she carried her thirty or so extra pounds like a middle-aged woman would. And even though she wore a cream color satin shirt with lots of sheen, her shirt was the only sheen about her. The social worker's olive skin looked tired under dried out makeup. Her eyes looked tired behind dark-framed half glasses. Her hair looked frazzled, and she sighed as soon as she saw Shaye strut in wearing Adam's high heels.

As Marabelle, behind her desk, sighed and looked up at her, Shaye smelled a lingering odor of breakfast waft off her. Shaye imagined Marabelle Sanchez getting her kids up this morning, sending them off to school. She imagined her wishing she could stay home with them, rather than listening to another hard luck story from another female drifter who had carelessly thrown away all the things in life Marabelle cherished.

"Phoenix House isn't accepting any more homeless," Marabelle Sanchez informed Shaye before Shaye got to utter a word. "Just abused women. And you don't look abused."

Shaye forgot to lower her eyes like a good abused woman probably would have. But she pulled her light colored hair away from the side of her head, revealing the enormous reddened bruise that now showed from Danny's gun butt. She held up one bruised wrist backward, like a dog showing its paw.

The social worker set down her pen- more like threw it. She sighed and motioned for Shaye to have a seat. Then she gathered papers, lowered her eyes and went on to explain the Phoenix House program with all the animation of a scratchy recording.

"This is transitional housing," she said. "The intention is to first make sure you're safe from the man that's been abusing you, and then take care of you. That means get you off of drugs and alcohol, get you back on psychotropic meds if that's what you need, get you medical care and get you trained for a career. How does that sound?"

Shaye didn't think she needed to really dignify any of this with an answer.

"If you get through that part of the program, and I mean *if*, because our rules here are really strict..."

Shaye interrupted now. "I can follow the rules," she'd said.

The social worker nodded. "Well then, when you complete that part successfully," she said, suddenly seeming to warm to Shaye a little bit, "then comes the fun part. We help you save money, help you find a job and find an apartment in the community- help you transition."

She had seemed just a little perkier now, so Shaye thought it the best time to ask her question. "Like with Mami Ramierez from Flamingo Park?" she asked innocently. "She once used to be a hooker. Do you help women like that?"

Marabelle Sanchez sighed again loudly. She also made a point of looking Shaye up and down, obviously believing another down on her luck prostitute sat in her office right now. "We used to take in women in the sex trade, yes. That's not our focus now. But if you want to stay, you're welcome to... What did you say your name was? I can see you've been abused, so we're here to help you."

Impishly, Shaye introduced herself as Lorrine Danielo. She thanked Marabelle for offering her help, and then switched back to her line of questioning. "So, Mami Ramierez, you did help her? You got her off the streets. And out of the life?"

Marabelle gave a "humpf", gathering together the stack of Shaye's papers with none of the blanks filled in, and briskly paper-clipping them together. "Mami Ramierez is dead, Lorrine. You knew that, right?"

"I heard that," Shaye said. "But some of us girls in the park were friends. We heard before that sicko got to her that you guys turned her life around. And Mami was pretty hardcore and all, wasn't she?"

The young social worker shook her head, not seeming to like the unflinching curiosity in Shaye's eyes. "You know," she said. "The police came in here asking questions about Mami, too. What they don't realize is, this is a battered women's shelter. Everything is kept ultra confidential..."

"But Mami's dead," Shaye protested with a small deliberate show of attitude.

"And that's why I can tell you, yes we did help her, Lorrine. And I want you to pass that on to other girls, so we can help them as well. It's never too late."

"She's dead, though," Shaye repeated with a pout.

The social worker shoved papers at her with a sound like a growl. "Lorrine, Did you see Mami when she first came in here? Because I did. Filthy and ragged and letting men use her for ten dollars and a beer. Let me explain something. Elvira, or Mami as the girls started calling her, had problems even expressing herself when she first came in here. She'd keep her head down and hide underneath her long hair. Two years later Mami was dressing in suits, she'd learned word processing and we placed her with a staffing agency as an executive secretary. She was earning fourteen dollars an hour, Lorrine. That's more than I make here!"

Shaye saw fit to slouch, holding the papers on her stomach and looking sullen. "I don't think I could go that far."

Now the round apples of Marabelle's cheeks lit up pink with a little fervor. "If Mami could, anyone could. Mami started helping all the other girls, especially girls of Latina background. And she really became an inspiration to them. She became a close friend of mine, in fact. And I saw her all the time even after she graduated."

"Was that because you're Latina also?" Shaye pried. "Is that why you guys had a lot in common?"

Marabelle the social worker seemed not to know how to take the question. In fact, it seemed to send her off on some weird line of thought inside her own head. She gestured with her hand. "*All* woman are sisters under the skin," she said. "That's what we say here at Phoenix House. But for you, blond haired and blue-eyed..."

"My eyes are green," Shaye put in, just to fluster her.

"But you're a gringa, and some Latin girls would feel like you couldn't understand them. Or that they couldn't understand you."

Shaye had crinkled her brow. "So was Mami one of those girls? Is that what you're saying?"

Marabelle shook her head, as she scoffed. Then she glanced around almost furtively, as though making sure no one was listening in.

"Mami was just the opposite," she said finally. "Her old clientele in the park were mostly immigrant lawn workers- mostly Mexican. For that reason, I think that Mami was fed up with men from her own country. She helped the other girls, yes. But all she wanted was for them to stand up for themselves and act like American women..."

Her hands slashed the air in gestures that couldn't express all she was trying to say. "You have to understand, there are so many traditions for women of Mexican descent. It's expected that they act subservient to their men, and that they support their men's 'macho". You have to be brought up in our culture to really understand. I think Mami wanted to reach out to her sister Latinas, especially there in Flamingo Park. But I think she wanted to bust those myths, once and for all. I'm not saying that I agree with her, Lorrine- in fact I'm more of the school of thought that says to celebrate our culture. But I think she was trying to help the girls here at Phoenix House to go beyond their Latin heritage and, instead, to embrace all the opportunities they had as American women. Just as she had..."

Shaye eyed her after her speech and the two women simply did not click together. Marabelle stood and reached out her hand to shake. Because of the risk of germs, Shaye had to putter around and avoid it. This did not improve their relationship any.

"Well I'm truly busy right now," Marabelle told her, cutting their conversation about Mami Ramierez off completely. "In that packet is all the paperwork we'll need to get you registered as a resident here at Phoenix House. Then we have to do a drug test, and then get you a clinic appointment to test for venereal disease."

Shaye's eyes popped. "You're kidding, right?"

"Almost one hundred percent of our residents test positive for something," Marabelle said priggishly. "It's your choice though, Lorrine. Either you take a simple physical. Or else you go back out there to the man that abused you."

Shaye's eyes darkened like an artic sea. But, since she wasn't going to be spending the night here anyway, she supposed she should be more complacent to get her chance to speak to the other girls. "What about the paperwork? What were you saying about that?" she choked out.

The social worker led her out with an unwelcome soft sweaty hand on her bare arm, trying to act motherly to her, while at the same time obviously disliking her. Shaye felt sad, as though she really was Lorrine, the perverted cop-battered victim, coming in here looking for help and understanding, and instead being patronized.

Marabelle handed her the paperwork and a cold generic soda. She also tried to hand her a pen, vehicle of a thousand germs, which Shaye shrugged away.

"You might as well fill these out in the dining room," Marabelle had said, impatiently bending over her thick belly to retrieve her pen that Shaye had let fall to the floor. Although she was so much shorter than Shaye in the heels, she looked up and practically glowered.

"These papers usually take hours to fill out- with an experienced social worker helping. But today we got in some cases that are a lot more needy than yours. If you really want to get checked in today, Lorrine, you can sit down at one of the tables in the lunchroom and work on the paperwork yourself. I'm quite busy today, but I'll make time to see you around four-thirty if you get through those papers- and you're still around…"

The corridor was tiny and stuffy, and sweaty delivery men with boxes on pallets kept pushing past Shaye, stopping only to gape at her legs and her hair and her large pert breasts braless in the peekaboo woven shirt. Shaye felt trapped.

On the walls the shelter posted checklists of what to do if you were being abused, how to know if you qualified for food stamps, how to know if you should get tested for HIV. Shaye saw bus schedules and clinic schedules and postings for jobs at the local day labor agency. Then there were posters with photographs of kittens in visors and bulldogs in baseball caps and even a gecko in a princess tiara. Each featured an inspirational saying about being a woman.

Then Shaye had to run the gauntlet of the dining room, having to be examined by all the women's eyes, starting with the most troubled new women at the table closest to the corridor. At the next table was a group dressed a little butch, a little gangsta and they eyed Shaye with some challenge. Beyond them at the far end of the hall, Shaye found a table akin to the one in high school where all the popular girls would sit.

Six women sat at the table, an even mix of white, black and Latina skin tones. Unlike the females at any of the other tables, these women were animated and laughing. One girl seemed in charge. She was about twenty-eight, with casually trimmed shoulder length black curls and an hourglass figure that twisted invitingly as she moved. Even though she was in a room filled with one hundred man-hating woman, her body looked like it was made for loving men.

Although she was black skinned, her features were delicate Latina and her voice boomed with a strong Spanish accent. In other words, she was a throwback to all those old myths that women like Marabelle the social worker and Mami the reformed hooker despised.

Shaye grinned to herself, wondering how she could make a place for herself at the table with these alpha bitches of Phoenix house.

The Spanish looking girl finished bouncing out of the kitchen holding a greasy wax paper wrapped takeout meal on one of the house's trays. It looked like something she had bought in town to serve to her friends as a little appetizer before the main, bland, Phoenix House meal.

Women at other tables looked around with jackals' eyes as they scented the takeout food, Mexian empenadas, while they were simply being warehoused with their butts on splintered benches and no control of when their meal came.

These six women, with their happy giggles like girls at camp, had probably graduated and now enjoyed all kinds of privileges. It seemed like a strange hierarchy- the sorority girls of abused and drug-addicted women.

But the sense it made is that these must have been Mami's Ramierez's closest friends. Now Shaye stood inches away from their table.

One older black woman, with shorn platinum hair and a silver ring that pierced her lower lip, turned her wrestler type body toward

Shaye. "This table's taken," she said. "Except for girls that already graduated the program."

Shaye thought about offering a trade of smokes or liquor but there was the chance that these girls really cherished their recovery. Instead, she thought fast and offered as bait something that any girl would like.

"I got my old man's credit card," she lied, just loud enough that the all women at the table could hear. "Before I get checked in here and they confiscate it, us girls can go on a shopping spree! And you guys can buy as much as you want; I really want to screw him."

The women seemed taken aback for only a second. Then the one with the piercing instantly became her buddy. "I own a van," she said. "I can drive us, as long as the social workers don't hear about it."

Now the pretty Hispanic girl smiled, beaming her warmth over Shaye and she encircled her in one arm. "So, this is our new amiga. What's your name Honey? Mine's Tori."

Shaye greeted her, trying not to swoon at the smell of the greasy food that was being waved under her nose.

"Let's eat our food before we go," Tori said. "You can have some of my empenadas. And if you miss lunch here, I'll treat you to lunch at the mall. I've got a good job now, and I can do that," she added, with a twinkling smile.

Shaye wanted to get some information out of the six women before they found out that she really didn't have a credit card. About all she found out on the drive was that they had all known Mami. In fact, they had spent practically every day with her for the past two years. Tori said that Mami had been her very best friend at Phoenix House, and Shaye felt vindicated that she had made the right decision trying her bluff with these women.

At the mall Tori, teetering on heels, asked to run to ladies' room before the girls descended on Glamorama, their favorite store, which featured racks and racks of outrageous club wear, every piece under ten dollars.

For a reckless moment, Shaye almost considered shopping at Glamorama. She had fifty dollars of Adam's money in his pink purse, and she fantasized dressing up for him tonight, really wild, for their expected rendezvous. She could dress like a real trailer tramp and see if it rocked his world. Or maybe it would just make him laugh. Even seeing that would really be a pleasure.

A part of Shaye tugged her toward the clothing emporium. But the part that needed to stop the serial killer made her follow Tori in the other direction, hoping for some compassion, along with answers to her pressing questions.

In the ladies' room, Tori bitched about her period cramps and banged around in the stall changing her pad. Then she came out and slicked layer after layer of blackberry gloss over naturally pouty lips in an otherwise unspectacular face. She watched Shaye gingerly reapply her own makeup. Adam's makeup actually.

Shaye caught Tori's eyes looking at her. "Tori," she confessed. "I don't really have any credit cards. I was just feeling nervous in the shelter, and I wanted to ask you girls some serious questions."

Tori laughed out loud, showing big white teeth. "So, you a liar, too, as well as a ho!" She glanced over at the stalls, bending to check that no one was in there, and then she came up by Shaye, and then laughed again. "It don't matter. My homegirls will just shoplift shit at Glamorama anyway. It's what we always do…" She leaned back against the counter adjusting herself so she didn't topple over in her extremely tight jeans. She took a piece of gum, and snapped it a few times. Then she asked Shaye seriously. "So what're your questions?"

And then she proceeded to tell Shaye all she knew about Mami Ramierez.

Chapter 14

When she returned home, Shaye found Adam barefoot at their kitchen sink, washing out fancy wine glasses and wearing men's soccer shorts and a tank top. The shorts showed off the sleek muscles in his legs. And, as he turned, the tank revealed his succulent, perfectly proportioned pecs washed in sunlight, which filtered in through the slatted window over the sink.

Adam and Shaye eyed each other knowingly, and his lips slid into a sly smile even as both his cheeks blushed.

"You look good," he told her.

Shaye let her long cape of hair swing free, meanwhile bending to try to unhook the heels. They were still on for tonight or Adam wouldn't be here. But he was here, just like he had promised.

Despite the fact that she really wanted to do this, Shaye's heart raced at what felt like four hundred beats a minute. She felt her face flush completely, even worse as she bent down.

"Your shoes are killing me, Adam,"

Instead of just joking around, Adam left a pregnant silence that made her look up. "Why don't you leave them on, then?" he asked. "You may not be on your feet for long."

Making no comment, but hearing the sound of her own audible breath, Shaye sidled toward him, finding the graceful movements of a cat in the high heeled shoes, even as they shot pains all up her shins.

205

Adam drank in her every move, standing confidently like the man he was, after all. He prepared drinks- a wine spritzer for him and sparkling water with a cherry and a starfruit slice in it for her.

Shaye took the drink from him and every sensation felt heightened. She felt the cold wetness on the side of the glass, a slick sexy feeling. She lifted the drink and felt tiny bubbles jump and tickle her nose and she smiled. Adam's face was only inches away now.

She marveled at his soft skin and his dark enticing eyes under thick black lashes. She'd had always been fascinated by his face, she realized. In fact, she'd never desired her ex-husband a fraction of the amount she had always been attracted to her enigmatic best friend.

Shaye took a sip of the drink. Then she tried to be cute and take a sexy nip of the maraschino cherry. Adam did her one better. As the cherry sat clutched between her swelling lips, Adam reached his own lips forward. He brought his lips against hers, sliding as intimately and as wetly as if they were having sex. Then he clicked his white teeth against hers with a tiny sound magnified only by the intensity of the moment.

And he bit off half the cherry. He pressed his lips against hers again, sliding deeper, and he slid his tongue in her mouth, exchanging his piece of cherry with hers. Shaye helped him, sliding her tongue expertly and wickedly in compliance. They ate their pieces of cherry, sliding them back and forth while moaning and tasting more and more of each other, while Shaye lifted one long leg up around Adam's waist.

Making out now, melting completely into each other, Shaye felt totally debauched. It was fitting that, after the years of almost dying, the forced celibacy, the abandonment by her husband and the shriveling up inside as a woman, this would be the end of the drought. This sex that was going to be more amazing than her wildest dreams. It only figured that Adam, who had always loved her so perfectly as a friend, would prove extraordinary here, too. That Adam could deliver.

Shaye threw her hair back, wantonly and raggedly drawing in gasps of air and Adam assertively ran his hand up the back of her skirt and clutched her buttocks. He lifted her up, and she felt the chilly vinyl stick to her the naked parts of her ass cheeks. Then Adam worked his fingers inside her, assuring that she was wet.

He slipped his face under her hair right up against her throat. "I love you, Shaye," he murmured, his words like fire.

And then he crushed his body against hers, impaling her with his hard on, as he pulled her closer on the stool. Shaye spread her legs and let him have her. She reached for his lips with hers, melting inside and out and then she gave a little gasp and her eyes flicked to his.

"Don't worry, Baby," Adam whispered, sliding out and replacing his hard-on again with his fingers. "I've got protection for us. I just wanted to go in for a second first this way, just to feel it. Just to feel us together, Shaye."

Shaye leaned her face against his sweetly, brushing her velvety skin against his. "We've always been together in one sense or another, haven't we, Adam?"

Adam smiled, taking friendly nips of the bottom of her lip, and the sides of her cheek. Her slid her up, cupped against his body, with her legs locked around his lower back. And he spun her gently as he carried her toward his bedroom. "We've always been together," he asserted. "And tonight I want us to be together every conceivable way."

The next day the two policemen in black leather jackets hurried through the sun drenched Florida airport- Officer Glenn Chow with a hectic flush on his smooth cheeks, and an excited half smile as he sorted through his ticket folder- and Officer Frank Danielo striding behind protectively- glancing around for potential trouble and carrying Chow's bags.

They walked as far as they could together, and Chow's plane to Mexico City was already boarding. Danny sorted his partner out with the luggage, the tickets, a cell phone and instructions for how to retrieve his weapon at the Mexican airport.

"I'm so excited about this trip," Chow repeated for the hundredth time since Danielo had driven him down from Oceanside. "You're still sure you don't want to go?"

Danny shook his head. "This is your show, Buddy. You're good at this kind of thing. More diplomatic than I am, certainly. And you always wanted to do some investigative work, so I figured this could be your chance…"

Chow's voice came out breathless, as he stowed everything away in the proper pockets prior to handing in his boarding pass.

"Well, thank you again, Frank. And tell Mayor Walker thanks also."

"No problem, Glenn. Just make sure to keep those cell phone batteries charged. And remember, you'll be out of range of cellular towers most of the trip so keep in touch with the local police and stay diplomatic up there in the mountains. Trust your Mexican guides, but don't trust 'em too much, if you know what I mean. And sleep with your gun- but don't sleep too deep…"

Chow nodded politely, but nervously. "I, I think I better catch the plane now…"

"Stay away from the water… And the women," Danny added.

Chow lifted his hand in a smiling salute as he backed away, toward the pretty blond employee waiting to take his ticket.

"I'll do it all," Chow said. "Just like you say."

"And dammit," Danny called out, making Chow turn again. "Make sure not to tell the suspect's family that you're looking for a killer. Tell them he won the lottery or something."

Chow nodded again, and Danny laughed. But then Chow called out something to him. "Danny, make sure to keep our witness Vicki safe- just in case I don't come home with the suspect." He winked at Danielo in friendly fashion. But suddenly Danny looked a little grim.

"I got it under control," he said, as he turned to walk away.

And then he growled to himself, under his breath. "Unless those bozos in Oceanside do something to fuck it up while I'm here at the airport."

Shaye and Adam lit candles around the room, and they made love all night long. At six in the morning, the candles were just starting to burn down, replaced by the first hints of dawn.

Shaye rode Adam, swinging her hair to let it trail over his chest and then back to sweep the tops of his thighs. She grinned and caressed the two gold nipple rings; she had always craved so to touch these.

"How do you feel, Baby?" he asked her. "Do you feel good?"

Shaye closed her eyes and nodded, to show her pleasure. Then she opened them to watch his pleasure at her ecstasy.

"I've fantasized about touching your chest like this for a long time," she murmured.

Adam raised his brows. "You have?"

Shaye nodded, with a blush as she slowly rose up and down, working him.

Adam caressed up and down the smoothness of her hips and thighs, he ran just the tips of his fingers across her belly, making her shiver.

"You know how I feel," he said. "I totally cherish you. I remember seeing you that first day in the hospital when they wheeled you in after surgery, strapped down like some female tiger that might claw everybody. You were just a little scrap of a thing, Shaye. To give you pleasure like this, to actually watch you smile like this, it blows my mind."

Two silver tears leaked out unselfconsciously, one stream trailing from each of Adam's eyes. Shaye became all choked up herself, and she fought it. "Don't do this Adam," she said. "Let's just feel healthy now. Because we are. The day is beautiful and everything feels like it's fixed."

Adam sucked back his tears and acted sexual like she liked by planting a kiss on the tip of his finger, then on her lips. He did it again, touching his fingertip, in turn, to each of her nipples.

"I just want you to understand something, Shaye," he said with such seriousness that she stopped moving for a moment. "I'm not doing this just because you're Shaye Taylor and you're beautiful. That's so far from it that I can't even say."

"I know what you feel for me, Adam. I know that you've been with me through everything," Shaye said.

"And I will be with you, Shaye, even when you're a hundred years old and wrinkled."

Shaye giggled politely.

"But there's more to this than just that either. There's this chemistry..."

They glanced around together at five used condoms that littered the floor around the bed. "You and me, Shaye. We're good together. It's scary how good we are." Adam met her eyes with perhaps the most deeply sexual look she had ever seen in her whole existence. "It's one in a million. We can't deny that."

A question started to bubble up, and almost came out of Shaye's mouth. Instead, she rode Adam harder, and squeezed her eyes tight shut, swinging her hair like a blanket over herself, biting her lip and trying to block out everything.

The question was: how many men have you been with in your life, Adam? And, is that what you want? A guy and not a girl?

Shaye cried now as she rode her friend violently and even whimpered, but he was taking it a different way.

Adam arched up and came inside her again, his face looking beneficent, like some choirboy blessed with the sight of heaven. How could he seem so pleased if he was gay? How could he even do this to her, she wondered.

Shaye cared about Adam so much, but as their lovemaking finished she caressed his face, looking deeply into him with tremendous confusion. And his look seemed to reflect hers. He was so good, and so sexy. But did he practice that at Foxy Lady, going with male johns? Had Adam slept with Madeline, or Rochelle or even Candy Cane? Was that why all of them always liked to laugh at her?

She draped herself tiredly over Adam's body, and listened to the pounding of her heart. Meanwhile he stroked her hair and quietly sang her an old blues lullaby. Every single one of Adam's signals suggested that he wanted to stay with her for life. And now, the way he had made love to her unashamedly indicated that he might want to be her lover for life as well.

So why didn't he just say that?

If he did ask her to commit to him, Shaye wouldn't know what to answer, and Adam probably knew that. Could she love Adam for life and be his sexual partner if she knew for a fact that he was bisexual? If she would always be sharing him with men, even though he would never love them the deep way he loved her?

She lifted up, and the pain in her eyes must have showed as she desperately examined Adam's face seeking for answers. He was still inside her body, and all he did was rest his eyes on hers until she finally climbed off. But, before she could leave the bed, he stopped her.

"Shaye," he said. "Ask me anything. Ask me now if you want to."

Shaye glanced down at the floor, seeing the pink heels, the pink purse and the purple panties she had worn- Adam's girl's clothes, clothes that he would eventually put back on. Inside her raw and overexcited body, the strange pain clutched her heart like a fist.

For today, nothing was going to change. She wasn't going to ask that critical question. She wasn't going to ask if they were now girlfriend or boyfriend, or still just brother and sister. Maybe they'd go on as lovers and she'd never ask that question.

Wearily, Adam climbed out of bed with her. Pressing his lips against the nest of her hair, he walked behind her to the bathroom. Together, like sleepwalking, they rolled into the shower. They giggled, and Adam stood behind her slipping his hands underneath her breasts and over the nipples so that her breasts screamed again with excitation. Shaye gasped and leaned forward and Adam pressed against her from behind, groaning while he washed her.

Shaye leaned back, letting her soaked mop of hair fall into his capable hands. Adam lathered it vigorously, pushing the excess bubbles down her flanks. "You're like my little mermaid, Shaye," he said. "My little long-haired mermaid. I can't wait to make you breakfast. I can make you fluffy pancakes, which I can decorate with raspberries and some of that funky starfruit from yesterday, right from our own garden. How would you enjoy that?"

"It would be great," Shaye murmured, enjoying the incredible indulgence of being washed by a love like this.

But then she made the terrible mistake of thinking out loud. "I forgot to tell you all the stuff I found out at Phoenix House yesterday, Adam. All this gossip about Mami Ramierez. She definitely had a boyfriend. And she cheated on him with one of his coworkers. All because her boyfriend lost all his money. I think the coworker might have been paying her... You see, the motive for the murder could have been jealousy. And then it spurred the next murder somehow..."

Adam climbed out of the shower, and offered her a towel. Then he concentrated on rubbing himself down.

Shaye was too worked up to take the hint.

"Do you know what all of this means? If we find that boyfriend, and he comes from the Santasemana region of Mexico, then we've found the killer."

Adam now looked up, and looked her full in the face with an expression that was unreadable, but with a tilt of his chin that indicated he was protecting himself with pride, the one thing he held onto.

"When you say we," Adam practically choked out. "You don't mean you and me. You mean you and Officer Frank Danielo?"

Adam kept his chin stiff and Shaye finally understood why he looked emotionally destroyed.

She tried to shake her head, trying to shake all the confusion and pain away. "No, Adam," she said. "Not like that. I'll just e-mail him or something."

"Then work with Glenn Chow. Chow seems like a good cop, and he's ambitious."

"But Danny is the one protecting us."

Adam eyed Shaye with a look that seemed to say he could see everything. He touched her once again, simply to cup her chin. "There was something I was gonna ask you. But, you know what, Shaye? It's enough that you know I'm here for you. No matter what. I'll be your lover, best friend or whatever. And we don't even have to talk about lifetime commitment, because you know that's what we've got..."

Shaye nodded in total agreement, for this part was true.

"But," Adam continued emphatically. "I really don't want you to have unfinished business with Danny. So do what you've got to do and finish it. Be with him if that's what you want to do, or say good-bye if you don't..."

Shaye stamped her foot and dissolved into frustrated tears, rocking between both walls in the crowded little bathroom as she exploded in protest. "It's not about Danny and me!" she said. "I hate Danny. It's about the killer now, Adam."

Shaye's voice was made ragged by her tears and her heartbreak, as she stopped flinging herself around and instead sought out his eyes. As she spoke to Adam it was like she was articulating that thing that she hardly understood herself.

"It's about me catching this killer," she said quietly, but very intently. "You see, when those other people died from the e-coli- that housewife and that little boy..." A sob almost stopped her, but she continued. "... I could never understand why I was the only one that lived. I never thought I had any purpose. But now I see it. Maybe God let me live, Adam, so that I can save these lives here. I know they're just prostitutes that nobody really cares about. But *I* care now. And If I don't do this, then there would be no reason that my life was saved at all. Don't you understand?"

Shaye's eyes pleaded with Adam's. He took her by the shoulders gently and she saw that he did understand. And yet he steadfastly refused to back down. "Shaye," he said, with the same endearing, yet completely enigmatic expression he usually wore. "You know I'm a sophisticated guy. If you sleep with Danny and you even come to me fresh from that, it's not gonna throw me..."

Shaye's eyes practically bulged. Unlike Adam, she still *was* very much the innocent.

He spared a crooked grin. "I'm not saying I'd *like* that, Sweetie. I'm just saying, in the greater scheme of things, something like that doesn't so much matter. But there are some parts of you, Shaye, that I will *not* share, so just be clear on that. If you're determined to go to the library today to email him, I'm not coming home early."

Shaye gulped down her own emotion. She didn't know exactly how she felt, but she knew she hurt. It would be easy enough to just say she wouldn't contact Danny. But she couldn't let this case go now.

"I'm going to e-mail him, Adam. That's all. A few more days and this will all be over."

Adam leaned forward and kissed her on the forehead. "Well, come to my room late tonight and we can still make love, but let's wait to talk til then."

Shaye trembled. "You mean when the case is over?" she asked. She knew they both were referring to when she made a decision about Danny. The wrong decision, she knew, and she and Adam might not even be leaving this trailer together to go to Miami.

Adam stood before her now, seeming to hold all her emotion stoically within himself. "We'll talk then," he repeated.

Chapter 15

Nine in the morning, Shaye was the first visitor at the public library. And everything felt cold- the desk, the chair, the computer keyboard. The chill went up into her body as she sat down, and her empty stomach twisted as she thought of what she might be throwing away by touching her fingers to the cold computer keys.

Yet she sucked in a teary breath- and she did it.

"Dear Officer Danielo," she wrote. *"I am emailing because I have some information that might finalize the arrest of the Flamingo Park killer. Mami Ramierez had a boyfriend, Danny, as I tried to tell you the other night. As Willie Jeremiah witnessed. Her friends at Phoenix House didn't know much, because they weren't supposed to be dating while in recovery and Mami kept things quiet. But her relationship with this man was definitely serious.*

They were engaged to be married, and he was very involved in Flamingo Park- possibly he owned some land. Or maybe he was just knowlegable about developing land and building. You know the lot on Caiman St. - the murder scene? It wasn't chance them being there together.

They had serious plans to buy the Caiman St. lot together- or for him buy it for her, I think. And then they were going to build a community center there, with a park and a chapel. They were planning to save the denizens of Flamingo Park. Everything ties in now- the crosses, etc. and I think I even have the motive of why he finally killed Mami, as well as killing Josie Swank. There's a lot more, but I'd like to know that you can use this information..."

Shaye turned around to chat with her friend the librarian when, five minutes later the computer dinged, indicating she had a message. It was a reply from Danny. His email address, "rockincop" left no doubt.

"Friend," it read.

"Thanks for being the bigger person and contacting me first. Number one, I won't keep you in suspense, and I'll tell you that we've had some crazy big developments in the case. Glenn Chow is in Mexico right now. We found out more about the rooster claw and he's going to the town where it was made, a tiny town on a mountain near an ancient silver mine.

By tonight, we might have the killer's name. And there's some other stuff seriously too classified to mention in email. I really want to fill you in. More than Chow, you've been my partner on this one..."

Shaye knew Danny was sitting somewhere at his computer right now, waiting, so she bit her lip and emailed him back.

"Have you ever heard of the Seven Deadly Sins, Officer Danny? And is there any one of them you don't have? So why should I trust you to meet you in person?"

The reply took a while.

"Shaye, if I took the time to make amends for every single thing I did wrong to every person in this life, it would take a lifetime. In fact, it will. It's called Step Nine and it's a program I'm supposed to be working, but momentarily forgot," Danny wrote. *"Please don't let my shortcomings get in the way of solving this case. If we can work together to solve this case, you and I can save lives- and finally contribute something to this world. And I know you want that, too.*

I'll come by tonight. Why don't you have Adam and the crew there? That's fine with me. Let's just say the other night didn't happen, Shaye. You and I are still living, so I guess we should have a sense of humor, put our own problems in perspective and pretend like it didn't.

"What do you say?"

Shaye grimaced, even as she smiled and wrote back simply, *"Well, you owe me a T-shirt."*

Danny's reply came quickly. *"And you owe me some handcuffs."*

Shaye stood up and stretched. She honestly didn't know what gave her body such a sense of release- the glorious lovemaking with Adam all last night- or this sudden rapprochment with Danny.

She stretched her arms all the way up, so that the pretty camisole she had chosen for today rode up, showing her sleek tummy, and she yawned with a smiley face like a cat's.

"Done so soon?" the librarian inquired.

"Yes, I am," Shaye said. "In fact, I think I'll go down to the beach."

Shaye breezed in to the trailer all tanned and windblown, and found Adam waiting for her. He gave a little smile that was half knowing wink and half smirk, but he ducked out of the way agilely when she tried to kiss him, pretending to busy himself baking.

"So, Shaye," he asked her, with his back turned, playing Martha Stewart juggling a tray of fresh-baked croissants. "Is the cop from hell coming over here tonight- or not?"

Shaye reached up and struggled to undo her nest of salt stiffened hair that she had piled into a bun for her walk across Flamingo Park on her way back from the beach. "He emailed me that something was happening with the case," she tried to explain. "Something that he wanted to explain to us in person..."

Adam, who looked dashing in a white silk blend designer shirt open to the belly with his nipple rings peeking out, simply smirked again as he hopped up onto the counter. He licked his fingers from a croissant, and then tossed it in Shaye's direction.

"Heads up!"

Shaye caught it and looked at him poutingly.

"I wasn't inquiring about Danny's latest screw up with his case, just whether you've invited him over, which you have." Adam sighed, playing the part of "Adam Ant", the mercurial nightclub entertainer, acting like he didn't care much and affecting a definite lisp. "I just don't want to leave you here alone with him if he's gonna rape you or something..."

"Adam..."

"Anyway," he said, waving his hands flamboyantly. "I traded shifts with Candy Cane so I could at least greet him at the door. If everything's alright, I'm gonna fly."

Shaye leaned back against the sink and gnawed on her croissant. Suddenly she was being made to feel like a disobedient teenager. "It doesn't matter, Adam. Why don't you just stay while he's here?"

She felt a sense of vertigo for a moment, when she thought it was so clear that Adam was acting wildly jealous. But then, why didn't he just come down off the counter and kiss her? And why was he going to work to dress up and dance erotically as a woman? Why didn't Adam just ask her to be his girlfriend, if he wanted her not to get involved with Danny?

She gestured helplessly. "Or... I don't know... what do you want anyway?"

Truly, Shaye didn't know what she wanted at the moment, and her stomach cramped painfully on the food. All she wanted was that feeling she had out on the beach alone today. A feeling of freedom- combined with an abiding sense of safety.

Adam shook off her comments, flicking his head like a southern belle. "Just... well, guess what, Shaye?" he said breathlessly. "We might be going to Miami before this weekend- if you want to... I mailed Jeff Freeman some money, and I asked him to buy us fake ID's. I talked to him today, and he said he's sending one of his bartenders to Little Havana to buy them for us tonight!"

"For real?" Shaye asked, feeling suddenly like a fresh ocean breeze washed her. "But how about the police down there? And how about your dad's private investigator?"

Adam gave a little grin like a cat scrunching up its chops. "All gone, Jeff told me. Apparently my father's grown tired of wasting his money looking for me. Maybe he's ready to accept the inevitable when I come out of hiding this summer. Or maybe he just thinks I'm dead."

Adam winked and Shaye retrieved a bottle of spring water from the refrigerator and raised it in a toast. "Well, let's drink to him then."

They both grinned widely at each other, unable to help it.

"Seriously, though," Adam said. "I also looked at used cars today, and I found a dealership right up on US 1 with the perfect thing. It's a seven-year-old Dodge Caravan. Burgundy. It's a minivan, Shaye. Not tres chic or anything but it's got low mileage, and I drove it around their parking lot and the engine sounds good." He giggled. "Not that I'm the car expert. But it only costs two thousand. Which I'll pretty much have after tonight."

"You *do*?"

Thoughts warred in Shaye again. Why had Adam kept this from her? With all that money, they could have been out of here already and she wouldn't have been sexually molested by a demented cop!

They didn't really need a vehicle. Just the ID. And what kind of work had he been doing to get so much money anyway?

Adam brushed her question away with a gesture in the air.

"Being an entertainer, Shaye, instead of a waiter, I make lots of money. And the music producer gave me some money. It's a long story. The important part is, we'll be able to get out of here. Jeff says just watch the mailbox for those documents..."

Adam's glance burned into her like daring her to challenge him. Just then, at the worst moment, came the knock on the door. Adam made a burlesque face of surprise and lightly leaped from the counter, dancing and singing the theme song from *Cops*.

He flung the door wide, singing to the unspectacular sight who stood outside, head bowed, clutching a paper bag wrinkled and sweaty from his hands.

Danny wore blue this afternoon- a casual short sleeve shirt, jeans and no cop paraphernalia. He glanced up ashamedly at rude Adam who looked every millimeter the haughty trust fund baby he was soon to be.

"Adam," Danny attempted in greeting, and reached out his hand.

Adam spurned it. "You look different sober," he said.

Danny had clearly had enough. "And you look different as a boy."

Adam preened, making a pointed show of his disdain. "It's boi," he said. "Spelled B-O-I. You wouldn't get it," he added, backing off to swing the door open. He also turned an unreadable glance to Shaye for the briefest second.

Shaye didn't know what boi, spelled B-O-I, meant either. She heard Danny's boots scuff on the first metal step.

"Is Shaye here?" Danny asked. "I'm supposed to see her."

Adam grimaced, briefly delaying the inevitable. What he said seemed for Shaye's benefit as well as Danny's. "It depends upon which Shaye you want to see. If anybody liked Trailer Park Shaye, that one's gone, thanks to stress. So before you flip out seeing supermodel Shaye in the flesh, just remember it's a defense- so actually, it's sad. Come on in. Just don't slip on your own drool..."

Adam backed off, Danny climbed up into the living area and Shaye cringed, feeling embarrassment herself. Danny turned and stared at her speechless, clutching and turning his little paper bag. Shaye followed his eyes as they made their slow trip down her body. First, he took in her gleaming facial features enhanced with high sheen makeup, just like she had copied from her swimsuit model days. Shaye lifted up her chin in an attempt at pride and self-protection as he stared.

Danny's eyes gently caressed her prominent collarbones, which he'd never seen bare, except the other night. Shaye had changed into an ornate litte camisole-style shirt that belonged to Adam. It was the shade of port wine and it separated her breasts with triangles of fabric and stretchy, wine colored lace. With it she wore an airy flower-print miniskirt, rouched even higher up one thigh with a dangly little string. She'd borrowed a silver belly chain from Adam and she wore it slung flirtatiously low over her naked belly button. And her shoes were spiky four-inch mules- in the color of some exotic tropical fruit.

The silent scrutiny lasted a full five minutes. They could all hear each other's breathing. Shaye became impatient with being a centerpiece like this. After all, there were people possibly dying around here. Why were they all acting so ridiculous?

"Danny," she breathed. "These are just Adam's clothes. It's no big deal."

All eyes watched Danny for his reply.

He sighed.

"You know what," he said. "I think I liked them better on Adam. I miss Trailer Park Shaye…"

"Oh, get real," Adam mumbled, sounding a bit like a cat hissing. "But since he seems harmless without the courage of booze, I guess I'll get dressed for work. I've got a bus waiting out there…"

He tried to swish off, but Danny stopped him, catching him by the arm. "You know, as a police officer, I advise you carry your female clothes in a bag tonight, Adam. It's really not safe walking around out there dressed up right now." He glanced at Shaye in the kitchen. "Seriously. Not you either, Shaye."

Adam huffed and extracted his arm.

Frank Danielo headed over to the living room and plopped down on the couch- a seat he was very familiar with.

"Could I please have both you guys in here for a moment? There's something I want to tell you both about. And I wasn't comfortable sharing it over the Internet."

Shaye walked toward him woodenly. She sat down a distance from him on the very far end of the couch. Adam pulled over a bar stool and faced him.

"Is this where you say you want to arrest us?" Adam asked.

Danny shook his head. He extracted a bent photo from his jeans pocket- a photo that Shaye noticed from a distance contained a thin-faced young woman with long shiny black hair.

"Oh my God," she breathed.

Danny reached out a hand in a placating gesture that didn't connect. "No, she's not dead, Shaye." He rubbed over dark eyebrows and slightly swollen eyes that looked like they had seen more crying than sleep in the past two days. Now both Adam and Shaye looked at him raptly. Even Adam gave full attention.

"Her name's Victoria Cruz," Danny said. "Vickie C. is one of her street names. The girl came up from Miami with her pimp, who, believe it or fucking not, thought that this territory was wide open now because girls were dying! So anyway, I was driving... the other night," Danny continued, his voice dropping to almost imperceptible when he said that part. "... When Vicki jumps out from the woods onto the hood of my car... She's our secret weapon now, guys. No one in the press has an inkling that we have this witness. It's a big amazing secret..."

"Lots of secrets," Adam commented.

"Too many," Danny agreed. "Vicki Cruz thought she was pretty keen. After all, she picked up on the fact that one of her new johns could be the killer. She got in his car and then he started acting strange and all preachy. Suddenly switches from English to talking to her in some Mexican Indian dialect..."

Shaye looked up. Danny nodded. Adam also stared, perhaps in some amazement, remembering all Shaye had deducted about the suspect.

"Shaye is good, Adam," Danny confirmed. "I spent three years as a New York detective and I know. When you guys clean up your messes, maybe someday Shaye will have a career as a cop."

Danny had to face two extremely strange expressions.

"Anyway," he continued, "the suspect picked Vicki up in a rental car. Then he drove her to a vacant lot, showed her a little altar he had made and started blessing her in that Indio dialect. That was all it took. Vicki got spooked and ran. But before she got away he managed to rake her with something..."

Again, Adam and Shaye both looked up.

"It had to be the rooster claw," Danny said. "Although she didn't see, because it was dark. The assailant didn't really give chase after she escaped. But Vicki crouched in the bushes by

Caiman St., using Kleenex to stop the bleeding on her hands, and trusting no one around here until my squad car drove by."

Danny relaxed a little and he sat back in his seat, confronting two pairs of suspicious eyes. "Unlike some people, Vicki Cruz talked to me for a bit and decided that I was the only person she could trust. She hadn't seen the suspect well enough to make a good police artist's sketch, but she said she could identify him in the flesh with no problem- she remembered how he felt and smelled and sounded. He acted regal, she said, and respectful, until he took it upon himself to ritually execute her...

"And Vicki wasn't going for that. Neither did she want her name advertised in the press as a witness. We compromised and she allowed me to arrest her for prostitution. She was sitting safe and sound in jail. And then the wires in the department got crossed. Somehow she got offered bail and, even though we'd agreed she wouldn't post it, apparently she did. They cut her loose when I was at the airport dropping my partner off for his investigative trip to Mexico..."

At the mention of the trip, Shaye's heart literally warmed, and tension faded. For a second, despite all the horrible circumstances, she felt that she was helping something to go right. "That trip worked out?" she asked softly.

Danielo nodded. "I had to let Chow take the credit for your detective work, Shaye, so he could go. That was the only way."

Shaye shook her head, and then nodded. "No, yes, of course. That's great, actually."

"I came back from Orlando and I found Vicki Cruz gone," Danny said. "Nowhere to be found in town even though we borrowed three units from Oceanside to help us search. Then she had the gall to leave a message for me that her pimp had posted bond and she knew how to keep safe; she was still in the county for her court date, but miles out of town, she said." Danny made a violent gesture of helplessness. "Dammit, I'll tell you. I basically tore up our little locker room when I got that message. Things in such a mess anyway with my marriage. Plus me flushing a year of sobriety with booze down the shitter, 'Eden', that night partying with you and your friends. And then the next night. Acting in a manner unbecoming to an officer."

Adam sniggered, and lifted up his chair with a flourish. "Danny," he mumbled, turning on his heel to go retrieve his work things from the bedroom. "You are your own worst enemy."

They watched Adam walk out and then Danielo took a deep breath and expelled it suddenly, remembering to relax his grip on the paper bag he was mangling. "Shaye," he said, reaching it out towards her all the way because she sat stiffly, not budging. "I bought you a T-shirt."

Shaye let him hold his arm out straight, waiting for Adam to leave earshot. Her eyes stayed level with Danny's, even though the lids weighted with sudden tears when she spoke. "I'm seeing someone now, another guy."

Danny's arm dipped for a second, but he lifted it and still extended the bag. She watched tears leak from his already swollen eyes. "Whatever," he said softly. "I'm doing my ninth step in my recovery. I'm making things right. You're probably lying anyway. But you've got every right."

Shaye examined his dark brown eyes, the flush on his cheeks, the dark stubble on his chin so different from Adam's smoothness. She couldn't deny the sincerity of this fallen detective's expression. It seemed like his whole soul was tied up in hers. It almost could make her forget the whole world for a moment.

Shaye allowed herself a smile. She took the bag and pulled out a brand new folded souvenir T-shirt. Then she dropped the bag and shook out the shirt, noting with some pleasure that it was quite oversized like the last. In a way, just like Adam and Danny, she felt a little sentimental attachment for "Trailer Park Shaye". Those first obsessive weeks, innocent of the murder case, had seemed like happy times in a strange nostalgic way.

"Put the shirt on," Danny urged, sucking back his emotion and allowing himself to smile now, too.

Shaye took time to really look at it. Then she sputtered out a laugh. "Danny, this is a dolphin! Mine was a shark!"

Danny crawled over by her, now that her relaxation seemed to make him feel welcome. He grinned, and pointed at the dolphin's getup. "Yeah, but look here," he teased. "This guy is wearing a hula skirt, and he's got this cool Margerita in his hand…"

Shaye gave him a playful push in the arm. It felt perfectly natural. Her hand remained on his hard bicep muscle for a second too long.

"My shark was surfing, Danny!"

"Well, see, this guy's more welcoming. That guy would eat people."

His cheeks flushed more as he teased her. They pushed into each other jokingly and Shaye pouted, able to hear a tone of light flirtation in her voice. "The only thing they have in common is they're wearing sunglasses..."

Suddenly, she saw Danny look up. Adam stood by the kitchen island stiffly, just staring at them.

"Keep an eye out for Vicki Cruz when you're out there, man," Danny requested. "Why don't you take her picture and show it around amongst your friends tonight?"

Adam padded up to take the photo. To Shaye, he seemed all frozen up. But to the world, he'd just seem gay, in the emotional sense of the word, if a bit wry and cynical.

"Well why not, Danny?" he said, tucking the photo into a very tight slacks pocket on his hipbone, the sight of which made Shaye's own pelvis tighten in remembrance. "I doubt you'll be using it much tonight."

Adam gave the door just a little slam on his way out.

Danny raised his eyebrows. "I swear to God I won't try to sleep with you, Shaye, or touch you in any inappropriate way. Can't Adam see now that I'm sober, and I'm sorry?"

Shaye shook her head, and flopped back against the couch. "It's not that," she said. "It's complex," Danny heard for the second time that night. "You wouldn't understand. So please don't worry about it."

Danielo shook his head. "Well, let's get down to some work," he said. Shaye got up and retrieved her forensic research file from the bedroom. And she decided to be polite and bring back a plate full of fruit, cheese and croissants for them to nibble on during the dinner hour.

They leaned their heads close together, distractedly munching the food while they flipped together through every page of the research on the murder weapon that Shaye had produced on the county library computer.

She also retrieved the borrowed history books and explained the whole "silver heel" legend in detail, as well as the warrior personalities that were prized for centuries in men of that region.

"Wow," Danielo said. "I tried to explain some of this to Glenn Chow, based on what you managed to tell me the other night- but this is really freaky stuff. He's supposed to call me on my police mobile phone tonight. He's staying down at a hotel in a village at the base of that mountain..."

"El Viejo? The mountain with the silver mine?"

"That's right. El Viejo was the definitely the name. The village is called Rio Loco."

"Crazy River?"

"Is that what it means? Even though I police this park, unfortunately I know not a word of Spanish. Have you learned any, Shaye? Maybe it could help."

Shaye looked back sheepishly, and didn't know exactly how to answer. "I remember my husband speaking fluent Spanish whenever we went to South Beach for Catalog shoots. And some of the beaches in Mexico and Venezuela. Back then, Danny, to tell you the truth, I hardly even spoke English. I mean, Riley did all the talking. He ordered in all the restaurants. He even chose my clothes. I was such an idiot. I traveled constantly to all of these wonderful far off places, and I never even got to talk to the locals."

"Don't be so hard on yourself," Danny said and he reached out instinctively to pat her leg.

They both made note of the gesture and Shaye watched his hand until he removed it, basically in slow motion.

But he kept a cockeyed grin on his face, looking over her skimpy skirt and tiny flowery shirt, and the way her breasts asserted themselves standing out braless under the wisp of brushed fabric.

Every breath made her hardened nipples rise and fall.

"Oh, Danny," she finally admonished in exasperation, dropping the completed file on the coffee table. "Are you going to faint or something?"

Danny chuckled. "You know, my wife Lorrine's really pretty, too; did I ever tell you that?"

Shaye felt suspicious, as she often felt lately. "You specifically said I was the most beautiful woman you had ever seen in the flesh-your quote. So how do you account for that?"

He grinned. "You've got a good memory. The thing is, Shaye, you're the most beautiful woman *I've* ever seen, personally to me. And that's no lie. But Lorrine stands her own out in the world. She was head cheerleader in our high school and she won a few beauty contests back in our little rural county in Michigan. And she still keeps her body nice with no real effort. I imagine there are guys out there who bought posters of you in your swimsuit days, but if they saw you here at your most down and out, they wouldn't realize it was the same girl. It's all about who's on top, I guess."

Shaye gave a dry little laugh, actually liking what he had said. "That's what modeling is," she agreed with him. "All smoke and mirrors. I just hope you can look at me and not be swayed and attribute some terrific personal qualities to me that I just don't have."

Danny's eyes crinkled at their corners as he smiled. "Truly," he said, taking the liberty to adjust one wispy stray strand of her hair. "I look at you, Shaye, and I'm totally entranced. I love your soft green eyes that remind me of a female cat skirting the edges of society. I love your hair that mesmerizes me…"

He tried to pull it down, but Shaye lightly slapped his hand away in challenge.

He pulled away and put his head down in his hands, his hands on his knees. When he came back up it was with his face all rubbed and ruddy. "Let me explain this weirdly, Shaye. Let's say that you weren't a special person inside. If all I saw was your looks, I'd still be fascinated, I admit it. I'd probably love you even if you *were* just some Barbie doll like Adam's friends think, with nothing inside…"

There was no way to prevent it, the comment about how little the "girls" thought of her was enough to hurt Shaye, the subject of being an empty beauty was such a soft spot for her.

Danielo watched her flinch, but continued. "But here's the thing. And I want you to seriously understand this for all eternity. Shaye, if I knew you and you were exactly the same girl in personality, yet really ugly- I'd still be here tonight. Not just working with you on this case, but also telling you that you're beautiful. Because that's how I see you."

"In other words, that I'm God?" Shaye joked.

"I was just wondering," Danny ventured to ask her now, lifting up the hem of her floaty skirt to indicate what he was talking about. "Now that you're dressing up again and all, and you're back to a normal weight, are you planning to go back to modeling?"

Shaye cocked her head and looked at him like he was crazy. She'd been telling herself for a year now that the reason she would never go back to modeling was her changed looks. Really, it went so much deeper than that. How could she ever go back to a career like that which had no meaning? She realized it right now sitting here on this shabby couch, next to this neighborhood boy detective wearing too much aftershave.

If she did ever have a career again, shouldn't it be something that actually helped people? And why on earth had she never stopped to ponder that simple point before? Had she been truly brain dead? She couldn't even claim poverty or privation as to why the glamorous world of fame had lured her. She'd just pursued her career following Riley and hardly even realizing she'd become famous.

She sighed and told Frank Danielo a white lie, only a portion of the truth for a moment. "Danny," she said. "I don't know how to say this. Lots of women are pretty. But the camera can do cruel things, and a lot of great girls fell by the wayside where I succeeded. Just for the tiniest little problems. A bit of cellulite, an old acne scar, the way someone's nipples tilt..." Shaye blushed furiously as Danny glanced down there, obviously entranced by the tilt that he saw. "My body changed when I got sick," she explained bluntly.

"But you gained back the weight," he said. "You're five nine, Shaye, and you weigh like a hundred and ten pounds now. Isn't that perfect for a model? Don't they want you to be thin?"

Shaye sighed so that it shook her frail frame. "Danny, a swimsuit model is different than a fashion model. All-natural, my measurements used to be thirty-four double D breasts- twenty-four waist, thirty-four hips. Look, this is so embarrassing to talk about... Photographers and stylists used to stand over my breasts, measuring them, recording every angle, pinching my nipples to make them blush, rubbing in moisturizer and makeup, making sure that the gooseflesh didn't stand out too much when they threw ice water over me..."

Danny, looking clueless, gawked between her face and her breasts now.

And Shaye was able to look him in the eye and continue without breaking down. "The point is- my breasts have changed... when I lost the weight. At one point in the hospital, at the worst, I weighed seventy-eight pounds. It wasn't just that everybody thought I was going to die. But my illness ruined the firmness of my breasts. That was why Riley left me, because I'd lost my marketability.

"Tropical Sun was a corporation, so Riley took all the company's money- even though it was all money made on me. He reinvested it so I couldn't touch it and then he divorced me before my continued hospital bills could deplete his personal assets.

"I remember, Danny, one day when I was barely lucid in intensive care Riley came in and poked at my breasts. 'You're not special anymore,' he said to me. 'No longer one in a million.' And he meant my breasts. Because that was my fame."

"Shit," Danny said. "Is that why it bothers you so much when I act like a male pig? Because your husband treated you that way?"

"Who knows?" Shaye said. "All I know is that my breasts came back 34C and the firmness is no longer there. The skin is loose. I also have scars up by my collarbone where the hospital put in a central IV line and three larger scars on my stomach from surgery. It's all ridiculous, I know, but it means I can't model."

Danielo stared at her with an intensity Shaye had to admit she liked. She could see him thinking and pondering, really focusing on her.

Finally, he spoke, "Well, why don't you just get breast implants then, like ninety percent of other models? You're so beautiful, Shaye. You're not just one in a million. You're one in a hundred million..."

"I don't *want* to model!" Shaye suddenly declared. Her voice was so sharp it seemed to cut through the room. She breathed in, gathering herself. Danny had made her admit the truth now, out loud, to both of them. "I don't believe in it anymore," she said.

Danielo respected her emotion and remained quiet for a bit. They both chewed on cheese and grapes until she settled down. Then he took one of her hands, as much a friend as a potential suitor.

"I'm actually glad you don't want to model again, Shaye," he said. "Because I have a proposition for you, but I had no clue where your heart was. What I want to suggest is that you go to college and learn police forensic science.

"I really think I can help you and Adam get rid of the charges against you so you don't have a record. Then, after you get your college degree, I could help you get work. I think it would be a great career for you, but I was afraid to suggest it to you because you're so glamorous."

Shaye flashed him a pitying look. "It's not that, Danny. But do you really think I could do professional work like that and not fail? Just like I've failed at everything else in life? I'm even afraid to drink water out of the tap, or go to the toilet without perching above the seat."

"But you do great forensics work," Danny persisted. "Glenn Chow even agreed with me. I told him the research on the murder weapon came from one of my regular informants, and he thought I was lying and I got one of my old supervisors in New York City to help me. You get it? My partner thought I used a whole *police* department to do that computer simulation and trace it to the town in Mexico!

"You do brilliant police work, Shaye. And you pick up things like learning to speak Spanish so quickly it's scary. You're an incredibly intelligent girl..."

Shaye's ears echoed so that she thought she was going to faint. In her whole spoiled, coddled and rarified lifetime, she'd heard a lot of things. But she'd never once heard those particular words before!

Chapter 16

A little while later, Glenn Chow called Danny and the two police officers spoke for about a half hour. After Danny signed off, repeatedly admonishing his partner to be careful, he seemed satisfied with the way the evening was going.

"My partner found the name of the silversmith," he explained to Shaye. "Chow told me everybody walks around those towns wearing silver medallions. And they're suspicious people, none too friendly. He had to talk to each person for hours, through his Spanish-speaking guide, to gain their confidence. Then he'd examine their individual jewelry. No rooster claws to be found, but after two days he started winning people's confidence. Eventually, the locals in the mountain towns mentioned an old man, who's like a kind of a Mexican Indian warlock. The guy supposedly lives in a handmade hut at the mouth of the mine, forging magical silver amulets and doing spells, Chow told me. His name is Delgado Ortiz."

Danielo took a moment to write the name down on the outside of Shaye's file.

"Get this," he said, eagerly, while Shaye listened in true fascination. "If the townspeople want to talk to Ortiz, they don't bring money. They have to bring him ceremonial gifts- including a chicken roasted underground in a clay oven. For real; that's their custom."

Shaye felt lost in the mystery and she giggled. She hated the fact that people were being killed, yet she couldn't help loving this intricacy that she could lose her own problems in, perhaps forever.

It was easy for her envision the mountain and the old man. She imagined him with long gray hair down his back and darkly tanned skin, shaping the barely cooled molten silver with blackened hands. And she could almost smell the exotic spices wafting off the offering of roasted chicken.

"They really give gifts of chicken?" she asked with a giggle. "Because they did used to worship poultry there."

Danielo nodded. "Well, I know this type of thing makes sense to you. To my partner, also. But I'm just too impatient," he said. "Anyway, lucky for all of us, fifty dollars is a fortune to them there. Because that's what it will take for Chow's guide, who's putting him up in Rio Loco, to get another family in the mountain town of Ascension to make the special chicken recipe…" Danny laughed. "I kid you not, this shit is for real."

Shaye nodded, looking more appropriately serious than he did. If the old myths and customs of the Santasemana region were so intricate, it made sense that a man like the killer might have perverted it all, hallucinating strange motives and shadows and totems that compelled him to violence after something that happened in this park set him off.

"I'm just glad that I was able to help," Shaye said. "I just hope all of this effort in Mexico really will lead us to the suspect."

"Glenn Chow thinks it will," Danny said. "More than one person told him the legend of the rooster with the silver heel, but they told him only a special man would be allowed to wear that medallion. And Delgado Ortiz is the only man who could make the amulet correctly, becauses he's descended ten generations down from the silversmiths who made the original design.

"Anyway, my partner is different from me. I like the nitty gritty of police work most, and he likes the details. So this is all right up his alley. He's got his ceremonial chicken baking in its clay oven in the earth overnight. Tomorrow morning, his guide with carry him on a donkey back up to Ascension- a completely inaccessible town he said, where you'd think even a mountain goat would have trouble getting to. Just before sunrise, Chow will pick up the roasted chicken. Then he carries it, by foot, to Ortiz to present it at daybreak…

"Since Glenn Chow can't speak a word of Spanish, the guide will follow him. But he'll only approach the silver mine if Ortiz invites. I told Chow to do like the missionaries in Africa used to and bring some American candy and trinkets, just in case the chicken isn't enough!"

He laughed at his own politically incorrect humor, and Shaye had to chuckle with him.

"So, I guess it could work out alright," Danny summed up. "Chow's gonna probably call around ten in the morning, and then we may have a name to put on our killer." He ducked a little to make sure Shaye's eyes met his. "I'd like for you to ride along with me in the squad car tomorrow," he said. "If Chow emails me a name and a photo, I think you could help me find him. We can put you in the back seat, so anybody looking will think you're a suspect. Would you want to do that, Shaye?"

Shaye felt surprised everything now seemed to be going okay. In one way, riding in Frank Danielo's squad car as he trolled for the killer was the most dangerous place in the world she could be. In another way, that was the single way that the killer could not sneak up on her. And being taken by surprise was the thing she feared most of all.

"Okay, I'll ride with you, Danny," Shaye said. She stood up and stretched so that her cop friend was staring directly at her belly button.

Demurely, she tugged her camisole down, trying to cover her bare skin. She stretched again, but not fully. "If Chow's gonna call you first thing, and we're going to go out looking, then maybe you better get some rest now."

"What time is Adam expected home?" Danny asked her.

The question made Shaye nervous, for she realized how the hours alone and fearful stretched ahead of her. But she wasn't much for lying.

"Maybe three," she said. "Something in that area."

"Well, don't take it wrong," Danny said. "But I'd like to stay over here."

She raised her eyebrows.

Danny stood up facing her, and he cupped her chin and then let it go. "I won't try to force you to sleep with me," he said. "But I made this cassette tape to show you how I feel. And I'd be honored if you'd let me kiss you ..."

Shaye began to puff up in a show of justifiable outrage, once again feeling a dip in the rollercoaster.

"But it doesn't matter," Danny said, talking over her silent objection. "As a policeman, I'm really afraid with our witness,

Vicki Cruz, wandering the streets. Our suspect has a new reason to want to kill now, nothing to do with his ceremonies and only to do with protecting himself. Word might have got out, Shaye, that you were interrogating Willie Jeremiah. Or that you've been talking to me. Who knows? I just can't have you sitting in this trailer alone tonight."

Shaye wasn't really afraid of Frank Danielo. In ways she wasn't even afraid when he'd come after her the other night. But tonight, definitely, she saw the concern of an alert cop in his eyes.

"I can sleep here on the couch," he said. "Then you and me can take off first thing in the morning..."

He was able to hold Shaye's eyes for a long while.

"All right," Shaye agreed finally, not really minding having an armed police officer to guard her for the night. After all, she was a girl who would have liked to sleep guarded every night. "Give me a minute."

Danny sat down and grabbed the TV remote, flipping between channels.

Meanwhile, Shaye brought him out an armful of blankets and sheets. "These are very clean," she told him. "They're ours, not the ones that came with the trailer."

"That's fine," Danny tried to say.

But Shaye spoke rapid-fire, her nervousness quickening her speech. "This is a big new bottle of water for you, completely sterile." She set the water down on the coffee table. "A here's a fresh new guest towel, just for you, and a new tube of toothpaste. I'm sorry, but I don't have a toothbrush to go with it. But there is a new soap for you in the bathroom in the morning..." She rattled on, neurotically, hearing the edginess in her voice.

Danielo stood up, drew her in for a warm hug and then let her go.

"What about your wife, Danny?" Shaye asked. "Isn't this kind of strange?"

She saw tears fill Danielo's eyes again, at the mention of Lorrine. "Shaye, we're divorcing," he said. "I told her I wanted to divorce the other night when I got home from here."

Shaye's eyes popped open wide. She did have feelings for Danny. But she'd never told him, so he couldn't possibly have told his wife there was something between them. She must have been cocking her head inquisitively, because Danny warmly patted her hair.

"It's not just because of you, Shaye. I've realized that Lorrine never really loved me. When I was a success in high school, she fell in love with that guy. The guy that would take her out of our town, and go to the big city. But Lorrine never understood my addictions and she never forgave me for the shame I put her through in New York. Since then, I think I've made her skin crawl."

Danielo sighed, and took Shaye's hand as he spoke.

"I would think," he said, "in a certain way, you could forgive your man if he was that screwed up, Shaye, even if he betrayed you. More than my cheating, or my alcoholism, I think it's my vulnerability Lorrine really disliked most of all. But you know, I believe in love. And if you love someone madly, you'd want to work with them no matter where they fall to. I guess that's what I'd like to think."

"I guess I agree," Shaye said tentatively. "I guess I feel that way, too." The closest thing she knew to real love was with Adam, and they certainly loved each other unconditionally. Or did she? Did she really accept Adam's cross dressing? Shaye's mind struggled with this as Danny gazed into her.

"What I realized that night, when I was here," Danny said, "is that, for everything I did to you, you forgave me. I could see it in your eyes, because, in some way, you deeply care about me. Somehow, ambivalent as you are, Shaye, you manage to care about me more than my own wife ever did..."

"Danny, I never said..."

He cut her off gently. "You don't have to say it. You do care, though. And I care for you so tremendously that it's crystal clear that the whole rest of my life was playacting. So, even if I never saw you again, it was time to tell Lorrine that we didn't belong together. I think Lorrine was actually relieved when I told her, Shaye. And she's going to be fair about letting me see Shari. So I think it's for the best of all."

"Oh," Shaye said. "Oh."

She attempted to back up, to leave him politely to his own emotions. But Danny reached out and took her hand, trying to hold her back. "Just let me play the cassette," he said. "And then maybe you'll let me kiss you good-night."

Shaye retrieved Adam's boom box for him, feeling like a little bit of a traitor as she did it. In her mind she reminded herself that nothing physical was going to happen between them. And yet her whole body trembled as she stood before Danny.

Danny maintained the almost reverential silence as well. He sighed, and bent to feed his homemade cassette into the boom box. The tension and the expectation in the room was so strong that it made hairs stand up all along Shaye's body. She felt chilled, but also hot- like this was the hottest place in Florida- a hundred degrees and unbearable. Shaye fanned herself with one hand, watching Danny curiously and really not knowing what she would do.

He stepped up to her and let out a little breath that she felt against her lips. They stood almost the same height and eye-to-eye. Danny let her look right into the depths of him, just like a dark haired little boy, in a half-darkened room, sleepy before bedtime.

Suddenly, the music exploded. The song Danny had taped for her was *"What Do I Have to Do?"* by Stabbing Westward. She'd heard it before- an insistent message of apology from a man who'd done wrong, a man who was shamed and who'd now do anything for his woman. And now Shaye couldn't ignore the power of the message.

Danny took her by the arms, singing along as he stepped even closer, commanding her to look deep inside him. Along with the song, which spoke for him, he apologized. He sang almost in a whisper, caressing up and down her arms so her skin jumped like she was feeling sparks.

Danny went down to his knees, intimately caressing Shaye outside her flimsy sexy outfit. His fingers just grazed her hardened nipples. He rubbed his warm face and light beard stubble over her sensitive belly. Then he nudged her floaty skirt away with his cheek, rubbing his face against her closed thighs.

He lifted his face; his eyes and lips looked beseeching and moist. His voice roughened as he sang along with the words that he'd memorized, offering to do anything for her if she'd just give him one more chance.

Finally, as the music crashed around them, he grasped Shaye's raspberry colored heels, and lowered his head to plant several kisses on her insteps and her painted toes before he sobbed out the last words.

Slowly, he rose to his feet. And Shaye helped him up. She wondered if some of the emotion that showed in his eyes showed in hers also. Because Shaye couldn't deny what she felt for Frank Danielo. Something about him shook her and spoke directly to her heart.

So who was her soul mate? She had given the bulk of her adult life, and all her loyalty as a woman, to Riley Taylor. Now she had to admit that she felt so much more warmth for this police officer that she had only met a few weeks ago that it was staggering.

And then there was what she felt for Adam.

Shaye hated to even go there in her mind right now. She sensed that a relationship between herself and this man who now gazed at her, giving her his all, could be healthy. She pictured them years from now as a happy young suburban couple who liked to take care of their home and joke around with each other, who would laugh and smile a lot in bed, who would cuddle together in front of the television on the few cold winter nights in Florida and who would face life's challenges with a little difficulty- but with love.

Shaye pictured Danny standing by the barbeque grill in the backyard of their imagined home, and turning to face her with the same kind of warmth and curiosity his eyes showed right now. She imaged him carrying her across the threshold of the same modest three-bedroom ranch house on their wedding day. She imagined, on a crisp winter weekend, going out on a quiet river branch in a kayak, and rowing together in sync as she pointed out Florida manatees in the water around them. On Valentine's Day, she imagined buying Danny cute brushed cotton sleep pants with little hearts all over them, and then videotaping him wearing her gift.

These were all things Shaye, with her life of photo shoots and red carpets, had never actually experienced, yet some part of her had always craved it.

She let the images run through her mind as the song by Stabbing Westward played yet again, but this time more softly. She let herself reach out and she lightly brushed the stubble on the side of one of Danny's cheeks as he stood up before her. His eyes implored her and she wondered if he could possibly read her fantasies.

Danny leaned his forehead down to lean against hers. Their noses touched and their breath moved in and out of each other's parted lips as if they were in the rhythm of making love together, not just swaying in time to a song.

"Tell me you don't have any feelings for me," Danny breathed. "Tell me I'm crazy, and that I imagine what I sometimes see in your eyes."

Shaye breathed in, and almost choked on air. Her eyes watered. "I do have feelings," she admitted, wanting to squeeze her eyes so tight shut that she could prevent the consequences of her words from happening.

Danny just breathed out in relief. She felt his strong slightly barrel-like chest push out against her. Determinedly, he released the clasp from her hair to free it and then he hid his face in the nest of her hair. Meanwhile, his hands caressed her all over, just lightly brushing her nipples from the side.

She felt his warmth through his clothing. One of her hands wandered to his side to gently caress him, brushing over his gun, and this excited her more. There was no denying what man she was with, or the fact that this was real.

"Shaye," Danny breathed, as his song for her played once again. "If I say I love you, the words might come out sounding cheap." He looked up into her face, leaving off his sexually teasing caresses to squeeze both of her arms. "But I only said those words to one other woman in my life and that was Lorrine. And they weren't totally true then. I know that now. I really love you, Shaye, tremendously, like a guy like me never even deserves to feel in this life…"

They swayed together dumbly to the beat of the music, both seeming mesmerized. Shaye felt so incredibly confused right now she couldn't bear it.

"When I first saw you," Danny continued. "I saw your eyes and they made me think of everything intriguing, everything mysterious and timeless. The amazing thing, Shaye, is that it wasn't until later that I understood you were so objectively beautiful. Because I was already totally and completely in love with you regardless."

She opened her mouth to protest, but instead she admitted, "I felt a lot for you, too."

They gazed at each other and then Danny leaned forward and softly kissed Shaye. They didn't share any tongue. They just shared the amazing warmth that made her close her eyes, while the warm and relaxing sensation dropped down her body, down her legs, all the way to her painted toes, which curled in excitement.

They pressed their lips together for a while, feeling their hearts thudding against each other. Shaye intertwined her sweaty fingers with Danny's like a high school girlfriend. When they disengaged, their lips seemed to stick together; they parted so gently, and it took so long, that they actually felt the bond break. Shaye then laid her head against Danny's muscular chest, like she was coming in to safety out of the harsh cold world. And he collected her in his arms.

"I'm not stupid, Shaye," she heard him murmur. "I know that you and Adam have your own life and that he wants to take you out of here as soon as he gets the money together."

Shaye gulped around a lump in her throat, knowing that it was true. Danny brought her head up with both hands under her chin so that he could look at her. "I know that a thousand men will tell you they love you in this lifetime. But I want you to know that what I say is true."

Shaye tried to duck her head, but Danny held it up.

"It doesn't matter if you move away," he said, "because you've already changed my life. But I want you to stay, Shaye, and I want to prove to you that I'll take care of you. I'll never look at another woman. So don't even worry about my past, because that's all ridiculous now, in light of what I feel for you. I'll be a good man, and a good cop, because I know you feel that's important. And that makes me realize how important it's always been to me, too."

Shaye finally disengaged. "It does mean a lot to me, Danny. I guess I always sensed that you were a good cop. That's why I probably approached you and took the chance I did. But you know my limitations. You know I'm confused. I really don't know what you expect me to do."

"Marry me, Shaye," Danny said, staring her directly in the face, "as soon as my divorce goes through. Until then, live with me at my house and go to college for forensic science. Forget your whole other life and take a chance."

Shaye took a little step back, almost stumbling on her heels. Danny rubbed her arm encouragingly and he gave her a little smile. "You don't have to do it, Blondie. I'll love you no matter what you do. But there is one thing I want," he said. He grinned and dug something out of his pocket- a little jade necklace in the shape of a Chinese calligraphy letter. He cupped it in his palm for her to see.

"This character symbolizes courage," he said. "I found it at the same shop where I got your T-shirt."

Shaye looked down, intrigued.

"Because the thing I most love about you," Danny said, "is your courage."

He allowed Shaye a moment to gape and look shocked. "Me?" she asked.

Danny smiled. "You're more courageous than anyone I've ever known. I've watched you from when you got here, struggling with fears of the littlest things. And yet you've come out like a heroine, wanting to save lives…"

"Maybe it's just to keep myself from being afraid," Shaye ventured. "I certainly don't see myself as courageous."

Danny slipped the necklace around her neck, and kissed her on the forehead. "Maybe some day you will see it, and you'll understand. But for right now, Blondie, I feel blessed just to know you…"

Slowly, Danny backed away from the kiss, and he sat and settled down under his blankets on the couch. Shaye stared at him, with one hand on her courage necklace and the other self-consciously fixing the shirt that had come up over one of her nude breasts while he was touching her.

Danny winked. "And I bet you thought I was just gonna try to screw you tonight!"

Chapter 17

The next morning- El Viejo Mountain Pass, Santesemana, Mexico

Alternating streaks of gray and dark purple ringed the crest of the stony mountaintop, the colors suffused through the halo of morning mist. Sounds echoed in the vastness, the scrapes of the mules' hooves, the men's backpack frames clanging against the tan rocks that lined the trail and the occasional softspoken command given by Officer Chow and his native guide.

Officer Glenn Chow wore a buckskin vest, a colorful blanket over his shoulder and a rickrack decorated sombrero identical to that of his guide. But, even with his serious Oriental countenance it did not look ridiculous, but rather elemental. The deep abiding silence around the mountain made everything more profound and both men lifted their eyes at the piercing cry of a wheeling hawk.

"We are almost there," the guide said to Chow in broken Spanglish. "Almost at the Casita Ortiz," he added with a grin.

Indeed, they spotted the shack that was built into the mountain. They didn't notice the dwelling on its own merits- actually there had been brushpiles that were larger along the trail, all appearing to be the same composition and design as the home the wizard Ortiz had lived in for almost all of his eighty years.

No, what stopped both men in their tracks- the mature Mexican villager as well as the ambitious young American cop- was the sight of a giant forged silver cross standing tall as the very first rays of daylight struck it. This cross stood in the very center of the path to

241

the entrance of the mine. At ten feet tall, it was several feet higher than the roof of Ortiz's ramshackle dwelling.

Out of respect the guide stayed back. Glenn Chow approached the cross, padding softly and with appropriate reverence. He set the ceremoniously roasted chicken in its ruddy clay oven decorated with ancient designs down directly before the cross. And then he looked up in wonderment at the work of Delgado Ortiz's lifetime. Yes, this full size cross must represented untold wealth in silver, and it could have been brought down the mountain and sold to the finest cathedral, where it could have been viewed by thousands. But here, standing as an intricately carved sentinel to the mine of its origin, it truly seemed to beckon, and welcome, God himself.

"Buenas Dias, Senor. Te gusta El Viejo?" a husky voice said behind Officer Chow.

Chow looked back at a hardened looking old man, dressed in traditional clothing. His eyes flicked over the man's smiling leathery face, his traditional handmade clothing and long gray hair braided in thin strands with colorful dyed leather. But none of this made much impression. For Chow's gaze remained riveted on the item that the man leaned on like a staff- a five-foot long, five pronged spurred garden rake! The tines of the rake were forged of silver--and lovingly shaped into the likeness of a rooster's claw.

Adam walked into the trailer at three twenty that morning and headed straight for the couch. He wore a black, body-hugging cocktail dress with tiny sequined scales that sparkled like water and a forties-style slit that sashayed as he advanced. His eyes were heavily smudged with kohl-style eyeliner and, with his hair short, he resembled Liza Minelli in the movie *Cabaret*- vintage feminine and innately tragic as he stood with hands on hips staring down at the man sleeping on his couch.

Officer Danny stirred and, half asleep, tried to grab for the television remote that threatened to slip off his hip, down his back and onto the shag carpeting.

Instead, Adam grabbed it away and bitchily shut off the television that was showing snow.

"Don't let me disturb you," he said to Danny.

If Danny had looked up right then, he would have seen the two tears that made Adam's ripe eye makeup even fuzzier. But it took him a moment to get turned around and gather the cover comfortably around him.

"What's up, man?" he croaked to Adam in a sleepy voice, yawning like this was the best sleep he had gotten in a long time and he was about to slide back into it.

"I should ask you what's up," Adam said. "Why are you sleeping here?"

"Shaye and I are going out first thing in the morning looking for my witness. I didn't want to leave her here until you got home. What time is it anyway? What took you so long?"

Adam had no answer for that, but he shook his head and then flicked his dress, heading away to his bedroom. "Go back to sleep, Danny. Who am I to interfere with police business?"

Danny stopped him. "Hey Brother," he said. "You look pretty tonight."

Adam faced him again, just for a second, with his expression souring at Officer Danny's lame attempt at political correctness. "You're such an asshole," he said, in lieu of goodnight.

At the first real morning light, Shaye got up and lightly crept past Danny sleeping on the couch with his police radio tucked under his chin and his white tube socks sticking out of their blanket. She made her way across the living area, dodging creaky floorboards and she padded into Adam's bedroom, wearing the new "shark" T-shirt and stretchy gym shorts.

Adam was wide awake, shirtless, leaning back against the headboard with his arms crossed- obviously stewing.

Shaye tried cracking a smile. "We've got police protection," she attempted.

Adam's face, washed clean of makeup, seemed to glow purely in the morning light. "I noticed," he said.

Shaye stepped over to the bed, remembering their recent wild lovemaking, and feeling lit up with just a bit of that passion again. Adam sensed the feeling and he blinked his big auburn eyelashes, as though trying to protect himself from her intensity.

Flirtily, Shaye lifted the T-shirt up on both sides, showing Adam a glimpse of her smooth tan sides. She did a tiny little dance step like a stripper for him and, as he climbed to the edge of the bed, she stepped up between his bare legs. She lowered her head and kissed Adam gently upon his hair. "We could still make love right now."

Adam tilted his head up, engaging her with eyes like sultry molten fire- a level of emotion that tugged at her in ways that Danny could never make her feel. Shaye started to climb up on Adam's legs and Adam gasped, struggling with his own emotions, even as he lightly grasped both of her hips. With his head tilted up to hers, they stretched forward to kiss.

And just then they heard a crash in the kitchen.

Adam pushed Shaye away, abruptly shifting to a harsher-harshly feminine- persona. "Shit!" he said. "That goddamn cop of yours!" He started for the doorway, and then leaned back in. Shaye saw the problem. A large visible hard-on in his tight boxer briefs. He snatched a towel to cover it and then ran for the kitchen.

Shaye followed and found the two men bickering at the coffee machine. Danny, shirtless and hairy, with his white T-shirt tossed over a strongly chiseled shoulder, worked at the coffee machine with two mismatched mugs laid out on the counter before him. Shaye smelled coffee grounds, some of which had apparently spilled on the counter and floor.

And Adam bumped Danny out of the way none too gently with his hip.

"What are you doing here?" he demanded.

"We're going out to drive around all day. I wanted to make breakfast for Shaye. And some coffee."

Adam let out a loud, "Humpf!" and turned to Shaye long enough to roll his eyes. Then he squared off facing Danny. "Shaye can't have coffee, even if she says she wants it..."

Danny raised his brows like Adam was just being silly. But Adam's intensity made his expression freeze. "She suffers from bleeding ulcers, Danny, and coffee is just one of the items that can set the condition off. That's also why she can't have liquor- or any spicy food."

Shaye stood there and watched Adam explain the demoralizing truths. "I watch every single thing Shaye eats," Adam continued. "Because she's not under medical care anymore. Not that all their care helped her much... she was dying in the State Hospital. She's actually been healthier here..."

Danny turned to Shaye with his brows raised. "Is it true?"

Shaye sighed. "Yeah. Adam's right. I wasn't just mentally ill. In fact, the only reason they said I was so crazy was that they called me paranoid about my illness- and especially about doctors."

"And suicidal," Adam added as he began to pull food from the refrigerator. "Just so you know who you're toying with like everything's fun and games."

Fearless in Florida

Danny stood there looking helpless and shocked, and Adam turned to Shaye. "Would you like some hot cocoa, Sweetie?"

Danny stepped forward. "I can make the cocoa. Now that I know not to make coffee, I won't."

Shaye literally stamped her foot before she could catch herself. She straightened her posture to look a bit more mature. "I'm not an invalid!" she said. "I'd rather both you guys just thought I was nuts. I can get my own breakfast here!"

Neither man listened and Shaye hated to approach closer in the flimsy T-shirt and sleep shorts that suddenly made her feel shy. As Adam and Danny tried to shoulder each other away from the counter full of breakfast food, Danny's telephone suddenly trilled.

Everybody stopped moving as Danny pressed the phone against his ear, trying to make out the staticcy call.

"Oh my God," he said, his face seeming to lose much of its tension. "For real? The rooster's claw! So what's the suspect's name? I don't understand. Oh. Oh shit. Okay. All right. So talk to them and call me back. Be careful. And don't tell them he's wanted on a crime."

He clicked off his telephone and looked between Shaye and Adam. "Delgado Ortiz, the old wizard silversmith guy, he definitely sold a rooster's claw hand rake. In fact, he uses one himself. Glenn Chow just saw it. Glenn just left him an hour ago."

Shaye gasped. "So it's all really real?"

Danny winked. "As real as a heart attack, Baby." He turned to slap some cheese slices onto two dry English muffins, and then cupped them in one hand. "Delgado Ortiz told Chow that he only sold a rooster claw, years ago, to one other man, a young man descended from many generations of chiefs of their old tribe- a man who is quite tall and light skinned, resembling an American. This young man, he said, was from the town of Ascension, and everybody knew him because he was different. He seemed fated to become a leader..."

Shaye held a hand to her heart as she leaned up against a barstool. "This sounds exactly like my guy, then. The one that dated Mami Ramierez."

"That's what Chow says," explained Danny. "This guy had big dreams for a community where people still live like they did two thousand years ago. But he knew the world was changing. His plan was to go to America and create some kind of haven for Mexicans there. He was only nineteen years old when he left his town, but he

245

truly thought he was going to change the world. Step one was to go to America.

He had a trade- he was a master gardener. And he already spoke impeccable English, which he had learned down at school in Rio Loco. Delgado Ortiz stresses that this young man was a warrior, and that he had no doubt he would succeed and do great things. The young man told everybody he loved that he planned to be gone a very, very long time, perhaps forever. And he had the personalized rooster's claw rake forged for himself as a good luck talisman, and an eternal reminder of his heritage."

Shaye bit her nails, as Danny wrapped up the two makeshift sandwiches in napkins, and snagged a quart of their orange juice to guzzle from the carton.

"Something doesn't sound a hundred percent right," she said. "This guy is Mexican, from that kind of tiny village. So wouldn't his family know exactly where he is now if he had traditional values? Wouldn't he see the well being of his family as paramount?"

"Glenn Chow, and his guide, plus a few of the local police officers are heading out to the family's chicken farm in Ascension now. It was the local officers who patched through Chow's call to me."

Shaye raised her eyebrows and looked toward Danny almost in an appeal. "Did the silversmith tell Chow the suspect's name?"

"Jorge Colon," Danny said.

And Shaye literally jumped- for everything fell into place. She remembered the white landscape truck and the man riding in the passenger seat with forearms like stone and the gaze of an eagle. She remembered the lawn worker who propositioned her telling her how this man had been thrown off an important job in the region just because he was Mexican…

Shaye realized that, more than once, she had stared directly at the serial killer.

"Danny," she breathed. "I know him! I've seen Jorge Colon. Everybody calls him George around here. He owns a landscape business. And a big white Mack truck." She reached out in a gesture towards Adam. "Remember?" she asked him. "Remember me pointing out that truck?"

Shaye stepped up closer to Adam, and he rested a hand gently on her shoulder. "I do actually remember, Sweetie," he said. "Maybe we really need to get out of here now."

Danny glanced inquisitively in Shaye's direction. "Now?" he asked her. "Shaye, you need to come with me. If this suspect's in the park, you can point him out!"

Shaye stood directly between the two men. She squeezed her lips tight in a pained expression and then turned to Adam. "I can help him," she said. "I recognize Colon. I have to go."

Adam looked between them, with real nervousness showing. Neither backed down. "At least let me make a decent breakfast for Shaye. Something healthy."

Shaye touched him on the back and said, "I'll get dressed."

Shaye took only two minutes and then came out dressed oldschool in jeans, Keds and the new T-shirt, which she viewed as lucky. Adam sat on a bar stool with a dishtowel clutched in a fisted hand and a faraway expression on his face.

Shaye looked to him questioningly. "Danny went out to the squad car," he explained. "And he took those cheese sandwiches. He said he didn't want to wait for me to cook breakfast because he already made food for you. He could take care of you, as he put it."

Shaye's head started to spin. Maybe she really did need food, good food like Adam had suggested. She suddenly felt afraid of going out there with Danny and confronting the killer. But she'd come so far now that she couldn't even tell Adam how afraid she was. Like an adolescent, she felt committed to the freedom she had demanded now, even if she didn't know if she wanted it.

"Adam," she attempted, her voice breathless. "If we don't do something to stop this killer, then he could come after us. I feel so tired of running at this point. Always running seems worse than anything."

Adam nodded his head slowly and his eyes looked very dark and ominously shiny, like a once big fire that had been hastily tamped down. "Do what you have to do, Shaye," he said. "Danny's waiting for you..."

Danny drove the squad car for the first ten minutes chewing on his English muffin and talking animatedly on his police radio.

Shaye quietly worked on eating her muffin, washing it down with water from a fresh bottle that she carried. She felt very bad about how she had left Adam- so bad that she almost wanted to cry. And she made a few glances backwards before Danny made the turn and they swung onto Flamingo Beach Parkway. Shaye couldn't wait until she could get home tonight, and Adam would be back from his job at Foxy Lady and she could apologize.

But she sensed already that today might prove to be a very long day. "First stop is back at the station," Danny said to her, twisting around to talk. "I'm going to see if I can get a paper photo of Jorge Colon that we can show to people here in the park. So far, they say they've got no matches on any crimes for him in Florida recently. They're checking other states and Mexico right now…"

"Can you bring up the photo on your computer right now?" she asked. "Even before we get to Oceanside, I can tell you if he's really the man I've seen."

Danny sighed, shrugging his shoulders as though he felt ashamed. "I don't really know how to do it," he said. "Glenn Chow can ride around and play with that computer while he's driving, and make it useful… Maybe you could do something."

In the back seat, Shaye wrestled the computer out of its case and balanced it on her lap while Danny swung in and out of traffic to speed their ride to Oceanside. "Tell me your passwords," she said to Danny when she was ready.

He had to rummage in his glove box to find the little piece of paper where he kept his passwords scrawled, making the ride even more erratic. Then he called them out to Shaye. She had Colon's photo up within seconds.

She sighed, and the breath rattled in her throat. "It's him," she struggled to say. "It *is* him." And then she fought down a sob. She was staring at the driver's license photo of the lawn service owner. She had stared directly into his face once before. And that glance had made something within her vibrate in disturbance just as seeing his high cheekboned visage in the driver's license photo did now.

She had *noticed* Jorge "George" Colon. She had noticed him before the death of Josie Swank. So, theoretically, if she had voiced her suspicions to Officer Danny back then she could have prevented that death. And yet never once had she suspected Colon as the Flamingo Park serial killer.

No- and Shaye laughed at herself sneeringly now- she had suspected one of his leering pint-sized former workers. She'd suspected the lawnworker when he crouched outside her window counting money. And then when he'd tried to get her to sell him her body up there by US1, she'd gone postal- throwing trees at the man and chasing him away while he screamed at her in Spanish.

Meanwhile, the truck carrying the actual killer, a man with hands steady as steel and eyes cold as ice, had simply driven away.

Now, Shaye angled the computer screen toward the front seat, struggling to keep it steady as Danny weaved at sixty-five.

"Here he is," she said. "Here's George Colon. What you don't see in this picture is that he's tall. He has very athletic muscles. He stares a person in the eye and doesn't look down..."

Danny shook his head at the photo that was obviously unfamiliar to him. "You know, it's funny," he said. "I spend so much time looking at the known lowlifes around the park, that I might have totally ignored a cleancut guy that owned a business. I don't think I've ever seen this guy."

"Danny," Shaye breathed, "I'm so sorry. *I* saw him. And I actually noticed him before the second murder. Maybe if I had done something then I could have stopped it..."

Danielo pulled out some Wrigley's gum and crushed a stick between his white teeth thoughtfully. Then he offered one to her, even though she waved it away. "You can't punish yourself for stuff like that, Shaye. What you don't understand is that we don't even have enough evidence to bring Colon in at this point anyway. Police work is a complicated thing."

Shaye plastered herself up against the wire mesh as Danny came to a short stop in the City of Oceanside Police Parking Lot.

"What do you mean you can't arrest him?" she asked. "I reconstructed the rooster's claw rake. And then we connected Colon to it... Isn't that enough?"

Danny turned to look back at Shaye pityingly as he gathered his stuff.

"Shaye, honey," he said. "First we need to *find* the weapon. And some of the victims' blood on it would be really helpful. Then we need to connect Colon to the victims. Just him driving around the park when you saw him was no crime."

Shaye felt antsy and agitated in the back seat, and it didn't help that she was now locked in, as Danny commenced climbing out in front of the police station.

"Look," she said to him through the crack in the open door. "Bring your picture. And I can find his one former worker. Maybe he can tell us exactly where Jorge Colon is. Seriously, it's worth a try. So please hurry."

Danny snapped his gum and winked. "No, Blondie, I was actually gonna dilly dally around in the station for a while and eat some donuts. Maybe you should play some video games on that thing or something, and get comfortable!"

Shaye grasped the computer tighter and glared out at him with spite, even though he probably couldn't see back in through the semi-tinted glass. He had left the motor running, along with the air conditioning, so at least she could breathe.

Even so, a panic attack dimmed her vision for a few seconds. She woke with her panties damp with urine and her chin on the top of the laptop screen. Apologetically, she wiped some of her drool from the little laptop lid. She swelled her nostrils a few times, breathing in the astringent and frigid air-conditioned air. Officer Danny could have been gone five minutes or forty-five for all she knew. But all she could do was get to work. At least the computer, her weapon of choice, was sitting on her trembly legs.

Shaye attempted to hack into the Department of Motor Vehicles to get information on Jorge Colon's work truck. But her efforts proved worthless and she was sure, when Danny returned just a few minutes later, that his had been much more productive.

He came out with a leather folder overstuffed with papers, as well as little bag from Dunkin Donuts just for spite. He had white sugar on his dark lip fuzz, and he happily grinned.

"Jorge Colon's work truck is a 1987 Mack Bulldog, registered right here in the county. I've got all units in the area searching for it right now." He patted the file. "I've also got an 8x12 photo of Colon, blown up off that shot in the license."

"That's great," Shaye said, "you could show it around. Even if you don't find him today you could at least warn people..." Her voice was hopeful.

Danny backed out of his spot rather carefully. When he was back in traffic, heading back to the familiar turf of the park, he sighed again. "You're not making this overly easy for me. But I think you know better. Jorge Colon's not a suspect at this point, so we have to stick to calling him a witness. Do you think you'll be able to handle that?"

Shaye felt helpless and queasy, maybe from the breakfast without stomach-coating milk. Or maybe it was being tossed around in this car, utterly helpless in every fashion.

"Danny," she asked. "What would it take to make Colon officially a suspect?"

He laughed. "Well, definitely if we could catch him in the act."

"There is that," Shaye said glumly.

"More realistically," Danny said, "if we find Victoria Cruz, she can identify him as her assailant. We can convince the local judge not to give him bond on her beating. And that will keep him in jail for a while."

"Okay," Shaye said, a little hesitantly. She hated the idea of waiting for something that they couldn't be absolutely sure would happen. Instead, she had a better idea. "Danny, how about if I could find Willie Jeremiah in the park? And what if he could connect Mami Ramierez with the photo of Colon? What if he could identify Colon as Mami's boyfriend?"

Danny met her eyes in the rear view mirror. "Well, then we'd be a little closer to calling Colon a suspect," he said. "So how about we go looking for Willie Jeremiah?"

There was a hush as the squad car slid into heavily shaded bower that was Caiman St. in midmorning. "This is where Jeremiah hangs out," Shaye said, leaning forward and keeping her voice hushed as well, as if it mattered with the window closed. There seemed something dramatic, almost gothic, in the situation, and every breath seemed to make a noise as it drew in through Shaye's throat.

"I don't know why he'd hang out here," Danny said. "Considering it's just about the prime place for him to get arrested for vagrancy. To tell you the truth, after that day you sent me after him here, I haven't seen him since."

Shaye drew in another almost painful breath. "I think he still comes here for the night- to drink. Then he lights a campfire to make his morning coffee. He seems pretty set in that ritual," she asserted.

Just then, as the squad car progressed at around three miles per hour, and Danny opened his window to let in heavy swampy air, they both at the same time caught a whiff of campfire smoke.

The smoke drifted in a silver thread out from the wall of slender saplings and tangled brush and vines alongside the canal. Then they caught sight of a dark ragged figure standing up and abruptly tamping out the campfire, trying, too late to hide it from them.

"Yo, Willie J.," Danielo called out. "Come on out here. I need to talk to you."

Instead of responding, Jeremiah silently turned and scuttled away through the woods. If someone hadn't known he was here already, they might really have thought they hallucinated and the vague human form they had seen was only a spirit.

"Oh crap," Danny said, struggling to extricate himself, and Shaye had to beg him, "Let me out!" for the door was locked- she was a "prisoner" after all.

Without wasting time to argue, Danny released her door, and Shaye sprang out. She outstripped him, streaking across the slippery sandy grass and diving without hesitation into the brush. She ran the same route she had recently walked, through the shortcut behind trailers and alongside the canal.

Ahead of her Willie Jeremiah ran, panting and cursing. But he did not move lightly like Shaye did. His clumsy combat boots wedged under slim wooden brush that blocked the path, and his loose uniform shirt snagged on thorns. He even yelped once, loudly, as a low palmetto frond lashed the side of his face.

"Shit, mothafucka!" he exclaimed.

Finally, panting, he fell back against the wire dog kennel in Darlene's back yard while the four slavering pit bull mixes inside rocked and rolled. They snapped their jaws, seeming to smile about it, and then choked back their excited drool, eyeing Shaye and Jeremiah expectantly.

Willie Jeremiah rolled his eyes, playing up every inch of his discomfort.

"What you want?" he demanded of Shaye. "What you doin' bringing that cop here?"

"And what are you doing crossing over crime scene tape, Willie?" Officer Danielo demanded as he stepped up. He adjusted his gunbelt officiously, while trying to give his breathing a moment to calm down after struggling through the woods.

Jeremiah straightened up, brushing off his coveralls. "This a free country," he said. "Man can sleep wherever he wants, long as he ain't commiting no crime."

Danny opened his mouth to argue, but Shaye stopped both of them. "Willie," she said. "Officer Danielo needs you to look at a photograph. You can save lives."

"And how many innocent lives got taken in Vietnam? Where was you pigs during that time?" Jeremiah started in.

Again, Shaye interrupted, taking control of the situation by gesturing for Danny to hand the witness their blown-up photo of

Jorge Colon. Her legs felt weak at the moment, for, so far, even though they had proven that Colon was likely to own a hand rake in the shape of a rooster's claw, there was no concrete connection between him and this trailer park. If this strange man who liked to camp at the crime scene positively ID'd the photo, then there would be a firm connection, and then all of this would be real.

"Here," Danny said to Willie, extending the photo out to him. "Just let us know if this is the man you've seen with Mami Ramirez."

Jeremiah snatched the photo bitterly out of Danny's hands. Then he held it forward in front of him, squinting at it. He grumbled to himself, with his words indecipherable. Then he said finally. "I need my readin' glasses. Can't come runnin after a man, get him all riled up like this... This here's police brutality. Violation of a man's civil rights. And me a veteran..."

Danny rolled his eyes skyward and laughed. "Come on, old man," he said. "Let's go get your glasses."

The three of them trudged through the brush, with the sounds of birds and skittering lizards waking up around them.

Danny was first at the miserable campsite, and he circled around it, checking it out. Shaye came to stand shyly beside him, and Jeremiah lowered himself down on his milk crate, retrieving a tin mug of now cold coffee from the dark coals. He took a noisy sip, and put his coal-smudge fingerprints all over the photo.

He sighed.

"I can't be exactly sure, Chickadee," he said to Shaye, making a point of handing the photo back to her, rather than Danny. "Ain't nuthin says this can't be the guy. Black hair and all. And the same skin color. Could be white- or could be Mexican. But that daddy was arrogant an all. I'm over here, an he telling me he gonna take my home away... You know, tha's all I was seein at the moment- was the way he held himself?"

He phrased his statement as a question, and looked up at Shaye almost with an appeal.

Shaye tried to stay gentle with him, with her own feelings all in turmoil. "But it could be him?" she asked. "You're reasonably certain?"

Danielo squared his shoulders, looking antsy. "What it comes down to, Willie, is will you testify on it in court? Or am I gonna have to drag your belongings out of here today?"

Shaye marveled at how Danny's dark eyes could look so honest and good and yet sometimes he could say things like this, in the course of his job, that were nothing more than threats. And ridiculous ones at that. Why would he even want Jeremiah to testify if the man wasn't sure? Was Danny really that confident in her investigative work? Even so, and even if it was flattering, she didn't want him intimidating this stubborn old homeless man who had trusted her several times already, when trust was not his usual habit.

"Danny," she said. "Even if Willie can't ID the photo, he could still ID Colon out of a lineup when we pick him up."

Willie Jeremiah wrinkled up his smudged dark face and winked at her. "Tha's exactly right. The 'man' here didn't bother askin'. Show me Mami's ole man in a lineup, an I can sure as hell identify that motha there!"

He leaned back and laughed to himself, his eyes glazing over as he poked at his dead fire. The laughter, and the smoke, followed them as they retreated from the crime scene, and then Jeremiah called out, "Hey, Offica Danny."

Danielo glanced back over his shoulder.

"You datin' her?"

Shaye and Danny were equally stunned, and their identical wide eyes told the story, despite the fact that they said nothing.

Jeremiah grinned ear to ear, displaying his big white false teeth. "Well," he yelled out, "you got yourself one real sweet girl!" and he raised his coffee cup in a cockeyed salute.

Shaye marveled at this scene that seemed so strange and elemental. The air seemed to vibrate like the cicadas that buzzed in the grass, while electrical transformers lined up not far down the road thrummed with their own strange energy.

Jeremiah now retreated back into the world of his own mind, humming and singing and muttering to himself in a low tone that sounded like gibberish. She and Danny backpedaled toward the squad car. And then Danny looked to her with softness in his expression and he shrugged.

In invitation, he reached out a hand to her. With only the crime scene, the overhanging trees and the strange homeless man as witness, she let him take it. And they held hands as they walked out from the Caiman St. murder scene together.

Chapter 18

Danny grinned in the rearview mirror as they both climbed back into the squad car. "See, even General Willie Jeremiah thinks we make a good couple. So you have to give in to it sooner or later!"

Shaye ignored his bright spirits, glancing back at the mostly hidden campsite as they pulled away. "Why do you ignore him living like that at the crime scene?" she asked. "He's in danger. So why don't you do something?"

Danielo paused to start a new stick of gum. He swung into traffic on US1 and gave the gum a snap, then glanced back at her again in the rearview, with his eyes more shadowed this time.

"What makes you think I *haven't* done something?"

Shaye, feeling chided, stayed silent while Danielo made a series of calls on the police radio regarding the Mack truck registered to Jorge Colon. From what she overheard, the truck had been recently sold to a dealer, right after the Josie Swank murder, leaving another dead end.

Danielo sighed. "Last time you sent me out there chasin' after Willie Jeremiah, Shaye, we kept him at the station for a coupla hours. I did some police work and found out he wasn't just telling tales about that Vietnam veteran shit; he really is a veteran. So I called a social worker in to talk to him. Willie's the kinda guy who refuses to live in a homeless shelter..."

"I know that," Shaye said, feeling a little sad that she had put Danny on the defensive. But she was shocked at what he said next.

Fearless in Florida

"The bad news is, Blondie, Willie's still gonna be living out on the streets for a little while more. But the good news is, we got him signed up to receive his veteran's pension in a few months- decent money, so he can afford an apartment. And believe it or not, good ole bad cop me actually said Willie can have his paperwork sent to my home so he can have somewhere to use as an address for now."

Shaye gulped. "Sorry, Danny," she said. "Sometimes I don't know who to trust these days."

Danny wiped his forehead that had become sweaty from the exhausting morning, and it was still an hour short of noon. He drove with more attention to the back seat than the road ahead.

"You know, Shaye, sometimes a person puts up a certain image or façade that fits them so well that everybody else really believes it. Like really, deep down, to the core. I know my partner Glenn Chow sometimes suspects I'm a dirty cop, some kind of caveman at heart... It's disappointing..."

Danny shook his head. "I wasn't always the 'bad cop', you know. In fact in New York City, it was the opposite. My partner was this older dude from Staten Island, really cynical and rough around the edges and I was always the golden boy, the football hero from a small town. I used to act so squeaky clean and so kind to people, Shaye, that everybody joked that I could never succeed working Vice."

Shaye raised her eyebrows, wondering why she was even taking the time to get to know this man, and why she was even caring what made him tick. But she was, and when she thought about Danny, his emotions and his pains and his dreams, her focus went off herself and her stress went away with it. It felt almost as though she was a normal girl again, sixteen years old and wondering what colleges would take her with her great extracurricular activities and all her parents' money weighed against her less than stellar grades.

But instead of having to face up to college, Shaye Celestia Banks, the amateur beauty queen, had been "discovered" by famous Hollywood Talent Agent Riley Taylor. Shaye never had to face the embarrassment of attending a less prestigious college than all her more intellectual friends. For she had never gone to college.

And now it felt as if the whole wild ride might never have happened. No fame, no photo shoots, no red carpets or scandals in the gossip rags. No e-coli bacteria that tore her body and mind apart.

Now she was just a young girl again, wearing shorts and Keds and a silly dolphin design T-shirt, listening to her first boyfriend talk about himself, attempting to make her understand him. They were riding in his car together, after kissing for the first time last night.

The only problem here was of course that it was a police squad car, and Shaye's pretty face and skeptical eyes were separated from Frank Danielo by wire mesh intended for suspects. A barrier intended for fugitives- which she happened to be...

Shaye let out a little shuddering noise. "Do you ever wonder, Danny," she asked, "About just turning this squad car around and, instead of driving in circles looking for Jorge Colon, just bringing in the fugitive that you have right here locked in your back seat?"

Danny shook his head side to side, but didn't dignify Shaye with an answer.

"I'm not exactly driving in circles," he said. "We know Colon owned a landscaping business here in Flamingo Park, so I'm looking for landscapers. Anybody who might know him, like that one guy you mentioned. So maybe you could help me, instead of having your pity party right now."

His tone stung. Shaye spread her palms against the mesh. "Okay," she breathed. "I don't really have a problem believing you used to be a nice cop. And I want to get to know you better, Danny... I do. I'm very comfortable with that."

Danny didn't answer, but he gave her a thumb's up signal, a gesture of peace. Then he hunched down in his seat, peeking out alternate windows as he made a U-turn to head back north on US1. He was looking intently at anything that resembled fresh landscaping, or workers out and about.

Shaye helped him out, even though telling the story of her last encounter with one of the landscapers made her blush.

"Last time I saw this guy," she explained, "he was planting saplings near the new shopping center across the street from Flamingo Beach Parkway. And what ended up happening was a little embarrassing."

Danny insisted that Shaye tell the whole story- up until the part where she told him how she threw the saplings. And then he enjoyed breathless laughter at her expense. He then made the left where Flamingo Beach Parkway turned into Flamingo Road west of US1, his expression turned sober and they both carefully examined the quarter-mile long swale where new green grass flourished. Half the saplings had unfuruled platter-sized neon green leaves while the other half had wilted.

"Shaye Baby," Danny said. "The landscaping right here looks pretty much completed to me. And inside the plaza too..." He gestured broadly at heaps of bruised earth where heavy machinery rumbled up and down the dunes. Steel and brick skeletons towards the back didn't even yet resemble the commercial buildings they would become. "All I can see is construction workers right now," he said. "You figure the landscapers moved on?"

Shaye truly didn't know the answer. "The impression I got from the man I talked to," she said, "was that this was some huge job. So maybe the landscaping team will come back later on to work up near the plaza, once the dirt is evened out and once the buildings start to go up. But truly I don't know."

"Well, here's my next plan," Danny said. "I know a spot a further up US1 where some of the undocumented day laborers hang out mornings when they're looking for work. As soon as I pull up with this squad car, I know they'll scatter. But I can go through the alleyway in back to sneak up. If you can spot the guy you met that used to work for Colon, I'll come on foot and detain him so we can question him. If we don't find him, maybe you can talk to some of the others in Spanish, Shaye, and find out where Colon's crew is hanging out now. You think you're up to helping me?"

She thought for a minute. "I'll do it," she agreed, feeling utterly fearless for some reason. "But I don't know how that guy's going to accept me after me attacking him and throwing trees last time he met me."

Danny grinned. "Well, maybe he'll think you reconsidered about the prostitution. In fact, maybe I should just use you as a decoy and do a vice sting."

Shaye slapped the mesh between them. "Screw you, Danny!" she admonished.

Danielo reported their whereabouts to his headquarters on the radio as he slid the car into a narrow alley where weeds brushed against both doors. He jounced over a pothole and settled into a stop. From this angle Shaye could just glimpse the crowd of short dark skinned men standing out by a telephone pole near the curb. Danny slid out of his side of the car and helped her out. He directed her to duck as they both slid forward, blocked from view by the nose of the car.

"Do you see him?" he whispered.

Ten or so men milled around, gesturing and laughing and sometimes blocking each other from view. They were all short and dark skinned, and all wore work clothes just like the man she was looking for had worn on both occasions she had encountered him. But she noted something special.

"Look down," Shaye whispered. "See those gray ostrich skin boots. I think that's him. His hair is slicked back today, and last time I saw him it was messy and down over his forehead. But I definitely recognize his face, Danny. I'm sure."

Danielo squeezed her shoulder. "Okay," he said, "follow me. The other guys will scatter as soon as they see me coming. You just need to get "your guy's" attention. Just tell him in Spanish to sit his ass on the curb and put his hands on the ground."

He carefully straightened and helped raise Shaye to her feet. And then he boldly walked out striding in the direction of the landscape worker with one finger pointed straight at him.

"Senor!" Shaye meanwhile called out in Spanish. "This police officer needs to talk to you. He says sit on the sidewalk. Do it now. And put your hands on the ground."

As Danny predicted, the other men ran off in all directions.

Her guy stood out like a wide-eyed little owl, perched unsteadily on his new ostrich skin boots. Instead of looking alarmed at the uniformed officer's approach, he pointed at Shaye.

"Esta mujer esta loca! She's crazy; she's dangerous," he said in Spanish, sputtering so that spittle flew from the corners of his mouth. "I didn't do anything wrong!"

Danny swaggered up to him and pushed him impatiently down to the ground. Then he looked to Shaye. "What did he just say?"

"Nothing, just that he's sorry about how he treated me."

Danny smirked. "Yeah, right, I'm sure. Just tell him we need to find out about his boss, Jorge Colon."

Shaye translated. The lawn worker looked from her to Danny and back to Shaye with shiny skittish eyes. "What do you want to do to me?"

"Nothing," Shaye said impatiently, and then took the liberty of adding, in her best translation. "As long as you give us the information about Colon. We need to find him."

The lawnworker visibly trembled before them. Again, this time Shaye could smell his musky sweat, a product of standing out all morning in the sun in dark green coveralls. She took one dainty step back as he faced her.

"Colon not my boss no more," he attempted in English.

"Where is he, then?" Danny demanded.

"Donde esta el?" Shaye translated.

"I told you," the lawn worker said to her, returning to his native language so he could talk faster. "Mr. Jorge got thrown off the job. Some of us guys stayed back with Mr. Pete. Then Mr. Jorge was angry with all of us. We don't know where he went. We haven't seen him."

"What did he say?" Danielo asked, standing loomingly over the lawnworker in a show of physical power to compensate for his lack of understanding the language. Shaye explained in detail what the man had said.

"So who's Mr. Pete? Ask him."

Shaye did. The lawnworker fired off a helpful string of Spanish. Shaye grimaced, trying to process all of it. "Pete Andersen," she explained to Danny.

She looked around her and realized that they had begun to acquire a crowd of onlookers. Their audience included young teenagers with bare feet leaning on rusty bicycles, two skinny Indian clerks from inside the convenience store and several sewer workers with reflectorized strips on their vests who had paused in their work to gape. A few locals with battered vehicles slowed as they passed, but did not stop.

Shaye spoke hurriedly, yet kept her voice soft enough that she hoped the onlookers would hear nothing. "It sounds like Andersen was Colon's partner, and he took over the landscaping company. This guy thinks that Andersen is still at the construction site on US 1. He's just doing designs now, and planning, with a few white guys. But when the asphalt is complete he told the Guatemalan crew to come back to work on the grass and trees for medians in the parking area. Supposedly Andersen works out of a tempory trailer on the site."

Danny took a step back and inflated his lungs with a contemplative breath. The lawnworker looked curiously between them again.

"Is this guy legal?" Danny asked Shaye. "What do you think?"

"He told me last time he is legal," she said. "That's why this Andersen hired him. Apparently there was some kind of discrimination against the Spanish guys on the crew that weren't citizens and Colon's partner got rid of them."

Now Shaye looked to Danny expectantly. And so did the lawnworker down on the curb, watching his every move. Danny made a simple gesture, reaching out his hand with his palm open. "Tell him, if he's a citizen, then he'll have no problem showing me ID and a green card."

Shaye explained, and the lawn worker dug in his pockets, mumbling to himself. Frayed lottery tickets, condoms and crumpled cash fell out on the sidewalk, and he gathered them back in. He finally handed Danielo his ID and Danielo glanced at the two cards. Then he gestured for the worker to rise and follow them back over to the squad car. The same onlookers still stood around staring and the lawnworker walked with his shoulders slumped, as if deeply ashamed.

At the car, Danny checked back in with his base, and then stepped back over, extending the cards for the lawnworker to take them back.

"He's clean of any warrants or past arrests and his documents are in order just like he said. But don't tell him that. Tell him we'll look favorably on him if he's willing to testify against Colon."

Shaye was sure her distaste for his police methods showed. She had a bit of trouble translating this time, but the lawnworker seemed satisfied. He backed off saying, "Okay, okay." But then he raised his finger and pointed. And it was straight at Shaye.

His lips parted in an expression that was almost a leer, yet he looked quite nervous as he stumbled and backed away. "Ella es un diablo. I'll do anything, I'll comply with you cops," he said, in Spanish. "But keep her away from me. That one is a she-devil!"

Then the lawnworker hurried away, stowing his documents back in his pockets and rubbing his sleeve across his nose.

Shaye lowered her head and blushed again, heading hurriedly for her back seat in the squad car. But Danielo delayed a minute in letting her in. As Shaye cringed back against the door and the onlookers stared, he winked at her. "So, what was that he said back there? Sounded like he said something about a devil. And he pointed straight at you."

Shaye responded by giving a little simper, just the kind she knew he would find endearing. "Actually," she said, "it was just like

Willie Jeremiah. He was just commenting on what a nice couple he thinks you and I make…"

Danny's next stop was outside Shaye and Adam's mobile home, after cutting through a narrow sandy track that wound through the woods from behind the convenience store. Shaye felt a little surprised, for she had assumed they were going together to interrogate Jorge Colon's former partner, Pete Andersen.

"What's up?" she asked.

Danny shook his head and craned around to look at her in the back seat. "I love having you with me, Sugar," he said. "And we could get away with it with guys like that lawnworker and Willie. But, with Pete Andersen, I first have to check on him with the county to see if I can find some vulnerabilities in his business. And, Shaye, there's the chance he could possibly be involved in the killings…"

She mulled the idea around in her mind, something she hadn't considered.

"Well, isn't that more reason I come?" she asked. "Can't I help you? After all, your partner's in Mexico. And I can recognize Colon if he's hiding somewhere on the construction site."

"Shaye, a guy like Andersen can complain," Danny said. "He can say I had someone with me during his interrogation and that could make what he told me inadmissible."

They both took a quiet moment to think about the situation, and then Danny narrowed his eyes. "You know what? I'd really like to have you with me, Shaye. And I'm willing to take a chance- but only if you dress up like a businesswoman, someone official, and you don't say anything about who you are as I question him."

Shaye sighed. She felt tired and her stomach felt a bit queasy. Even with Darlene's family- the men back from jail again- and all their wild dogs up and wandering the street, her little trailer still looked like a sanctuary to her. Somewhere she could take a nice warm shower and catch a quick nap. Shaye stifled a yawn and let her mind, rather than her body, make the decision.

"I can do that, Danny. And I definitely want to go with you."

"So," he asked, "does Adam Ant own any clothes for a businesswoman- or only for hoochies?"

Shaye couldn't help but grin. "Why, did I look like a hoochie to you last night?" she teased. "Because that's about the most demure he owns."

Danny smacked his lips. "Well, it worked for me, Blondie." He laughed. "But I guess it's not the look we're aiming for. How about if I take you to Wal-Mart?" he volunteered. "I'll treat you to a career outfit and you can pick us both up some takeout lunch. Meanwhile I'll run back up to Oceanside and run the permits and licenses on Pete Andersen's business."

Danny talked quick and drove quick, making a left turn onto US1 that seemed to leave Shaye's stomach behind. He excused himself and then talked furiously into his car phone, lining up information for when he reached the station in Oceanside. Shaye felt a little wobbly on her legs when he let her out in the enormous discount store lot.

Before leaving he pulled her to him for a kiss, slipping his tongue inside her parted lips for just a second. Then he stuck some rolled up bills in her hand. "Buy the whole she-bang," he said. "A nice little suit, heels and don't forget a bra. We don't need Andersen staring at your titties. And Baby," he said. "I'm craving a hot dog for lunch. Can you get me one from Crazy Dogs? Put whatever on it you want. And get something for yourself, too."

Someone beeped at the parked squad car, and he cursed under his breath. "Motherfucker- I ought to arrest his ass! Anyway, Shaye. I gotta go and I can't take you to the station. I'll pick you up outside here in about a half hour. Okay?"

Danny wasn't actually asking, and Shaye never actually answered. He pulled away and she stared forlornly after him, wondering if she looked anything like the prostitute he'd had dealings with the day she tried to blackmail him. What must people in the parking lot think?

Slowly, she slid her head to look in one direction and then another. The weak sun glared off hundreds of vehicles. Thousands of them, some pulling in, others pulling out. Carts clattered around her in every direction, loaded high as shoppers dodged the parking lot traffic. Shaye noticed how the giant warehouse-like building before her blocked the light.

And it blocked any breeze as well. She smelled spilled gasoline, mixing with the odor of popcorn from a machine outside the store that played jangly carnival music and flashed red and silver lights. Shaye raised a hand to protect her sensitive eyes and something whooshed past her, almost taking one of her ears- a shiny SUV/van combo.

She stumbled and another vehicle bore down on her, a red pickup with a rebel flag and an American bulldog with a pendulous tongue hanging its head over the truck bed. This truck, also traveling at highway speed, almost clipped one of her ankles.

As it drove off, jouncing over a speedbump, Shaye observed how the dog shared space in the back with a box that contained a new fifty-inch screen television in a labeled box. And yet the truck didn't even possess a muffler.

Shaye gagged on its fumes and then saved herself by stepping out of the way of the next speeding vehicle. Up on the sidewalk, she shuddered in the sudden chill that hit her as the store's automatic doors opened for her. She followed the crowd into a lobby filled with the sharp echoes of voices, the scents of cheap cologne and human body odor and the unimaginable clatter of shopping carts pushing over uneven glazed stone floor.

An old man with a bright blue tunic and a face full of infectious looking eczema surprised Shaye, sneaking up on her, vigorously patting her back and announcing, "Welcome to Wal-Mart!"

Shaye's face went a shade paler, as more blood escaped her head, impairing her functions even more. She stepped into the store, pushed in by the crowd.

There seemed no end in sight- just glaring lights, glaring flooring, glaring ductwork and silver carts streaking like meteorites aimed straight at Shaye. Children screamed and parents threatened their lives in voices as harsh as wolves. Banners and garish inflated toys- grotesqueries- waved before Shaye's eyes. Red revolving lights flashed atop registers where people lined up so tight that their bodies and features and purchases blurred.

"My God," she mumbled to herself. "My God."

She had simply walked in here, blindly trusting Danny. But she'd never been to a Wal-Mart before. In fact, she had never even heard of one. Maybe, in her modeling days, she could have stepped out of her limo and walked in here with some girlfriends and none of this would have disturbed her. After all, she used to party the nights away in nightclubs even more crowded. But, in those days, Shaye did all of her shopping in upscale boutiques.

She uncurled her hand now, looking at the money Danielo had given her. Another irony. Fifty whole dollars. She rolled her eyes around in even more panic. How was she supposed to find a business suit in here for that little money? In her previous life, this amount of cash wouldn't have even covered the bra. So why had

Danny dropped her here rather than the thrift shop? She'd done better shopping there recently, not so overwhelmed by all the fear- and all the people.

Shaye drew in a little fortifying breath and, as she padded carefully down Wal-Mart's main aisle, she tried to block out the maddened bargain shoppers in her peripheral vision. She wondered if things had been easier for her in the thrift shop because it was less crowded- or because Adam was there.

She finally reached some racks of women's clothes, which smelled sickeningly of the plastic used to pack them. She didn't care what she purchased, even if it was bright red or bright purple polyester like the first few outfits she fingered. Couldn't these pass for business clothes if she was desperate?

And where were the bras?

Shaye stretched her neck and peered and a booming announcement exploded right over her head that made her shake.

"God," she breathed again. "See me through this." She prayed to make it through this ordeal in the discount store, a much more dreadful challenge than the meeting scheduled later on with the partner, and possible accomplice, of a serial killer. Really, it was very hard for her to envision that appointment actually taking place. For she was caught in the now, in this dangerous moment that seemed like it would never let her go.

Why hadn't she stayed with Adam today, she wondered. Why had she gone with Danny, who didn't even understand that this was a bad place? Danny probably shopped here every day, just like all these other young families rushing past. But Adam loved Shaye enough to deal with her problems. Adam never brought her to a place like this- because he knew. So what else might Frank Danielo expect of her? And was he really even a friend?

Shaye uncurled her sweaty palm. At least she could go and get him his hot dog. Her strategy was to find, and tackle, the lucheonette before the noontime rush. Then she could come back here and buy the clothing with whatever cash she had left.

Shaye crept in between racks of women's clothing, plastic jewelry and men's clothing trying to dodge some customers who appeared red-nosed and sick. She got the feeling that some of them stared at her strangely. But she didn't mind. She just hoped they kept their distance. She skittered across the slippery floor, wishing for something to hold onto or lean against.

But there was only another stream of jangly carts. She yipped every time one got too close, moving like a soldier dodging bullets. And then she minced her way across the sticky threshold of the Crazy Dogs snack bar. She gasped at the smells, the big red sign and the vats full of steaming chilies and pepper toppings. The teenage employees wore pointed red and white hats that resembled barber poles. One of them, a pale acne-faced girl who weighed no more than ninety pounds handed a steaming hot dog with all the fixings to a customer- and then she wiped her nose with the back of her hand!

Shaye gagged. Fiery blood rushed to her head, throbbing and blurring her vision. Next a pain knifed through her stomach. She bent double, running to find a restroom, as all the faces and merchandise became a whirling blur of color before her.

She found a ladies room. She felt her way along the wall and dived in, almost knocking over a line of women. It was dim in here, and it stank. The smell of old urine hit Shaye's nostrils like pure ammonia. But it was too late to care about cleanliness. She slipped on a spill on the floor and slid down before a filthy toilet, vomiting out her meager breakfast. Then she clutched the toilet lightly and peered in. Seeing the vomit ringed in strings of blood, she began to sob.

Her ulcer was starting again. She struggled to her feet and leaned back against the cold greasy stall wall, sobbing soundlessly and clutching her stomach. In other stalls, women flushed, yelled at their kids, gossiped and produced unspeakable odors. Outside the reeking ladies room, another announcement came over the speaker.

Shaye prayed to God to die. Somehow she was still holding Danny's fifty dollars. She stuck it in the front of her shorts waistband, swallowed another sob and licked some pink blood off her lip. She took their private cell phone out of the back of her waistband and used it to try to call Adam, not Danny.

She was sure Adam could somehow find a cab, get here and take her home. Adam would know what to do to take care of her stomach. And he'd walk in here right past all of the women, just like a girl himself. Then he'd lift her up and carry her out like a man. And then later, when all was allright again, he'd do her like a man- so deep and so skillfully that she could momentarily forget everything. Shaye chuckled to herself like a madwoman. For she was getting no answer at their house. Adam wasn't home.

Officer Danny found Shaye huddled outside in the corner of the store's cement wall and a big brick planter. The weird thing was that, even though Shaye was an unusually tall girl, she had folded herself up so tightly that Danny had to make three passes of the squad car to even find her. When he did, he stopped the car in traffic again and ran to her- with an expression of horror on his face.

Birds had found Shaye. Delicate little sparrows perched on her knees and one balanced on her index finger. She stroked this little one absently, while the others dined on old spilled popcorn that had accumulated in her corner. Shaye's eyes looked glazed and she breathed in shallow pants like a cornered animal, as shoppers passed by her with no attention.

Shaye looked up at Danny as he approached her. "I'm sorry. I didn't get the suit," she said. "I... I didn't get your hot dog either. I got scared in there. Maybe we were wrong. Maybe you really shouldn't be around me. I... I just got overwhelmed..."

Danny sat down on the edge of the planter and absently petted Shaye's long hair. He looked off at some preschool girls in shorts happily buying popcorn as their twenty-something mother fussed over them. And his eyes filled with visible tears.

"Sometimes I feel like an idiot, too, Shaye. I know that I love you," he said. "But only a week ago I came here shopping with my little girl. My child. And everything seemed easy. Sometimes I feel crazy, too."

Shaye seemed like a contradiction, huddled in her filthy corner with her lap full of sparrows and her big eyes peering out like a famine victim, while she tried to talk wisely as a woman.

"We don't have to do this, Danny," she said.

"Yeah, right," he said. He looked off into the crowd like he only partially perceived them. "I love you and we *do* have to do this... Let me go inside and buy the stuff. Will you be okay sitting out here for a few minutes more?"

This time no one beeped at his squad car with its flashing lights and wide open door. Shaye petted her smallest bird and didn't meet Danny's eyes. "I threw up a little blood in there," she confessed.

His eyes showed panic and indecision. "Are you all right?"

Shaye licked her dry lips. "Yeah," she said softly. "It was just a little. Not a hemorrhage. I've had those before and I know."

Danny tried to gently lift her to her feet. "You know, I'll have to take you to a hospital if it's usually bad like that. They'll get you in immediately if I bring you."

Shaye got to her feet and sat down on the brick ledge. "Please don't ever say the word hospital, Danny. Because I will never again, in this life, go to one." Her eyes turned steely. "Shoot me first," she said. "But I will never go to a hospital again!"

They sat with their shoulders and hips leaning against eachother, both looking at the police car and the backdrop of the milling parking lot. Danny reached for his cell phone.

"Who are you calling?"

He waited out a few rings, and then shut off the phone and shook his head.

"Who was it?" Shaye asked.

"Adam," he said. "But he wasn't home."

"I know," Shaye said. "I already tried him."

At her request, Danny retrieved her bottled water out of the squad car. Then he took only ten minutes inside Wal-Mart to choose her outfit, and he also brought out a pint of all-natural vanilla ice cream, the only food she said her stomach could tolerate.

He then drove her in the front seat of the police car, glancing at her like she was an invalid about to expire as he made a few turns to an area she had never seen. It featured a grassy riverbank with native vegetation and graceful overhanging palm trees. And, right at the moment, they had the special little pullover to themselves.

Shaye laughed. "Another place you take your women?"

Danny helped her out of the car, and he set her up comfortably in the shade with her ice cream and Wal-Mart bag. He made a place for her on top of a blanket he usually used for crime scene victims. And then he huffed as he sat down beside her and took off his shoes.

He ruffled her hair.

"Feeling any better?"

Shaye nodded, and she let a few miniature spoonfuls of ice cream slip down her flaming esophagus. "It's no super big deal," she said. "I got scared in the store and this was on top of having some orange juice at breakfast. Adam usually takes care of what I eat because I guess he cares more about me than I care for myself."

Danny looked at her curiously and then they both looked out at the shimmering, mellowly rolling water. "Well," he said, "that's nice of Adam and all. But I think you need to start caring and start taking care of yourself. Adam fusses over you like a mother hen. Yet the guy's only twenty years old, right?"

Shaye nodded, shyly.

"Well, that doesn't seem healthy," Danny said. "He needs to live like a young guy and find himself a boyfriend, not constantly keep fussing over you. Don't you think, Shaye?"

She could see that he meant well, but his words stung immeasureably. No one in their right mind could have imagined that she and Adam had been making love. Danny was just sincerely trying to help.

"I would feel sad," he said, "if you went with him to Miami just because you felt you owed him something, or vice versa..."

"I know. Adam made me want to live, but now it's my responsibility to keep on living, you mean."

Danny leaned forward and kissed her on the forehead. "Don't feel bad," he said. "I'm sure you've been a great friend to him also. You've just got to watch your diet more. And I'll help you build yourself up, just like he says."

Danny stretched and lay back, leaning his head on his arms. He seemed satisfied that Shaye was regaining her color. He chewed on the end of a weed and winked at her.

"So, you think I bring women here? What would you say if I told you that I haven't screwed a woman in almost a year? It's part of my recovery in Sex Addicts Anonymous. A year of abstinence..."

"Wait. You've been with those prostitutes..."

"Hand jobs and stuff," Danny said. "I stuck to the letter of the law."

Shaye's lips crinkled in a smile.

"That's not exactly abstinence."

Danny didn't mind. He smiled too. "For me it is," he said. "I took it seriously. I'm not about to fall back into my illness." He rolled on his side, looking at her flirtatiously. "Unless you want me to, that is."

Shaye and Danny looked at each other softly. And then he snaked out a hand to her and they intertwined their fingers. He drew her attention to the water. "Let's eat our ice cream and chips now, Shaye, and let's have a beautiful picnic. Because I don't know how beautiful the rest of our day may turn out."

She nodded in agreement and they pointed their faces toward the breeze, watching the bright blue water, the waving palm fronds and a gliding white egret, which looked like a white flag on the air currents.

"By the way," Danny said. "The only woman I ever brought out here before you was my daughter. Whenever I get the chance, I like to bring her here fishing…"

Chapter 19

An hour later, landscape boss Pete Andersen's eyes fastened on Shaye's cleavage even as Danielo interrogated him. And the big blonde haired man seemed an exact opposite of his business partner Jorge Colon.

While Colon was intense, yet classy, his six-foot-two business partner Pete Andersen looked like a big overgrown twelve-year-old, eager to investigate life with no hesitation and no shame. Andersen had a large head, a big toothy mouth, which he seemed comfortable letting hang open while gaping at pretty women and a gangly body sprawled in a new leather desk chair.

Almost everything in this trailer office looked and smelled brand new, including the teak and glass topped desks for the two partners. Andersen's passions showed on the wall behind him, including oversized posters of long-limbed Scandanavian bikini models that looked like they could be sisters to him.

His other life passion was obviously parasailing, with colorful framed photos of bright sails and sunny seas on every other available wall, interspersed with plaques he had earned in competitions. Shaye let her eyes rove over all of this while Danny verbally pursued Andersen.

"Mr. Andersen, I've checked you out with the County like I said. For a landscaper, you sure hold a shitload of money in escrow accounts. Millions in fact, and we all know money is always the number one motive for violent crimes… Even in front of sex," he added pointedly, scowling at the way Andersen drooled over Shaye.

With obvious regret, Pete Andersen pulled his eyes away from her body and sighed. He took up a peppermint stick out of a glass container on his desk and waved vaguely, indicating that Shaye and Danny could help themselves. Then he narrowed his eyes, looking about as calculating as he was capable of doing with his boyish features.

Unfortunately, his innocent looks were no more than natural heritage, and his looks did nothing to indicate his questionable morals. In the car on the way here Danielo had filled Shaye in on all Andersen's recent business manipulatings- including disposing of a bunch of undocumented workers and the business partner who had founded the company just as it won a multi-million dollar contract.

Shaye and Danny sat gingerly in the desk chairs and Shaye crossed her legs. Danny cleared his throat, waiting as patiently as he was cabable of for the landscaping contractor's explanation.

"Number one," Andersen said, pointing at Danny with his peppermint stick. "You cops just can't accuse anyone of anything. I've already talked to my lawyers about this, and I'm covered, perfectly covered. I don't even have to talk to you."

Shaye went pale. She could feel her insides quivering. What if Andersen really was involved here? She hadn't prepared for that. But Danny moved in, jaw and white teeth jutting like a little bulldog.

"And what is it that you don't have to talk to us about?" he asked. He got to his feet and wandered over to the other desk, the one Shaye assumed once used to belong to Jorge Colon. The empty desk featured an silver filigree cross on the wall, as well as a collection of exotic plants, now all dried and dead.

What she hadn't noticed was a photograph in a carved silver frame lying flat on its face in the center of the abandoned desk. But Danny got to his feet and retrieved it. He tilted the photograph so all could see. Shaye gasped and Andersen grimaced.

"I love how cocky you suspects are, Pete" Danny said. "This is a cozy photo of the three of you guys. You, your ex-partner Jorge - and Mami Ramierez. In better days, that is. When Mami was alive!"

Andersen shook his piecey outdoor adventure's hair out of his clear blue eyes. "I had nothing to do with what happened to her!"

Danielo shook his head ruefully, and glanced to Shaye. "Oh, this is rich," he said, "better than expected."

Truly it was. With every word he said, Andersen was walking deeper into a trap that they hadn't even set. Before this moment, Shaye hadn't even thought Andersen knew anything about Mami Ramierez.

And the next thing Andersen said, leaning forward man-to-man, really made her gasp.

"So what if I screwed Mami Ramierez a few times?" he said. "She was an ex-hooker. And old Georgie needed to be free of her anyway, before the bitch took him for everything he was worth."

Pete Andersen paused for a moment, looking into Danielo's face, as if for understanding. Shaye couldn't believe what she was hearing.

"I know I took George's business," Andersen said. "And I know I fucked his woman. But it was all really a favor to him. George was too altruistic, with his dreams about giving most of what he earned back to some community center in Flamingo Park. All it took was a few calls to some of my new buddies in County Government, and they could see that giving contracts involving public roads to somebody that wasn't even a full citizen didn't make much sense..."

"But Jorge Colon was in America legally, wasn't he?" Shaye interjected.

Andersen laughed and stretched his legs out to the side of the desk, seeming more comfortable now. "Oh, he was legal, detective," Andersen said. "But not a full citizen yet." He raised a hand to point vaguely in the direction of Flamingo Beach Parkway. "You see, the swale on this project is jointly owned by the county and a private developer..."

Now he swung his arm to cover three compass directions. "There are big plans here, a multi-use development that's going to encompass twenty percent of the undeveloped commercial zoned property in the county. And our- I mean *my*- company is signed on to landscape all of it..." He gathered his lips as though tasting something very piquant.

Danielo interrupted. "Brother, so now we know all about how you scored that landscaping contract and took over a business that was never yours. But I'm not deeply concerned with any of that. I'm conducting a murder investigation and I want to know what happened to Mami Ramierez!"

"Mr. Andersen," Shaye asked quietly, "where is your ex business partner, Jorge Colon right now?"

Andersen swept his glance over her breasts quickly, and then he met her eyes. "Well, that's the million-dollar question isn't it? That's what everybody wants to know." He slid a hand down to a desk drawer and Danielo responded instinctively by touching his own weapon at his side.

Andersen reached out his big hand in a gesture of peace as he laid a small handgun on his desktop. "This gun's legal, dude. I never had to carry it until Georgie started making his stupid threats."

"Threats?" Danielo asked.

"You know, all about that honor stuff. I told him, Georgie, it's business. The county won't let our company work as long as you're running it. So I might as well benefit. Somebody needed to take over. And George had plenty of cash to go his way with. He started this lawn service himself without ten bucks in his pocket. Now he had probably eighty or a hundred thousand saved up. He shoulda called it quits and just went back to Mexico. But he didn't even want nobody knowing he was a Mexican all those years. It was bullshit."

"What specific threats are you talking about, Pete?" Danielo asked. "You understand we're conducting a murder investigation?"

Andersen sighed and Shaye leaned forward, feeling there was some intimacy in what he was going to say next. Suddenly, the young looking man in his thirties looked very weary.

"There's no way I could've known what would happen to Mami," he said, as much to Shaye as to Danny. "George acted macho and all, but all Spanish guys act that way, ya know? And he started with all this really crazy talk, like quoting some old wizard in his Mexican village, tryin to make me scared when I took the business from him." He sighed again, and rubbed some kinks out of his knobby knees. "None of that even worried me..."

He then tilted his head, indicating Shaye. "Dude," he asked Danielo. "Would it be possible for me to just tell you the rest of it? Maybe the lady detective wants to look at some evidence or something while we talk..."

Danielo rolled his eyes towards Shaye, indicating that she should comply. He didn't bother to inform Pete Andersen that she was not a police officer and, for a moment, Shaye felt very warm and fuzzy. She willingly stood, stretched out her long legs and slowly made her way towards Jorge Colon's deserted desk. She didn't really intend to touch any evidence, for anything she handled she assumed would be inadmissible.

But she doubted Jorge Colon had left much evidence behind. If he killed Mami Ramierez, it probably happened as a spontaneous crime of passion. The reed crosses at that crime scene could have been created quickly, after the murder.

The Josie Swank crime scene was more elaborate, and he had probably planned her funereal display in advance. Something had obviously been unleashed within Jorge Colon. But it seemed to Shaye that, whatever that was, it had stayed dormant all the years, exploding only after his partner, Pete Andersen, had betrayed him.

Andersen now leaned forward, talking to Danielo in a confidential, secretive and somewhat smarmy voice, like men talk behind their hands to buddies at strip bars, and he gave a helpless little snort of a laugh. "The funny thing was," he said. "It wasn't just Georgie that went crazy with all his intense Mexican Indian mumbo jumbo. But then his streetwalker girlfriend shows up at my door…"

He noticed Shaye glance his way, and paused, with a stern look on his face, until she made a show of turning and examining Colon's desk calendar, which still featured last month.

Right away she saw Colon's meticulous appointments noted for all aspects of his lawncare service, with workdays running seven days a week from five in the morning until ten o'clock at night. She doubted very much that his partner, right now attempting to say everything in a whisper, kept up those same kind of hours.

"Mami comes to my door," Andersen said to Danny, "to my condo at the beach. And she tells me that George betrayed her, and now she wanted to betray him…"

"Wait a minute," Danny said, "if anyone betrayed anyone in all of this, I'm sorry to say, friend, but that really seems like you."

Andersen laughed. "Mami Ramierez once used to be a hooker, right. And then she turned into some reformed saint. But she was still only after the money…"

Shaye felt gooseflesh, like a little cape ringing her upper back as she listened to Andersen's words. Meanwhile her fingers caressed Colon's collection of plants, now dried and desiccated. She looked up at the beautifully carved silver crucifix attached to the hollow temporary wall and noticed also a sepia photograph. A family dressed in traditional Mexican clothing stood with their burros before a small shack at the foot of an almost mystical snow-topped mountain.

This had to be the Santasemana region where Colon was born, Shaye was sure, and the mountain El Viejo. Indeed, it looked beautiful. This particular photograph could have been taken rather recently and just stored badly. Or perhaps it dated from Civil War days, depicting ancestors of Colon's that were long dead. The beauty of it was that none of that mattered, for time seemed like it stood still in the tiny mountain communities that ringed the peak of El Viejo.

Jorge Colon, in his hours he spent doing paperwork in this shoddy temporary trailer, must have felt a little like a caged animal. But his dreams had been enough to make him soar, and sustain him. Colon had dreamed of making Flamingo Park, Florida a magical place just like his home region, a place of sanctuary for good men like himself fleeing the poverty of Mexico. A place that would give people a chance.

And that was apparently what Mami Ramierez wanted, as well.

Shaye looked at Colon's calendar, noting meetings scheduled with realtors; the local zoning board, regarding a land use change and the bank- all relating to the purchase of the lot on Caiman St. There were also scheduled meetings with lawyers, regarding forming a non-profit agency, or land trust. According to his partner, Jorge Colon had been driven off and told he had to return to Mexico, before some of these meetings could take place.

"Mami Ramierez wanted money," Pete Andersen continued, "to turn parts of Flamingo Park into a community center and a sanctuary for Spanish hookers, or something flaky like that. I didn't really get into it. I mean, that was all George and her used to discuss, and I thought he was stupid agreeing to throw away all his money into her harebrained scheme."

Shaye glanced back under lowered eyelashes and saw Danielo grit his teeth. "But of course you already had plans to take over the company," he said. "So Jorge would never be investing his money in that stuff anyway."

Andersen couldn't restrain a large-toothed grin. "So was Mami so much better?" he snickered. "She coulda just gone back to Mexico with George. Instead, she said she wanted me..."

Breath caught in Shaye's throat as she caressed a little silver letter opener of Colon's featuring a cross and a rooster claw.

"Mami wanted to fuck me," Andersen said baldly, "in exchange for me taking over and giving her the money for her project." He chuckled to himself. "Dude, I mean, you're a man of the world," he said, nudging Danny's arm. "People know your reputation. Somebody offers you some experienced pussy, you take it! You can appreciate that, right dude?"

He chuckled again, and dropped his voice even lower trying to hide from Shaye in her Wal-Mart suit and messy updo put in place by Danielo at the riverbank. Apparently, the disguise made her seem professional enough that it worried Pete Andersen.

Shaye sat down slowly in Jorge Colon's worn leather desk chair, feeling the outline of his body, and fancying she could also feel his warmth, and perhaps the growing fire of his rage. If just listening to Pete Andersen with his greed for money and "experienced pussy" could enrage her like this, than what had it done to his former partner, a man obsessed with religion, honor and revenge?

Danielo flexed his arms out now, seeming uncomfortable himself. Shaye knew in the sinking of her heart where all of this was going. And Danielo probably suspected, as she did, just how easily the murders could have been prevented.

"Mr. Andersen," he said, slowly and carefully. "You are off the record here, as we discussed. But, in a moment, I'm afraid we may have to go on the record. So you better have excellent alibis for both those killings if you plan to continue talking to me."

"I told you," Andersen said. "I'm already covered. The weekend Mami got killed I was away in Key West competing at a parasailing tournament. Four days. It took me a while to even find out she was killed. And for the other one, that other hooker way back in the trailer park, I had people staying in my house at the time. I still do. My mother is in from Minnesota on vacation for the cold weather, and the girl I'm dating was staying with me also."

Danielo slowly shook his head, while Shaye pretended to occupy herself peering out a parted miniblind at workers milling over the construction site. A brand new Mack truck parked outside had replaced the one that Colon had sold. Shaye doubted very much that the tire treads of this one could match those found at the Josie Swank crime scene. But perhaps the treads on the old one could. But for now, Colon had given up the truck, which could have been a way to track him.

Apparently now he was on foot. And he was quite familiar with the outdoors. He could probably move freely anywhere in the bounds of Flamingo Park if his compulsion to kill fallen women had kept him around. In fact, he could be crouching outside this trailer window right now, Shaye thought, and she shrank back, with an involuntary gasp.

The men hadn't heard. Danielo was quietly berating Andersen, obviously needing to make an effort to keep his voice down. "But why in the hell would you sleep with Mami Ramierez, Pete? Wasn't it enough that you took away the guy's business that he built? Why'd you have to take his woman, too?"

"Oh, hell," Pete Andersen said. "I don't have to answer that to you. My lawyer told me I don't have to tell you anything. But I actually wanted to help, in a way. Mami Ramierez pushed herself on me, thinking I was gonna hand over hundreds of thousands of dollars for her cause! I mean, no ass is that sweet!"

His voice boomed a bit, but then he struggled to keep it even quieter. "I mean, no offense meant, but there are girls out there that look like your partner... Look at her for example." Shaye felt her skin crawl as he pointed in her direction. "If I wanna spend all my money, I'll find myself a gorgeous girl like that. No retired whore is gonna snag me."

Andersen leaned back and patted his chest like a young gorilla might. In a way, more than his partner, the impassioned and insane serial killer, this young man with no morals disgusted Shaye.

Danielo cleared his throat, glancing at Shaye with some warmth, obviously glad she was keeping quiet, despite Andersen's outrageous comments.

"Andersen," Danny said wearily. "If there is anything at all you can tell me about where Jorge Colon is right now, I need to know. There's no more playing around now. You say he made threats on you? And on Mami Ramierez also?"

"Just on her," Pete Andersen said, now including Shaye back in the conversation as well. "He showed up at my house one day, looking for Mami. He called her a fallen woman, a fallen angel, and said he wanted to send her back to sainthood. Look, I thought it was all just craziness. I knew he didn't actually want to fight me. We were friends and partners too long. And he must have known Mami wasn't worth anything. I told him to get out of America before immigration seized all his cash savings. I even offered to help. Look, the man was a little pissed off about his woman. He was speaking ninety percent in Spanish. And I don't understand that shit..."

Shaye and Danny both sighed in unison at his incredible bigotry.

"You know, some of the shit creeped me out a bit, though," Andersen said. "George kept talking about making his fallen woman into a saint, and all about The Day of the Dead, or something. I thought he was just trying to bother me, just playing with my head. I just humored him, you know. So I told him where Mami was, staying in a hotel down US1. I told him her room number, and that all she wanted was money if he wanted to get back in her good graces…"

He looked between Shaye and Danny with the expression of a bad child that wanted to be told he was good.

"Look, I had my *mother* at my house," he said. "What was I supposed to do about my Mexican partner turning crazy? Why would I suspect he killed Mami? Why him and not some real lowlife out of the park? Georgie was always a good guy, you know? Not some suspected killer."

"Well, I'm afraid you're going to possibly share some responsibility in this, Andersen," Danny said, with some disgust cutting through his voice. "Unless you help us now."

"I will help you," Pete Andersen said. "You don't have to threaten me." He stood, stretching to his full height, and stepping in the direction of Colon's desk. "I want to help you guys now. I can tell you all Georgie's friend's names. I'll show you his church and where he lived and where he kept his bank accounts. If George did this, I really want to help."

Andersen bent and pulled a cardboard box out of a locked cabinet. He piled it with notebooks, day planners and stacks of loose papers. He pulled the box onto the floor, swinging it around to make it accessible to both of them. "This is his stuff. I know it's late," he said, "but this time, I really want to help."

And then Danielo's phone rang. Shaye swung in her friend's direction, and watched his face go pale.

With no ceremony, he scooped up the box overflowing with Colon's possessions. He tugged her arm. "Come on, we've got to go," he said. He didn't bother with a formal good-bye to Pete Andersen. All he said was, "Don't leave town. And you better make sure you're available if we need you."

Danielo didn't talk to Shaye for the first few minutes they drove west, with the siren screaming.

"Where are we going?" she finally ventured, as she swayed off balance in the back seat.

"Out by I-95," he replied, with his expression closed and shut down. "To the truck stop out there. A crime scene..."

Shaye rubbed at her face with thoughts swirling through her head. From the way Danielo was acting it seemed all their investigating today had been too late, and they were heading to the scene of another murder. At the same time, Shaye didn't understand the sense in it. From what Pete Andersen just told them, everything Jorge Colon had done so far made sense, in a twisted fashion. But a murder at an interstate truck stop wouldn't fit.

"Danny," she tried, "can't you tell me?"

He met her eyes in the rearview and she saw softness there now, but also something dark and deeply troubled. "Shaye, honey, I can hardly talk about this," he said. "Oceanside PD has an unidentified dead female in her thirties, sprawled on the pavement at the truck stop in the middle of fifty big rigs. She has long black hair and she died wearing a white plether miniskirt and halter." Danielo gulped. "It's Vicki Cruz, honey. I know it is. They're calling me to see if it's my witness. But I know it's her. I failed her, and somehow Colon got to her."

Shaye drew in a breath. "*We* failed her, Danny," she said. "We should have figured out everything about Colon sooner."

A driver Danielo passed driving along the shoulder gave him a dirty look, and Danielo turned up his lip in a sneer. "You're not the cop, Shaye. Glenn Chow and I should have brought this guy in days ago, long before Vicki Cruz."

Shaye found it hard to explain why she felt so culpable but, almost from the beginning, she had felt an inner assurance that *she* was the person who would have to stop the Flamingo Park killer-somehow.

"Danny," she tried to explain. "I'm the one who understands Jorge Colon best. I'm the one who stared into his eyes in between when he killed Mami Ramierez and Josie Swank. What I saw there, Danny, I don't know if I can even explain. But it's a feeling I've empathized with- so I know it. A feeling of righteous indignation, and of something being taken from me."

"But you're no vigilante, Shaye. And you're not psychotic. You're nothing like him!"

She bit her plump lower lip, tasting strawberry lipgloss that she had forgotten she was wearing. "But if I *was*," she persisted. "I mean, I understand the concept of going to extremes. I understand all the strange places a person's mind can take them when they perceive themselves as a victim. Jorge Colon spoke about turning Mami Ramierez into a saint. Picture this, Frank- his whole life he went up against obstacles. He lived an almost mythical life up in those mountains. Life was harsh. Yet magical. A lot like those old legends."

"We're almost there," Danielo interjected. "I'm just gonna hop on the highway to go south one exit…"

"Okay," she said. "I'll try to express what I'm thinking quickly. Why I think he killed."

"Well he killed Mami Ramierez for obvious reasons," Danielo said. "Sex and money. Sex because she went whoring with his partner. Money because his partner stole everything from him. But why turn into a serial killer? Why kill Swank? And how about my witness, Victoria Cruz? Do you see her as part of the larger picture, too, Shaye?"

Shaye sighed, her mind whirling, as Danny blatted the siren to get past some traffic on the exit ramp. It was a long shot, but she felt confident. Touching the evidence, touching the silver rooster claw letter opener she now held sheathed in plastic wrap in her pocket, she felt she had an insight.

"I think Colon wanted the world to be a better place so his life would have meaning," she said. "If Mami was larger than life, first an angel and then a demon and finally a saint by his intervention, then he hadn't been cuckholded, but simply a part of some larger spiritual process. Danny," she said, only now putting it together confidently in her mind for herself. "Josie Swank was Mexican also. She had to be."

"Nobody ever said Josie Swank was Mexican," Danny stated while negotiating the parking area crowded with trucks. "She came from Texas originally. She changed her name ten times, and changed her appearance a few times, too."

"But the town she came from sat twenty miles from the Mexican border. I'm sure of this, in my heart," Shaye said. "She was Mexican. That's the key to it all. Another Mexican girl who sold out and turned on her heritage. Colon might have chosen her for her long hair because of the superficial resemblance to Mami Ramierez, who I think he was madly in love with…"

Danny had slowed the squad car to almost nothing, turning to peer at Shaye as she continued.

"I think he fell madly in love with Mami," Shaye said, "just like he went over the top with everything. And then Josie Swank. He probably knew that she was HIV positive. He wanted her to be a Mexican saint again, not a fallen porn queen, living in the back room of a trailer and fearing for the future of her children. Danny, Jorge Colon, in some sick way, probably thinks he's *saving* these women."

At the truck stop Danny nudged the nose of the squad car out of the opening of an alley by a loading dock, just far enough that they could both see the expanse of pavement ringed by several Oceanside patrol cars with flashing lights. And then he gulped, like a man personally involved.

"So what about her?" he asked, indicating the twisted form before them, a little puddle of shiny white clothing and shiny black hair floating on a sea of gray asphalt. "Why do you think he killed Victoria Cruz- a sarcastic, tough-talking little scrap of a hooker- who came to me trusting me, begging for my help? Is it because she's Spanish? Is that why he killed her? Or because she had black hair? Or was it just cause I actually thought I could help her?"

Shaye reached forward, laying a hand on the mesh between them in an attempt at comfort.

Danny shook his head, trying to ignore it.

"Shaye, I can't have you here," he said. "I have to go identify the body." He came around to open the door and look deeply and intently into her eyes. He squeezed her shoulder, as if apologizing for his harshness. Then he bundled up her T-shirt, shorts and sneakers. "You better put on your old outfit, Blondie. And wear these sneakers so you can run if you have to. There's a good chance Colon could still be here somewhere, watching us right now…"

He swung his eyes to include the concrete and steel truck stop building, the gaping truck wash and all the grumbling rigs themselves, which surrounded them in shadows and diesel. He squeezed her shoulders together in a quick hug. Then his eyes blazed into hers.

"Shaye, I don't know if Colon even wanted to kill Vicki Cruz the first time around. If what you say is true, he was just interviewing her, deciding if she needed him to 'save' her. But then she ran away and she became a witness."

"It looks like he just ran her down with a vehicle today, from what I see here. There was none of his usual ritual. He only killed

Vicki Cruz so she couldn't testify... Now word on the street is that you've been working with me, Shaye. So even though your hair is blond... do you understand what I'm saying? Can you deal with what I'm getting at?"

Shaye faced Danny with her green eyes wide, but her shoulders straight. "Death came for me once," she said seriously. "And I beat it. So just tell me what to do now." She quickly swept the truckstop with her eyes, considering hiding places. Danielo assessed what she was doing.

"I want you to hide yourself right now, Baby. Blend in until I'm done. You see the cops out there? I see twenty already. And the FBI's coming too, now... Because I screwed this one up... Can you hide from all of them, Shaye? Can you blend in, and stay around but not be seen?"

Shaye nodded. If anything, hiding was what she was great at.

Danielo now bent down and pulled a small, shiny black pistol deftly out of his sock. He handed it to Shaye, tucking it down on her side and folding it into her hand.

"Do you know how to shoot?"

"I can figure it out," Shaye said, sensing deep inside that her life had been lined up to come to this.

Danielo glanced around both directions, looking hungry like a watch dog desperate to protect her. "If Colon comes after you, Shaye, make sure he dies first," he said. "If he turns up, and he corners you somehow, call me first. Or call out to any cop. It doesn't matter if you go to jail; because your life's more important.

"And don't go chasing shadows. But if you're alone and Colon comes after you, Shaye, you make sure he dies first. Okay, Honey?" He leaned forward to plant a wet kiss on her cheek. "I gotta go now. If he's still hiding in this place, I'll find him. Stay safe and I'll give a call when I'm ready to pick you up. I'm trusting you Shaye..."

He stretched out a hand to her in good-bye. Then he ran out to the pack of milling uniformed officers, yelling out to them. "You guys, close off this truck stop, now! We're checking every single truck and nobody leaves here. And call the FBI. They need to get people at the airport. Hold back any flights to North Central Mexico! Do it now! And get me some K-9's!"

He reached the group and Shaye backed off further into the shadows. From there, she watched Frank Danielo shoulder past the other officers, skid to his knees and gather up the limp body of

Victoria Cruz. He held her as gently as if he had just discovered his own murdered child.

Chapter 20

Shaye stood amidst the crowd of onlookers awhile later, feeling a strange safety in being part of the warm mass of people. It was suicide in many ways for her to stand here, she knew, just as it had been risky for Frank Danielo to leave her here. Shaye was a fugitive wanted on several felony charges and now she stood, amongst slack jawed travelers munching chips from the truck stop rest area, only feet from two FBI men in sleekly tailored suits.

They mumbled to eachother, on and off the phone with Officer Glenn Chow in Mexico. Meanwhile Danielo ran around seeming to show up in ten places at once. He gave orders to the FBI men, who seemed to defer to his authority and he dispatched uniform officers from Oceanside to interview witnesses who milled together listlessly under the hot sun, matching officers with onlookers as though he was the men's supervisor.

Then he broke it all off to chase down an eighteen-wheeler that was trying to skirt the barricades.

"Police. Stop, or I'll shoot!" he shouted. "What the fuck are you trying to do?" he yelled as he hopped up to grab away the driver's keys. The truck's brakes whined to a halt, and Danny pulled the obese driver down to stand flatfooted and wheezing on the pavement.

"Did you kill that girl?" he yelled, pointing back heatedly at Victoria Cruz's body.

"I didn't kill that damn hooker!" the middle-aged driver yelled back, while rubbing in a nervous irritation at his white beard stubble. "But I got a load of frozen food here that's set to go to California. I can't sit around for your damn investigation!"

Shaye sidled over to one corner of the crowd in order to hear better.

"And how come you know she was a hooker?" Danny asked, slanting his eyes down in suspicion.

An answer came from an Indian man wearing a truck stop apron, apparently the restaurant manager. "Those lot lizards come around this truck stop all the time," he said. "I tell them to get away, or I call the police like you! But always more, more come. I can't stop them. It's not my fault. We need more police patrols…"

Danny swung his impatient glance at the manager, obviously dismayed at having his interrogation interrupted.

"Lot lizard is right," the truck driver scoffed. "Knockin' on a man's windows so he can't sleep. Then charging eighty dollars for a friggin blowjob. It's not my fault she got run down in front of me. Just before this happened, the bitch was chasin trucks all over this lot, just tryin to flag em down!"

"You son of a bitch," Danny mumbled. He looked over the giant dewy sliced orange and the can of frozen juice displayed on the side of the man's truck. "You turn my stomach!" he said. He gestured over for one of the uniformed officers to come to him.

"I've got a witness here," he told the cop. Then to the trucker, he snarled, "You'll be lucky if your employer SunJuice doesn't fire you for this. Entertaining hookers in your rig... And I'll make sure they're informed. What I don't get though…" he said, as the uniformed officer prepared to take notes. "…Is how you could see the woman running around, trying to flag somebody down for help and you didn't even let her back into your truck"

The trucker mumbled inarticulately so that his jowls trembled. "I didn't think she needed no help. I just thought she was acting crazy."

"But yet you tried to run that barricade when you saw police talking to witnesses. How come? Unless you killed her?"

The man choked on an ungracious sob, and then he trembled with tears sheeting over his reddened face, looking much like a pink pig crying.

"I saw a guy chase her and run her down. Okay? I didn't see the guy's face, but he drove a new silver F350 pickup, and he wore a cowboy hat. He chased her with the truck in circles all around the parking lot, and then he ran her over- one-two-three times-maliciously like that," he blubbered. "When I saw, I... I got scared. I was with her just before, and I thought maybe he'd come after me. I just wanted to get out of here..."

"Well, Mister, forget driving to Cali," Danny said to him. "Next place you're going is down to the Oceanside Police Station to finish this interview. Meanwhile..." He raised his voice again, calling out to a different officer. "I need an APB on a new silver F350 pickup. Murder suspect is armed and dangerous. Report it at the roadblocks and at the tollbooths. The vehicle might have front end damage, possibly blood, so I want people stationed at the nearest gas stations, also anywhere there's a hose or a car wash."

One of the FBI men called out to Danielo, and Danny swung in the man's direction. But then he turned back for a second to the young Oceanside officer and the fat trucker. "Take this SunJuice fuckhead's keys," Danny advised the officer. "He watched a murder and said nothing. Get his statement down at the station, and then keep him until the FBI guys and I get there... Dudes, I'm coming," he yelled to the two closecropped FBI professionals who seemed like they were his age, yet his juniors by far in experience.

When Danny happened to turn his eyes in Shaye's direction for the first time in thirty minutes, his eyes looked ancient and weary. He gave her a wink and a subtle thumb's up signal and Shaye cracked a tiny ghost of a smile.

She had used their private cell phone to try to call Adam, both at home and at the Foxy Lady. At home there was no answer and, at the club, the only person who picked up was a cleaning guy who said he knew nothing, and that most of the entertainers weren't even in yet.

Shaye sighed, watching Danny circle around once again, this time standing in the shade for a moment in a whispered conference with the FBI men. Then he turned back her way for a second and his eyes seemed totally lost.

His expression looked so pained that Shaye instinctively took a step back. She felt the void inside herself, too, as a sudden ache in her stomach.

As long as Danny was busy, he seemed to be okay, running on adrenalin. Now, suddenly, his pace slowed and stiffened.

He was heading back to the body of Vicki Cruz, his witness, the woman he had promised to protect and then failed.

The crime scene people had arrived wearing booties and gloves and masks. Two of them, a slim man and a slim woman, circled the body, glancing up at Danny with what seemed like smiles behind their masks. They photographed Victoria Cruz, and laid rulers gently over different angles of her body, noting their measurements down meticulously and taking more photos. Everything the two did seemed coordinated together in a graceful, and silent, dance.

Their movements held Shaye transfixed, as Danny stood over them looking on with pain and horror, revealing more emotion than a cop should probably show. But that was Danny, all fire and emotion.

He had said that Shaye would do well as crime scene technician. She could be cold and meticulous, like the two technicians were right now, inserting little bits of evidence in little plastic bags and carefully sealing them. Measuring how far the white bone stuck out of someone's collarbone, ringed in blood. Delicately, with white plastic gloved hands, moving aside locks of glossy black hair, like photographers posing a fine lady for a portrait, yet instead exposing a red torn opening in her skin and a white protruding bone.

Shaye gaped in fascination. She looked at Victoria Cruz's pinched little ferret face, her smudged red lipstick and the cheap plether halter stretched flat over size A breasts.

Every line in Victoria Cruz's body looked stringy and tired, like a burnt up meth addict with too many miles on her. Her hair was long, long long. Like a long story, it stretched all the way down to an unnaturally bent calf and the bottom of a well-scuffed sandal.

Shaye's drew a breath as she examined the sandal, and her eyes traced the hair in all its folds and valleys up and down, up and down.

Jorge Colon had saved this victim from herself after all. Shaye stood twenty feet from Vicky Cruz, and yet she felt as though she was reaching out and touching her cold bony body. As though she was lying down, curling on the pavement beside her. A throwawy woman, finally killed. A fallen woman.

Like Shaye.

That moment everything seemed to stop for Shaye, except staring at the victim. For she had sold her body, too. And she was finally remembering it.

Forty minutes later, Frank Danielo grabbed Shaye by the arm, oblivious, even though her body had turned physically icy in shock.

"C'mon, Blondie," Danny whispered under his breath. "I told the FBI dudes some cock and bull story about me having to get you out of here because of you're a witness with long hair. They think I'm taking you to a police station in Flamingo Park, and we don't even have a police station there, so I better move. I'll get you home, lover..."

He glanced at Shaye, at her blond pale visage that seemed now to be carved of stone. "You okay, Baby?" he asked.

But the question seemed purely rhetorical. He quickly tucked Shaye into the back of the cop car and then spun out of the truck stop at seventy, deftly skirting one of the barricades he'd had erected. "We found a coupla more witnesses to the silver pickup," he babbled excitedly to her. "If Colon got it washed down, I'll bet he'll tuck it away in Flamingo Park somewhere. A fucker like that would like a new truck like that F350 too much to just abandon it. And if Colon is hiding out in the park, I know every little spot. I'm gonna find him tonight, Shaye! I'll drop you off with Adam, and I'll leave a gun for you guys for your protection..."

Shaye said not a word.

Danny still didn't notice. Now he drove at eighty, with lights and siren blasting, weaving smoothly through four lanes of rush hour traffic.

"Colon may try to drive the truck to Mexico," he said. "And we've got the border alerted to look for him. He's definitely our man. You got that so right, Shaye. Starting with the rooster claw. Colon contacted his family in his village yesterday, and they immediately reported it to Glenn Chow. Colon told them he's on his way home, bringing them all his money, enough to last a lifetime. And get this, the sick fuck told them he's also bringing with him his bride, who's got beautiful long black hair..."

Shaye stared out the window blindly.

"My partner Glenn was supposed to play it cool. But instead he told the family the truth. Luckily they're religious people so it all worked out. They agreed to turn Colon over to Chow whenever he comes home. They said they'll be able to talk to him and he'll go peaceably. So even if I don't catch him here tonight we *will* stop him Shaye, wherever he tries to run. We *will*. Vicki Cruz deserves that much…"

The squad car tore up grass pulling to a stop on their trailer lawn, and Danny helped Shaye inside, along with her bundle of clothes from Wal-Mart. When he bought them seemed an eternity away. Right now she couldn't even recognize this young, dark-haired uniformed officer who hustled her inside the sour rattly mobile home, dim even in the daytime.

For Shaye felt she had died back there on the rest stop pavement when her memories came back.

For a second Danny glanced at her strangely. He rubbed at her arm, trying to rub away the coldness. Then he glanced around the shadowed room. "Adam!" he called out. "Adam Ant? Come out here if you're home…"

When he got no answer, Danny rushed through the house, checking all the rooms.

"Baby, Adam's not home," he announced.

He stopped short when he saw the way Shaye stood stiffly facing a blank paneled wall. "Shaye, are you okay?" he asked. "Did that crime scene get to you so much? I'm sorry I left you alone. I just freaked out myself. I thought Jorge Colon was still in the crowd, or hiding out in one of the trucks or something. I felt I failed Vicki Cruz, and maybe I could save somebody else if I acted quickly. I've still got to try…"

Shaye gave no response. Danny gently pushed a wisp of her hair behind her ear. "What happened?" he asked, his own voice starting to turn cold with apprehension. "You didn't see Colon, did you? He didn't threaten you? Another body? Did you see some other woman dead? Shaye, you're starting to frighten me now."

Shaye suddenly looked to Danny, focusing. She saw herself reflected in his eyes, tiny and big headed, like a little girl with a garish T-shirt and straight blond hair that seemed to stretch forever. She liked this distorted silhoutte that, to her, resembled Alice in Wonderland.

If that was all she could be, then it would be okay. If she could just be an eternally lost and confused little girl again, a silly blond haired child.

She shifted her focus now, away from the reflection, to stare at the worried man.

"I understand why I need to help the victims now," she breathed, her voice soft and raspy. "Colon's killing prostitutes, and I … I was one of them."

Shaye felt her eyes pleading with Danny in expression only. It wasn't his comfort she needed as much as she was pleading with the universe and with God. Danny's eyes immediately reflected her pain and longing. Maybe he felt disgusted, too. She *wanted* for him to be disgusted. She wanted only to vanish off this earth, now that she remembered. Shaye sunk down to the carpet, grasping onto Danny's leg, leaning her head against him, in a position and in a place she had never imagined herself.

Danny stroked the top of her long messy hair and she attempted vaguely to shake him away.

"I never would have sold myself for money, or publicity or anything," she said. "But my husband forced me to. I did it for him. I didn't know what to do…"

Suddenly, wet sobs rolled out of her. Her tears and drool drenched Frank Danielo's pants, while her fingers grasped his leg like claws. Levels of grief erupted out of Shaye like a burning volcano she hadn't even recognized was there. Since the hospital, since she had almost died, she hadn't remembered. But there were burning horrible secrets in her life even before then. She realized now she *should* have died.

"Oh, Danny," she cried out in a sob that sounded as much like retching as weeping. "I sold myself three times, three different men. That I can remember."

Danielo tangled his hand in her hair and his own tears streaked down his face as he now stared to the wall.

"I'm not mad at you, Shaye," he said, sniffing the tears back. "Not at all. And not disappointed. I'm just sorry for what I've done to hookers myself. I've done worse things in my life than what you probably ever have…"

"Don't you see?" she squealed suddenly. "No prostitute *wants* that kind of life." She looked up, suddenly pleading. "They don't want to die, either. And they don't want to do something so stupid that it makes them die. They just think that maybe somebody will help them; maybe somebody will save them. But their lives don't matter in the end…"

Danny squatted down next to her and he tried to lift her chin as she stared forward, again blindly.

"Will you tell me what happened, Shaye? Will you give me a chance to help you?"

Shaye pulled her legs cross-legged and hung her head down, like a little girl confessing to her concerned father. "Adam doesn't even know this," she said. "Because I just remembered today, when I was staring at Victoria Cruz in the parking lot."

Suddenly grief ripped through her for the once-daring hooker Vicki Cruz, with her hopeless dreams of travel. Shaye wailed out loud for the world's loss of Vicki Cruz before she ever got to prove that she was a good woman.

Shaye's eyes now burned with the agony of her own fiery tears. "Danny," she said. "I prostituted myself to Shaun Dayne."

Danielo creased his eyes, responding with the initial starstruck response that three hundred million other people in the country might.

"*Shaun Dayne the movie star*? You're shitting me, right?"

A few minutes ago Shaye had almost lost track of the slender thread of life. But her mind remained focused enough now to give a grim little laugh.

"So that doesn't make me a prostitute? Because it was Shaun Dayne?"

Danny flopped down on the floor by her, struggling to shake off the conditioning of celebrity magazines and gossip TV. After all, the year her husband had offered Shaye's body to Shaun Dayne as a publicity stunt, Dayne had been voted *People Magazine's* "world's sexiest man".

Danny now shook his head as if to clear it.

"You really fucked Shaun Dayne?"

Shaye sucked back her tears with a snort. A thread of self-respect was returning. She hardly knew where it came from. But she knew she felt bitter.

"At this party," she said, "Shaun and my husband were feeding me pills in a hot tub all night long- Ecstasy, tranquilizers. I didn't even like drugs, Danny, but I was doing whatever Riley said, drinking champagne and getting silly. I was wearing this new bikini from the *Tropical Sun* catalog that had real gold coins sewed into it- and Riley made me stand up and do a sexy dance to model it. I remember the tub was up on this really high redwood deck with a view of the ocean, and the waves were going crazy because a storm was brewing out at sea."

Shaye laughed in a strange, almost psychotic way, reliving how she had laughed that night. "There were no bodyguards up there with us because Shaun wanted privacy. He had just left his wife, and we were the first friends he told and that night he said he wanted to get totally drunk and stoned and act crazy. So we were all pretty messed up, all acting kind of crazy and Riley was encouraging it. At one point I had to climb down one level to go into the woods to pee, because I was too stoned to even make it into the house. Riley followed me and stuck a condom in my hand."

Shaye gulped and laughed, uncontrollably. "Oh, Danny, I didn't even know what he wanted at first. Then he told me that Shaun had asked if he could fuck me. But what Shaun didn't know was that there were photographers in the woods. Paparazzi. Riley had set it all up. It was his grand plan. He told me to go back up there and let Shaun do whatever. Riley grabbed my chin in his hand, Danny. For the first time since we'd been together he hurt me…"

Now tears squeezed out of Shaye's green eyes that had darkened with bloodshot little veins- and righteous rage.

"Riley told me the photos they could get would be worth millions of dollars to us," she said, "and he told me I needed to go back and keep my breasts and my hair showing for the photographers because they were my best features. Oh, and show off the bathing suit, too. And he told me he would kill me if I didn't do it."

"What?" Danny breathed incredulously, with almost no sound coming out. "He said he'd kill you?"

"That didn't matter," Shaye said. "Riley owned a pistol, yes, and I knew he could sometimes get violent. But all I cared about was what was implied. Not that he might kill me. But that he would leave me. Riley was all I loved in the world. And I would've held the gun while he pulled the trigger if that was what he wanted. I was nobody, and I needed him…"

Shaye stared ahead broodingly for a long time, recalling the incessant crashing of the waves that night and remembering the feel of the handsomest man in the world impaling her in time to the surf, as though the whole darkened planet conspired against her.

She had awakened the next afternoon in a ten grand a night hotel suite rented out by Shaun Dayne, with him already long gone. A bellhop from the hotel staff barged in and flashed off another photo, bringing her back to consciousness as it flooded her eyes with glaring light. Her first thought was that Riley would be glad for that, too, for it might also end up in the tabloids.

She couldn't blame her friend Frank Danielo for his next insensitive question. Shaye knew many people would have asked it.

"I'm sorry, but what was it like being with Shaun Dayne?"

"It hurt," Shaye snapped. "He was big, and I didn't want him. I only wanted my husband. I didn't know until that night that sex could hurt that way." Her eyes seemed to come alive, and they peered intently into Danny's. "But I guess I deserved it. Riley was right. Photos of me and Shaun doing it in the hot tub came out in all the tabloids immediately. And the press blamed me for the breakup of Shaun's marriage, although it didn't happen that way really. But the publicity made me famous.

"I was nobody before, and then I became the most famous swimsuit model in America. I sold my soul, Danny. My husband made me sell my soul that night…"

The trailer was getting dimmer as the day started to turn towards evening. Danny rubbed at his eyes, and he and Shaye squinted at eachother for a long time, saying nothing.

Finally, he sighed, attempting to get his legs adjusted better in his squatting position.

"You know, maybe you think you sold your soul," he said. His exhausted tone made her aware that her troubles were not pressing compared to the murder investigation he was delaying every second that they talked. And he made her feel patronized, even while trying to to be kind. "But you're too innocent, Shaye," he continued. "You still don't know what it's like to a streetwalker. You slept with one guy. These girls sleep with ten guys a night, and not all of them the handsomest movie star in America…"

Shaye's eyes looked glazed. She wanted to make her point more strongly, but she hardly felt she had the energy. She knew Adam would understand better and she wanted to tell him now and finally have light shown on all the dark corners of her life. Maybe that would finally give her mastery of her fears. But Adam Ant was nowhere to be found at the moment, and Frank Danielo was her only friend.

"Believe me, I'm not trying to make light of it," he said. "But I just don't think you have to go out chasing a prostitute killer because you think you owe something to hookers. You're not one of them, Shaye."

"There were other guys," she broke in, letting herself slip back down into the dark vortex of memory she had discovered looking at Vicki Cruz's dead body today.

After all the years, now she was finally talking. Now she was trying to command it all. Now it was no longer horrors recalled from a shameful nightmare. It was her past, which she must now own. Shaye realized this dark shadow would never go away now until she could find some way to live with it. And make the best of it, as well. Shaye *did* have to save the hookers, she realized.

Wrong had been done to her. And she hadn't fought back then. She hadn't even tried to stand for good. In fact, she'd never tried to stand at all, not for anything in her whole life. So what made Shaye Taylor special? Maybe only the fact that her strange past would make her determined to stop these crimes -more determined than anyone in the world could be- even Danny.

She lightly touched his shoulder, and she thought she experienced him flinch back almost imperceptibly. For now that she revealed the past to him she had stepped over a line. She was no longer untouched and no longer possessed her sanctity. The funny thing was, because she was beautiful and because her first john was the country's favorite movie star, her friend thought it was more acceptable. But even so, his body reacted instinctively, pulling away.

"Danny," she said, "once or a thousand times, there's no essential difference once a woman sacrifices her body."

Danny moved his head- it could just as easily have been shaking or nodding. All that was clear was that he was having a hard time with everything right now.

"I remembered everything standing out in the parking lot today," she said, "looking at Vicki Cruz. When I got sick two years ago, I was in a coma briefly- actually, I was legally dead. Then there were certain facts I didn't remember once I woke up, and the doctors said that was to be expected. But, you know, I didn't lose the memory about Shaun Dayne then. Because it happened over a year *before* my illness. I had *already* forgotten. *Before* being sick."

Danny narrowed his eyes. "But you remember everything now?"

Shaye nodded. Oddly, even though it felt she carried a tremendous and serious weight now, she also felt more real, and more grounded.

She pulled Danny's wrist over to check his watch. "I know you've gotta go, honey," she said, calling him that for the first time. "But I really want to tell you these things."

"I do have to go," he agreed. "But I want to hear your story, Shaye. There's still some good daylight left, so we've got a few minutes. Just as long as I can check the park for Colon's truck before I have to go up to the morge for Vicki's autopsy."

Shaye smiled, attempting to acknowledge his patience and his caring. And she plowed ahead, revealing the past, as she now felt compelled to do.

"After I slept with Shaun Dayne," she told him, "later the next day, the photos of me with him in the hot tub came out. Within a few days the photos weren't just in the *Sun* and the *Enquirer*, but a less racy shot also made the covers of *Us* and *People*. My photo was featured in more magazines than I kept track of, and the whole world knew me in the space of a week.

"*Tropical Sun* sold out of that bathing suit with the gold coins within ten minutes on our Internet site." She twisted her pouty lips into a wry little smirk. "Both kinds sold- ones with fake gold coins for $38 each, and the real ones with real gold coins hand sewn, for thirty-eight hundred. For the next few weeks we sold thousands more of the cheap suits each day. Because I guess every woman in America wanted to look like Shaun Daynes' booty call!"

Danielo laughed politely, just as Shaye had needed him to do.

Shaye sat back against the couch, bracing herself. "Everything went crazy after that. Riley had investors lining up for the Tropical Sun Swimsuit Company and meanwhile people were inviting me to model all over the world. I started getting interviewed on talk shows on national TV... For real. It used to be that Riley and I always made less money than my parents used to. Now, suddenly, we entered a completely different league. We started traveling all over the world with me wearing designer clothes and designer diamonds. And, for that 'fifteen minutes of fame', everyone in America knew my name."

She caught Danny giving her a strange look. "Well, okay, I didn't know it," he said. "But I bet Lorrine did. She used to follow every move of Shaun Dayne. She used to worship him."

With a little dark humor, Shaye said. "Well, I hate your wife."

"That's good," Danny said. "So do I. I guarantee Lorrine wouldn't have minded being Shaun Dayne's booty call if she got rich by it. Lorrine's all about what people think, and I hate that.

Knowing you, how genuine you are, only makes me realize that more."

"Anyway," Shaye said, "the strange part is, all of my new famous lifestyle came because of that night. And yet I made myself forget the night completely. I focused on the fact that Riley approved of me, and I tried to be the glamour girl he wanted even though it never really felt right to me. All the clothes and parties and publicity took up all my time. And then it happened again with another guy- but this one was so much worse. Have you ever heard of Milton Orpheus, Danny?"

He looked a little blank. "I've heard of Orpheus Films," he said. "Is he the movie producer?"

Shaye nodded. Gooseflesh crept all over her bare arms and legs, and she had to press her folded arms tightly against her stomach to ward off sudden pain. This second memory sickened her so much more than the first, and the last of the episodes was even worse. She could hardly breathe as she told what she remembered happened with the movie producer.

"Riley had me go to Milton Orpheus' house in Malibu... And he was so old..."

Shaye was overcome by chill and she started shaking, so that her words couldn't come out. Danny slid over and rubbed her arms, kissing her softly on her hair. "Baby, it doesn't matter what you've done. I've done worse. Nothing you tell me will turn me off on you, I swear."

Shaye nodded, fighting the shakes. It helped that Danny was forgiving. But the pain of her memories was so much more enormous than that.

"I wore a leather bikini that night," she said. "And a long gold sable coat. And I supposedly went there to do a 'private modeling' session for him.' She gulped. "Milton Orpheus was seventy-five years old. And I was twenty-two. Danny... I... he did everything to me. Touched me all over. He ate me out. He couldn't get inside, because he was impotent. But he tried... I don't know. Honestly, I don't know.

"Unfortunately, I was sober at that time, no drugs. My head was perfectly clear. I remember wanting to die, and when I came home I went into our bathroom and dismantled a safety razor. I cut my hands doing it and I never got to finish... it was so ridiculous. Riley barged in, and he beat me up then for putting scars on my body..."

Danielo rocked her.

"Well, you know, it's allright, though, Shaye. The funny part is, you've lost fame and millions of dollars. But you've turned into this seriously amazing woman. You're a little quirky and a little crazy, I know. But you're a real person now. And a guy like me can love you. Your best friend, Adam, loves you. Lots of people in Flamingo Park love you immediately. Adam's transsexual friends love you."

"Madeline hates me," Shaye broke in. "For all that I was."

Danny grinned, and planted a friendly kiss on her nose. "Minor technicality," he said. "The point is, you have a new life now. We both do."

Shaye swung her eyes around at the glum view inside the trailer, wishing she really could have this life, wishing it was that easy. She really would settle for any kind of happiness. But she was the kind of girl who, out of weakness, had betrayed herself and others.

"I cheated on my husband, Danny. Something I never thought I could do."

Danny faced her with an incredulous expression. "The bastard pimped you out! To everyone in showbiz. So how can you blame yourself?"

She nodded, and continued. "Well, surprise surprise. The day after my vist to Milton Orpheus, Riley got a phone call. Orpheus wanted me for a picture. That was no surprise in itself, since it's why Riley agreed to send me there to 'entertain' him. The funny part is, have you ever heard of the film *Killer Bet*?"

"Sure," Danielo said. "Lorrine and I hired a babysitter to go see it. It was about this old thief- Paul Newman- initiating a young thief- Matt Damon, right- at these casinos on the Gulf. And there was a love triangle with the girl. I don't remember who she was- but she was a real sex kitten- kept going between one of the guys and the other..."

"It was Scarlett Johannson," Shaye said. "That movie helped make her famous."

She paused until Danny looked up. "And?"

"That part would have been mine. Milton Orpheus offered me a role alongside two of the best respected actors of all time. And I never acted a day in my life. Orpheus liked my boobs and my hair that much. Just like everyone else, he liked my boobs and my hair..."

Danny shook his head, as though to clear it.

"So, what happened, Blondie? I don't understand. Or, wait. Was that when you got sick? When you got the e-coli? Was your husband mad because you lost the movie role, and that's why he left you?"

Shaye snickered, almost choking on her own saliva. Her stomach cramped so badly now that she doubted the ache would go away. Yet she was reluctant to get up and scuff over to the kitchen to even try to find some milk or something to soothe it.

"I cheated, Danny. For real."

He looked at her appraisingly. "I can't imagine you cheating. You're so afraid of sex, even now."

Shaye's head whirled. Men always had a problem with imagining her doing anything bad. And Danny was clueless that she had been sleeping with Adam. So was she cheating on him? Was she officially Danny's girlfriend now that he had separated from his wife? Or was she Adam's girlfriend? Which one was she betraying?

Yes, she used to hate sex after Riley had made her do the things with Shaun Dayne and Milton Orpheus. After she turned on sex, she suspected that Riley had started cheating on her, because he no longer enjoyed making love to her. But no, she had never desired to cheat on him. No matter what he did to her, no matter how disrespectful or cruel he acted, she had always been faithful-minded.

Until that last weekend.

"Danny," she said. "I was signed up for a starring role alongside actors making twenty million each for *Killer Bet*. I was contracted for three million. And the only reputation I had in show biz was for being silly and empty-headed. A human Barbie doll, like Adam's friend Madeline likes to call me."

Danny scoffed. "Well, so, is that really different from any Hollywood starlet?"

"The point is," Shaye said. "A lot of people were out to get me. Riley was extremely good at PR, and he'd navigated this far, accomplishing the impossible, even with his questionable methods. But he was afraid we were going down. He found out that *People* magazine hired an investigative correspondent named Matthew Siegler. I had no idea who Siegler was at the time, but everybody who followed world politics knew him.

"Siegler didn't usually deal with celebrity news. He did exposes on the government and that type of thing. But *People* hired him to do an investigative report on me and my movie- just before the movie started filming. The article was going to emphasize how corrupt people like Milton Orpheus were- all in the guise of an in-depth interview of me. Anybody who read between the lines would know Orpheus hired me because of the casting couch. It was meant to place the whole movie industry in a bad light...

"Riley explained all of this none too kindly because his spies at the magazine had clued him in to it. Siegler didn't actually intend to interview me and make me famous. His plan was that I was so stupid that he'd interview me and get me to share my life history- and then he'd write the article sarcastic and the whole world would laugh at me- and, because of me, they'd hate Orpheus."

"I'm not sure I understand where this is going," Danny said, surreptitiously checking his watch. "I'm sorry."

"Two more minutes," Shaye assured. "The story's not complex. Rumors had it that, even though Matthew Siegler seemed like a nice educated guy, he liked to travel the world and try out kinky sex- geishas and that type of thing. Riley wanted me to turn the tables on Siegler by seducing him when he did the interview, and that way he wouldn't write anything bad about me, or the movie.

"Danny, I'm a shy girl at heart... With the others, Riley told me to dance in a swimsuit. That's something that, unfortunately, I've had years practicing, so I'm pretty good at. But I'm not sexually confident. Riley wanted me to go hang out with some journalist that hated me, and then throw myself at him like some sexual vixen.

"This time Riley threatened to hurt my parents if I didn't comply. I know it sounds stupid, but I guess I was stupid at that time and believed anything. But, if I didn't still love Riley, I wouldn't have gone along with it; the threats didn't matter. But I forgave him everything, even wanting to hurt me. I really believed he knew best..."

Danny just shook his head.

"Okay, we're almost to the end," Shaye said. "This is what I remembered in the parking lot this afternoon. *Killer Bet* was going to start filming in Gulfport, Mississippi on and around the new casino ships. And the whole town was throwing a party to start it off. Riley arranged things so Matthew Siegler would meet me there. Instead of meeting him at a restaurant, I was supposed to surprise him at his hotel room. Then I was supposed to sleep with him and persuade him to cover me positively in the article. As soon as it was over Riley wanted me to call him so he could come out and we'd party together at the 'Mardis Gras in Gulfport' for two days before the filming started.

"Well, I came out to Gulfport with this bagful of costumes, all this freaky stuff, for the Mardis Gras party where I was supposed to hang out with some of the other models from *Tropical Sun*. And I wore one to Siegler's hotel room that night. It was this 'dark angel' thing Riley designed, with shredded black lace, and kohl mixed with diamond dust rubbed under my eyes and my hair frizzed all out," she gestured to show him, "with black confetti and black tinted glitter all through it...

"I was supposed to look like this gypsy seductress, like the one from the Cher song called 'Dark Lady,' Riley said. When I told him that the song was before my time and I didn't even know who 'Dark Lady' was, he slapped my face and called me an idiot. I remember it now, Danny. So clearly..."

Shaye felt sudden anger build inside again, like some guardian angel stood on her shoulder now that could have protected her from her husband's abuse all along. How could she be so much wiser now than back then?

"You know, I don't know anything about the song now either," Shaye said. "But I guess I could have faked it..."

Danny gave her an agreeable grin.

"Okay," she said. "I said I was naïve. Anyway, I went to Matthew Siegler's room, tottering on my six-inch heels. Riley wanted me to try crack cocaine to build my confidence, but I said no. Instead he gave me a bunch of caffeine diet pills which was bad enough. I was speeding out of my brain and I got sick and threw up on the plane ride to Mississippi.

"In Gulfport, I knocked and Matthew Siegler swung his hotel room door open and he looked truly surprised to see me there, instead of the restaurant where we were supposed to meet. I tried to act sexy and intense and say all the things Riley had rehearsed with me, but all I could process was the way Siegler stared at me. He was fairly young- thirty-two, which was closer to my age than Riley was. But he looked boyish. He was known for that friendly face that everyone said made him a good newsman.

"Instead of seducing Matthew Siegler, the moment I saw him I immediately fell apart. I just fell down on his floor and started crying, with my costume falling half off. I cried for like an hour straight. I confessed to Matthew what Riley wanted me to do, and I said I didn't care if he wrote bad things about me, because I deserved it and I really wasn't good enough to act in a Hollywood blockbuster..."

Danny leaned up against the couch next to Shaye, looking from one small window to another. He gave a little laugh in sympathy. "And I bet Siegler was a man after my own heart, Shaye. I bet I can guess where this was going."

"He knelt down by me," Shaye said, remembering everything now, seeing only the past in front of her eyes. "He touched my face and he touched my costume. He kissed me. He kissed every tear away and he kissed my hair down to the tips of it and my legs all the way down to my toes. He told me he thought my husband was more evil than some of the foreign dictators he'd interviewed. He offered to feed me dinner and he offered to have me move in with him then and there to protect me from Riley."

Danny chuckled along with her in sympathy as she told the story. Shaye hoped he didn't hate her for the story of yet another man falling in love with her. For the end, which was so horrible, came only two days later.

"Matthew Siegler offered to marry me if I would leave Riley," she said. "And he said the only expose he was going to write was one of Riley meeting me at age sixteen and cheating me all throughout my career. Matthew told me I never had to sleep with him or anyone else that I didn't want to... And he had such kind eyes."

Danielo punched her playfully in the arm. "I've got kind eyes, too."

"Oh, screw you, Danny," Shaye said, pushing him back. "This is hard enough to tell. You don't know the end."

"Did you fuck him, Shaye? Is that what you're going to tell me?"

Shaye was blind to the dimming trailer, the floor they sat on and her friend, Frank Danielo's police uniform. She remembered that other dim room. She remembered herself and Matthew Siegler embracing on the carpet and him pushing aside her crazy costume, while the sounds of the street were shut out. She remembered him softly touching her cheek, softly running his lips over hers; she remembered breathing into his breath and telling him that it was all okay.

She didn't have to touch him, Siegler said. No matter what, he was writing the article in her favor. He said Milton Orpheus had probably chosen her for the part because the old producer must have noticed her heart, not just her body. And this was more news than another story about the casting couch.

So she knew she didn't have to make love to him.

But Shaye did it anyway. She let Matthew Siegler make gentle love to her there on the floor of his hotel room, running his hands under the lace of her mystical costume and marveling at her beauty. Shaye let herself enjoy the sweet lovemaking that gave mutual pleasure, rather than the wild electric sex she'd had with Riley that always left emptiness inside her- casual sex even though they were married.

She let her hesitant plump lips become greedy, kissing Matthew Siegler over and over as they rolled up into the bed and made love over and over again and again. Just like she and Adam had, she realized. So maybe she wasn't as shy as she thought, she pondered now. She'd had that passionate side in her even then. She'd just been sidetracked by five decadent years with Riley.

Even recalling making love with Adam now, she felt a sexy twinge and she then felt shame for thinking that way even as she sat next to Danny. The horrible part was, she wasn't even clear on which one of them she was betraying. She hadn't even wanted a boyfriend right now- just to be free of her fears. In the past month she had come back alive, it seemed. And then everything had immediately spun out of control and she wished she could slow it all down.

Despite her shame, Shaye looked Danny in the eye and went on.

"I slept with Matthew Seigler again and again," she said. "Even though I no longer had to for the article. And I allowed him to fall in love with me. We ordered room service and ate chocolate éclairs that we rested on our bare bellies as we lay in bed. It was such a warm feeling, Danny. Something I hadn't felt in so long...

"And then I remembered Riley, and I called him at like two in the morning. I told him some lame story that Matthew's flight hadn't come in yet, and he believed it. He just yelled at me that I better not eat anything and let my stomach look bloated. He didn't want me to look bad for fucking Matthew, he meant, or for photos when I hung out at the parties the next days. It disgusted me! But I shook it off and laughed about it, and ate more éclairs and snuggled in Matthew's arms. I was there cheating on my husband, Danny. I was doing wrong. And I didn't even feel bad about it!"

"Whew," Danny said, shaking his head. "I don't perceive you did wrong to that pimpin bastard, Shaye." He laughed. "But the funny part is, look at the men you end up fucking. First a

Hollywood star, then a Hollywood producer- and then a famous news correspondent. Was he rich also?"

Shaye stopped for a moment and her voice turned cool. "I don't know if he was rich, Danny. I think informing the world about important issues was the thing he cared about in his career."

"I just wonder about something," Danny said. "You said a few days ago that you were seeing somebody after I hurt you. And I thought you were lying, you know, trying to play on my guilt. But now I don't know. *Did* you see somebody else?"

Shaye looked at him flatly.

"Shit," Danny said finally. "You really did." He paused and thought for a while. "I guess it was my own fault for treating you like I did. But you don't ever have to spend a minute with anyone else again. No matter how infatuated, I guarantee no guy can love you like I do, Shaye. This newsman might have thought he loved you. And this other local idiot might think he loves you now. But I'm here, Shaye. I've seen you get crazy like you did today. And I've never even fucked your beautiful body yet. I love you as my best friend, and as my detective partner. And just stick around. Watch me love you all your lifetime. You don't ever have to try anyone else..."

Danny wound down, breathless.

"Danny, this is now," she said. "And that was then."

That, indeed, was another world. A voodoo world, like the strange Mardi Gras festival the community was celebrating in the streets. Local vendors had come from all around the region, invited by the city for a sprawling out-of-control street party infested by news media from all over the world.

She and Matthew Siegler had made love three more times the next morning, and then they wandered down to the bustling streets that had been closed off to traffic. Shaye had skipped along with bare feet, wearing Matthews' T-shirt and soccer shorts. She drank home-ground chicory coffee and gorged with him on quirky shaped pastries at a crowded sidewalk café. He bought matching woven leather sandals for them at a street stand and a bracelet of chunky beads for Shaye that was supposed to be lucky for good health.

Hah, she thought now. There's no good health when the devil is after you. When you have sinned, like she had.

While plucky marching bands squealed out jazz in the street before them, Matthew Siegler pressed Shaye into an alleyway, and he made love to her there, greedily possessing her lips while they humped out in the open. He said the words, "I love you," more times than she had heard them from Riley in the proceeding year, even though she got the declaration from strangers in her fan mail every day.

Her fans always wrote, "I love you; I love your tits, I love your hair."

Matthew said he loved her soul.

Afterward they staggered out, hand in hand, and started getting tipsy on wine. Then Matthew bought her a white gauze peasant dress with tiny mirrors sewn all oven it, and she changed while he shielded her with his body. Her three model friends from Tropical Sun met them at noontime and that afternoon they all acted giddy together, rushing through the city and partaking of every funky homegrown delight they could.

The girls all draped themselves over Matthew, who they thought was the first cool guy their friend Shaye had ever hung out with. Didi, Chantique and Melani, who was the oldest at twenty-one years old. Like Shaye, they each carried big tote bags and unihibitedly changed silly Mardis Gras style costumes at will.

The four girls danced to Zydeco music in the streets, interlocking hands and swinging crazily, circling Matthew. They got their hands painted with henna and colorful glass beads braided into their hair. And they spontaneously kissed the cheeks of old local men, black and white.

As evening fell, Shaye wandered into an odd little shop at the edge of the party that advertised "medicinal remedies". While her model girlfriends waited outside changing clothes again, and Matthew vanished into a dark aisle to retrieve a red blood red rose and a jar full of creamy rose smelling "love potion" for her, the proprietess pulled Shaye aside.

The woman had smooth cappachino-colored skin and lively black eyes, and she wore amulets along with tatters of burgundy velvet and gems and beads woven into her knee-length corded hair. She smelled like hay mixed with spices- a perfume of her own making, just like her love potion. And her age couldn't even be guessed at. Shaye found herself staring.

Before Shaye could move in the aisle crowded with pottery and candles and figurines, the woman reached out a surprisingly cool and gentle hand to cup her cheek. Those eyes stared into hers and Shaye could still see them now, here in this room.

"You must become fearless, Princess," the woman said. *"No man can do that for you. You will die. Or you will become fearless!"*

Matthew found her there with the woman staring at her, and Shaye leaned back easily into his enfolding arms. *"Tonight,"* the woman whispered as they parted, but Shaye was no longer listening.

Their group tried seafood and more wine in a crowded pub, and Matthew kissed Shaye whenever the crowd was thick and they could get away with it. Her girlfriends only giggled for, even though Riley Taylor was their agent, too, he'd been cruel to them also and they owed him no loyalty.

The five young people strutted, arm over arm, through the street party. One of the city's squares featured an ornate illuminated fountain, a band and an announcer and a crowd of photographers. As camera flashes went off, the girls jumped into the fountain, totally hectic and abandoned with their hair flying and their faces glowing from their day in the sun.

Shaye spun under the starlight and the streetlights, dancing like a gypsy woman, with her new white gauze skirt swinging out around her. Then she staggered out of the fountain, embraced by her friends, wandering in a warren of streets. After midnight they walked down to join ceremonies at the edge of the sea, mystical ceremonies involving flowers and chanting and fire. Shaye squinted her eyes and thought it looked like voodoo and she loved it all and felt completely entralled. Somewhere down the tight warren of streets she smelled the musky smoke of local cooking. Anticipating the savor, wanting to try it all, she and her friends and Matthew ate strips of barbeque with their hands, licking sauce off each other's palms.

They ate from twenty different stands that night, a morsel here and a morsel there, letting the food drop into the dust when they were finished. But Shaye was the only one who ate the fatal hamburger, the one piece of meat containing the strain of e coli that killed four other people. It happened that weekend with Matthew.

Early the next morning, in deliberium, with a hundred and six degree fever, Shaye lay on the white sand beach in her wet gauze dress with bloody vomit spurting all over the beautiful white fabric and all over her beautiful long hair.

A concerned male face stared down at her along with her friends. Shaye keened in pain and sputtered out the confused words of madness and illness, recognizing no one. That morning was the beginning. It was the end. And she hadn't remembered a bit of it until today.

Chapter 21

Frank Danielo rubbed his eyes, and hung his head. He absorbed the story for a few minutes. Then he looked Shaye in the eye. "I know you're hurting. I know. But I've gotta go to look for Colon now. Come with me?" he asked, standing up and extending his hand.

Shaye wasn't able to give an answer.

"I can't leave you here." Danny shook his head regretfully, like the whole situation might be too much for him. "So what do you want to do?" he asked her. "Do you want to try to call Adam again?" He reached the telephone down to Shaye.

Without words to him, she dialed Foxy Lady. The bartender answered. Rather than giving her Adam, he put Madeline on the phone. And Madeline laughed raucously in Shaye's ear. "Adam Ant doesn't want to talk to you tonight, Barbie," she said, slurring her words. "He's mad at you."

Shaye could hardly cough out her words. "Madeline, tell Adam I'm sorry, okay. Just please put him on the phone to let me know he's okay."

Madeline scoffed again, "You ain't his mama. Adam don't have to answer to you. So leave us alone!"

Amidst the booming noise of the bar, Madeline hung up on her.

Shaye's words came out quiet and rusty. "I guess Adam's mad at me, Danny. I don't really even know if he's there at the club. Madeline says he won't talk to me."

Danielo sighed. "I can't leave you here right now, even with the gun. It's just not safe. And you're distraught, Shaye. Let's go out there and take a quick look around the park. Then I have to go to the coroner's, so I'll drop you at my house."

At another time, Shaye would have protested. She wondered if Danny intended to leave her at his house with his wife. The whole idea seemed bizarre and troubling to her and, even though she felt unable to speak, her eyes must have registered her doubt.

Danny reached out his hand more urgently. "It's the safest place, Hon," he said. "Just for tonight."

He gazed at her intently until Shaye responded and took his hand. Then she let him pull her up. Shaye felt limp and wrung out. It was hard to be clear what day or time it was, what the exact problem with the serial killer was or where she fit into the whole scheme of the world right now. The only thing that she was sure of was that she felt bad- and very weak.

Danny took a moment to write another brief note for Adam and he left it on the counter. Then he gently guided Shaye out of the trailer and he locked the door behind them.

Everything seemed quiet when Shaye followed Frank Danielo into his house an hour later. He lived in a family-oriented suburb that could have easily been located in any city in the country, in any state. Lawns and landscaping were well cared for here, and some of the residents bothered with white picket fences and fancy mailboxes. On the other hand, second cars spilled out of single-car garages, parked in the driveways or out on the street where carpentry projects or kids' Big Wheels crowded the driveways.

No one was out at the moment at this time around twilight, but Shaye could envision kids circling the cul-de-sac on bicycles at most hours of the day. Everything looked a little crowded and a little strained- the evidence of young working families like Danielo's straining at the seams in every sense of life.

Danny helped her out of the squad car and their slamming doors seemed to make an odd thud in the muggy air. Not that there was anything sinister about the neighborhood. It all just seemed staged and unreal. Shaye didn't even know what street she was on at the moment.

Danny caught her looking around and winked at her. "Not exactly what you're used to, huh?"

Shaye really didn't know how he meant that- did he mean she was more at home in the lowly Flamingo Park trailer where she lived now? Or was she referring to neighborhoods like her parents' in Westchester County New York where hired gardeners, not the fathers of the families, took care of the landscaping, and where cars were safely tucked away in three-car garages?

Whatever he meant, he still wasn't getting any commentary out of her. The weight of the world was too much upon her

She trudged along behind him as they stepped between hedges onto a ruddy tile strip that sat under a shaded overhang, and Danny unlocked the front door.

It was only then, as they stepped over the threshold, that he thought to inform Shaye, "Lorinne's not gonna be here tonight. And she's in the process of moving all her stuff out for good. Even if she did pop in on you, just tell her you're my girlfriend. She already knows, and she won't give you any problems."

Shaye faced Danny in the dim living room where nothing looked distinctive. The room could have been a stage set for any suburban home and any young cop's family. She noted the ice blue brocade sofa, loveseat and ottoman- expensive, but in a style that was more popular a few years back.

Since the family had only moved in here less than two years ago and the furniture looked brand new, Shaye was able to infer something about the woman who had chosen it. Lorinne Danielo obviously liked pretty things- possessions that she strained to afford, and she thought would impress her friends. Unfortunately, though trend influenced, the woman was not cosmopolitan. Next time she went to redecorate, in a new home with a new husband, the new choices would also be perfectly matched- too perfectly matched- too expensive for their budget and, again, two years behind the cutting edge.

Shaye cleared her throat and she looked into Danny's dark shadowed eyes with suspicion.

"So, even in the midst of chasing a killer, you found time to tell your wife I was your girlfriend?"

Danny headed to the kitchen, abruptly snapped on a fixture that hung above the all purpose counter/bar- the utilitarian hub of the house- and scooped up mail that had been left for him. He huffed at Shaye as he impatiently ripped open a letter.

"Yeah, right. All I'm doing is trying to ruin your life Shaye! You know, I didn't say you *are* my girlfriend. I just said I told her. I know the deal with us at the moment. But I had to say something that Lorrinne can understand. I just wanted her to know that you're not a one-night stand. I happen to own this house, all in my name and I'll keep it after the divorce. So if I give you a key, I want her to know you belong here. That's all."

The information was coming at Shaye too suddenly. She didn't feel at the moment like she belonged here. She trembled with chill, even though the house was stuffy. She had always liked the manly smell of Frank Danielo, his physical warmth and his woodsy aftershave. But this house didn't smell like him. Shaye sniffed out ingrained cooking odors, anitseptic floor cleaner, perfumed air sanitizer in the living room and a miniscule hint of woman's perfume.

Shaye turned her head and looked over a child's art stuck on the refrigerator with bright alphabet magnets, and family photos that she couldn't quite make out from where she was standing. The counter featured a full fruit bowl, a fine crystal statuette of a robin made to hold toothpicks and a squat dried florist's bouquet.

In the silence, Danielo finished up with his mail, and then observed Shaye looking at everything, with her teeth pressed into her lip and the laser focus of someone examining a crime scene. Danny looked like he'd gotten a bitter taste in his mouth. He sighed and tapped her on her shoulder.

"Snoop in here all you like, Shaye. What you see is what you get, same as with me…"

Danny stepped over to the refrigerator, and retrieved a few photos for her. The first portrayed a bright-eyed little girl with shiny black hair, snapped hugging the neck of a carousel horse at an amusement park. The next few showed Danny with his daughter at the park, looking like a happy kid himself. Father and daughter looked flushed and silly with their flashing dark eyes and big white teeth, smiling broadly into the sun.

"That's Lorinne with Shari," Danny said glumly of the next photo. "You won't find many pictures of the both of us with our daughter."

Shaye gingerly held onto the next photograph of Danielo's wife and daughter, which looked like it was taken at a mall, at Glamour

Shots. Lorrine was also black haired, and she was undeniably pretty, as Danny had said.

Shaye caressed her finger over Lorinne's rose petal complexion and satiny black hair, cut perfectly to frame her face, making her look modern and edgy. Lorinne wore a fake diamond studded dress watch and real one-carat diamond studs in each ear. With her tight petite body that, even in the photo, seemed to bristle with unspent mischief and energy, she appeared to be anybody's perfect high school sweetheart.

Without comment, Shaye frowned towards the father/daugther photos, which Danny now held. "So who took those?" she asked.

"Jealous?" He snapped his gum teasingly and then shook his head. "Actually, Glenn Chow took them. He's the one comes with me to take my kid to Orlando."

Danny leaned over to paw through the refrigerator. It was a close reach to pile sandwhich makings- ham, cheese and a cellophane-wrapped head of iceberg lettuce- on the butcherblock counter.

"No," Shaye said, trying to redeem herself. "I just thought that you and your daughter looked truly happy. She's beautiful, you know. A little angel. And, from the way that she smiles, I think that I can see she has a good heart. She's definitely your daughter..."

Danielo concentrated on preparing two sloppy sandwhichs, but he bit back his lip and grinned with fatherly pride. "Shari is good hearted," he said. "And, like you say, she's definitely mine. She lives in the present, and sometimes she finds it hard to see the bad in a situation..."

Danny slopped greasy mayonaisse onto his sandwich, and he noticed Shaye grimace. "None for yours?" he asked. She shook her head and he handed the sandwich to her dry, along with Kool Aid in a chilled sculpted glass, with plenty of cloudy old ice from the refrigerator's icemaker.

The sandwich smelled great, for Shaye was ravenously hungry. But the ice, just like ice from a third world country, seemed suspect. Shaye could smell a faint plastic odor above the Kool Aid. And, although she wanted to trust the cleanliness of the glass, the only one she could really trust to clean a glass according to hospital standards for her was Adam Ant. Her best buddy, her roommate, her lover, who she walked out on to spend the day with another man...

Shaye gulped, and it tasted almost as though she had swallowed some tears. Meekly she slid the cold sweating glass filled with red liquid back across the counter. Danny, wolfing down his sandwich, took a moment to notice. Then he fluttered his soft eyes under his fringe of dark lashes and it almost melted Shaye's heart- even as she knew he'd probably be disappointed in her.

"I'm sorry," she said.

"What's wrong with Kool Aid?" he asked, but only factually, not angry.

"I don't trust your ice maker," Shaye muttered, genuinely ashamed. "Do you have anything canned?"

"Beer." Danny winked. But Shaye was in no mood to smile.

He bent back into the refrigerator. "Take one of Shari's juice boxes," he offered next.

Shaye took the little cardboard box of apple/grape juice from him. She stabbed it with its little white straw and then sucked down three quarters of the box instantly- totally dehydrated.

Danny watched her strangely. "I'm sorry, Shaye," he said. "We got so busy and I forgot you'll only drink bottled drinks."

"You don't hate me for it?"

He ruffled her hair. "That's not something to hate somebody for." He looked incredulous, as though surprised that someone, like her husband, might have actually hated her for her weaknesses and her fears. "I have to go now. The coroner just called that he got Vicki Cruz's body."

Danny gathered keys, radio and gun from the counter where he had rested them and tilted back his head to swallow down his Kool Aid. "It may be a long night," he said, leaning forward to kiss Shaye on her forehead. "Have the run of the house," he told her. "You can take a shower, and take a nap. If you want clothes, all my stuff is in the guestroom and that's my room now, so you can sleep there. Okay?"

He backed toward the front door, and watched Shaye strangely. The house was almost dark, except for the yellow fixture swinging above her. She wondered if it made her look like a beautiful movie star to him, under the studio lights, or more like one of his suspects in an interrogation room.

She felt it was time to say something kind; she finally remembered that chasing Jorge Colon might put Danny at risk, too, even though he acted like it was nothing. "I'll see you later on," she said. "Be safe, Danny. Be careful."

He replied with a soft little smile. "Eat your sandwich," he said. "And take some milk."

Danny activated the house alarm before he left and then turned his key in the lock from outside, locking her into safety.

Shaye ate her sandwhich in distracted nibbles, with no bite bigger than a grain of rice. It took her over an hour, perched halfway on the now warm vinyl of the stool like a frightened bird. She gazed out at birds fluttering in the back yard, which she could see through French doors and past a vast dark screened-in area, which she assumed was a pool.

But Shaye stayed rooted in her spot as complete darkness settled throughout the house. Time seemed to have no meaning here and even the repetitive clicks of manual numbers turning above the older range did not disturb her- just served to hypnotize her further.

Shaye wondered if Danny had left the autopsy yet, and if he'd had any success finding Jorge Colon yet. She doubted it. As soon as he found him, he'd said he would call her. She checked their private cell phone to make sure it was fully charged. Then she glanced over at the home phone in its own corner of counter space. He certainly knew where to call her, she reflected. So did Adam. Danny had left his home number and police cell phone on the note on the counter.

Shaye's dreamy gaze was distracted again, just looking into darkness. She had a sinking feeling of something bad happening with Adam, but she didn't know what, or how. And she felt so weary right now.

Just on the other side of her counter, in the living room, Shaye stared at a TV screen five times as wide as the one in her trailer- a slick dark expanse. But she felt she liked to leave it blank. She slipped from her stool with no sound, as though compelled to keep quite, and she let her hand trail over a few objects in the living room- the back of the couch, a big pillar candle, which contributed to the vanilla and jasmine smell, a miniature wooden table with a skyscraper built of wooden building blocks. The control box for the house's alarm glowed neon red in the distance.

Shaye's Keds made no sound as she slipped out of the wood-floored living room down the hallway. She ran fingers along the narrow walls, lightly touching hanging art, and experiencing the textures of little area rugs under her feet.

Shaye felt her way around the tile wall of the bathroom, where a blue tinted nightlight resembling a minature lantern glowed. She snapped on a regular light, and saw reflected in the mirror a giant photograph of Lorinne in a bathing suit, clutching Shari's hand. The photo, matted in powder blue, was tinted an odd shade of black and white, deliberately altered to look old. Behind Lorrine and Shari she saw buildings that looked like old casinos. If Shaye had to guess, she would assume the photo was taken in Atlantic City, obviously by a professional photographer.

It must have come from "the good old days", before Danny's scandal in New York City. Lorrine looked positively dewy- and unmistakeably luscious. Her eyes curved like a cat's, with full makeup. And the somewhat old-fashioned swimsuit emphasized her tiny hourglass figure. She resembled surfing movie stars like Natalie Wood, dangerously attractive in a breezy girl-next-door way.

Shaye thought about the fact that, just when this photo was taken was probably when Danny had first been promoted to detective- and transferred into Vice. This was also when he had hit bottom with his sex addiction. He had told her he usually went with prostitutes and sex-industry workers. But he'd also had trysts with female police officers right in the station, women he met in the subway, a girl who sold him espresso in the mornings and, at the worst of it, a teacher at Shari's day care five minutes after he had dropped his daughter off. He told her he'd cried in his car for an hour after that last incident, determined to seek help. And he would have gone to a meeting immediately, but a massive drug sting ripened right then, and he had a spectacular afternoon's work making arrests.

He'd celebrated the successful drug bust by treating himself to one last time with his usual massage parlor girls, swearing to himself that he'd find a sex addicts' meeting as soon as he got cleaned up and got some sleep. What he didn't realize was that he'd done so well on the drug bust that he had a sleazy reporter from the *New York Post* following him, wanting to get a story.

The reporter had got a story, all right, and one very memorable photo. Danny had hung his head, and told Shaye that he always tended to be unlucky like that.

Yet he still held on to this beachside photo, a shrine to everything that was beautiful and powerful in his wife, up in his bathroom. Shaye gazed at it backwards in the mirror.

After they separated a few days ago, Danny had probably not taken it down because he was lazy. Or because it was pretty. Or because it also showed his daughter. But Shaye couldn't look at it right now. So she turned off the light, and then bathed furtively in the blue nightlight glow, standing in the tub and washing with sea-themed guest soaps, feeling like a bag lady that had invaded a normal home.

After her spongebath, she left wet footprints on the tile, carrying her shoes in one hand and slipping down to the hall to the guest room. She found it by smell. Unlike the master bedroom, whose cold flowery smells seemed staged, this room smelled of closeness and wood and leather. Moonlight illuminated the small space with its full size bed and desk in the corner. Shaye glimpsed framed photographs in a pile face down. She lifted the top one and found a pretty wedding photo. A few down, at the bottom of the pile, was one of Lorrine posing seductively in a red and white Christmas teddy.

It was clear that once Frank Danielo had adored his wife, or at least desired her. But no more, obviously. The only photo he kept displayed here where he slept now was one on the bedside table- his stiff police academy photo- the one Shaye had seen in the newspaper. Seeing his pride in this made her feel sad.

Shaye sat down on the edge of the bed, holding the photo within her crossed arms and looking out to the moonlit sky. She remembered her recent nights in Flamingo Park, with what sounded like howls of violence filling the air. Here it was so quiet. She could hear her own toes as she crossed and uncrossed them on the rug. She wished that Adam would call her. She wished Danny would call.

Eventually, her muscle tone relaxed. Hardly realizing, but not fighting the tiredness, Shaye slumped back into the bed.

Danny woke her, breathing gently into her face, and he slid his nude body gently over her in the darkness. He gently slid his arms along hers, raised her arms over her head and captured her hands.

"This is the police," he teased. "You're under arrest."

Shaye felt herself melt into his warmth, hardly able to distinguish where he ended and she began in the enclosing darkness of his home- this safest of places she had been brought to after all the trouble of the past few years.

Shaye sighed into Danny's face and flexed her body against his, squirming and then giggling against his neck.

Danny's body tensed with passion. He brushed his hands, one at a time, up and down her sides, feeling her slim waist under her T-shirt and her long sleek thighs. "I like you in my clothes," he said, as they caught a rhythm and started moving against eachother.

So much had already been said that now it felt right being quiet together. They simply murmured and stretched and twined their bodies around eachother, giggling and curling their toes. Danny stroked his fingers through Shaye's hair, and then he slid his hands down, lightly teasing the sides of her breasts through her T-shirt-actually one of his.

"Oh," he teased. "I love your tits, Shaye. I love your hair. Is that enough? Can I be with you?"

Shaye pounded on his back in mock anger. It was too dark to see, but had he been able to, he would have seen her grin. Playfully, she nipped one of his ears as she pulled his head down to rest on her chest. "I'm glad you're home," she said huskily.

Danny lifted his head up and kissed her softly on the lips.

"For real, Shaye. I'm only a few weeks shy of a full year of abstinence. But I'd give that up to make love to you. If you're ready..." He cupped her chin and stroked her cheek with a finger. "Are you ready, Angel?" he breathed. "Do you want to?"

Wistfully Shaye stroked along his well-carved back and his hard buttocks. It would be so easy, yet immeasureably hard, to go through with this. Shaye wanted this passion- and yet she was nowhere near ready for it. In ways she loved being held by this man, who a few weeks ago was only a stranger. At the same time, she felt she could hardly breathe.

She squirmed under him, protecting her chest with her arms.

"I care about you, Danny," she said tentatively. "I care about you tremendously." She clutched his shoulders for emphasis. "But I don't think I'm ready to do this right now. Not tonight."

Danny shifted his weight, but still held onto her, pressing every inch of himself against her, from his pounding heart to his hairy calves, never depriving her of his warmth. Their breath seemed to flow together as they spoke, neither voice more than a whisper.

"Just tell me if I'm crazy," Danny said. "As soon as you get your head together, will you go back to someone like that newsman in Gulfport? You never told me, did you fall in love with him then? Did you ever start a relationship?"

Shaye shook her head in the darkness, clinging to Danny and trying to dispel the old demons.

"It was nothing like that," she breathed, trying to explain and feeling herself twist with the shame she had to face. "I just liked somebody caring then. It was nothing like what I feel for you, Danny. This is definitely real."

Danny ran a hand down from her forehead, over her eyelids and over her lips in a gesture of mock chastisement. "Silly girl," he said. "You ought to just do it then, get over the hump and allow someone who really loves you to make love to you. Finally see what life should be. Take a chance on our future, Shaye."

Shaye shook her head in the darkness. "Please wait."

"Okay," Danny breathed. Gently he guided her hand down to touch his hardness. Then he pushed it up against her through the clothes. "I can make you come, though," he said. "Would you like to feel that? We can just play like this and come together."

Shaye didn't answer in words, but she clutched onto Danny's back and wrapped her long legs around him, letting him move like he wanted to. Meanwhile she parted her lips and accepted his, joining in a smoldering kiss that matched her wetness down below. She arched her back, stroking her pelvis against his hard-on and making him moan, while she groaned and sighed in unison with him.

Getting even hotter, and losing even more control, Danny curled up around her. "Shaye, I love you," he said. "I want to stay faithful to you forever. I wanted you from the first minute I saw you..."

His last words came out in sputters as his body tensed around hers in his climax. Shaye finished, too, but more quietly. She grasped Danny's strong shoulders and let out one big breath as she felt all the day's tension and fear release. Then softly, she let her body form against his.

She waited out a few hundred pounding heartbeats, hers and his. Then, hoping he was asleep, she admitted in a whisper, "I wanted you from the first minute I saw you, too, Danny."

Shaye woke the next morning as soon as it was light, and she propped up on an elbow so she could caress Danny's face while he slept. His brown eyes fluttered open and his lips slid into a relaxed smile.

"Hey, so did you find out anything more about Jorge Colon?" she asked him.

Danny shrugged and pulled himself up higher to lean his head against the headboard, while gently resting a hand on her back. "Not really," he said. With a wince, he added, "Vicki Cruz was definitely murdered. The coroner confirmed she was run over back and forth several times. She died in agony, but I guess Colon didn't care..."

Shaye shook her head, and gently touched his face. "I'm sorry, Danny."

"Later on, I was riding with Stephen Wren from the FBI. They detained a guy at the Orlando airport who they thought was Colon and they brought me out to see him, but it was the wrong guy. Then we came back and checked out an old address of Colon's, a mile from Flamingo Park, but it seemed abandoned..."

Danny got to his feet and respectfully pulled a towel around his waist, sleepily standing over Shaye and rubbing his hairy stomach. He pointed at the cardboard box of Colon's possessions that Pete Andersen had given them yesterday.

"The good news, Shaye," Danny said. "Is that you can look over every item in that box and see if you can find any clues. I brought it home for you. The bad news is that I'm going to have the FBI dude with me again this morning. Until I can lose him, you'll have to stay here. Is that okay with you?"

Shaye crept over to the edge of the bed.

"What about Adam?"

"I called your trailer two hours ago, just before I crawled into bed with you," he said. "No answer." He stepped over to the bedside table and tried again from that phone.

Shaye tensed, and felt her stomach turning over as Danny stood there listening to repeated ringing. Maybe Adam was sleeping she tried to tell herself. Maybe he had gone back out with the "girls" when he got the note from Danny about her being here. Maybe he was furious. Maybe he was jealous, even though he had never said anything about wanting them to be more than the friends they had always been.

She knew Adam resented Danny because he took her attention and affection, even though she still wasn't sure exactly what Adam wanted with her. But she did know it broke his heart yesterday to see her leave with Frank Danielo.

"Danny," she said, looking up pleadingly. "You need to find Adam. Possibly he's also in some danger from Colon."

Fearless in Florida

"Adam probably just had a hissy fit," Danny said levelly. "No offense. But he's probably just upset that he might lose his roommate and best friend if you stay here with me instead of going to Miami with him. So he probably just had a "girls night out" getting drunk with Madeline and Rochelle. I wouldn't worry."

No matter what he said, Shaye could see from the tenseness of his posture that he was worried, too. There was just too much horror in Flamingo Park, especially after he just lost his witness, for him to remain unconcerned.

"Danny, please find him," Shaye said. "I'll stay here if you do that. Please…"

"Okay, Baby," Danny said. "No problem. I'm supposed to pick up Stephen Wren at eight." He indicated the doorway with a friendly leer. "Do you want to come in with me now and take a shower?"

Shaye looked around her at the brightness of the room, and she felt light and bright herself- almost like she had been chosen to be spared from everything. And now she just craved to be purified. She had been thinking of the swimming pool peripherally since she had seen it last night.

"Could I swim?" she asked. "Would that be all right?"

Danny smiled and gave a little laugh. As he did, his face seemed to light up.

"Sure you can swim," he said. "Wear yourself out. Swim nude if you like. Or, if you're shy, Lorinne's got bathing suits in her top drawer."

Backing towards his shower, Danny watched Shaye grimace at that suggestion and he laughed. "Then, nude it is!"

Shaye slipped into the cool, leaden colored water as carefully as a nymph out of Greek mythology, or some other tortured female creature with its own agenda. Her hair caressed alabaster buttocks and long slender thighs and she walked regally down the steps, her long fingers just skimming the water.

She immersed herself with not a splash, slipping like a five-foot alligator into its watery element, a place where silence was essential. Then she drifted toward the deeper water, floating with just a few movements of her fingers, as though unknown currents pushed her. The chill waters almost stopped her heart, yet her immersion woke her up to necessary insights, she felt. She gazed up at the limitless gray sky through the screen enclosure, timing the morning to the in out out of her own breaths.

321

Shaye paddled on her back in circles, enjoying the Zen-like condition, envisioning herself a natural creature like an alligator, or a long slippery gray salamander. She could feel the silvery water as it parted along her sides like silk. One stroke, then another and then another. This is all there was.

Danny came forward from the house with his hair slicked back, getting adjusted with a bagel and cream cheese which he stuck in his mouth as he tied on his gunbelt. For a few seconds he simply stared at Shaye, as if awed by her mystery and majesty.

She watched him out of slitted eyes, but finally deigned to open them and look at him innocently.

Danny gulped. "There's bagels back there for you. And you could make yourself eggs. And go through that box of Colon's stuff, please. Call me if you find anything."

Shaye paddled over to the edge of the pool, crossing her arms so that Danny looked down into her naked cleavage and at the long tendrils of hair that fanned out in the water behind her. She looked at him questioningly about the whole situation, yet she didn't challenge him.

He read her concern.

"I can't tell the FBI they can't ride with me, Shaye. If we don't nab Colon by afternoon, I'll try to find some way to come back and get you. Okay?"

Shaye gave a deliberately ambiguous smile, one that was knowing and seductive.

Danny rolled his eyes, as he stuffed some bagel into his mouth. "You make me crazy, Baby. But I gotta go…" He walked off into the house, jingling keys. Then suddenly Shaye heard him exclaim. "Oh, screw it. Just what I needed!"

He hurried back to the edge of the pool enclosure. Shaye still leaned up at the edge.

"Shaye," he said. "I hate to ask you to do this. But Lorinne just drove up with Shari. For just five minutes, can I get you to hide? If you want to meet them, I'll let you. But…" He gestured vaguely-there was the problem of Shaye's lack of clothes.

Without giving an answer, Shaye pushed back, and then she lowered her head neatly below the stone edge of the pool. Like an alligator, only her eyes and nose showed above the water. She didn't resent Danny. She would have done this on her own. For there was no question that hiding was the thing she did best.

Fearless in Florida

8:00 a.m. that morning- Oceanside Hammock, FL, five miles from Flamingo Park

A slim dark-haired figure ran through the misty morning woods, slapping green saw palmetto fronds and splashing dew. This figure wore an odd costume- white and silver baroque fairy wings and a silvery green jumpsuit. And, although so delicately dressed, they ran with desperation.

In pursuit followed a man, huffing and pounding the earth, while the fronds swished as they parted before him like the rice paper of a geisha's fans. His body was sturdy, and his panting was the only sound besides early birdsong and the brush of wings on fronds.

The two figures ran up a subtle rise in the land. There, in between native shubbery, stood four rusted metal pillars connected by cables- the legs of the old Oceanside water toward.

As the pursued climbed this rise with pursuer nearing, he suddenly turned- revealing Adam Ant's heavily made-up face, reddened from crying. The kohl that ringed his eyes ran down his white face powder, emphasizing his agony.

"Leave me alone!" he cried out, pointing a slender finger at the man in accusation. "I'll kill myself, but I'll never let you touch me!"

Chapter 22

Shaye could just barely hear Danielo greet his wife and daughter at the front door. Then she listened to the girl tromping through the house near her, singing to herself. Shari didn't come out here, and her singing stopped briefly. Shaye guessed she was looking for something to eat in the refrigerator. She heard a stool scrape back. Having found nothing in the fridge, Shari had probably decided to climb up to get some fruit.

Then she heard a harsh female voice call out, heading this way. "Shari, put that stool back! Go in your bedroom and pick up some of your toys. We've gotta go!"

Now Lorrine stood right by the French doors. Great, Shaye thought, plastering herself harder against the pool overhang and feeling the dampness, feeling herself freezing or turning to stone like part of the hard ceramic tile. Part of Shaye wanted to peer up and look. But much deeper instincts, almost animal instincts that resided deep within her, told her to be still.

"So, the movers are coming this weekend, Frank," Lorrine said, "to pick up everything. Do you think you'll be ready?"

Danny approached the vicinity as well, although he didn't sound as close as Lorrine. Maybe he was trying to lure her away. "Take whatever you want," he said. "I'll survive. Just leave Shari's bed and some toys for when she visits me on the weekends."

Lorrine scoffed. "Are you sure your new girlfriend won't mind?"

"Why do this now, Lorrine?" Danny asked. "You're the one who's planning on buying a house with your boss. You were in his bed the day after I broke up the marriage. So why the double standard?"

"Because you're the one dating some scanky informant from the trailer park, that's why!"

Shaye listened to Lorrine's heels pound down on the tile by the door like sharpened daggers as she paced. She wondered vaguely what the woman would think if she found the "skanky informant" soaking naked in her swimming pool. But Shaye felt beyond caring. There were bigger things. Lorrine's anger and concerns paled next to the inestimable power of a serial killer.

"Do you have to do this right now, with Shari in the other room?" Danny protested.

"Why not? Shari knows what kind of man her daddy is, what kind of loser. The whole world knows that, Frank."

"Oh, goddamn it!" Danny suddenly raised his voice, a deep wounded bellow that Shaye had never heard, not even when he yelled at suspects. "Would it be different if I dated a supermodel, Lorinne? Someone that used to screw Shaun Dayne? Would *that* make you respect me?"

"Oh, please. No supermodel would ever look at you, Frank! You just love the hookers and losers. Pathetic women, that's all you care about."

These words stung, or maybe it was the chlorine in the pool. Shaye felt her eyes burn. She thought for a nanosecond about simply breathing in the water- what a peaceful way to die. But clearly, she wanted to live. She had other women depending on her now for their lives.

Meanwhile Danny's voice shook the house. He didn't seem to care if she heard, if his daughter heard or if half the neighborhood heard.

"Fuck your uncaring heart, Lorrine! I'm fed up. Did you knw the Flamingo Park killer just murdered one of my 'loser' informants yesterday? I watched them autopsy what was left of her after he ran her over three times…"

Suddenly, Danny was interrupted by his little girl's clear voice. "Stop it, please, Daddy," she asserted in a bell-like tone.

Shaye splayed her fingers on the pool tiles, trying to press closer and hear more. Her heart suddenly pounded as the little girl's voice approached closer to her. "Don't be mad at Mommy. She just doesn't understand what it's like to be a cop. You told me that. Remember? You said that's why you guys are divorcing. So why are you getting mad?"

Now Shaye listened to silence. From down the block, she heard the droning of lawn machinery. Or maybe it was a mosquito right up near her ear that had somehow gotten through the net. Since being in this house she had lost much sense of perspective.

Now she didn't have to hear the words exactly. Danny said, "Come here, Shari," and then he must have lifted his daughter, for soon she was giggling as he cooed and murmured to her. "Daddy's little girl is so wise," he said. "Wiser than both of your parents. I love you so much, Shari. Honey, here, let Daddy make you a bagel so you can take it with you to daycare. I doubt Mommy bothered to feed you…"

Lorinne's spike heels hit the kitchen linoleum. "You know, Frank, you don't understand. When Louis and I get married, Shari will be able to eat anything she wants for breakfast, lunch and dinner! And she'll have a housekeeper to serve it to her because Louis' house is a mansion compared to this dump. He already makes four times more than what you ever will, even if you ever get your promotion."

"Whatever," Danny agreed. "I really can't talk at the moment. I was just out the door to ride with the FBI. We're still looking for the serial killer today. In fact, I'd feel better if you don't go anyplace alone until I apprehend him, Lorrine. Seriously. Particularly stay away from Flamingo Trailer Park."

Suddenly, Lorrine laughed- genuinely- and her laugh sounded quiet pretty. She really started cracking up. "And why would I want to go *there*, Frank?"

Shaye heard Lorinne let out more of her tension. Silly laughter bubbled out of her, until her daughter giggled too and, finally Danielo laughed as well. He was humoring his wife, Shaye knew. But she could also hear how tired he was of fighting.

"Come on now, Lorrine," he urged. "I seriously have to go now. Let me help you carry out the stuff you wanted today."

Shaye heard quiet for a bit. Then she listened to them shift some items around in the living room, bumping the front door against the wall as they carried them out.

Danny appeared for a second at the break in the French door. He pointed back at the house in the direction of Lorrine and made the "crazy" sign, wiggling a finger around his ear. Then he winked at Shaye, smiled goofily with a hand on his heart, pointing at her with the other. The next second he tapped his watch and held out his hand in the command for "stay" as he backed away still smiling at her softly, until she could no longer see him in the dimness of the interior.

A few more minutes passed, and Shaye should have felt sure she was alone. Instead, she sensed another presence.

She paddled backward in the pool and she stretched up until she saw who was watching her. Little Shari stood in the doorway, holding a bagel and a stuffed bear that was bigger than she was, and staring intently. Standing silently like this, Shari looked perfect, with clear white skin and shining eyes, shiny shoes and an old-fashioned red curdoroy jumper. She reminded Shaye of herself back in kindergarten- a guileless, yet powerfully curious, little girl.

Despite the fact that she was naked under the water, Shaye felt no shame or negativity. Her face relaxed into a big completely spontaneous smile in response to Shari Danielo's curious stare.

Shari smiled, back. Then she raised her hand shyly, stifled a little giggle and, before she ran off, wiggled her fingers in a secret farewell.

Danny left a few minutes after his wife and daughter. Then he telephoned Shaye not even a half hour later as she swam in the pool nude, gliding around its edges like an otter or a mermaid at dizzying invigorating speed. It took many rings for the cell phone she had left atop Danny's shorts and T-shirt to break into her reverie, and a few more rings for her to sort out what the sound was. She dredged herself up over the edge of the pool to retrieve it, feeling the weight of water soaked in her hair as so heavy that it might drag her back down if she didn't fight it. Her wet fingers slopped water all over the phone.

"Yes?" she breathed.

"Don't be worried," Danny said to her, with his voice breaking up a little. "I'm out at the old Oceanside water tower. And, physically, he's fine now. But there was an incident out here- involving Adam…"

"What do you mean *physically fine?*" Shaye demanded. "What happened, Danny?"

Danny sighed. He called out something to someone in the background, probably another cop. A few beats passed, and his answer came out right against the phone. He was hiding things, it seemed, tense almost beyond his breaking point.

"Please don't get upset, Shaye. Adam might have a broken wrist, possibly a broken collarbone. That type of thing. He just attempted suicide and I saved him. But now Oceanside cops are taking him for a psych exam, right after his X-rays at the hospital.

"And there was another man involved, an older man. It's not really clear if Adam attempted to harm the man, or if the man tried to do something to him first. We're taking the man in for questioning, too."

Shaye almost stopped breathing with the horrible thought. "This guy, whoever he is, could *he* be the killer? He tried to hurt Adam?"

"The serial killer's still out there," Danny said, "and I can't even look for him this morning until I get this situation with Adam cleared up." He seemed to press his mouth closer onto the phone. "It's not even my jurisdiction, Shaye, but I butted in. I called Oceanside and asked if they had any calls involving someone matching Adam's description, and this situation was happening right then, so they let me help.

"And the guy I've got over here's no killer, Shaye. He's just some sleazy rich faggot record producer who doesn't want to tell us his name. Adam cut his hands up with some tweezers, and now the guy's going crazy. He wants the cuts on his arms fixed up, but doesn't want to go to the hospital in case the newspapers will print he's a fag..."

"If that's Adam's record producer guy... Oh my God," Shaye said. Her heart sank for her friend. In a way this was worse than him meeting the killer. Adam had just encountered an agonizingly shoddy end to his dreams. All her fault, she knew. Adam never would have been out there with that man if it weren't for her.

Danny confirmed it. "The best I can gather from what the producer told me is that Adam has been performing privately for him for money for the past week. Probably Adam trying to save up to take you to Miami... But tonight- actually this morning- Adam was dancing for the producer in some frilly fairy costume. And then the producer announced to Adam that he was in love with him. Apparently Adam snapped then and went totally crazy on him.

"Shaye," Danny said, and Shaye could hear the tremendous tenderness and concern in his voice. "Adam was acting really crazy. He climbed up the front of the tower wearing these giant silver angel wings..."

"Like something out of Shakespearean Theater?" she asked. "*A Midsummer Night's Dream*?"

"Yeah, something freaky like that," Danny confirmed. "I didn't even know if it was real when I saw it. The Oceanside cops were sure Adam was serious about jumping and the producer was wailing and crying. All I could do was start climbing the back of the tower.

"Adam jumped when I was still a few feet below him, Shaye, but his costume snagged. He broke some bones dangling, but I caught him before he could fall the rest of the way. Then I carried him down."

Shaye gave a little sob. Danny had unfortunately described the scene so vividly that she could clearly envision it. Except the fact that she was the missing element. She hadn't been there.

"Did Adam say anything?" she asked. She hardly knew what she hoped for. Maybe just forgiveness.

"Adam was lucid, Shaye. And, thank God, we agreed neither of us would mention you to anybody. Ever. That's about all there was. He wasn't in great shape. He did say one thing, Shaye. He said he was sorry. And he said to tell you he loves you."

Danny asked Shaye to promise that she wouldn't show up at the hospital and ruin everything. And she promised, but she was really hardly listening when he signed off.

Forty-five minutes later, Shaye still circled the pool in the rythym of nature, seeking some solace or inspiration, when Danny called her a second time. He told her Adam's father was flying in by private jet to come to the hospital, and he warned her again not to show up.

"I think I can help Adam," Danny said. "His father called me just now from his limo on his way from the airport and we had a long conversation. Dallas Underwood says he feels really guilty and he says he'll get Adam a great lawyer for the charges from New York. First we can get Adam declared unfit for trial, and we'll say he was so mentally unstable that he kidnapped you or something. I can help you guys as long as you continue hiding out, Shaye."

"Okay, I'll do that," she said.

Hide. Hide. Hide. Once again, hide. The only thing she was good for. In the end her being with Adam had only hurt him anyway.

"But I can't just stay at your house forever, Danny."

Danny's voice came out harsh with his overwhelming stress.

"You know, *I'd* be the one to go to jail for that, Shaye, not you. But I don't care. Just please sit tight now. There's no choice. My partner Glenn Chow's flying back in tonight from Mexico. Chow and I will spend all night looking for Colon and hopefully we'll catch him. But please promise to stay at the house, Shaye. I need to know you'll be safe."

Ideas and images swirled in Shaye's head. The whole progression of events ran through her head, all of the scenes, from herself and Adam first coming to Flamingo Park, to the image she visualized of Adam jumping from the tower this morning.

"Danny, I'll stay safe. So please go back to Adam now," she said. "Help him. Smooth things out with his father. And don't worry about me. I'll be here when you come back. I'll be fine."

Danny signed off with a kiss. But Shaye had hung up before she heard. She pulled herself out of the pool and sat on the cool tile nude, in lotus position while the water slipped from her skin. She gazed in an almost Zen-like trance at the damp stones in Danny's empty flowerbed and the unnaturally bright green grass. She gazed beyond at the morning mist that still steamed in neighbor's yards. Birds flitted before her vision, two tiny azure blue birds that seemed to come from her imagination.

Like everything else, they occupied her senses for a second and then they were gone.

Shaye knew she couldn't just sit here. The next time she saw Frank Danielo wouldn't be here. It would probably be later tonight, at her trailer.

For she determined she had to go back. She would carry Danielo's gun. And she knew exactly where in his room Adam kept hidden their traveling money. At least two thousand dollars. Unless the producer had already given him more. But, for what Shaye planned to do today she didn't need more than twenty dollars. She simply needed enough to purchase a camera that would work with a computer, and three boxes of jet black hair dye.

Reaching for the hair dye was perhaps the hardest thing Shaye had ever done in her life. For the moment, it was not the crowds in the local Publix supermarket that disturbed her. It was the feeling of prickling on the back of her neck underneath her long mane of blond hair. The blond that was her one protection. Her arm shook so hard as she reached for the box on the shelf above her that she had to steady it. But she did steady it. And she took down the boxes- one, two three, definitely enough to turn every strand of her blond hair black.

Drawing in a steadying breath was hard, but Shaye did it. The people milling around behind her disturbed her, always too many. She wondered what it would be like when the new supermarket across US1 replaced this one. Theoretically, it had twice the square footage, so it should alleviate some of the crowds. But Shaye doubted it. She had heard the saying, "build it, and they will come". And that seemed to be true. Even when people knew they were in danger.

Shouldn't some of the people shopping here today stay away because of the killer? She glanced back at a young slim woman behind her, who wore a white T-shirt and butt-cheek hugging gray shorts along with perky white leather tennis shoes. The woman, who looked fresh and healthy, stood on tiptoes picking out a Glade candle air freshener, carefully selecting from all the colors and scents.

Didn't this young woman ever watch television? Didn't she realize that her hair and her age made her a possible target for a killer who struck twice within the past month less than a half a mile from here? Was the little candle she selected with such apparent enthusiasm really worth the risk to her? The young woman looked up from her candle, caught Shaye staring intently and batted her lashes in friendly greeting.

Shaye sighed. Oh, God, she thought. And it all came crashing down upon her. Once she had been without cares, too. Now, because of the burdens she carried, just because of the fear, she might be fated to provide this woman's salvation.

Shaye attempted to give the young woman a reassuring smile. Because of her state of mind, it may have more resembled a demented grimace. But perhaps her pretty face salvaged it. With one more smile, the young woman sauntered off.

Shaye locked her hands on her cart and turned toward the front of the store. It was afternoon already, because returning to the trailer to retrieve the money, then taking a bus into town to buy a Web cam and then getting back here had taken many hours.

These hours had given Shaye time to think. In a tabbed pocket in the chino shorts she wore today she carried approximately two thousand dollars in cash. At first she had debated leaving most of Adam's stash where it was. But then she thought wisely about the possibility of the police pawing through the trailer, trying to investigate Adam. There was no sense letting them get the money. She was sure Adam wouldn't want that.

Danny had called several times on the cell phone, reporting that he had met Adam's father and that the situation actually looked promising. But he couldn't let Shaye speak to Adam.

"There are doctors around everywhere, Baby," he'd whispered. "They want to take Adam into surgery to work on his collarbone. He's heavily sedated and he's... not himself," he attempted to euphamize. "He's not in any pain, Shaye, but I just think you'd feel better talking to him when he's feeling better..."

Danny was trying to protect her, she understood. She'd already seen her friend Adam when he went mad. And that's the state he must be in now. Shaye just hoped that his father might be gentle on him, and that Danny really could help him in a legal sense to perhaps get all the charges, the new and the old, dropped. Adam deserved it.

As for herself and their future, Shaye felt entirely lost. Danny hadn't even suspected that she wasn't still in his home the few times he had called her. He had sounded immensely preoccupied, and he seemed happy when she gave him a few leads she had gleaned from out of the box of papers, a few more people he could talk to who might help him locate Jorge Colon.

Aside from that, Danny was pushing for information on the new F350 that Colon had used to kill Victoria Cruz. There was always the possibility that Colon, although intelligent, had completely slipped up, using a real address to register the truck. Or maybe he'd used a credit card to purchase gas at the truck stop, which could perhaps be traced to a real address. And then there were witnesses at the truck stop who might possibly have seen Colon, or conversed with him, still to be interviewed.

Danielo was acting his old self, tenacious and inherently optimistic, and grasping at whatever straws he had left to stay on the trail of the killer. But Shaye thought, unfortunately, that she understood better how Jorge Colon thought and what motivated him. And, for that reason, she stood a better chance of capturing him.

The man was mad, was the key. And Shaye was also mad. So she understood obsession. She understood how real life could twist you around until the big threats seemed small, and the small ones could wring out your heart and crush your soul.

At the Publix checkout counter, she swung her eyes up to silver alien-looking bulbs that hung from the cavernous ceiling, hidden cameras, looking at her. Shoppers chattered and clattered, following eachother touching the finger pads of a shared debit machine that could bring illness and an end to their lives. And all they seemed to want to do was suck on lollipops and add a few more bars of candy and a couple more celebrity magazines to their already overflowing carts.

God bless them, Shaye thought, not entirely cynically. Gooseflesh sprung up over her bare arms in the air conditioning. A booming voice echoed around the store, coming from above. Not the voice of God, however. Just the store manager, announcing that somebody's car was about to be towed, and urging the shoppers to try the special on Palace Pork Rinds in the back of the store. Shaye glanced all around her, realizing that this was all the reassurance that most people got in life.

She sighed, paying with a hundred dollar bill, and collecting the change on top of a napkin she held as germ protection in her hand. The irony was that you would never know whether you had succeeded in this day-to-day struggle just to stay alive until it had ended.

Shaye wandered out of the store, feeling listless and abandoned.

Oddly, it felt in her gut as if she *was* grounded, as if someone *was* watching her. Not God, but a human presence. As opposed to most of these shoppers who seemed to hurry to escape their day-to-day fears and emptiness, Shaye sensed, all the way down to her tingling feet, that there was a real human presence around to whom she was very important. And she sensed this presence watching her.

She left the region of clattering carts and wiped-out teenage workers squatting by the wall smoking. She got far enough from the store that she was able to feel a breeze- able to watch the impish wind stir bits of rubbish in the untended hairs of long grass. Amidst the bright green grass, and the rubbish, several white seagulls and several shiny black crows picked for tidbits and she found the contrast in the colors strangely beautiful.

Shaye took a fortifying breath and squared her shoulders. As she jogged across Flamingo Beach parkway and angled into the trailer park at a fast walk, the feeling that she was being followed intensified. Shaye smelled something murky beside her, perhaps the canal. She noted that a new chain-link fence had been erected around the Caiman Street lot. Danny mentioned to her this morning that the owner, the same A&H Holding Company that owned their trailer, had done that to avoid more trouble and possible lawsuits.

Danny had also told her another news flash not known to the general public. Apparently Flamingo Park as such might not exist very much longer. Oceanside Mayor Adrian Walker, now a friend, had shared the information with Danny that, within the next year, the park would probably be annexed by the City of Oceanside.

This was not a problem for Danielo. He cared most about the safety of the denizens of Flamingo Park, not as much about their independence. And he was going to be working for Oceanside Police Department before then anyway. His job with Oceanside was guaranteed; and if he captured Jorge Colon, then he would be starting immediately as detective.

Well, by this evening, if Shaye's plan worked, Danny would arrest Colon and the detective job would be assured.

She had thought about it in the deepest way, and she really didn't have anything to lose. If it took setting herself as bait to guarantee everyone's safety, so be it.

She imagined Jorge Colon standing in her living room caressing through her long dyed hair with the tines of the rooster claw. She imagined him trying to end her life, posed before the little Web camera. He would never see the camera and, whatever he did to her, at least his crimes would be caught on tape. Stacked up against all the good she could do, Shaye perceived her life as basically expendable.

She would fight, of course. And she thought she could even win. She'd have Danny's pistol hidden underneath long pants. She planned to hold Colon at gunpoint, and then call for Danny to remove him. Of course, Shaye would probably be removed as well, for she was a wanted fugitive. It was likely that, when she called, Danny would have his FBI partner with him. How long before Shaye, a witness, became a suspect?

So, if she was able to attract Colon, whatever happened, she would lose in some way. But she thought about perspective again, and she held the value of her life quite lightly.

Even now, she thought she heard soft footsteps padding along behind her in the woods. If someone lunged at her across the asphalt right now, she could pull the gun and shoot. But she didn't think they would. Colon would have no need to chase a girl with blond hair. After all, he was completely ritualistic. Killing Vicki Cruz, who was emotionally stable, wouldn't have satisfied him because it didn't further his mission, so he'd have to go after another victim that met all his criteria. He would want cops to see that he wasn't an ordinary killer, but rather a savior, a changer of hopeless prostitutes into saints.

Everybody thought Colon might head back to Mexico right now. But Shaye felt a conviction that he couldn't go until he left on high note, as he would see it. He'd want to make clear that he only killed because of a divine mandate he believed he had been given.

Seeing a new young woman embark from the County bus with a shake in her hips and a lost look in her eye, as well as the longest sleekest hair he had ever seen in this park, would be exactly that last encounter he was waiting for before he would depart. Shaye felt sure of it.

It wasn't likely that it was Colon in the woods behind her now; more likely it was just one of the park's assorted derelicts and troublemakers. Byron Hanes and Troy Reid were both jailed, but she spied two other teens vanish around the corner of Caiman Street, looking like scrub dogs tucking their tails.

A pickup with a trailing bumper rattled by, and a muscular guy in his thirties leaned out, and pursed his lips at her in a smacking parody of a kiss. "I wanna lick them long legs, Baby," he called. "I gotta tongue like a lizard!"

Inside the truck, his buddy snorted with laughter. Shaye thought she recognized the guy, this time wearing a red bandana tied over the top of his head. When he'd yelled out to her a month ago, his bandana had been blue.

The two men carried some sort of rusted gas tank, and rusted tools, in the back of their rusted truck and they turned down a dirt track called Alligator Lane, probably on their way to do a filthy job for customers who were probably poorer and more desperate than they were. Shaye looked around at some of the trailers whose metal edges jutted in between untrimmed brush. She knew that there were many people in power who believed this area shouldn't hire handymen and carpenters to keep shoring up these rotting buildings, but rather demolition crews to tear them down.

At what price was independence worth it? People in Flamingo Park could still say they owned houses and could still make their own decisions. But if the park was leveled, literally down to the ground, and then filled with identical pink stucco condos and environmentally correct landscaping that flanked cute little parking areas, complete with floodlights and a guard gate... well then, would all evil be eradicated from the world?

What would happen to Willie Jeremiah, she wondered, stopping momentarily to link her fingers through the shiny mesh of the new fence around the Caiman St. crime scene. She strained to see into the darkened woods. But, of course, he couldn't be in there. The holding company would have ensured the area was empty before they fenced it in.

Shaye turned the corner and plodded through the gravelly dust of her own street, Manatee St. What would happen to *her*, she wondered. She followed a dirty-tailed skinny-flanked white dog, whose bad hips made him amble like a drunk before her- another one being fed by Darlene and her crew probably.

Spitting a stray hair out of the side of her mouth, Shaye contemplated that she might actually miss this place. Tonight might be the last time she would ever see this street, and this scene which had taken over her full reality so much in the past month and a half.

Would Adam ever come back here again? She doubted it. It was amazing and terrible how things could change so quickly and completely. Would Adam go back to his rich boy world, of country clubs and executive boardrooms? Or would he live out life, for real this time, in a mental ward?

Shaye shivered. It was hard to believe that Adam had helped her in all the ways he had and, at the moment, there was absolutely nothing she could do for him. She couldn't even be allowed onto to the hospital floor where he was being held behind locked bars.

She stopped before their mailbox out of habit, not because she cared about what might be there. But she did it out respect for Adam, because he religiously looked for the mail every day, just like he had done many of the daily chores.

Shaye stopped. Stuffed into the mailbox she found a fat manilla packet. She pulled it out gingerly and saw the postmark- Miami Beach.

"No way," she mumbled to herself, cradling the taped envelope carefully, and checking around furtively as she carried it inside.

A part of her had always thought Adam's promise of Jeff sending them the fake ID was no more than a fanstasy, a happy *Wizard of Oz* fairy story made up to sustain them. But now Shaye's heart pounded for, all along, it had been true.

She unlocked the difficult front door lock, checked the trailer quickly for intruders and, when she confirmed it was safe, she plopped on the couch and tore the envelope open over the coffee table. Amid shredded packing material, a slew of cards and documents poured out. Breathing rapidly, Shaye separated them out. Carefully, she picked out one card in particular, a Florida driver license with an old modeling photo of her smiling broadly, but featuring a new name- a completely new identity.

In the stuffy living room, Shaye practiced smiling and repeating the new name, and she memorized the new birthday. She could be this new and improved woman from this point on, this woman that nobody knew!

And now her plans for the day changed drastically. For now everything had changed.

Chapter 23

Shaye carefully tucked away the three unused boxes of black hair dye in her small bathroom, glancing at them pensively as she did. She then took a minute to stare at herself in the mirror. The green eyes that she saw there now looked surprisingly awake and alive. More so than when she was modeling, this looked like a face that a person would remember if they only saw it once. In a way, her fresh, yet hardened look embodied female strength. Her tight cheekbones were sun-reddened and her green eyes shone, a look that brought with it the presence of the outdoors.

And there were depths in this face that did not reveal themselves. Her strong bone structure, held stiffly, covered things she had seen and things she had known that she did not wish to ever have to share. Her face seemed to keep secrets, and sometimes she had trouble recognizing herself.

Shaye sighed, looking deeply into the inquisitive eyes under the old fly-speckled incandescent bulb. She didn't have to recognize herself now. She could be the young woman in the new driver's license, which she held tucked away safely in her shorts' pocket over her hipbone.

Shaye repeated the new name, her plump lips breathing it out as no more than a whisper.

Shaye knew if she called the Foxy Lady now Adam wouldn't be there. For Adam was in the hospital. This time yesterday perhaps she could have changed things if she had done something. But now, if she called, she knew she'd get the bartender. It would then be easy enough to get her friend Madeline on the phone- in fact

Madeline would probably grab the phone if she knew who was on the other end.

Shaye's tummy tightened up at her thoughts about the rivalry between them. She liked to think that she did not bear the bitchy transsexual any malice. For, if she did, then it made the plan she was running over in her mind even more awful.

Shaye washed her hands for the fourth time since coming in here and then glanced up a bit too knowingly at her face that told no secrets before pulling on the bulb's rusty chain and immersing the bathroom back in darkness.

What she was about to do was for the good of all; it was police business if she had actually been a police officer. No, Danny might not approve it. The FBI man might not either. But they could not have the final say. For they did not understand the Flamingo Park killer like Shaye did.

Jorge Colon would have never come after her, even if she dyed her hair, she realized now, lowering herself on the bed that sank down under her and putting her chin in her hands in a thinker posture. There was still plenty of daylight, but night would come soon. And the killer was hungry.

Shaye sighed, and nibbled at an already demolished fingernail. She had to get up then and then wash her hands, and then brush her teeth. She had to stare at her face again in the light. Just for good measure, she dabbed at the insides of her lips and cheeks with some rubbing alcohol. The taste was so intense that she almost gagged. What a way to kill germs! How ridiculous some of the things she did, she pondered.

She walked out and sat down again heavily on the saggy old bed and she found that her heart was pounding violently, almost as if she was being hit with boxing gloves in the middle of her chest with each beat. She curved her back submissively to get away from the pain and her head spun.

She could just lie down. She could just leave this idea, and maybe Danielo and his FBI friend really could snag Jorge Colon on his way to Mexico, or maybe Glenn Chow could pick him up someday down there. But Shaye doubted any of that. Colon had been too smart for everyone all along. He had gone from living in one of the most remote, and poorest, villages in Mexico to being a man of substance in America, with legal standing and an expertise in his business. He'd had grand plans for transforming all of Flamingo Park, thwarted only because of his partner's betrayal. And then he started killing women right under everyone's noses. He even managed to purchase a brand new F350 pickup to execute the only potential witness to his crimes, Victoria Cruz.

Was this man going back to Mexico? If so, would he only hole up in the ancient town of his ancestors, content with that? Or would he again look for bigger and better things, establishing a new identity and a new business anywhere North or South of the border?

The fact that Colon had bothered to kill the witness, but not in his ritualistic fashion, indicated he didn't want any evidence left. So maybe he didn't plan to stop killing. Even with Flamingo Park crawling with police now- with Frank Danielo working with all of the Oceanside force and the FBI here and the story going out all over the country on the AP wires, even with more reporters and police sure to pour in- maybe Jorge "George" Colon still felt insanely confident. Maybe he still felt compelled to do his "life's work" of sending fallen women to heaven. Maybe he intended to make his stand here, killing as many as he could.

Maybe he knew something his pursuers didn't.

Shaye cringed, and gooseflesh rose on her arms as she thought about what she had intended to do right there in the bathroom. She had intended to put on a miniskirt, and go out with her long hair flying in the breeze stinking of fresh black hair dye and she'd planned for Colon to fall for it. But what she had forgotten for a while today is that what he did wasn't just a game for him. He didn't arbitrarily just select every black haired woman that walked by.

He only went after those who really were fallen. Who really had become lost and grotesquely sacrificed up their lives. Beautiful young Latina women who had thrown away every shred of pride and laid out their bodies at the altar of sin- and risk. Was Shaye such a woman? Not enough, she didn't think. She imagined Colon scoffing at her laughable disguise, and then perhaps running her down with the pickup truck because he might think the police had put her out as a decoy.

She pictured herself falling, cursing at the futility of her last silly effort as her fingers raked the asphalt. She pictured all her ravaged and repaired organs violently ripped open once again and her bright red blood spilling out, trickling from pavement down onto pine needle strewn earth. She pictured cars crawling past in the trailer park, not spotting her in the leafy shade made deeper and tunnel-like by night. She pictured the endless headlights noisily slashing past on US 1- all for nothing.

She pictured Jorge Colon driving on to restlessly troll the park once again.

But then she pictured him finding her target instead. The target she intended to put out there tonight.

Shaye breathed in with a shudder, for she could see no other choice as to what she had to do. In a way, Madeline had brought it on herself. Once, not long ago, she had been a pretty young boy in Puerto Rico. No one told Madeline she had to come to the States. No one told her she had to go through a series of operations to turn herself into a girl. And no one had forced her to become so absolutely bitchy- the kind of girl who prostituted "her" new young body to the absolutely riskiest of homosexual johns, and then insulted them, daring them to hurt her and then throwing rocks and clods of earth at their cars as they drove away.

No one told Madeline she had to snap and snipe at every other female, chasing away every potential girlfriend she had, other than her long-suffering protector Rochelle. And even Rochelle's patience was starting to wear thin.

No one told Madeline that she had to dance in risqué ways up on the stage of Foxy Lady, or to take johns into the bar's bathrooms for forty-dollar quickies or to drink more and more each night, to the point where she reeked of liquor every hour of the day and she teetered on her size ten heels. No one told Madeline that she had to drink until she literally fell down in the dirt, crying and slobbering like a baby, yet still yelling out insults at every passing woman and rattling her bracelets at every passing male, like a gyspy offering herself for sale.

And most of all, no one told Madeline that she had to make a mortal enemy of Shaye Celestia Banks Taylor.

Shaye shook her head roughly to clear it, and steadied her hands enough to lift the telephone receiver. She trembled and placed it down several times in a row, and she had trouble identifying the peculiar excitement that she felt. Did her body tingle like this because she had found a surefire way to entrap the killer? Or was it because she simply could not have found a nicer bait?

She shook her head again.

"I don't hate you, Madeline," she said outloud in the empty room. "But we have to protect others now, you and I. You always wanted to be a woman. And this is the horrible part of the sisterhood you signed up for. Women are vulnerable to men... You understand, Madeline. I think you must. This man, Jorge Colon, has been waiting for you. And I think he might just prove your salvation in the end..."

Of course, Shaye intended to save Madeline, not to let Colon kill her. She caressed the pistol that she now held tucked in the back waistband of her shorts. As soon as Colon spotted Madeline, as soon as he brought her here to the trailer and threatened her in front of the web camera, then Shaye could step in. She'd hold the gun on Colon and then Frank Danielo could arrest him and cuff him and take him away.

"I'll save you, Madeline," she said, directing her words toward the shiny telephone in her lap. "I'll save you, but first you'll have to save our sisters."

When Shaye finally made the call, Madeline answered the telephone behind the bar at Foxy Lady herself, like a definite sign. Shaye cleared her throat, finding the exact words to lure the reluctant- and highly stubborn- bait.

"Madeline, this is Shaye, Adam's Shaye. There's a serious situation out here at our trailer, a serious problem. I don't think it's entirely safe for you; I don't think you have the judgment. Maybe you should put Rochelle on the phone instead; I know how she looks out for you..."

Madeline chuckled, in such a deep sophisticated voice that she almost sounded like the man she was. "Trailer Park Barbie," she drawled drunkenly, and then translated not too kindly in Spanish, laughing again until she had to cough. "Just because I'm a woman don't mean I don't have any balls. I'm not giving up this phone to Rochelle, to let her talk to you. You can talk to *me*, Shaye!"

"Just tell Rochelle, please. Tell her everything I tell you," Shaye said, her eyes sparkling with the pleasure of this, like the patronizing high school cheerleader she was trying to imitate.

"Bullshit!" Madeline squealed, then hiccupped. Then she dropped her voice to a confidential whisper. "I ain't tellin' Rochelle nothing. Just, please, tell me what happened to Adam. I heard some gossip about that record producer trying to hurt him. And now Adam's not at work today. And I'm worried..."

Shaye made her voice a whisper, too, one girl to another. She even let out a fake whimper. She had to do what she had to do, if she wanted Madeline to get on a bus right now and come over here. And time was wasting.

"Madeline," she pleaded. "I don't even like you, but I think you're the only one who can help. Something bad happened with the producer, Adam's inside the trailer and he's gone crazy. I think he might try to hurt himself..."

Madeline snapped at her. "What? Are you crazy then, sister? Do something!"

"I can't help him," Shaye made herself sob. "Adam won't even let me come in the room with him. I think it's something about me not being gay..."

There was silence, and then Madeline scoffed. But her voice had turned a bit more compassionate.

"You're not even on the radar, Shaye! Sorry. But you're straight like some choirgirl from Kansas." Suddenly Madeline started crying, a bit more histronically than Shaye had managed. "Adam Ant needs somebody to love him, sister. Really love him, for what he is. What could you do, Shaye? Let me come out there- I can help Adam."

"He got a little violent," Shaye hissed, sounding to herself like Shakespeare's duplicitous Iago. "Rochelle won't think it's safe. She won't let you come if you tell her."

"I don't need Rochelle to get down to your trailer!" Madeline bragged. "I got money. I'll just take the County bus!"

Shaye let a few beats of silence go by. She glanced at her watch. "You'd have to leave now, Madeline, if you want to catch a bus. One passes Foxy Lady at about ten after three. But Rochelle won't let you get on it. She'll say men will bother you if you wear your sexy clothes from the club."

"Oh, fuck you!" Madeline said, the perfect one to be led into this trap. "I wear what I wanna wear," she asserted. "I just put some Jack Daniels for Adam into my purse, right now..." she grunted. "And Rochelle didn't even notice. I'm sneaky like that, Barbie. Shit- it's three o'clock now... and I'm coming out there, Shaye. I'll take care of Adam Ant."

Shaye almost fainted with fear at how easily this reality was coming true. Once it started, there would be no turning back.

"The door will be open," she said to Madeline. "Just walk in."

"Don't worry," Madeline said, in a confidential whisper colored by her Latina accent. "I'll come to your trailer and I'll take care of everything. Everything will be fine."

There was a smell in the air that late afternoon of woodsy smoke- almost like something being roasted. This smell, which drifted slowly from land being cleared in the west, hung in the misty air, along with tiny winged flies, which came out to mate in the spring. Madeline stepped down off the county bus, and the drop jarred her high heels and tight calves as she looked around suspiciously, reluctant to let go of the handhold.

She let go as the bus pulled away from her and her heels settled into spongy ground and damp spiky grass, newly planted and watered by Pete Andersen's crew. In the strange misty light, the shapes of the half constructed new plaza looked almost otherworldly, and Madeline squinted briefly in that direction.

"Shit," she said, shaking off her reverie and gathering herself for the walk through the trailer park. Although a bit disoriented, for she usually saw this area from the back seat of Rochelle's car, and usually in the wee hours of the night, she finally turned in the right direction.

She brushed away the "love bugs" with her brightly manicured nails, even as they died mating upon her, and she unstuck her gold heels from sinking into the wet ground. She mumbled to herself some self-pitying complaints in Spanish, something that came straight from her mother in Puerto Rico; other than these little curse words, Madeline didn't really know how to speak Spanish at all.

Parked further back in the woods, on an old logging trail behind the bus stop, Jorge Colon laughed to himself. "Mija," he said, under his breath. "This world must be too heavy for you in your pretty high heels. I can see your pain. But soon that will be over."

Colon was well aware that the hothead cop, Frank Danielo, was not far behind him. Danielo had been searching for him through the park, crisscrossing on and off all day. Sometime the squad car had been so close that Colon was truly surprised Danielo hadn't caught the faint glint of the silver truck not many feet away from him in the woods as he cruised intently again and again.

For a while this morning, something had drawn Danielo away from those rounds for a few hours, and that had only helped Colon. Then Danielo had appeared briefly again, but with the young man in a suit- probably FBI- riding with him and distracting him.

Although Colon had managed to evade his pursuer this far, it couldn't go on forever- Flamingo Park was only so big, and Frank Danielo was totally dogged.

Colon could have easily ditched the new truck, but something made him hold onto it. His actions seemed like he ultimately wanted Danielo to catch up with him, and finally ask him why.

Jorge Colon rubbed his weary eyes along the bony bridge of his nose. His head was filled with old mystical fables from back in Mexico, back in the Indian days. How could he explain why any more than he could explain the turning of the world? Some things just had to be made right, to be put back in their place and laid to rest.

He remembered going with his mother and laying down ritualized gifts at the altar near the high ridge of the mountain El Viejo. He recalled setting down bright red flowers and aromatic chicken roasted all day in the traditional clay oven. He recalled respectfully setting the gifts down and then watching the mists high up around the mountain's peak suddenly part.

There was so much ugliness here and so much melancholy. How could death be the ultimate hell, as long as it came with dignity?

Colon sighed. One more saint was necessary here, and had been all along, he realized. He had seen the object of his fascination from the beginning. The new girl, the loner, whose eyes were the color of the foothills of the mountain El Viejo half concealed in the light mists of winter mornings. She resembled the pale purple mountain flowers that lay in trembling blankets, the cool reflective gurgling of an uncharted mountain stream Jorge used to watch as a young boy or the skittish eyes of a little wild goat just before he raised his bow and it died in silence.

This mysterious girl was named Shaye. La Rubia he called her in his mind- the blonde. He first saw her moving down the grassy swale adjacent to the plaza with her loping gait just after he had started on his mission weeks ago. And her accusing eyes had made him want to stop everything as he stared at her and she at him.

Beautiful as she was, yet obviously deeply disturbed, she seemed an aberration. She ran around in Keds with skinned knees like a ten year-old girl. And she fluttered like a little moth, always swinging her eyes around as if afraid of being caught. And she had frozen and looked deeply into his eyes that day like she knew.

But how could anyone know? Even though, lifting his fingers underneath his nose like he had taken to doing many times each day, Colon thought he could still detect the brassy smell of his lover Mami Ramierez's blood.

Colon had seen the blonde Shaye a few times after that, making sure that she did not see him, yet feeling wistful and drawn to her. In a brief moment, seeing her look up at him, he realized that he had never seen such pain in a woman's eyes, not even in the eyes of his "saints" before he ceremoniously sent them to heaven. He could see that Shaye existed in that same mystical world of visions and pain that he did.

Gossip was easy for Colon to obtain. He was still well liked by some of the Mexican landscape workers he had employed over the years. They were all too willing to talk about women they saw in the park. Without cars, whenever they weren't working, watching women stroll the streets was what the lonely men liked to do. The men liked to lean up against the cage of propane tanks at the convenience store and comment on every female that walked by, most of them welfare sluts or out and out drug-addicted prostitutes.

At first, most knew nothing about the blonde. But then Colon got to hear a story of her attacking one of the men when he tried to offer her money for sex. "Loca" the men called her. Some said they were afraid of her. The story had made Colon laugh almost fondly. He couldn't kill this girl, Shaye, for she was pure! Her mind may have already escaped to ugly compromised places, but she kept her body pure. Thus there was no need to redeem her.

Jorge Colon thought about Shaye quite a bit after this, for she seemed to play a part in his fate, and he in hers. On the day he had to eliminate Victoria Cruz at the truck stop, he had been shocked to see Shaye in the crowd. This was not coincidence; she was his demon. Perched up in the rafters of the cavernous truck wash, Colon had observed her exchange a furtive hug with the cop, Frank Danielo before Danielo ran out to direct the search for him. And then Shaye had stood there underneath him peering around, sniffing the air for him.

Shaye was not meant to be one of the women he softly sent to heaven. But was she perhaps the one meant to send him there?

There was no doubt earlier today.

He had followed her into the grocery store, and noted as she turned down a particular aisle. When she left the aisle, he'd walked up to double-check exactly what she was purchasing. He'd then followed her, on foot, as she carried her paper sack protectively through the park. He knew what that bag was filled with- black hair *dye. So Shaye wanted to make herself a sacrifice and entrap him, perhaps feeling that risking her life was worth stopping his.*

Colon had felt rage mixed with pleasure as he followed Shaye. If she did it, if her hair became black like the other witch women, if she offered her body inappropriately, then could he bring down the silver rooster claw on her slender neck? She was setting a trap, he understood. But, did it matter? Could he really go back to life in Mexico, in his parents' village? He was now so much less, but also so much more than that.

It made Colon queasy imagining preparing the sacrifice of one that was not right, whose blood he would take when she was pure already. He envisioned the first rain washing the dye from the ends of Shaye's long hair, exposing the true blond. He had to shake his head to clear it, this thought was so disturbing and taboo.

Colon had hidden the truck, and followed her the last block on foot.

He had crept up in her backyard, where one of his workers always used to crouch to count the tips he was hiding and chew tobacco in the shade. Yes, Colon knew everything. When he hid there he glimpsed Shaye walk into her bathroom with the dye. But, an hour later, she sat with her back to him on the bed, slumped and still blond.

"Dammit!" he'd said to himself in English and he felt a sharp twinge of rage he hardly recognized. Suddenly, he felt peeved and frustrated. And then he'd overheard Shaye make the call.

"Oh, you little cunt. You little puta!" he'd whispered to himself, almost savoring how tricky and deceitful she could be.

And now he saw Madeline. It was surprising how tall and beautiful this young woman was, this bait Shaye had brought for him. He noticed how she stood out like a regal Latin American princess with her hammered gold bracelets banging against each other as she strode, and a lush fantastic mane of hair, shiny and frizzy and almost down to her flanks.

Madeline lifted her magnificently shaped chin as she walked, with her lips set in a perpetual pout, accented by lipstick. Colon was near enough to glimpse her doe eyes, partly shaded by theatrical lashes. And the look he saw there, although the girl was obviously young, seemed the weariest glance he had ever perceived in his whole existence.

She mumbled to herself in Spanish, little sullen curses about how unfair life was to her.

Colon felt a sudden tightness take over his abdomen, powerfully sexual, but so much more than that. In the next hour, he would bring the magical rooster claw down into her delicate creamy flesh, and end this fallen women's suffering forever.

Her electricity seemed to vibrate in the heavy smoky air; her cheap perfume smelled cloying. Everything about her said she was just begging to die. He watched her hike her tiny purple sequin miniskirt up even higher, deliberately displaying the very bottoms of her rounded ass cheeks. She bent, and caressed one calf for a moment, glancing around sloe-eyed to see if anybody was watching- any man who might want to buy her services- her body- and perhaps her soul.

A bottle of whiskey hung precariously half out of her purple satin bag.

"I'll protect you," Colon said outloud, as though she could hear it and it would comfort her. "You will never have to sell your body again, little precious, for your body will now soar with the angels."

Across the street, crouched behind a twenty-foot high mound of red dirt at the construction site, Shaye watched Madeline descend the steps of the county bus, and then look around briefly, adjusting her skirt like the uberslut she was before commencing to mince her way across US 1.

"I have to give you one thing," Shaye said outloud in Madeline's direction. "You're certainly dedicated to Adam. You're ready to give up your life for him."

Then she sighed, not liking her own brutal humor. No one was going to die here, she reminded herself, checking Danny's gun for the tenth time since she had been hiding here.

All that had to happen was for Madeline, on her half-mile walk in her glaring purple sequined dress, to catch Jorge Colon's attention, for Shaye now had no doubt that Colon kept tabs on the bus stop. This is where the local prostitutes plied their trade and he'd be looking to kill another prostitute. He certainly couldn't miss Madeline. Even though Madeline was born a man, with her slinky devil-may-care walk she seemed to embody everything overripe, and completely compromised, in woman.

Shaye didn't know why she disliked her so. Really, it wasn't entirely fair. True, Madeline was constantly bitchy. But it was more than that. Shaye sensed that the crush she had on Adam was more than just playacting. Madeline truly felt passionate, and truly seemed to melt in his presence. And Shaye was jealous. Maybe she was even jealous that Madeline would agree so easily to come out here, trying to save him.

Shaking her hair out to try to clear her head, Shaye suddenly got a glimpse of something pulling out of the woods onto US1. An extra large silver pickup. Shaye swallowed air, almost choking. It could just be coincidence, she thought as she mustered her resources and ran after it, still using the dirt mound for cover. Now she had to run across the highway, but the driver of the truck would be occupied in traffic.

Should she call Danny now? She could. He'd come flying through the park, chase down the truck as it drove and then haul Colon out and handcuff him. He would never allow him to get inside the trailer with Madeline. That would just be too dangerous. And it would have to be approved by his higher ups.

Yet it was necessary, Shaye understood with a tightness hardening her stomach. What good would all of this be if there was insufficient evidence and they had to let Colon go? Colon could move to a new city and kill again. Again and again. All of the forgotten women.

Sometimes someone had to make a sacrifice. In this case, Madeline would have to be uncomfortable for a few short minutes. All of it was fate. Even the way Madeline looked tonight, with her dress glittering like a beacon as she hiked across the highway, with Shaye following.

There was no way to see the truck now. Maybe it had been a hallucination. Shaye crouched as she jogged behind a hedge that backed up a slightly higher income community on Flamingo Beach Parkway. The light was beginning to fade, but all she had to do was follow the glint of Madeline's dress as she twitched her rump, trying to be an object of attention even in this sordid place.

The silver truck she thought she saw cutting into traffic on US 1 was nowhere to be seen now. Maybe it *had* been an apparition. Or perhaps, if it was Colon, he had now chosen to abandon the truck and follow Madeline on foot. Shaye crouched even nearer to to the spiky, newly trimmed hedge. If Colon was around, she couldn't let him see her. Not until she was holding a pistol to his head and snapping handcuffs onto his murderer's wrists.

"Ahh- a beautiful woman," Jorge Colon mused to himself, his coal black eyes going almost teary with philosophical gratitude as he gazed upon Madeline approaching Shaye and Adam's trailer.

"As the mountain stands tall," he intoned to himself, "she is like the river that runs round the mountain... As the land sleeps, she is like the yellow moon that watches over the land... She is the greatest mystery- and yet the greatest simplicity," he said, his voice breaking down.

It was not clear now whether Colon quoted the profound lines of an old Mexican Indian ballad, translated, or whether he simply spoke the poetic words on his own trying to justify his fascination with the young woman in the road. This fascination almost literally brought him to his knees.

Colon struggled to be quiet as he removed a large black leather tool pouch from the seat behind him and hooked it over his shoulder.

He took a breath, seeming to steady himself, and stepped away from the truck that he had hidden back in the greenery at the corner of Ibis Street. "What must be must be," he told himself. He adjusted the bag and moved forward in the direction of the young woman.

Shaye moved quietly enough not to wake Darlene's family's sleeping dogs in the makeshift kennel. Hiding in the deep shade behind Darlene's trailer, hunched between two propane gas tanks and a hot water heater, Shaye deliberately positioned herself downwind from the four pit mixes. But now she got to whiff every bit of their neglected offal. One of the dogs had suffered diarrhea and the others had tracked it all over the area; Shaye listened to the sickening drone of flies, in addition to breathing in the odor of the dogs' musky markings and the one dog's illness.

Added to the picture were some dirty soupbones, with little shreds of bloodied flesh still adhering, that the family had kindly thrown into the kennel for their companions. The flies buzzed these bones as well, as they were left to rot out under the sun. Shaye kept looking back in that direction- the bones that shone ivory in the sun, and the roasting coats of the sleeping dogs- white and red and piebald- and the scene brought up gooseflesh all over her body.

How could she doubt the wrongness of what she was doing? How had she come to this place in her life? And what harm would she be allowed to do here?

She could hear the dogs snoring.

Her view in front of her was almost completely obscured by young leaves, and she had to strain to see the street. She could almost forget that she was doing this; she could almost ignore the street in front of her. But that would be even more wrong, since she had already set this thing in motion.

Shaye looked up the street, in the direction of Caiman and the shortcut to Flamingo Beach Parkway. And she caught a glimpse of shiny legs strutting on golden heels. Her heart hammered. It was Madeline; she was coming. How amazing that such a profound scene could be enacted here at this time of the afternoon, and everything could seem so sleepy.

Just like the near comatose dogs that snored and stretched behind her.

Shaye felt something wet on her hand and heard a puppy snuffle. She looked down, but didn't let herself flinch as a half grown white pit bull pup covered her hand with its chill slippery tongue. It licked her gleefully, then crouched and rolled its eyes upwards as though to ask her forgiveness.

The puppy pumped its little rat tail, so that the whole animal shook and it continued at her hand, stretching its tongue even further, and wetting her down more. But Shaye stayed still with her shaking body and hammering heart, and the queasy feeling of oppression for what she had done- what was now in motion on its own as she hid behind the trees.

For a second, she tried to tell herself that the legs didn't belong to Madeline, but they did. She heard Madeline singing to herself in a breathy voice- of course, something retro, sounding like Blondie's "Call Me", with the name Adam Ant inserted into the words.

Shaye almost regurgitated, Madeline seemed so pathetic. Or maybe it was more that she felt so ashamed.

Shaye watched Madeline's high heels pause near their mailbox across the street. And then a man stepped into view. Slowly, like in a dream, Shaye crouched all the way down, so that the puppy saturated her lips with its desperate kisses, while it whined to her in an extremely high pitch like she was its mama.

Shaye ignored it. She knew the little sound did not carry. And its distress only interwove with her own. She felt stricken. She felt like groveling down in the dust by the trailer where she would be safe. Down low, at the very lowest point human life could offer, but safe.

For, across the street, right before her trailer, talking to Adam's friend, stood George "Jorge" Colon. He wore all black, stovepipe jeans and a worn, but immaculate, black linen shirt with the sleeves rolled up, showing his trademark muscles that appeared like polished dark wood. Shaye glanced down to his feet where black boots featured real silver spurs sitting up pertly right above the dust.

He approached toward Madeline with the stiffness and formality of an Old West gunfighter. Shaye noticed him adjust the black leather sack at his waist. A sack of murderer's tools and fancy Mexican funeral paraphernalia, she knew. It was all coming true, all like her sick fantasy.

In this dream that acted out before her, Shaye observed Jorge Colon gently reach his hand out to take Madeline's. He gently brought it up to his lips and kissed it.

"What is your name, beautiful lady?" he asked in Spanish.

Madeline responded by looking completely wide-eyed and nonplussed.

"You speak Spanish, don't you?" he asked, this time in English. "I can tell that you are Mexican. A true Mexican princess with no business being in this terrible neighborhood, and I can help you leave here."

Madeline lifted up her chin. Maybe it was with suspicion. Shaye hoped so. Madeline was big, born as much a man as Colon. All she had to do was push past him to get away.

Don't go into the trailer, Shaye begged Madeline in her mind, although it was complete hypocrisy. Her pounding heart slammed her chest exclaiming that she wanted Madeline to go.

One of Shaye's slippery hands, the one wet with sweat rather than dog drool, cupped Frank Danielo's cell phone.

Now that it was real, and Jorge Colon stood before her, she could call. Danny could get here in minutes to arrest Colon. Colon never had to go into the trailer with Madeline.

But he did. And Shaye let him.

As the pup's pleading heather colored eyes stared deeply into hers, Shaye trembled with remembrance. She remembered the silkiness of her lover Adam's skin, and the vividness of his sideways smile. She recalled Adam's charisma in the way he said everything he said, and his skill in how he slid his supple body along hers, licking her with the teasing tip of his tongue. She looked at their trailer from the front, with the serial killer and his potential victim standing before it.

That little front of the trailer, with the foliage closing off the private porch, could have looked quite cute. It could have been hers and Adam's home. Like any young couple "playing house", she realized now. If she hadn't worried so much about her own problems. Look at the way Adam kept things so pretty, like leaving a different colored Hibiscus flower in a chipped yellow teacup on the counter each morning, or preparing her the hot cocoa that she had grown to love.

And then making scorching crazy passionate love to her, over and over again, curling up in the too soft old bed in this dejected place they had claimed as home. They could have been a couple living here, happy in their forbidden passion, like brother and sister lost to incest.

Shaye's heart literally ached when she thought of how much she loved Adam. She thought of his sweetness when she used to curl up beside him in his narrow bed in the hospital and he'd cuddle her against his warm alabaster neck, ruffling her hair with his plump sensual lips.

She hadn't even known then how much she desired him. But she felt the tightness now, remembering, and it shamed her feeling this way as she watched Madeline about to be embraced by a killer. Shaye's hands drenched with sweat as she held tightly to Danny's gun, the dog nudging her dangerously.

"Oh, Adam," she whispered. "Adam Ant."

Images flashed before Shaye of his dark eyes, as warm as home fires flirting with her from behind heavy lashes, and his white teeth revealed in an electrified smile, only for her. She pictured his fingers intertwining with hers. And then sliding away. For he was gone.

Adam wasn't coming back to the trailer, Shaye understood and the true realization chilled her, feeling icy and wet on her like the water of the swimming pool this morning. She was essentially alone, for Adam was not coming back any time soon. In a very real way, Adam was no longer hers and things could never be quite the same.

His father had arrived in Florida, and had control now. Adam was in surgery. And then he'd be in restraints. His clothing had been taken, and he was no longer slim and graceful, but rather skinny and naked beneath a white and gray hospital gown. She felt like crying for him. And for herself even more. No matter how she wished it now, their sweet little life was not going to take place in that trailer.

Instead, this was what was happening. Adam had been sent to the hospital. And the killer of women was right now inviting himself into Shaye's trailer. The thing she had most feared, and she was the one making it happen now.

Watching the scene play out across the dirt street, she could have ended it simply by pressing a button on the cell phone. But Shaye slid the phone back inside her shorts' pocket for the moment, for she could only come out the other end.

"I'm Puerto Rican, Honey," Madeline laughed, with a rich Spanish ghetto drawl. "But if a man like you really wants to take care of me. I mean *really* take care of me- financially- I can absolutely be Mexican for you. Just don't ask me to talk any Spanish!" she laughed, as she allowed Jorge Colon to graciously help her up into the trailer with one hand on the small of her back. "Because the only Spanish word I know how to say right is fuck!"

Chapter 24

Shaye pushed away the puppy and the last loving swipe of its tongue, and she skittered across the dirt street faster than it could keep up. The dog sat back on its own side of the street, pot-bellied, whimpering and worried-looking. Meanwhile Shaye glided easily around the back of her own trailer without being seen. A thought flashed through her mind that in all her life she had never done anything like this, anything desperate. Even as a little girl, she had never played cops and robbers or hide and seek. She'd reached age eight, and her first kiddie beauty pageant, with never a scratch or a bruise on her soft pink and white skin.

Now her heart pounded, and she tucked damp hair behind her ears; every strong muscle tensed, and she ran low to the ground like an animal, furtive and glancing around in quick self-preservation. Her skin was fevered and slimed with a mixture of dog drool and yard silt, sprinkled on top with the reddish dirt of the street. Now, a new woman had been born and things would never be the same, for this felt natural.

Shaye flattened against the back of the trailer and, as she had rehearsed, climbed onto a cinder block she'd placed there earlier. Inside her trailer, through the dirt-crusted screen, she glimpsed shadows, a man and woman. Watching them like this, she could imagine they had come on a sacred purpose, some sacred ritual that they would both enjoy. Jorge Colon directed Madeline to sit in the chair that Shaye had placed directly in line of the laptop and digital video camera on the counter.

Madeline sat down gracefully and giggled intimately. It was almost as though the two inside were adults and Shaye just a child spying on them. Nothing horrible could happen here; just adults having their fun.

"You are beautiful," Colon breathed into Madeline's face. Shaye had to duck not to be seen. Gradually she inched back so she could observe, and Colon's eyes seemed to burn with rabid fire. They did not see her. They only focused on Madeline with curiosity and burning intensity. "The Lord has been watching you, you know. You are his little gem, Madeline, *mi hija*, my love!"

Suddenly, like a magician in proud form, Colon scooped his hands into his black leather pack, and then he anointed Madeline's head with big handfuls of red, orange and white flower petals. Madeline gasped, as though she had been drenched with water, and arched up her back toward him, letting a thousand petals fall.

"Oh my God," she said. "You scared me, lover. What are you doing?"

"Preparing a beautiful altar," he whispered.

Shaye gasped, hearing his words, but then bit her lip, holding back. For whatever he said didn't matter- recording his words was illegal and inadmissible; she had to actually film him physically doing something; the audio didn't count.

But wouldn't he do something? Wasn't he about to do something now? How could Shaye still lie to herself that this wouldn't happen? But still she did. There was still an aspect of unreality. She was pressed up against the sunwarmed metal wall of the trailer with no one even noticing her from the street. So, wasn't it possible that what was happening inside was simply one of her fears and one of her fancies? The window screen made things dim. Maybe Madeline was just in there alone, and Shaye was just fabricating the other image, made real just out of her own fears. Maybe all of it was just because she no longer had Adam.

Madeline chuckled, trying to show bravado, Shaye recognized, and tilted her head towards Colon. She took a big swig of her own whiskey and then held it forward to offer the man who leaned over her, blocking her into the chair with his arms.

Colon shook his head, dismissing her offer of a drink.

"You don't have to be afraid," he told Madeline.

"I ain't afraid." Madeline's laugh sounded a little like a bray this time. "I'll just get into trouble is what I'm afraid of, Papa. This is my friend's house. My friend Eden and her roommate Shaye. And Shaye's a real little bitch sometimes."

Colon's thin lips stretched in one direction in a tense parody of a smile. "I wouldn't worry about Shaye."

Shaye smirked in return, leaning back against the trailer with the gun lying cold on her thigh. Even at this moment, when she held Madeline's life in her hands, Madeline still disdained her.

"I shouldn't be turning tricks in here, really," Madeline mumbled.

Colon poured more flower petals over her head. Shaye could literally hear them falling; they sounded a bit like the benign brushing of the palmetto fronds here in the breeze outside. All of it brought gooseflesh up along Shaye's bare skin.

"*Mi Princesa*, my princess," Colon said. "You call this 'turning a trick'? *Mija!* This today is your destiny…" He leaned back, again posed like a magician, and then reached forward one hand with a handful of hundred dollar bills fanned out. There must have been twenty of them.

Madeline shook out her hair. Obviously, Colon had caught her attention.

"What do you want me to do for that money?"

Colon caressed her face gently, almost like she was a walking miracle embodied in her soft and hard flesh. "I want you to let go of all your fears. Remember that you are Mexican. Feel free to admit that now, beautiful angel. Let me purify you…"

Slowly, ceremonially, Colon slid beautifully tie-dyed strips of fabric over the bracelets on Madeline's wrists, he slid them over the feminine vee of her lap, over the back of her neck and her glossy black hair. As he did it, Shaye watched him close his eyes to ecstatic slits. She could only see Madeline from the back, but she imagined Madeline caught up in the trance of his spell, slitting her own eyes submissively as well.

She heard Madeline sigh, like she was releasing all her cares and all her sordid history.

Colon's voice keened, mysteriously and beautiful, just a few high notes teased by mountain breezes in an old Catholic song sung in Spanish. The song chilled Shaye's blood, but also fascinated her.

She watched Madeline slide in the chair, like a cat, brushing her long leg against Colon's hard side, flailing her big mass of black hair and arching her back, offering up her small breasts in their flirty décolletage. She sighed in surrender, while attempting to hum the ancient church tune with him. Meanwhile, George Colon tightened all of her bonds. He caressed each limb like it was fine alabaster, ready to be ceremonially carved. Then he unscrewed a small tarnished silver jar, decorated with a large red carnelian cross and he gently anointed Madeline's hair with glossy scented oil.

Through the window, the scent tightened Shaye's nostrils, like a light mix of mango, pomegranate and sangria- a scent that she would never forget.

Madeline finally lifted her head, as if just awakening, and Shaye listened to her sniff through both nostrils.

"What is this?" she asked, sounding more truly feminine than Shaye had ever heard her. "Are you just a john, really? Just here to fuck me, and just get kinky?"

Colon stayed silent, holding a cornhusk crucifix poised in the air. They both stayed silent.

Madeline cleared her throat. Her voice finally just came out sad and pouty, not even like she had the right to be terrified.

"I just got lucky, didn't I? I found you, and you're that serial killer?"

Colon carefully laid the crucifix on her heaving chest.

"It's nothing bad, Madeline. Your life was bad. You let men use your body like it was nothing... Nobody ever loved you..."

Madeline began crying.

"But now I will cover you in flowers. And, through the pain you will emerge beautiful. No longer a fallen woman, you will go to God a saint."

With a flourish Colon pulled out the rooster claw. Shaye saw the silver glint. For a moment he held it above his head, like waiting for God to send down lightening to energize the cold metal. And then he lashed it down at Madeline, taking the first swipe out of her arm.

"Yiyeee!" Her sharp cry tore from her throat as she rocked the chair. "Help me!" she screamed, choking on her words.

Shaye ducked down by the back of the trailer, taking her next rehearsed action. She hit the button on the cell phone for Danny. He answered on the second ring, and she was ready.

"Come to my trailer, Danny. I set a trap for Jorge Colon, and he's here now. He's killing Madeline! Come right now, Danny. I'm going in!"

Shaye heard enough to know he acknowledged her, but she didn't listen to his words. Whatever it was didn't matter. Madeline was screaming, and she had to go in.

She ran through the front of the trailer, and pushed through the unlocked door. Colon straightened up from Madeline and swung around.

Shaye aimed the pistol, but she couldn't shoot. Colon had a gun, too.

He aimed it at her, while his chest heaved and his eyes glinted.

"Shaye!" Madeline panted. "Save me! Shoot him! He's the killer!"

Before Shaye could respond, Colon had ducked around behind Madeline. He holstered his gun in his belt and then held the intricately carved cultivator up against Madeline's soft throat. The sharp tip of one claw nicked her skin, and a string of blood rolled down, like from a shaving nick.

Madeline's breath growled in her chest and she heaved her body up, vainly attempting to struggle free.

"Shaye, help me!" she begged. "Kill him."

Colon glared at Shaye so that she almost lost herself in the glinting black intensity of his eyes.

"That's right, Shaye, we finally meet. And kill me you must, for I am going to kill her. We will go together. You will shoot me as I tear out her throat. That is how God intended. But, if you kill me, you will have to let her die. And this way she can ascend to Heaven... My most beautiful love of all..."

Slowly and meaningfully, he slid the rooster claw to rest up on the fleshy center of Madeline's youthful pink-rouged cheek.

"No, no, not my face," she panted. "Nooo, pleeease..." Her sobs now came in bunches, incoherently. Urine trickled down her leg.

Shaye tried to line up a good shot, but she simply couldn't. Colon had left her only an inch or so above Madeline's head. She pictured trying to kill him and the shot going through Madeline's face.

"Colon," she heard herself say, the outstretched pistol trembling visibly in her hand. "This girl isn't actually a girl. She's a transsexual. She was physically born a man. So she can't be one of your saints. You have to let her go."

Colon raised one of his eyebrows, as his madman's eyes rested fully on Shaye's. "But that doesn't matter," he said, pleasantly. "I thought you understood me, Shaye. She will be the greatest saint of all. When I sever her jugular, and let her unclean blood color the crosses and flowers bright red, little Madeline will be washed clean. She will enter Heaven as a girl- a more beautiful girl than any other."

Colon's strong forearm did not allow Madeline to turn her head. But she rolled her eyes toward Shaye. Now she bled from a little prick on her cheek. Her heavily mascara'd eyelashes batted in a parody of fear and desperation, as eye makeup melted down her cheek to blend with the crimson spot of her blood.

"Shaye, help me, Shaye," she hiccupped.

"Shaye, observe it!" Colon commanded. "Watch her die!"

He lifted the rooster claw up in a broad gesture to slash, and Shaye sprang.

One leap landed her on top of Colon, and she grabbed for the claw. The three of them fell in a heap on the floor, Madeline screaming and kicking with her high heels and Colon struggling to regain control of the rooster claw.

But it was like the weapon was made for Shaye. Slicked with sweat and blood, it slid from Colon's hand, as Shaye kneed his face with her bony knees. He grabbed her hair, pulling her down, but she still had leverage. He swung out his hand and clubbed her on the side of her head, but she still pulled away.

Shaye had mastered the claw. Without thinking, she brought it down on Colon's weirdly grinning face, with his white teeth and sharp cheekbones. She slashed at the face, carving into it, trying to obliterate its evil darkness. She felt the cold silver claw break into his flesh; she felt it snag and listened to it rip, while the man below her groaned, growling at her like the evil entity he was.

Again she slashed, wildly ripping into his arm. She hit again in quick succession. Twenty times. Colon's blood sprayed onto her and onto Madeline and into the air. He roared and keened, and it sounded to her like the demons of hell calling. Colon hit and kicked her, but she didn't feel it. The pain only made her grit her teeth and cry with rage. She slashed again and again, so fast that the red and silver blurred and she could hardly see her hand holding the weapon.

They all rolled over the carpet together, Madeline screaming also, and still Shaye tore into Colon's body; the claw became an extension of her like a wolf's fangs. She growled with righteousness, tucked up her body, crawling on top of him and still violently slashing.

"Stop it, Shaye!" a voice commanded. "Move! He's aiming his gun!"

Shaye couldn't pay attention. She continued to growl, and slash.

But then a gunshot exploded right beside her. Colon subsided underneath her, his big chest sticking in the air, and his handgun sliding down and hitting the floor beside her thigh.

Frank Danielo stepped up holding his gun at the ready, and carefully checked Colon's condition. Colon wheezed, but with his last breath. Danny shook his head, and then holstered his gun and gently attempted to pull Shaye off.

She still looked down at the dark visage of Jorge Colon. His gleaming open eyes still looked observant, his bared white teeth still dangerous.

Madeline sobbed sweetly, like a woman, and allowed Danny to pull her to sitting position. "Danny," she said in awe. "Shaye saved me. He was going to kill me!" She glanced over at Shaye weirdly. Although grateful, she didn't seem quite able to look her directly in the eye.

Shaye uncurled her palm open, and looked at the intricately carved rooster claw, now coated with layers of congealing blood. She thought absently about contagious disease, and then wondered what that meant.

She lifted her eyes to Frank Danielo, in uniform. A policeman, her mind told her. Possibly her lover. Possibly not.

Her eyes flickered over his and he looked friendly and caring, not a danger. As her breathing returned to normal, and the cotton sounds retreated from everywhere, she made out that he was talking, and extending his hand as if to receive her weapon.

Why would she give up the rooster claw? Why now?

All the thoughts seemed to sluice down and around her, and Shaye noticed that her heart was hammering, and her hand with the weapon starting to shake. Did she just kill this evil man whose bloodied body she sat on? Did she really tear him to pieces with a *silver rooster claw*?

She glanced at Madeline, who seemed to be all right, and gave a shy little smile. Had she really protected, and done right? Or had she done horribly wrong?

Danny seemed to pitch his words to get through to her- a tone that made her look up finally, and focus on him.

"You didn't kill him, Honey. I did. But you saved Madeline's life…"

Shaye looked to him pitifully.

"You did," Madeline chimed in, with tenderness in her voice. "You didn't even like me, but you risked your life to save me."

Shaye felt a weight of cold stone seem to lodge in her stomach, for Madeline would never know that Shaye had set her up.

Danny ruffled Shaye's hair, and helped her to her feet. He kissed her gently on the top of her head, even though her hair was matted with Jorge Colon's blood. Then he stroked her hair, down her arms and down to her wrists, which he encircled gently with his fingers.

"I love you so much," he murmured. "You're such a good girl."

"She is," Madeline echoed, trying to straighten out her legs and shoes and stand up. "Shaye really is!"

Shaye looked toward Danny, crying out toward him, trying to see answers in his gentle eyes and flushed cheeks, in the anonymous blue uniform. She finally let him pluck the bloodied silver cultivator from her fingers.

"Listen," he whispered. "Madeline and I are going to say that you were never here. It was just the two of us." He looked to Madeline. "Okay?"

"Sure," she said, "whatever. I'll protect Shaye."

"Good," Danny said. "You have to get out of here, Shaye. I'll clean this," he said, turning the silver weapon in his hand, looking at it a little squeamishly. Who could help that, Shaye reasoned, after she had attacked the man like a wild animal, like a serial killer herself? How could Danny still say he loved her? But, apparently, he did. How would Shaye ever know if what she did was right or wrong, she wondered. It would be just another weight. Another terrible weight that she'd carry forever.

She groaned under it, trying to shake her head to maybe shake the ideas out, just for a moment. After all, she would have to run now, to escape the police whose cars she heard closing in on the park from US 1.

She allowed Danny to help her to the door. They stood in the fresh smelling shade of the banana palm. "You saved everybody; you're a hero!" Danny said, kissing her on her hair again. "Go somewhere and wash off now. You can go to my house. But hide. Hide for a while. Then it'll be okay." He rubbed her reassuringly on the arm. "Just stay away for a little while."

Shaye watched Danny's face blanche as the sirens wailed closer. She knew he cared more for her well-being than about just apprehending a killer, and the fact that he had just shot the man. But Danny would have a lot to live with for a while, too.

Shaye planted a kiss on her finger and comfortingly touched Danny's lower lip. "It's okay," she breathed. "I know where I'll go." She gave him one last look, and then twitched away, vanishing back in the foliage toward the rear of the trailer. She watched Danny square his shoulders as he walked forward to meet the cop cars that fanned around the driveway.

Damp green fronds, one by one, gently encircled Shaye's body, the gentle disturbance not enough motion to distract anyone as she faded away.

Chapter 25

*Three Months Later; Central Florida State Psychiatric
Hospital, Orange County, Florida*

Frank Danielo had a bit of trouble in the hospital gift shop deciding what to buy for Adam. He made his first choice outside, at the Starbucks coffee kiosk, where he bought a large latte drink with a five syllable Italian name. He couldn't picture a guy like Adam *not* being a big devotee of Starbucks, and Adam would definitely crave a fix of premium coffee after being locked up in here for three months.

What to buy for a gift was a little more troubling. Flowers or stuffed animals made Danny cringe. Even though Adam might like them, Danny just didn't see it as appropriate for a guy to purchase such things for another guy- even if the guy did wear makeup and fairy wings occasionally.

Danny picked up a fat new paperback, a very interesting detective novel, and he was about to buy it when he had to admit to himself that it was much more Shaye's taste than Adam's. He smiled to himself imagining how she might have enjoyed it. Then, after a moment of dreaminess, he realized that the elderly lady behind the counter was staring at him curiously, perhaps wondering what a cop in uniform was doing here in the gift shop.

Danny gave her a little smile as he approached the counter. He selected a magazine devoted to high fashion, hoping the lady behind the counter would just assume he was buying for a woman. She smiled beningly, and willingly gave directions on how he could get to Adam's ward. On the sixth floor, the top floor of the building,

Danny followed the signs for "T" Ward- short for "Transitional Ward". Adam had been transferred here when his doctors had decided he was almost ready to go home, and his focus on this ward was preparing for reentry into the real world. Danny was supposed to pick Adam up and drive him home on the day he would be released. But that was still a week from now, and there was really no need for Danny to show up in person today.

Except for the fact that he wanted to see Adam- and ask him a few questions.

Danny and the sweet-faced brown-eyed nurse behind "T" Ward's desk both examined eachother sheepishly as he signed in as Adam Underwood's visitor; the nurse was another one who seemed to find the police uniform inordinately interesting.

"You're his friend?" she asked. "Your Frank Danielo? The one who's going to sign him out when he goes home?"

Danny nodded. "How's Adam doing?"

The nurse stood up, lifted her hair off her neck to air it out, and smiled. "He's doing really great now. He was excited that he's getting a visitor. I'll show you how to get to his room. He's waiting there now..."

Even though the city of Orlando was a modern city with very much new construction, this wing of the State Hospital seemed old fashioned, with vaulted ceilings, polished wood floors and enormous, peaked almost church-style windows. The nurse accompanied Danny partly down Adam's corridor and then she pointed to a door at the very end of the corridor and let him walk the rest of the way on his own.

He passed patients wearing white hospital gowns and white terry State-issue slippers. Everybody seemed quiet, no talking except for the echo of a jangly television coming from one of the lounges.

Patients looked at Danny wide-eyed- the uniform again, and he shrugged off their stares, not even realizing that he was walking with his shoulders noticeably rounded. He had no problem locating Adam's room. For one, it was at the very end of the hallway, in a prime position for windows, probably finagled somehow by Adam's father's wealth. Then there was the decoration on the door- an ingenious floor-to-ceiling bird of paradise flower crafted out of different shades of construction paper. Adam had obviously used his time in arts and crafts here productively.

Danny tapped on the door, inclined to peak in the small window, yet politely holding back.

"C'mon in," he heard Adam call, the first time he had heard that voice in months.

Danny stepped in, and the first thing he saw was Adam's face literally lit up with excitement. Immediately, the look of joy deflated, and Adam lowered his eyes, hiding them with a few blinks of his long lashes.

When Adam looked up again, the obvious crestfallen look had gone, replaced with a more social and proper smile. He gave a sigh, and drew his legs up near him on his corner recliner. He wore new baggy jeans underneath his hospital gown, vintage purple converse sneakers without laces and a trendy purple crystal necklace. He looked very put together and healthy looking- Adam, in his male identity, at his finest. In his lap he held colorful craft papers that he was folding into designs, more origami like the flower on the door.

He threw a few of the little papers into the air to greet Danny- a flock of tiny white birds folded like ibis. Danny caught one, held it up between thumb and forefinger and grinned while squinting at the intricate design in the sun that washed through the curved floor-to-ceiling window.

"Not bad work," he said, "not a bad way to spend your time."

Adam giggled pleasantly. "My floor-mates here like to say that they wouldn't complain either if they were in my position- just killing time here while waiting to inherit a portion of a multi-million dollar company. I guess it's not exactly politically correct for me to feel sorry for myself."

Danielo gave an obligatory little smile and leaned back against the doorjamp, legs and arms crossed in a kind of Marlboro Man pose that he wasn't even aware of- it was an instinctive response to Adam and his sexual orientation making him uncomfortable. But he was obviously trying to act nice- and understanding. He cleared his throat.

"Well, I hope everything's okay, Adam. Hope you're happy about getting out of here. Your face kinda fell when I walked through that door."

Adam cleared off his lap and uncurled his legs.

"Yeah, well," he said, "my first reaction was that possibly my visitor was somebody else."

Danny sighed. "Actually, I wanted to talk to you about Shaye." He pointed towards the single bed, made up with military corners. "Okay if I sit."

"Please, be my guest," Adam said. As Danny walked past, he glanced at the Starbucks coffee and the magazine.

"I didn't know the exact protocol," Danny said. "But I figured you bring relatives in the hospital a gift and all..." He gingerly handed over the coffee, and then the weighty fashion magazine.

Adam chuckled. He looked at the cover model with a quick assessment, and tucked the issue into his lap. Then he gently pried open the lid on his latte, so carefully that the partially flattened mound of cream bobbed back up above the lid. "Ahh," he exclaimed, inhaling its aroma with theatric appreciation. "Thank goodness for life's simple pleasures, my friend. And thank you for all your sincere forays into political correctness." He giggled, holding the *Fashionista* magazine up. "I know it probably pained you to purchase this."

Danny chuckled, sitting down stiffly on the edge of the institutional bed.

"Adam, the very last thing Shaye said to me was to make me promise to take care of you."

Adam's usually luminous eyes looked clouded for a moment, focusing out the window. Then he looked back. "I don't think you're really obligated to take that to the grave or anything," he said. "I'd be happy to release you from it right now."

Danielo stared at him curiously, until Adam seemed made uncomfortable, and hid his youthful face behind the cream while taking a sip of his coffee. Eventually he was forced to look up.

Danny's expression reflected hurt feelings. "So you really don't want my friendship?"

Quite a few silent beats went by, and Adam just stared, and blinked his eyes a few times. He seemed to almost squirm in his chair.

"Frank," he said, using the detective's real name in a newly sober voice. "Suddenly I find myself at a loss for smart remarks. First, you saved my life back at the water tower. And now you're offering to sign me out of the hospital. This way I can have my own life here in Florida, rather than having to go home with my parents…"

Danny attempted to say. "Oh, that's nothing," but Adam waved his comment away.

"That's not what it's about," Adam said. "It's more the thought that you really are a good friend. And I'm just envisioning what it would be like to leave here and be totally lonely."

Danny's voice cracked a little in reply, and the corners of his eyes narrowed down in his own distress. "I know," he said. "I know exactly. There's been so many changes in my life. And it's not just that Shaye made me promise. It's more like, with all we've been through, it's almost like we're family."

Adam threw back his head and laughed, lightening the mood. Another patient in the hall echoed his laughter, probably stationed just outside the mostly closed door. Danny stood up to close it and then sat back down heavily on the bed, staring again.

Still smiling, with that beautiful, almost angelic look that Shaye so loved that transcended any gender, Adam slapped his magazine and coffee down on his little worktable and then confronted Danny.

"So, do you plan to keep beating around the bush for this whole visit, or why not just ask it? Why not just talk about her?"

Danielo literally gulped. It took him a moment to find his breath. "Adam, have you heard from her?"

Adam scolded with his look. Then he shaded his eyes with his lashes, and when he lifted his gaze, they looked darker. "Danny, have you?"

They both stared at each other moodily. Somebody screamed in the hall. They heard it through the door and Danny's gaze briefly flicked in that direction. Adam's didn't waver.

"Shit," Danny said finally. Then he went on, with difficulty. "I just thought she might have contacted you first, especially now, with you turning twenty-one."

"I don't think Shaye really cares about money," Adam said, attempting to hold his hand steady as he retrieved his warm coffee.

Danny noticed the shaking and Adam caught it.

"It's just medication side effects," he said. "I'll live."

Danny shook his head. "I don't want you to misunderstand. We both know that Shaye doesn't care about money. But since you guys had plans to run away and all... with your fake ID..."

"Well," Adam said. "We all grow up. And it's funny that I was the one to accept that first. That fake ID would've done me no good. Sooner or later I would have just ended up back here without my medication. Now, I've had a rapprochment with my parents, I'm willing to take a token role on their board of directors and I actually appreciate my father's business for once... So maybe Shaye was wiser and saw all of that before I did, Danny, and that's why she took the ID and ran."

"So then how about me?" Danielo broke in suddenly, his cheeks reddening, and his eyes suddenly looking fiery. "Why did she leave me? I'm divorced and alone..."

Adam's plump lip curled up on one side. "And also an Oceanside detective now, and a better cop than ever. Maybe Shaye was wiser than both of us."

Heat practically radiated from Danielo, he was so agitated, and yet he kept his behavior proper, respecting Adam's condition, and didn't leave his seat. "How can you be so philosophical about it, Adam?" he asked. "Do you really not care if Shaye ever contacts you? I stress about it every day."

"And I would've thought she'd contact you first, Danny."

Danielo squinted his eyes. *"Why?"* he asked, with true incredulity.

"Well, because you were fucking her at the end."

Danny sprung to his feet. Rather than lunging, he paced before Adam, glaring at him from different angles as he walked. "I can't believe you'd say that," he huffed. Finally, he sat down. His emotion made it difficult for him to get the words out of his throat. "It's not like that at all, Adam!" he said finally. "I love Shaye. I truly love her."

Adam stood and stretched his lean body. Then he perched on the overstuffed arm of his chair. He took a moment to look wistfully out the window and then looked back to Danny, his eyes soft and luminous.

"I know you love her, Danny," he said. "Because I love her, too."

Danielo shook his head. "I know you love Shaye like a sister, Adam... I know that..."

Adam waved his arm in front of him in an abrupt gesture, cutting him off. Nothing that could've happened outside in the corridor, none of the disturbing noises could now distract Danny from what Adam next said.

"I love Shaye, too," he confessed. "Like a man loves a woman. I'm madly in love with her and I've always been. That's how I can recognize that your feelings are sincere, Frank. Unfortunately."

Danny literally shook his head to clear it. He glanced down at his hands that rested on his knees, and both men noticed they were shaking. Right now it looked like he was just as ready to fall apart psychologically as Adam.

"What are you telling me, Brother?" he asked. His voice was so soft it barely came out, and it came out through gritted teeth. "You're not joking?"

Adam slowly shook his head. A blue vein throbbed in his pale delicate neck and he looked immensely slim and vulnerable. But he made an effort to hold his chin up proudly.

"I think you can figure out what I'm telling you," Adam said. His voice deepened with his seriousness. "I'm no more gay than you are, Frank. Maybe less, even," he added as a weak attempt at a joke.

Danny looked momentarily shocked and appalled, as much so as when he had stared at Shaye locked in bloody combat with Jorge Colon, Madeline caught up in their midst. He couldn't help tilting his head and narrowing his eyes, physically looking Adam over in a new light.

Adam sighed in exasperation. "Stare all you want," he snapped. "The other is just clothing. It's such a simple thing. I'm just a cross-dresser. It all about the costumes- nothing physical." He sighed. "Danny, the funny thing is, I would've never expected you to get it. But Shaye…"

While Adam's face looked immensely pained, Danny looked even more mentally strained and appalled.

"Shaye doesn't know, does she?"

Adam weakly shook his head. Now he had two bright spots of red on both alabaster cheeks. Another sigh shook his reedy chest, and he ran hands up to nervously fix heavily pomaded hair that wasn't at all messed up. His eyes seemed to beg for some kind of understanding, even as their fires had dulled. It seemed that, even in confession now, finally, there were still emotional parts of himself he wanted to hide.

"It's simple," he said, in a voice that betrayed the weariness of a much, much older person. "You can read it in books or on the Internet. Not all cross-dressers are homosexual." Keeping up his courage, he held Danny's gaze, even as Danny's gaze threatened to falter. This seemed very difficult for both of them.

"I don't know why I'm even weird when it comes to being a cross-dresser. But my sexual feelings for women are totally normal. I've had tons of female partners, and I love the female body. I mean, like a guy loves the female body. I love making love with women. And I do it really well," he joked, letting go of his sadness long enough to laugh.

Danielo's face blanched underneath his dark five-o-clock stubble. "I really don't understand, Adam..."

His reaction obviously pained the younger man. "You know," Adam said with an undisguised bitterness that was felt for more people than just Danny. "You act more queasy to look at me now than when you thought I was totally flaming. And you homophobic like you are..."

"I'm not... that... you know... homo-hater"

"Save it," Adam said. "The really sad part is about Shaye. I always had the crush on her. I loved her two ways. In one way, she was simply the epitome of feminine beauty. I plastered my walls with photos of her. And, if I could've looked any way in the world, it would have been blond and completely innocent like her."

"But you liked her as more than that, Adam?" Danny ventured seriously, again making an obvious attempt to protect the other man's feelings- and sanity. "I don't think Shaye knew."

"Of course Shaye didn't!" Adam said, his voice so cutting that Danny flinched. He saw the reaction and carefully modulated his tone. "No, she didn't know. It would have been so simple for her to just ask. But she respected me more than that. Shaye loved me so much that the simplest thing, she never asked. 'Are you gay? Do you fuck around with guys?' We told each other every secret, but I guess she never wanted me to have to embarrass myself with that one."

A beam of sun from outside suddenly broke through the clouds and illuminated Danielo's eyes to a glowing amber. But he seemed no less confused. "Adam, this is crazy," he said. "You knew Shaye for years in the hospital. You lived with her. Why didn't you just simply tell her, 'I'm not gay, and I'm in love with you?'" Suddenly Danny's eyes looked stricken. He was obviously processing the thought that, had she known, Shaye might have loved Adam back. "You were right there with her all along. Why didn't you simply ask her to be your girlfriend?"

Adam's soul seemed far away as he drew in a long breath. Minutes passed. "Let's see if I can explain this," he said, so softly that his voice almost couldn't be heard. "I guess I kept the truth from her because I so badly needed for her feelings to be real."

Danny raised his brows.

"We know that Shaye loves me," Adam said. "In the hospital I saved her life many times, and I became Shaye's whole world. I guess I had this fear... I guess I thought that maybe if I told her I desired her, she would date me, and maybe she would even marry me, just out of affection. Out of gratitude for all I had done..."

Danny looked dumbstruck, but nodded his head.

Suddenly, Adam trembled all over, and had to fight to hold back sobs. His lower lip quivered and he had to set down his coffee again not to spill it. "I wanted Shaye to come to me in true unrestrained passion. I wanted her to beg to be with me, and to desire me so much as a man that, in her heart she'd *know* I was straight, however I dressed. But I was an idiot," he said. "Now I may never get the chance to just tell her that I'm in love with her."

A cloud passed over the window, and both men sat in trembling silence.

Danny fiddled with his cell phone in his lap, resembling a sullen boy dressed up for cops and robbers. His voice cracked when he spoke. "Adam, you're not asking me to give her up?"

Adam gave a sardonic little huff. "Danny, why would I do that? I love Shaye. I know you love her, too. I'd want her to be happy," he gulped, "whoever it was with."

Danielo's eyes gradually brightened and he was able to smile. "But you agree it ought to be one of us, right? Not somebody else? We should protect her from that?"

Adam leaned over himself and laughed, an hour of tension finally cracking a bit. Then he sighed like someone who had just come out of a crisis of illness. "Danny," he said, once again straining not use a patronizing tone. "All I can wish is that either of us would ever again have a chance at making that decision. Is it possible? Have you found out anything about Shaye yet? Anything about where she might have gone?"

Danielo rounded his shoulders and sighed, obviously defensively. "I drove down to South Beach last month, Adam. And I found your friend Jeff Freeman that owns the nightclub. But that's a dead end also. Shaye's not down in Miami as far as he knows, and he doesn't know anything about the name on the ID he sent her. Apparently one of his employees just picked the ID's up from a street vendor in Little Havana, and Jeff sent them out without bothering to note the names."

Adam shook his head in disappointment as the information sank in. It seemed as though this hope that Frank Danielo would track Shaye down was one last thread that he had held onto, and now this was being stretched to the breaking point as well.

"I'm surprised you didn't search for her on police databases, Frank."

"Well, I did," Danielo said, with a sheepish ghost of a smile. "There are no new arrests- or deaths- under Shaye's name. And nothing likely that matched her physical description. It's hard, though. Did you know that Shaye never had fingerprints in the system?"

Adam smiled. "That's because our Shaye's such a good girl!"

Both men laughed and then, as the sun seemed to shift lower in the sky outside the floor-to-ceiling window, their expressions slowly became more solemn. It started with Danny, and then Adam observed his expression and mirrored it, respecting the silence. It appeared, thinking about Shaye's goodness, that Danny was forced to consider how she felt after attacking Jorge Colon.

That afternoon Shaye had glanced down at her own blood-covered hands, and the ends of her long hair tipped in blood. And when she had looked back up at Danny, her expression had been unreadable. She had looked like she was very very far away already.

After Danny had fired the fatal shot that day, the first time he had ever killed anyone in the line of duty, he did not have Shaye to turn to, so they could work through the experience together. Instead, he had found himself alone.

Glenn Chow had arrived back from Mexico that night and he had been Danny's greatest source of support, quietly going over paperwork with him, sharing pizza and smoking cigarettes and not pushing with too many intrusive questions. Chow had stayed at Danny's house through the night, not saying that he was worried, but yet refusing to leave his partner alone.

The following days had brought pep talks from some of the Oceanside force, whose ranks Danny would soon be joining, and from Mayor Adrian Walker. Immediately after the shooting, Danny talked on the phone every day with Adam, and with Adam's father, and this grounded him with a certain sense of connection and approval.

Glenn Chow came over almost every day for a while to help him repaint and refurnish the house that was empty of his wife's furniture, and to help with many neglected repairs. And even Lorrine called to comfort Danny, congratulating him on stopping the killer, and admitting that having to shoot a man in the line of duty was scary, entirely different than anything he'd faced in his police career when they were together.

So, even though he was fundamentally alone, Danny never really went more than a few hours without talking to somebody.

Shaye, on the other hand, probably was alone in the truest sense. His face showed the thoughts processing.

"Adam," he said, "you know I ask myself if it was right letting Shaye get involved in the case. After she attacked Colon with the rake, I could tell she wondered if she'd turned into some kind of monster. I tried to tell her she was a heroine, and I would have told her more if there was time. Even more, Adam, I think Shaye hated herself for the risk she put on Madeline- even though Madeline never knew it."

Adam replied with a cute sideways smirk. "Well, our dear Madeline won't ever know it; that's the saving grace. But I did get her to stop turning tricks- and to attend the occasionalAA meeting. Madeline thinks Shaye is a saint now. And, in a way, Shaye is. Even though she was the one to put Madeline in harm's way, she saved her as well. She risked herself to do it…"

Now it was Adam's turn to look agonized, to hide with the heel of his hand a few tears as he subtly brushed them away. "I don't know if I should have ever brought Shaye to Florida, Danny. I know I shouldn't have left her alone at nights the way I did. And it's funny that I never for a moment took the crisis with the killer seriously- I was too worried about other things."

"And I saw those other things," Danny said, as though to comfort him. "Shaye had one of her panic attacks in Walmart when she was with me. But I just never got the chance to help her."

Adam cocked his head, and bit his lip. "Let me ask you something," he said. "What would you do, theoretically, if she comes back?"

Danny raised his head and raised his eyebrows. "I'd ask Shaye to marry me, Adam. I already did. I mean, I mentioned it. I want to live my life with her, and give her the best life possible…"

He watched Adam watching him with narrowed eyes with a disturbingly sophisticated look of suspicion.

"… I know I can't give her the kind of money, or the kind of privilege you could."

Adam just looked even more perplexed. "Dude," he said softly, "it's not that. Don't you understand yet that Shaye is really physically sick as well as psychologically? The disease that she had, and the supposed health care she was given after it, did permanent damage to her liver and kidneys as well as her gastrointestinal tract, which she suffers with every day. Shaye's physical prognosis isn't good, Danny.

"All the doctors don't even know what to expect, because the strain of e-coli she had was so rare. It's amazing that Shaye's health seemed pretty good in Flamingo Park, but I constantly monitored her, Danny, every day, even when she didn't care about it herself…"

"I know that you did," Danny said. "I think it's cool you did, and I will, too. Whatever's necessary if she's willing to be with me."

Adam sighed and slumped, his very bones appearing loose and weary. "What are you going to do if Shaye's thirty eight years old and needs kidney dialysis, and she's no longer pretty?"

"I don't care if Shaye is pretty!" Danny roared. Then he swallowed his words, as a nurse poked her head in the door to check the disturbance.

Adam just grinned charmingly and waved the nurse away.

"I don't care that Shaye's pretty," Danny asserted again in a sharp whisper. "I love Shaye because she's my best friend."

Adam paled, obviously deeply stung by this particular turn of phrase. But he went on calmly, in the same kind of whisper as Danny's. "What about when she needs a kidney transplant, yet refuses to trust doctors? What about when she even refuses to take a prescription stomach medication to ease her agony, and you watch her spit up blood and then she lies about it? What about when she hates you if you try to help- when she says she'd rather die than see another doctor- and means it?"

Tears squeezed from Adam's eyes, but he held his chin up defiantly. And, even though Adam could embody passion and pathos simultaneously in his big dark eyes, Danny looked intense, too and met Adam's look with appropriate seriousness.

"I guess you would be there then to help," he said. "I assume you'd still be her friend, Adam. Our friend... Or am I wrong? Would you just want to go away if she chose me as her lover?"

After a few minutes warmth suffused Adam's cheeks in the form of a small flush, and he relaxed his pouty lips in an unguarded smile. "Unfortunately, you're right. Whatever happens, I'd still be Shaye's friend. In fact, my friend, I really like your optimism about her coming back."

Danny got to his feet, stretching out his back and straightening out his pantlegs. "Great," he joked. "At least you respect me for something now. Before I leave today, I'll sign off on your discharge paperwork so I can get you out of here on Friday first thing. But I don't actually know where you want to go. Do you want a ride to the airport to go back home to Westchester- or to go to Miami to meet up with your friend? The judge approved your leaving, and they'll probably finalize your sentence as 'probation with counseling', so you won't need to come back to Florida for the trial. Or do you want me to take you back to the trailer first to pack up your stuff?"

Adam stood up, his height just a little bit taller than Danny's, and he reached forward to pump Danny's hand. Then he gave a pleasant little laugh. "Don't die of shock or anything," he said. "But I'm not going back to New York- or Miami. I'm staying in Flamingo Park. Or should I call it Oceanside?"

"Yeah, that's right," Danny said. "Oceanside will annex Flamingo Park by the start of the New Year. And there are all kinds of plans to change and improve it. I'm one of the first to hear about everything because Mayor Walker is in and out of my office every day, sharing all the gossip. But how about you, Adam? How'd you find that out in here?"

He looked genuinely perplexed, and Adam seemed to put his sorrow on hold long enough to look as self-satisfied as some enigmatic housecat. "From my lawyer," he boasted. "My real estate lawyer, a buddy of my criminal lawyer."

Danny creased his brow.

"Real estate?"

Adam lowered his eyes demurely to the side in one of his old feminine gestures. "I'm not just going to live in Flamingo Park, Danny," he said, standing taller and more confidently. "I want to give something back," he said. "You know that vacant lot on Caiman St. where the murder took place? Shaye was always talking about it. How crazy Jorge Colon and his poor unfortunate girlfriend had plans to make a park and a community center there...

"Well, I have nothing but time now, Danny. First, I'm planning to build a little house for myself. And I'm already negotiating with the developer about making an offer on that lot on Caiman St. And then I'll build the community center there. While it's in construction I plan to go to Orange County community college for a two-year degree in counseling, and then I'll be able to work at the center. I can help the homeless, and drug users, even prostitutes... Madeline and the girls have promised to be my cheering squad. Even though I quit Foxy Lady permanently... And I think I'm going to give up cross-dressing, too."

Danny looked at him with shock. "Dude!" he said, for want of a more appropriate comment.

Adam grinned. "It used to be such a pleasure to me, an addiction, really. Now it brings back too many bad memories. I'd like to be free- and healthy- and then use the time- and my father's money- to make the world a better place. At least a little part of the world..."

Danny nodded, taking in all Adam's ambitious plans. As he approached the door, though, he looked at Adam from under lowered lashes- and suspicious brow. "And, in addition to wanting to save the world, you like the fact that you can wait around for Shaye, don't you? You *do* think she'll come back around to the trailer someday, don't you?"

Adam shrugged, caught out. "Maybe," he said. "I'm going to buy the lot, tow the old trailer away and build a nice little house. I don't have anywhere else to go."

Danny shrugged generously. "More power to you, dude. So we'll basically be neighbors, then. I can help you with carpentry when you start building your house. And, if you want, we can recruit Glenn Chow, work on the house for a few hours at a time and then all of us take a break and go fishing... if you're into that kind of thing now- masculine stuff... And I'll introduce you to Adrian Walker if you're really interested in all the politics in Flamingo Park..."

Adam grinned. "Sure, Danny," he said. "I'd be proud to hang out with you and get some stuff accomplished. At this point in my life I've got nothing but time."

Frank Danielo took one step into the hallway, which smelled of ammonia and rich dinner for a hundred cooking. But then he caught an unmistakable glint in Adam's eye, something different than anything he had ever seen. It was almost like Adam was smiling to himself, lost in some reverie, remembering something that, in itself, could motivate him to go on in life.

Danny stepped back into the room and slowly faced the younger man. He took a deep breath before asking his question. "Adam," he asked. "You didn't, did you? You know, Shaye and I, we were into each other, but we never... you know, we never actually made love."

Adam raised a cautious eyebrow. "For real?"

"We kissed," Danny said. And then he admitted confidentially, "and we made out, really hot. But she wasn't ready for sex yet, and I respected that... All along, Adam, I thought you were gay. But now, well, any crazy thing could be true. You and Shaye were so close..."

He looked utterly dejected and pained. And yet he looked ready to accept the blow, whatever Adam told him.

Finally he asked, "Did you guys ever make love?"

Adam stood just an inch or two taller than his new friend, Frank Danielo. And no one had to doubt that, no matter what he told him, Danny would still keep his promise to sign him out of the hospital, and even come around to his new home in the park to help him with construction.

But Adam frowned as he examined the obvious fear he saw in Danny's eyes.

"No, dude," he answered finally and assertively. "We didn't have sex... We kissed, similar to you guys. So it's still an even playing field for us."

Danny stopped, listened, absorbed. Then he punched Adam playfully on the side of his slim arm, as the breath he was holding released in a rush. "Well, no harm in having a little competition," he said. "I'll come pick you up on Friday." As he stepped into the hall he joked, trying to sound cheerful, "Who knows, maybe Shaye will come back by then!"

Danny waved, and then hiked down the hall in the direction of the nurses' station.

He didn't turn back or he would have seen a stream of silver tears slip down the bridge of Adam's nose.

Epilogue

Shaye Taylor had the Greyhound bus almost entirely to herself. That was the good part about the countryside here so far in the mountains and away from any interstate highway. Earlier, on her connections from Florida, she had been careful to travel very early in the morning to ensure that she was not crowded by any germ-infested passengers.

But now it was a quarter past eleven in the morning and the scenery couldn't be more beautiful. From her vantage point in the front seat opposite the driver, she examined panoramas of rolling farmland, with sheep and cows grazing like little black and white figurines set off charmingly against the emerald green grass. She observed old style wooden barns painted weathered red. Some had roofs adorned with painted advertisements for tractors or motor oil. In one of the farmyards a tow-headed boy and girl, toting straw in a red cart pulled by their pony, stopped by their pasture fence to teasingly wave at the bus as it passed.

Shaye blushed and her face relaxed into a broad genuine smile. Truly, it seemed that with every mile she was riding deeper into Norman Rockwell country, an area where time had stood still since purer sweeter times.

As the elevation changed, so did the countryside and the scenery. Although they were trailed by the rare vehicle that impatientiently passed them on the narrow mountain roads, sightings of these vehicles became rarer and rarer. Tight alongside the road now were the trees that the Evergreen area had been named for. Shaye flattened her palm up against the bus window as though she could feel them, their overhanging dark green boughs still cool and damp with the morning dew.

Shaye gasped with pleasure as they rounded yet another turn, this one revealing a small sapphire blue pond where a bald eagle lazily circled overhead.

Following her exclamation the bus driver, a wiry gray-haired man in his sixties, turned back to grin. "I love driving this route myself," he said, "so peaceful. Each time something different to see, like that eagle." He slowed the bus to point in that direction, so that the handful of passengers in back took the time to look as well.

Then carefully manuevering more winding roads, he drove on, continuing to chat. "There's not too much development out here," he said. "Mostly a great big state park, and lots of canoe rental outfits and campgrounds. Of course lately they've been gentrifying as they call it. Folks from the city settling into these planned communities, running from the traffic… and the crime…"

Shaye glanced down demurely at her hands. She understood exactly what the bus driver was talking about, and him mentioning it seemed almost like serendipity, the physical manifestation of her own dreams.

For, in her hands, she held a glossy booklet. The cover showed a smiling family bicycling through evergreen shaded forest pathways, their way illuminated by sunlight resembling liquid gold, just like the sun streamed through the real trees today.

After his accident, Shaye hadn't attempted to contact Adam. There would have been no way to do it without the hospital investigating her. Or maybe there would have been some way possible now- after all, it had been three months, and there was a possibility that Adam was already free.

But Shaye had not attempted to call. Instead, she had checked in during the one call she made to Frank Danielo. She'd asked Danny how he was and, after he'd squandered the seconds by saying, "I'm doing really good. I'm divorced and I'm an Oceanside detective now…" she'd cut him off. "Great," she'd said breathlessly, talking on a phone card in a bus station where Florida leaned up against

Alabama. "I don't have much time on this calling card. I just want you to know I'm fine. That's all I can tell you. And I have a request. I have a promise I want you to make to me..."

"What, Shaye?" Danny had attempted. "This is ridiculous. Come home!"

Shaye had spoken over him, coolly and assertively, even though her legs were shaking. "Danny, I want you to promise me that you'll take care of Adam for me. Not just now, but in the long haul. If you care about me, promise me you'll take care of him."

"Shaye," Danny had tried. "Don't do this. It's safe for you now. Everything is fine. Adam is so much better. The charges against you guys are down to almost nothing. Just come back!" Perhaps Danny had been crying for, over the miles, his voice had sounded like a melancholy song.

But Shaye broke in again harshly. "Just promise!"

"I promise, Shaye," he'd said, sounding as if she had interrupted what was probably a decent day by surprising him and making his heart rip out.

"Good," she'd said softly, almost a whisper. "Thank you." And that was all. Then she'd hung up, because she couldn't have talked a minute longer.

Shaye wanted to wipe a tear away as she gazed out at the dreamy scenery approaching her destination, the real-life Shangri La that would end all her pain.

Danny. And Adam. They were better off without her. They didn't know it. But she did. And time would simply prove it. Whether what she did was for altruism, to give them each a shot at an ideal future, or whether it was simply to allay her own fears, she might never actually be sure of.

She might never know, no matter how many nights she lay awake in mom and pop hotel rooms, or campgrounds, or National Parks or even the occasional section of posted woods where she had lain hidden, sleeping in her brand new tent.

Only the twenty-page brochure she held cradled in her trembling lap could make her feel sure now. *"Live Free of Fear,"* the caption over the happily mountain-biking family read. Opening the next page, as she had already hundreds of times, she smiled once again as she saw revealed a glowing panorama of subtly designed homes set to maximize privacy amidst colorful fall foliage and a lush carpet of green grass- a spacious pool and community building in the center of all and a high wall, punctuated by a manned security gate.

"Welcome to Safe Meadows, a planned mountain village, where peace and harmony prevail, removed from the dangers and anxieties of city life. A few select families can choose to purchase estate-style mountain homesites and luxury townhomes now and purchase a lifestyle free of the threats of big-city living. It's your turn to embrace a lifestyle of leisure and community- a lifestyle free of fear!"

Shaye held the pamphlet loosely, but her breathing revealed her depth of emotion. She brushed back her hair, now worn shoulder-length and dyed brown with subtle pink tips. Her clothing was different than the T-shirts and Keds of Flamingo Park, and also different from the flashy minidresses of her modeling days.

Her new ID, in the name Penny Chase, said she was twenty-six years old. Shaye had envisioned Penny as a graduate student with eclectic style. And although, as Penny, Shaye liked to dress in autumn-colored vintage clothes, she also looked fresher and younger than she had in a long time.

In the past few months Shaye had not spoken to many people face to face, but she had talked to some via the laptop computer she cuddled next to her. She'd actually earned a little money doing Internet research for anonymous customers around the country, and then she'd cashed the checks in the new name of Penny Chase. Truly, Shaye had begun to think of herself as Penny in her own mind. Penny, a capable young girl who could care for herself. Penny, who might someday be able to afford a home in Safe Meadows. Who might, even today, have enough cash to rent a townhome there.

This money was all Shaye had, balled up in a woven bag along with her laptop, a bottle of hand sanitizer and an embroidered wallet containing a photo of Adam Ant and her new Penny Chase ID. What Shaye planned to do after this month was over, she wasn't sure of.

But she stood up tall as the bus crested the last ridge and the glowing planned community came into view.

THE END

About the Author

Emma "Freeway" Lincoln writes sexy Florida suspense with underlying philosophical meaning. Emma and her husband- and soulmate- Ray are independent-minded, wide-ranging travelers who like to spend most of their time on the Florida beaches. They are also advocates for animals and the environment and have co-authored several dog books.

Other Books by Emma "Freeway" Lincoln:
Florida Justice, and coming soon two more books in the Florida Justice series

www.ingramcontent.com/pod-product-compliance
Lightning Source LLC
Chambersburg PA
CBHW071645260626
47170CB00001B/240